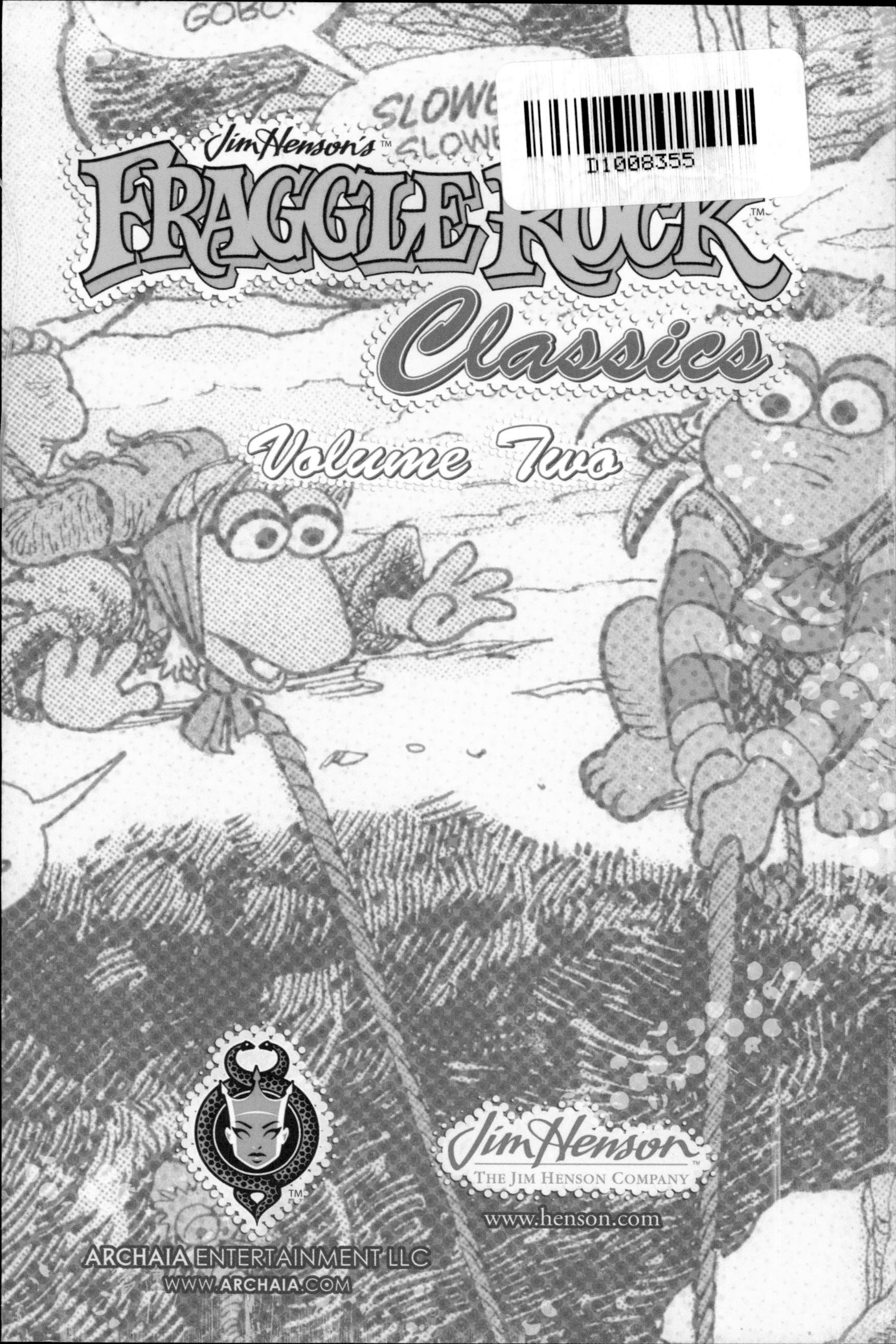
GOBO!
SLOWE
SLOWE

Jim Henson's™

FRAGGLE ROCK™ Classics

Volume Two

ARCHAIA ENTERTAINMENT LLC
WWW.ARCHAIA.COM

Jim Henson™
THE JIM HENSON COMPANY
www.henson.com

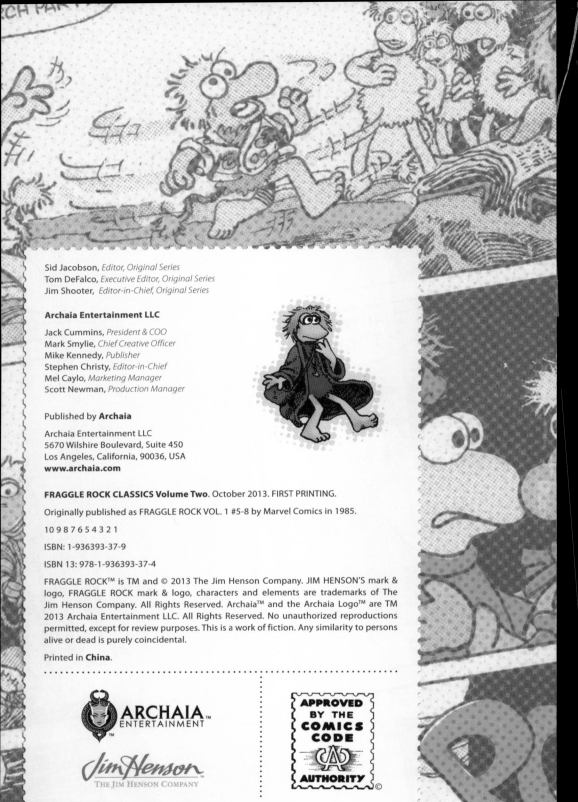

Sid Jacobson, *Editor, Original Series*
Tom DeFalco, *Executive Editor, Original Series*
Jim Shooter, *Editor-in-Chief, Original Series*

Archaia Entertainment LLC

Jack Cummins, *President & COO*
Mark Smylie, *Chief Creative Officer*
Mike Kennedy, *Publisher*
Stephen Christy, *Editor-in-Chief*
Mel Caylo, *Marketing Manager*
Scott Newman, *Production Manager*

Published by **Archaia**

Archaia Entertainment LLC
5670 Wilshire Boulevard, Suite 450
Los Angeles, California, 90036, USA
www.archaia.com

FRAGGLE ROCK CLASSICS Volume Two. October 2013. FIRST PRINTING.

Originally published as FRAGGLE ROCK VOL. 1 #5-8 by Marvel Comics in 1985.

10 9 8 7 6 5 4 3 2 1

ISBN: 1-936393-37-9

ISBN 13: 978-1-936393-37-4

Printed in **China**.

ARCHAIA™
ENTERTAINMENT

Jim Henson
THE JIM HENSON COMPANY

APPROVED
BY THE
COMICS
CODE
AUTHORITY©

Jim Henson's FRAGGLE ROCK Classics

Volume Two

Written by **STAN KAY**

Illustrated by **MARIE SEVERIN**

Restoration and Colors by
JOANNA ESTEP

Cover by
JAKE MYLER

Lettered by
GRACE KREMER & RICHARD PARKER

Design by
BRIAN NEWMAN

Edited by
REBECCA TAYLOR

Special Thanks to
BRIAN HENSON, LISA HENSON, JIM FORMANEK, NICOLE GOLDMAN, MARYANNE PITTMAN, MELISSA SEGAL, HILLARY HOWELL, JILL PETERSON, KAREN FALK, AND THE ENTIRE HENSON TEAM!

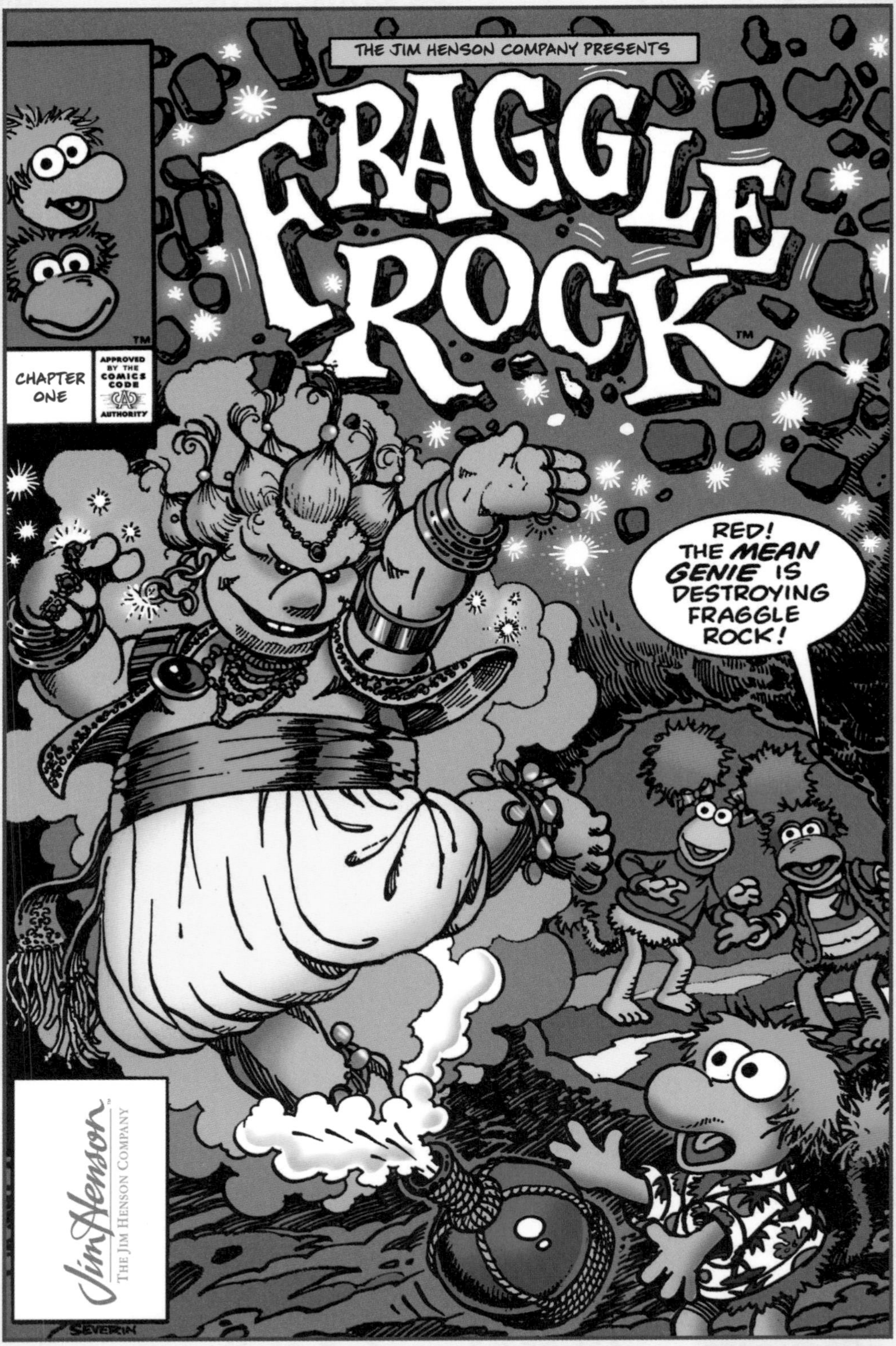
THE JIM HENSON COMPANY PRESENTS
FRAGGLE ROCK™
CHAPTER ONE
APPROVED BY THE COMICS CODE AUTHORITY
RED! THE *MEAN GENIE* IS DESTROYING FRAGGLE ROCK!
Jim Henson
THE JIM HENSON COMPANY
SEVERIN

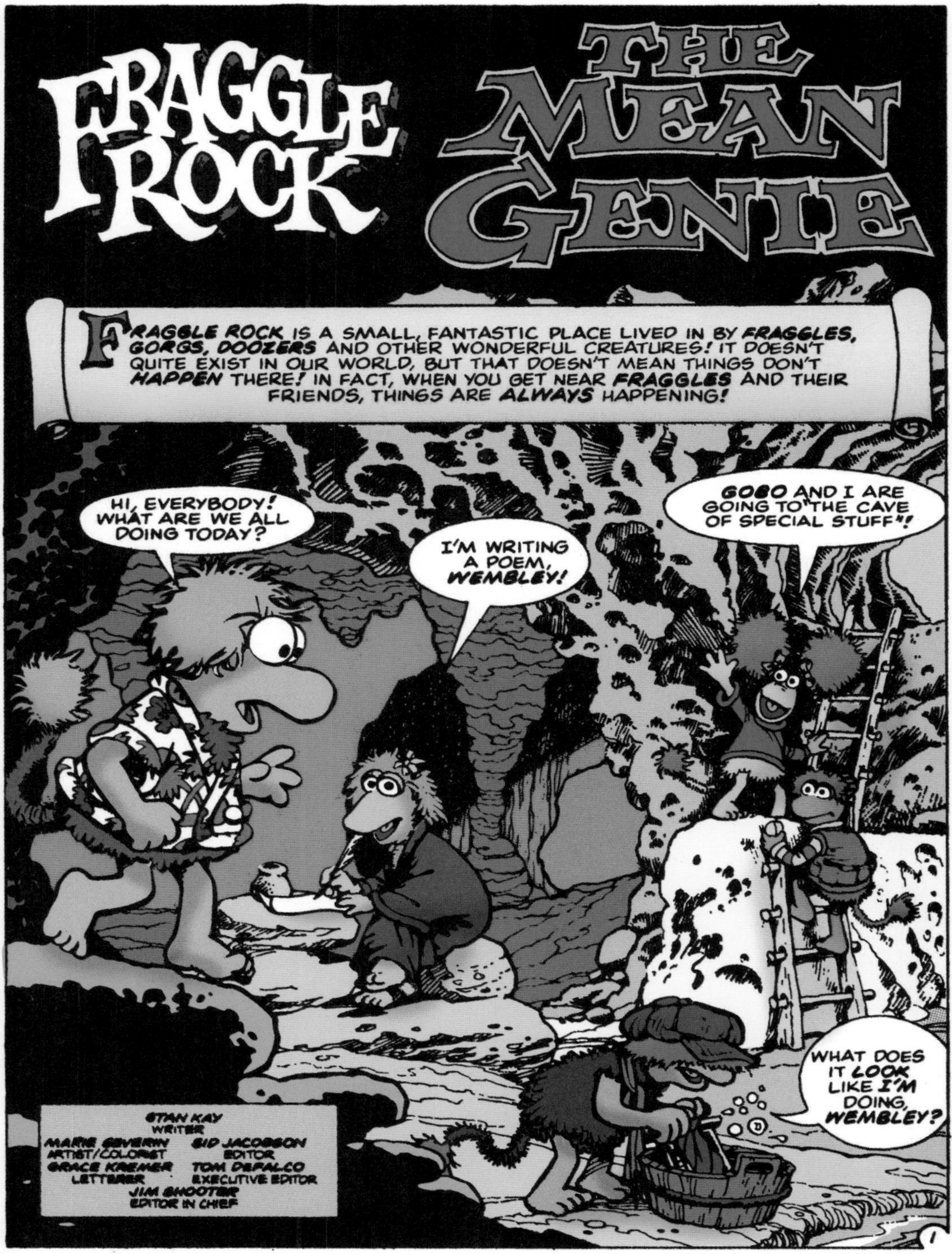
FRAGGLE ROCK
THE MEAN GENIE
FRAGGLE ROCK IS A SMALL, FANTASTIC PLACE LIVED IN BY FRAGGLES, GORGS, DOOZERS AND OTHER WONDERFUL CREATURES! IT DOESN'T QUITE EXIST IN OUR WORLD, BUT THAT DOESN'T MEAN THINGS DON'T HAPPEN THERE! IN FACT, WHEN YOU GET NEAR FRAGGLES AND THEIR FRIENDS, THINGS ARE ALWAYS HAPPENING!
HI, EVERYBODY! WHAT ARE WE ALL DOING TODAY?
I'M WRITING A POEM, WEMBLEY!
GOBO AND I ARE GOING TO "THE CAVE OF SPECIAL STUFF"!
WHAT DOES IT LOOK LIKE I'M DOING, WEMBLEY?
STAN KAY WRITER
MARIE SEVERIN ARTIST/COLORIST
SID JACOBSON EDITOR
GRACE KREMER LETTERER
TOM DEFALCO EXECUTIVE EDITOR
JIM SHOOTER EDITOR IN CHIEF
1

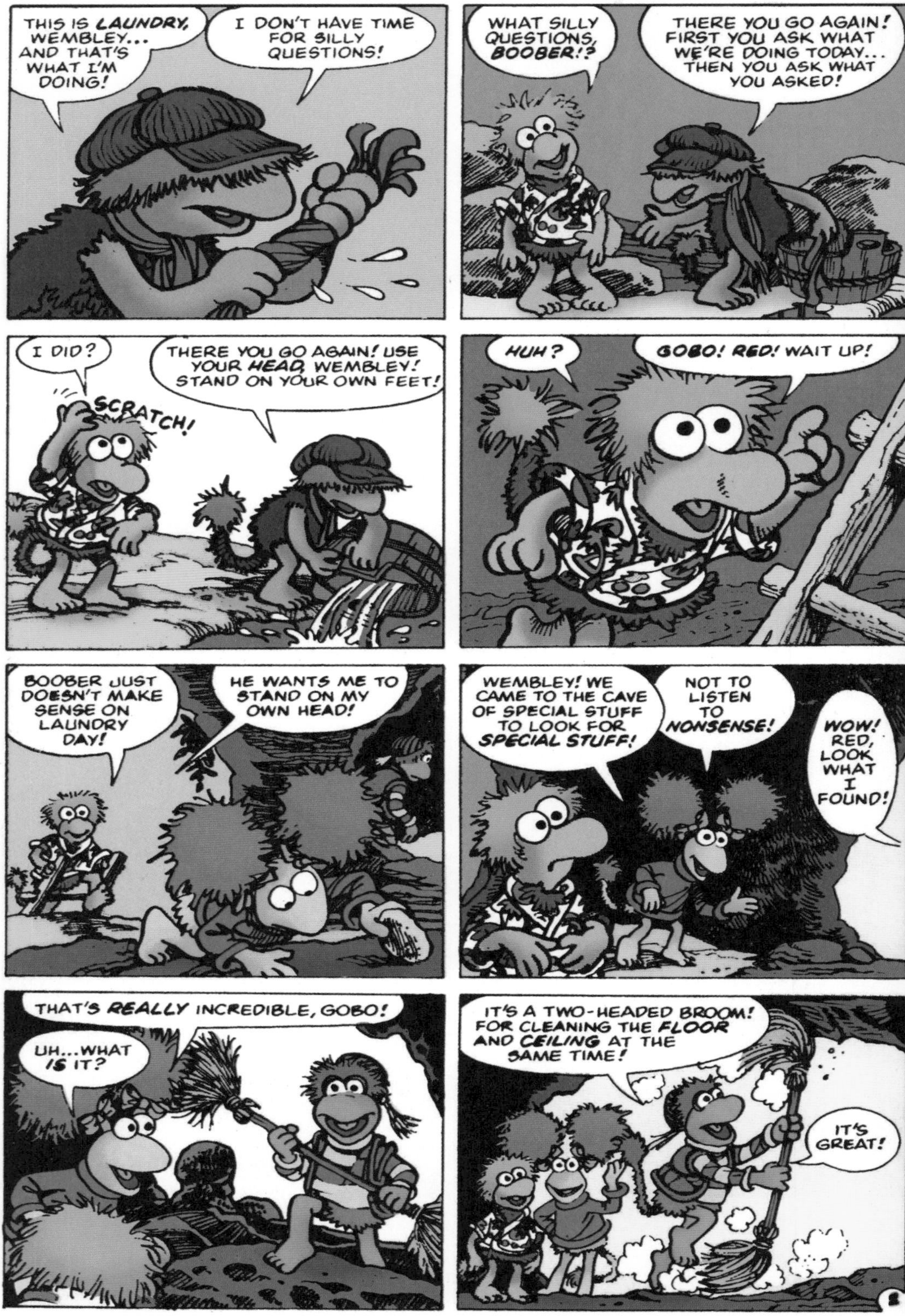
THIS IS LAUNDRY, WEMBLEY... AND THAT'S WHAT I'M DOING!
I DON'T HAVE TIME FOR SILLY QUESTIONS!
WHAT SILLY QUESTIONS, BOOBER!?
THERE YOU GO AGAIN! FIRST YOU ASK WHAT WE'RE DOING TODAY... THEN YOU ASK WHAT YOU ASKED!
I DID?
SCRATCH!
THERE YOU GO AGAIN! USE YOUR HEAD, WEMBLEY! STAND ON YOUR OWN FEET!
HUH?
GOBO! RED! WAIT UP!
BOOBER JUST DOESN'T MAKE SENSE ON LAUNDRY DAY!
HE WANTS ME TO STAND ON MY OWN HEAD!
WEMBLEY! WE CAME TO THE CAVE OF SPECIAL STUFF TO LOOK FOR SPECIAL STUFF!
NOT TO LISTEN TO NONSENSE!
WOW! RED, LOOK WHAT I FOUND!
THAT'S REALLY INCREDIBLE, GOBO!
UH...WHAT IS IT?
IT'S A TWO-HEADED BROOM! FOR CLEANING THE FLOOR AND CEILING AT THE SAME TIME!
IT'S GREAT!

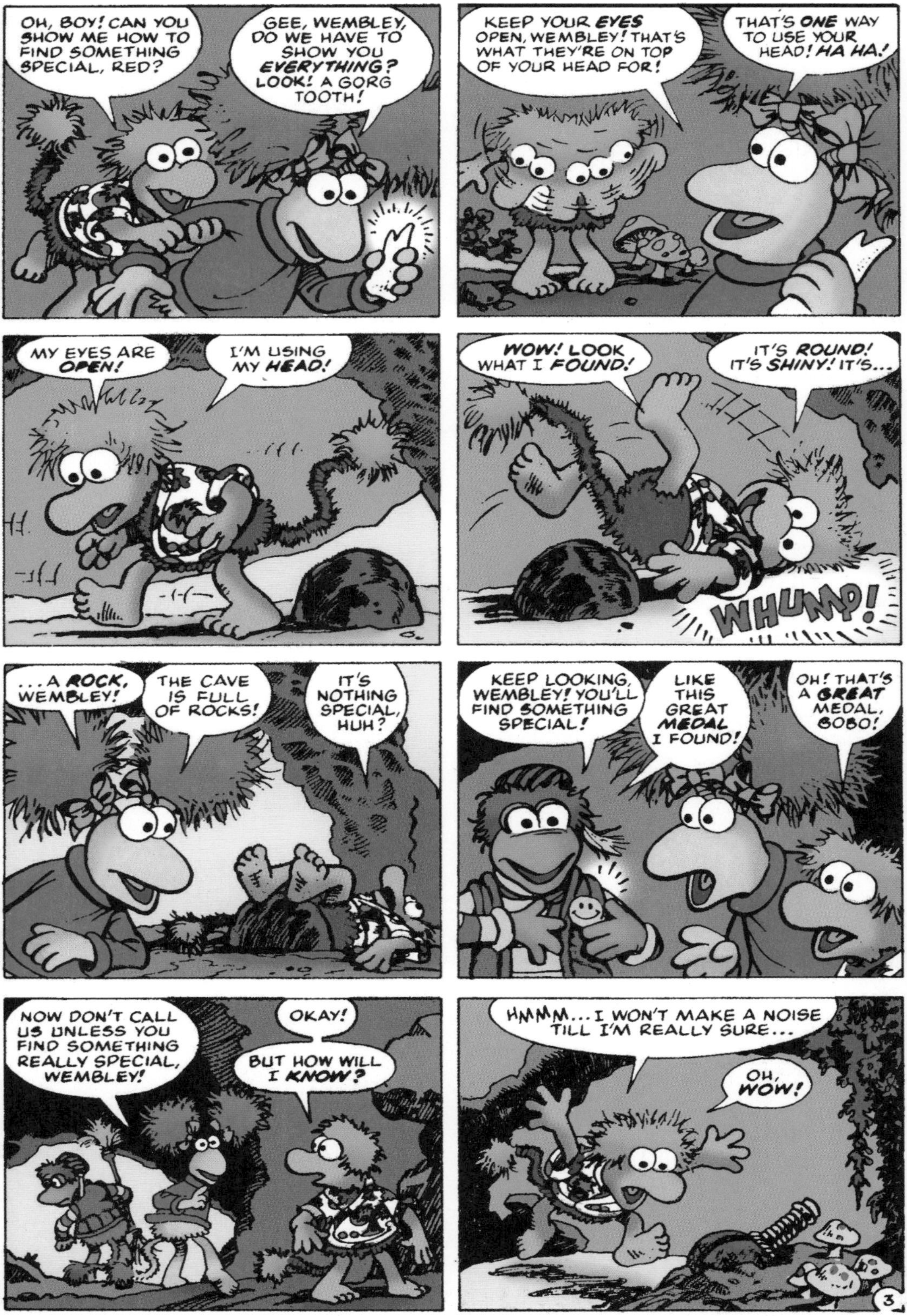
OH, BOY! CAN YOU SHOW ME HOW TO FIND SOMETHING SPECIAL, RED?
GEE, WEMBLEY, DO WE HAVE TO SHOW YOU EVERYTHING? LOOK! A GORG TOOTH!
KEEP YOUR EYES OPEN, WEMBLEY! THAT'S WHAT THEY'RE ON TOP OF YOUR HEAD FOR!
THAT'S ONE WAY TO USE YOUR HEAD! HA HA!
MY EYES ARE OPEN!
I'M USING MY HEAD!
WOW! LOOK WHAT I FOUND!
IT'S ROUND! IT'S SHINY! IT'S...
WHUMP!
...A ROCK, WEMBLEY!
THE CAVE IS FULL OF ROCKS!
IT'S NOTHING SPECIAL, HUH?
KEEP LOOKING, WEMBLEY! YOU'LL FIND SOMETHING SPECIAL!
LIKE THIS GREAT MEDAL I FOUND!
OH! THAT'S A GREAT MEDAL, BOBO!
NOW DON'T CALL US UNLESS YOU FIND SOMETHING REALLY SPECIAL, WEMBLEY!
OKAY!
BUT HOW WILL I KNOW?
HMMM... I WON'T MAKE A NOISE TILL I'M REALLY SURE...
OH, WOW!
3

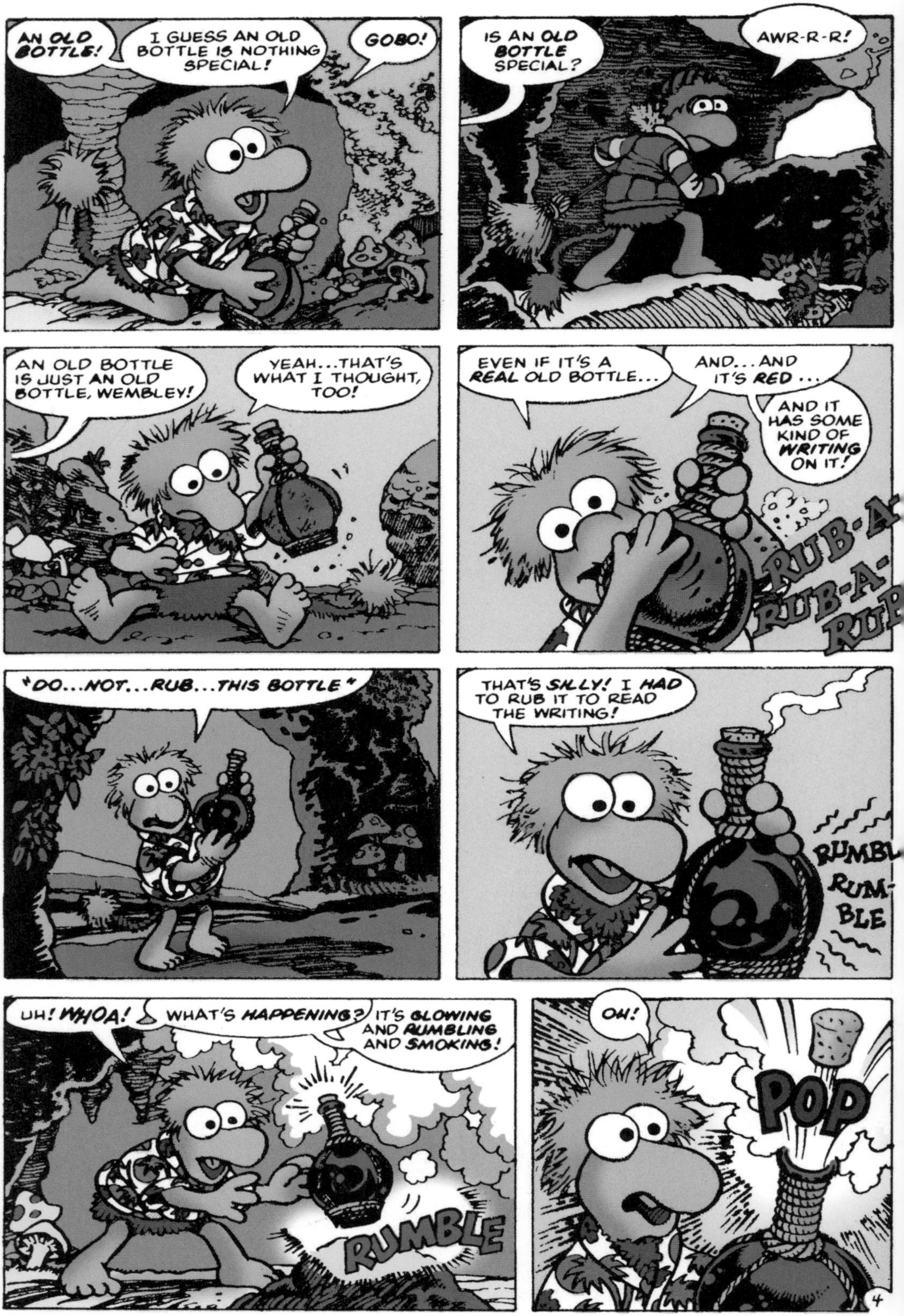
AN OLD BOTTLE!
I GUESS AN OLD BOTTLE IS NOTHING SPECIAL!
GOBO!
IS AN OLD BOTTLE SPECIAL?
AWR-R-R!
AN OLD BOTTLE IS JUST AN OLD BOTTLE, WEMBLEY!
YEAH...THAT'S WHAT I THOUGHT, TOO!
EVEN IF IT'S A REAL OLD BOTTLE...
AND...AND IT'S RED...
AND IT HAS SOME KIND OF WRITING ON IT!
"DO...NOT...RUB...THIS BOTTLE"
THAT'S SILLY! I HAD TO RUB IT TO READ THE WRITING!
RUM-BLE
UH! WHOA!
WHAT'S HAPPENING?
IT'S GLOWING AND RUMBLING AND SMOKING!
RUMBLE
OH!
POP
4

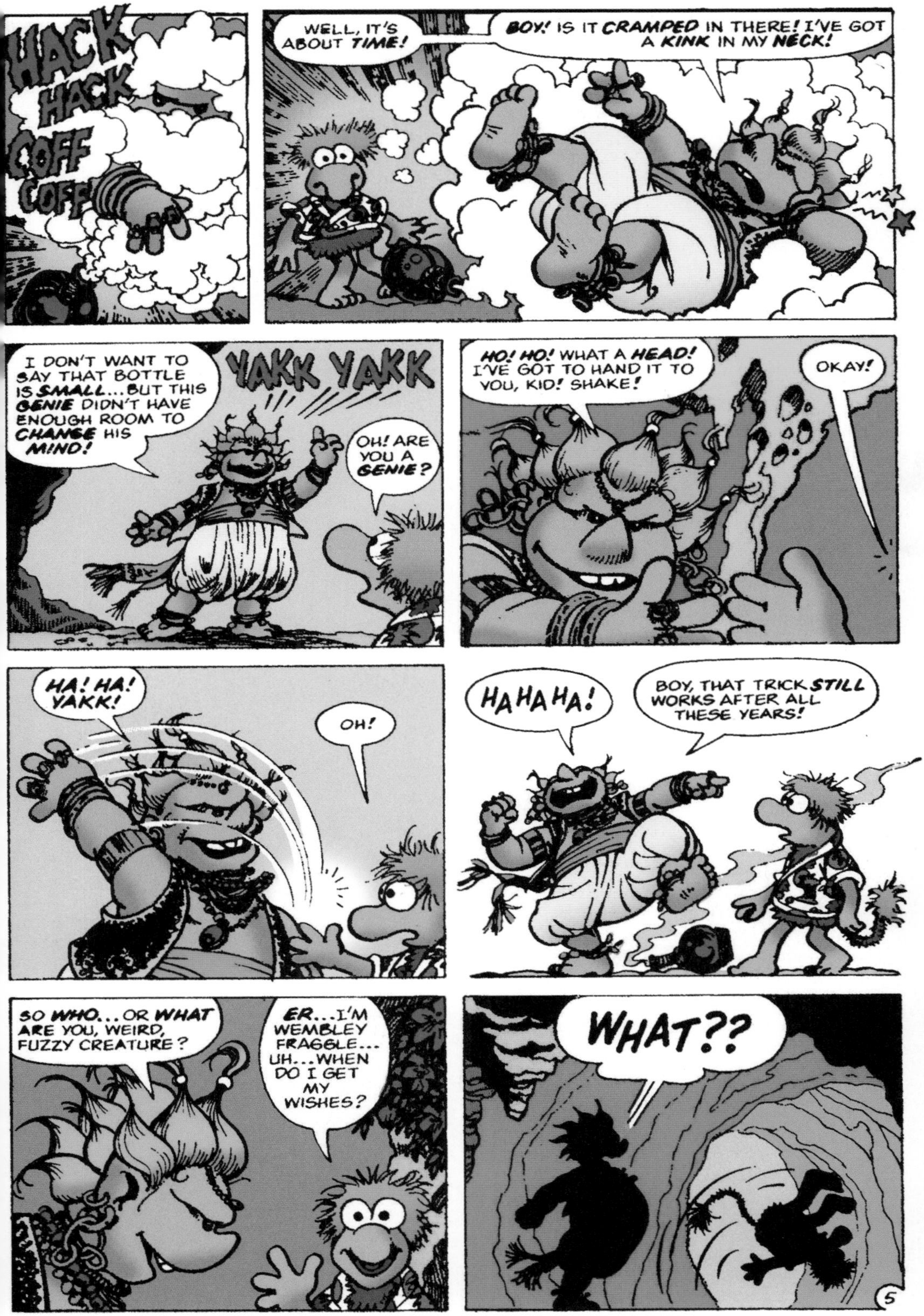
HACK HACK COFF COFF
WELL, IT'S ABOUT TIME!
BOY! IS IT CRAMPED IN THERE! I'VE GOT A KINK IN MY NECK!
I DON'T WANT TO SAY THAT BOTTLE IS SMALL... BUT THIS GENIE DIDN'T HAVE ENOUGH ROOM TO CHANGE HIS MIND!
YAKK YAKK
OH! ARE YOU A GENIE?
HO! HO! WHAT A HEAD! I'VE GOT TO HAND IT TO YOU, KID! SHAKE!
OKAY!
HA! HA! YAKK!
OH!
HAHAHA!
BOY, THAT TRICK STILL WORKS AFTER ALL THESE YEARS!
SO WHO... OR WHAT ARE YOU, WEIRD, FUZZY CREATURE?
ER... I'M WEMBLEY FRAGGLE... UH... WHEN DO I GET MY WISHES?
WHAT??
5

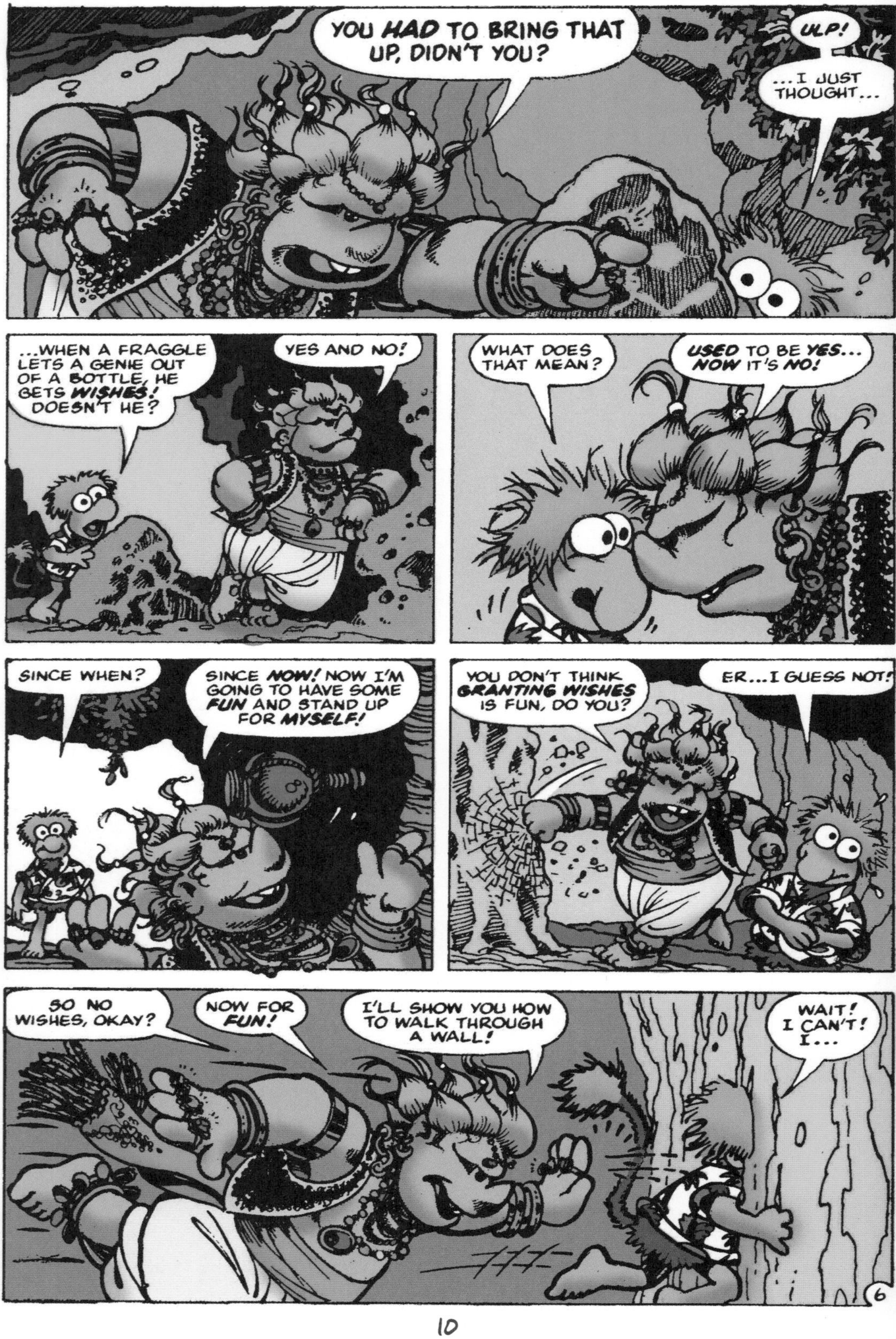
YOU *HAD* TO BRING THAT UP, DIDN'T YOU?
ULP!
...I JUST THOUGHT...
...WHEN A FRAGGLE LETS A GENIE OUT OF A BOTTLE, HE GETS *WISHES!* DOESN'T HE?
YES AND NO!
WHAT DOES THAT MEAN?
USED TO BE *YES...* *NOW* IT'S *NO!*
SINCE WHEN?
SINCE *NOW!* NOW I'M GOING TO HAVE SOME *FUN* AND STAND UP FOR *MYSELF!*
YOU DON'T THINK *GRANTING WISHES* IS FUN, DO YOU?
ER...I GUESS NOT!
SO NO WISHES, OKAY?
NOW FOR *FUN!*
I'LL SHOW YOU HOW TO WALK THROUGH A WALL!
WAIT! I CAN'T! I...
6

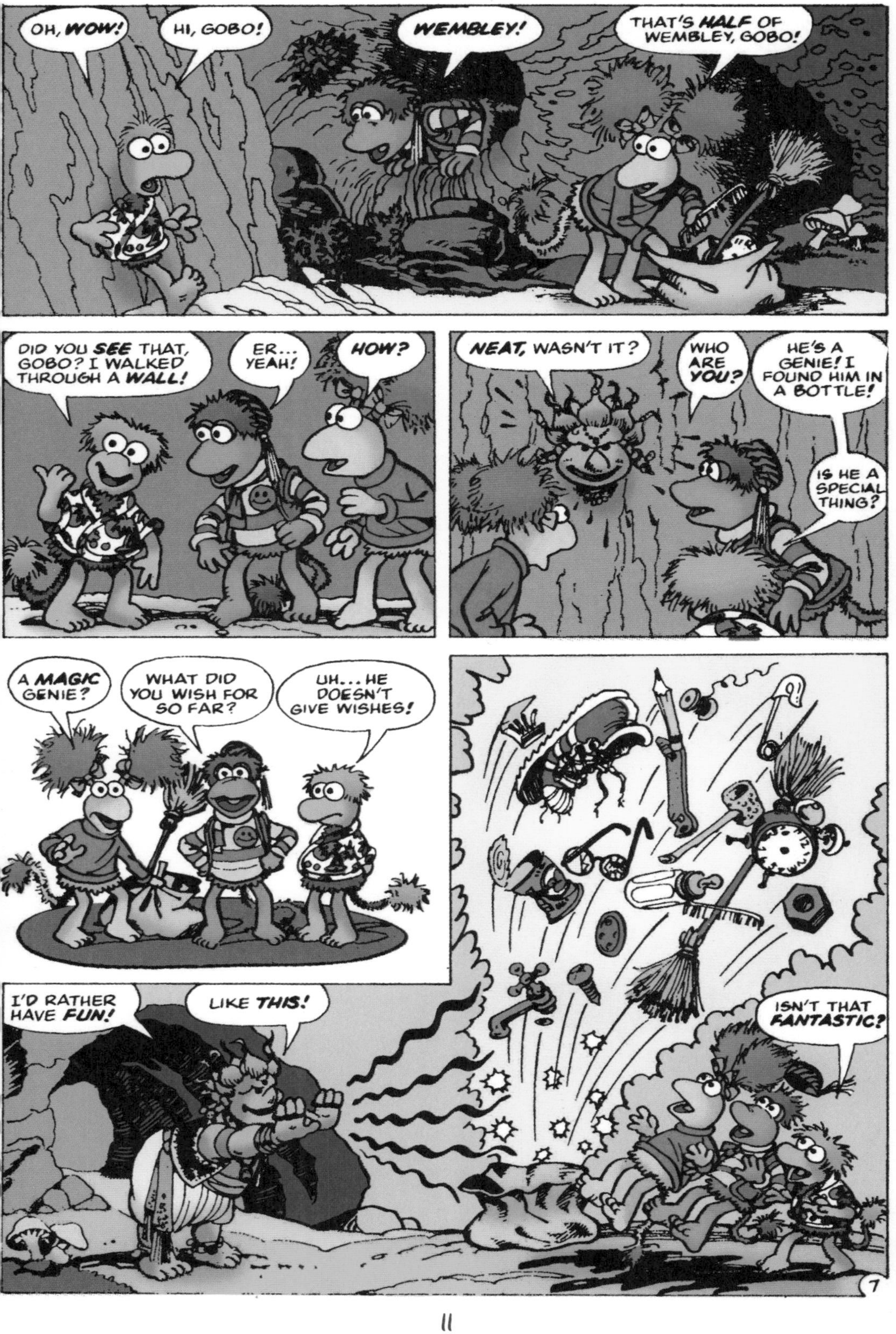
OH, WOW!
HI, GOBO!
WEMBLEY!
THAT'S HALF OF WEMBLEY, GOBO!
DID YOU SEE THAT, GOBO? I WALKED THROUGH A WALL!
ER... YEAH!
HOW?
NEAT, WASN'T IT?
WHO ARE YOU?
HE'S A GENIE! I FOUND HIM IN A BOTTLE!
IS HE A SPECIAL THING?
A MAGIC GENIE?
WHAT DID YOU WISH FOR SO FAR?
UH... HE DOESN'T GIVE WISHES!
I'D RATHER HAVE FUN!
LIKE THIS!
ISN'T THAT FANTASTIC?
7

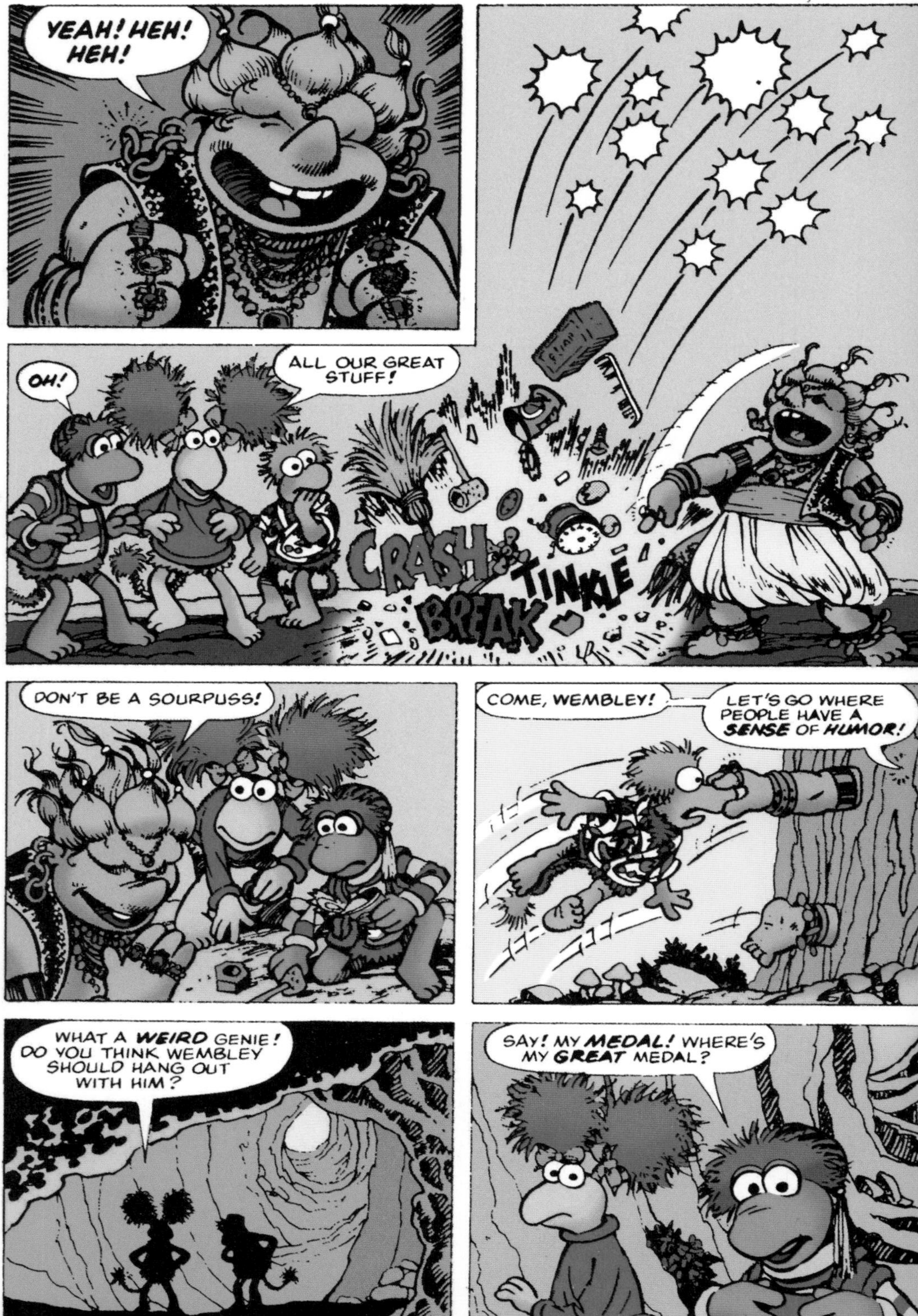
YEAH! HEH! HEH!
OH!
ALL OUR GREAT STUFF!
CRASH
BREAK
TINKLE
DON'T BE A SOURPUSS!
COME, WEMBLEY!
LET'S GO WHERE PEOPLE HAVE A **SENSE** OF **HUMOR**!
WHAT A **WEIRD** GENIE! DO YOU THINK WEMBLEY SHOULD HANG OUT WITH HIM?
SAY! MY **MEDAL!** WHERE'S MY **GREAT** MEDAL?
8

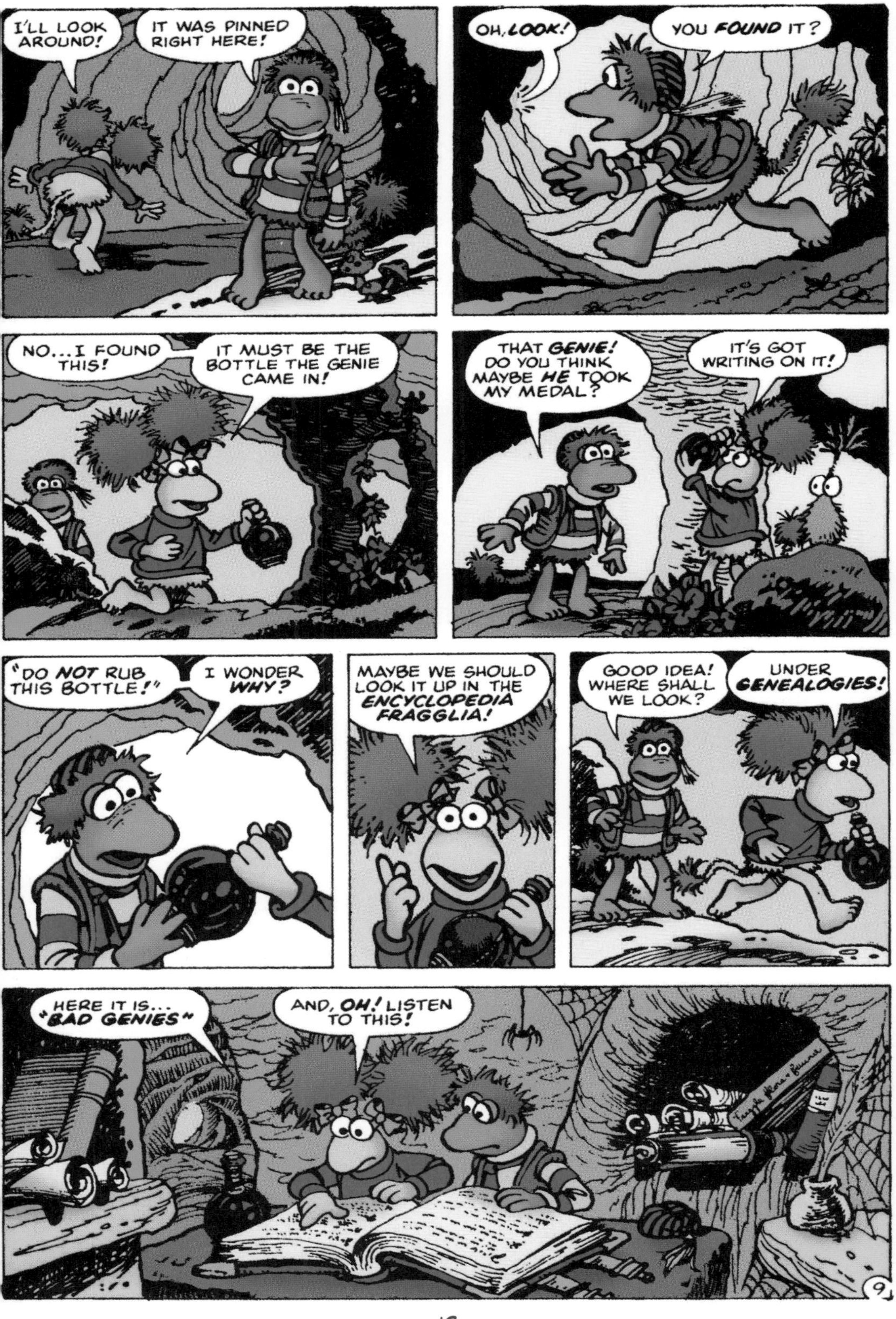
I'LL LOOK AROUND!
IT WAS PINNED RIGHT HERE!
OH, LOOK!
YOU FOUND IT?
NO...I FOUND THIS!
IT MUST BE THE BOTTLE THE GENIE CAME IN!
THAT GENIE! DO YOU THINK MAYBE HE TOOK MY MEDAL?
IT'S GOT WRITING ON IT!
"DO NOT RUB THIS BOTTLE!"
I WONDER WHY?
MAYBE WE SHOULD LOOK IT UP IN THE ENCYCLOPEDIA FRAGGLIA!
GOOD IDEA! WHERE SHALL WE LOOK?
UNDER GENEALOGIES!
HERE IT IS... "BAD GENIES"
AND, OH! LISTEN TO THIS!
9

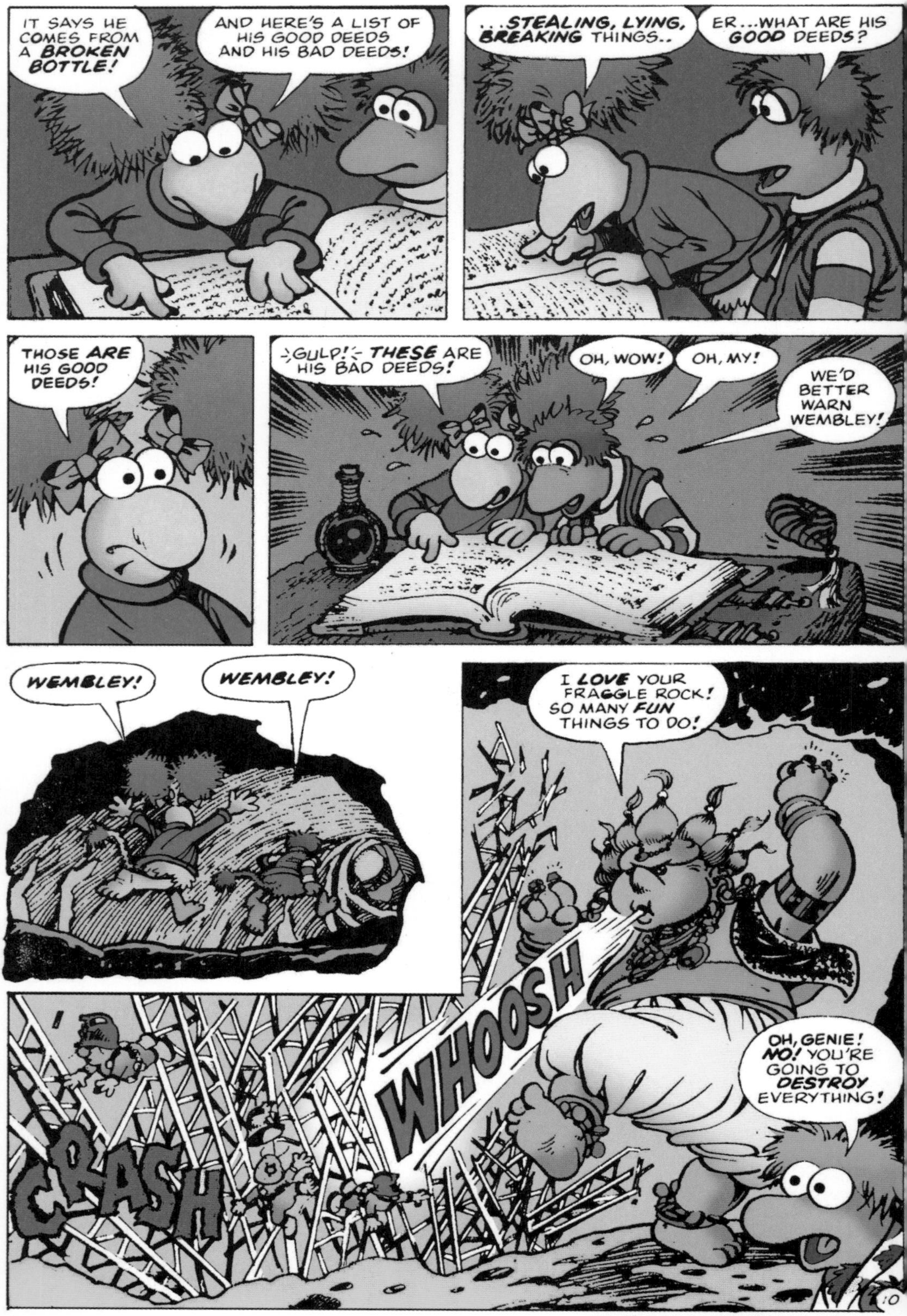
IT SAYS HE COMES FROM A BROKEN BOTTLE!
AND HERE'S A LIST OF HIS GOOD DEEDS AND HIS BAD DEEDS!
...STEALING, LYING, BREAKING THINGS..
ER...WHAT ARE HIS GOOD DEEDS?
THOSE ARE HIS GOOD DEEDS!
GULP! THESE ARE HIS BAD DEEDS!
OH, WOW!
OH, MY!
WE'D BETTER WARN WEMBLEY!
WEMBLEY!
WEMBLEY!
I LOVE YOUR FRAGGLE ROCK! SO MANY FUN THINGS TO DO!
WHOOSH
OH, GENIE! NO! YOU'RE GOING TO DESTROY EVERYTHING!
CRASH
10

CONTINUED IN THIS ISSUE...

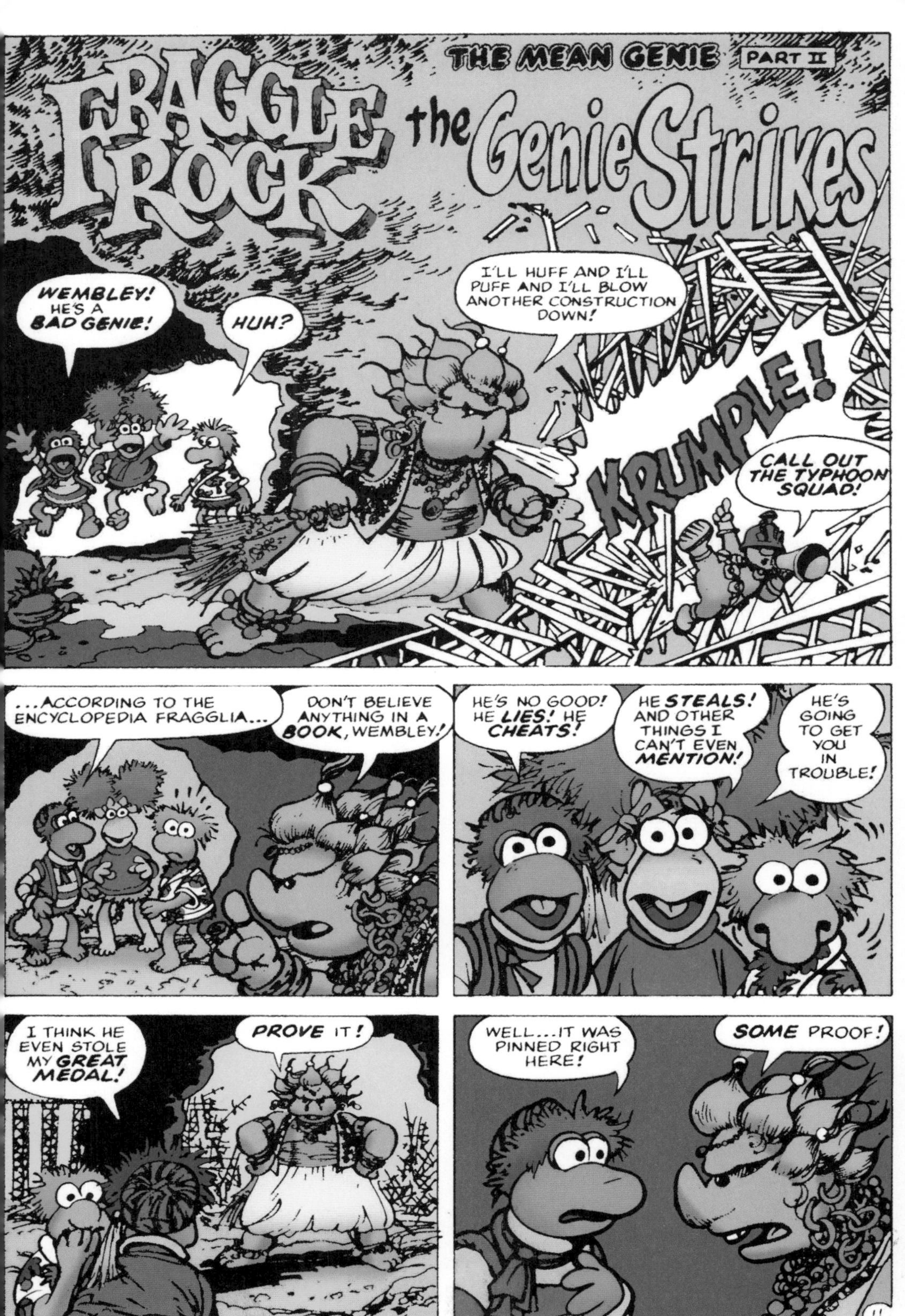
FRAGGLE ROCK
THE MEAN GENIE PART II
the Genie Strikes
WEMBLEY! HE'S A BAD GENIE!
HUH?
I'LL HUFF AND I'LL PUFF AND I'LL BLOW ANOTHER CONSTRUCTION DOWN!
KRUMPLE!
CALL OUT THE TYPHOON SQUAD!
...ACCORDING TO THE ENCYCLOPEDIA FRAGGLIA...
DON'T BELIEVE ANYTHING IN A BOOK, WEMBLEY!
HE'S NO GOOD! HE LIES! HE CHEATS!
HE STEALS! AND OTHER THINGS I CAN'T EVEN MENTION!
HE'S GOING TO GET YOU IN TROUBLE!
I THINK HE EVEN STOLE MY GREAT MEDAL!
PROVE IT!
WELL...IT WAS PINNED RIGHT HERE!
SOME PROOF!
11

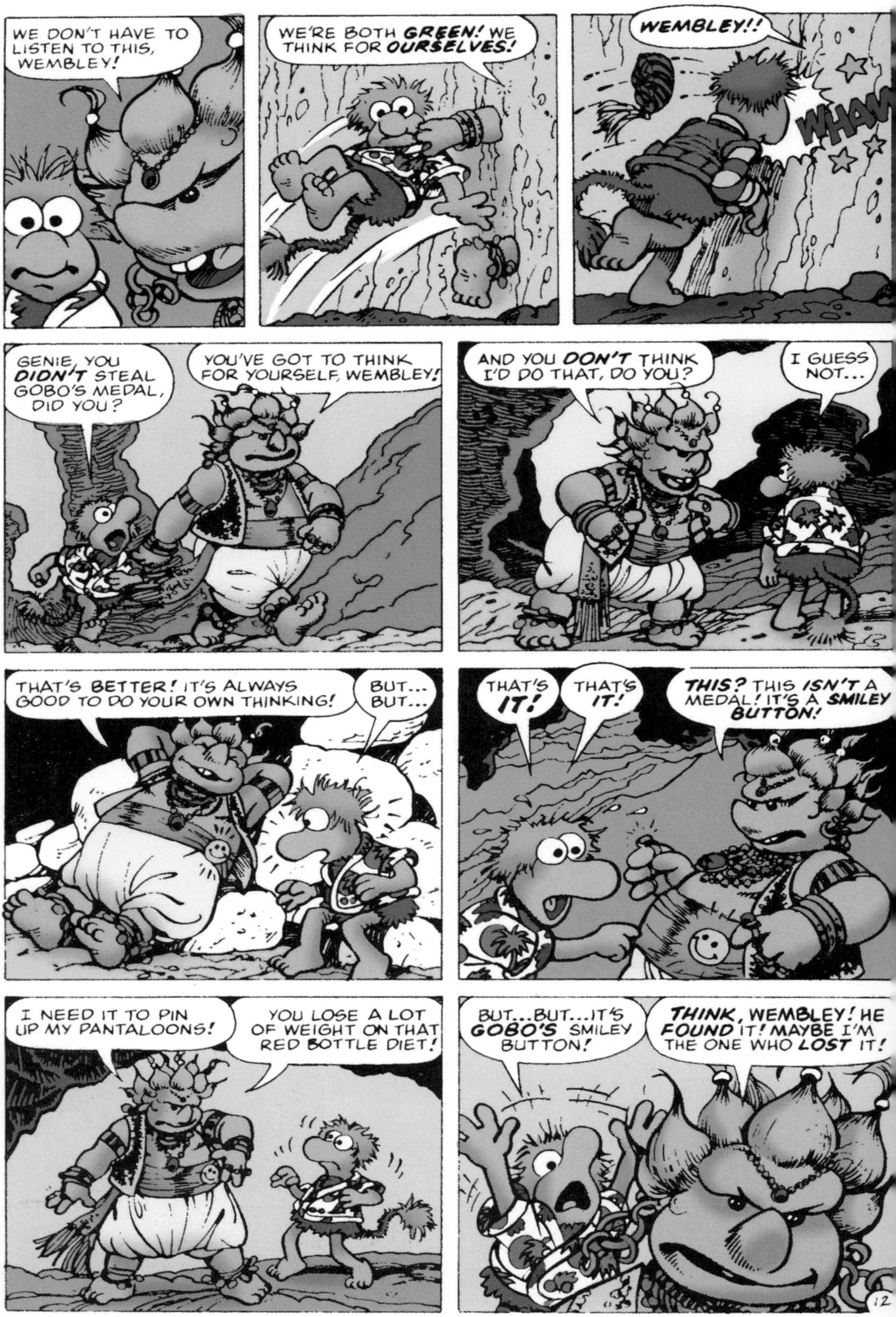
WE DON'T HAVE TO LISTEN TO THIS, WEMBLEY!
WE'RE BOTH GREEN! WE THINK FOR OURSELVES!
WEMBLEY!!
WHAM
GENIE, YOU DIDN'T STEAL GOBO'S MEDAL, DID YOU?
YOU'VE GOT TO THINK FOR YOURSELF, WEMBLEY!
AND YOU DON'T THINK I'D DO THAT, DO YOU?
I GUESS NOT...
THAT'S BETTER! IT'S ALWAYS GOOD TO DO YOUR OWN THINKING!
BUT... BUT...
THAT'S IT!
THAT'S IT!
THIS? THIS ISN'T A MEDAL! IT'S A SMILEY BUTTON!
I NEED IT TO PIN UP MY PANTALOONS!
YOU LOSE A LOT OF WEIGHT ON THAT RED BOTTLE DIET!
BUT...BUT...IT'S GOBO'S SMILEY BUTTON!
THINK, WEMBLEY! HE FOUND IT! MAYBE I'M THE ONE WHO LOST IT!

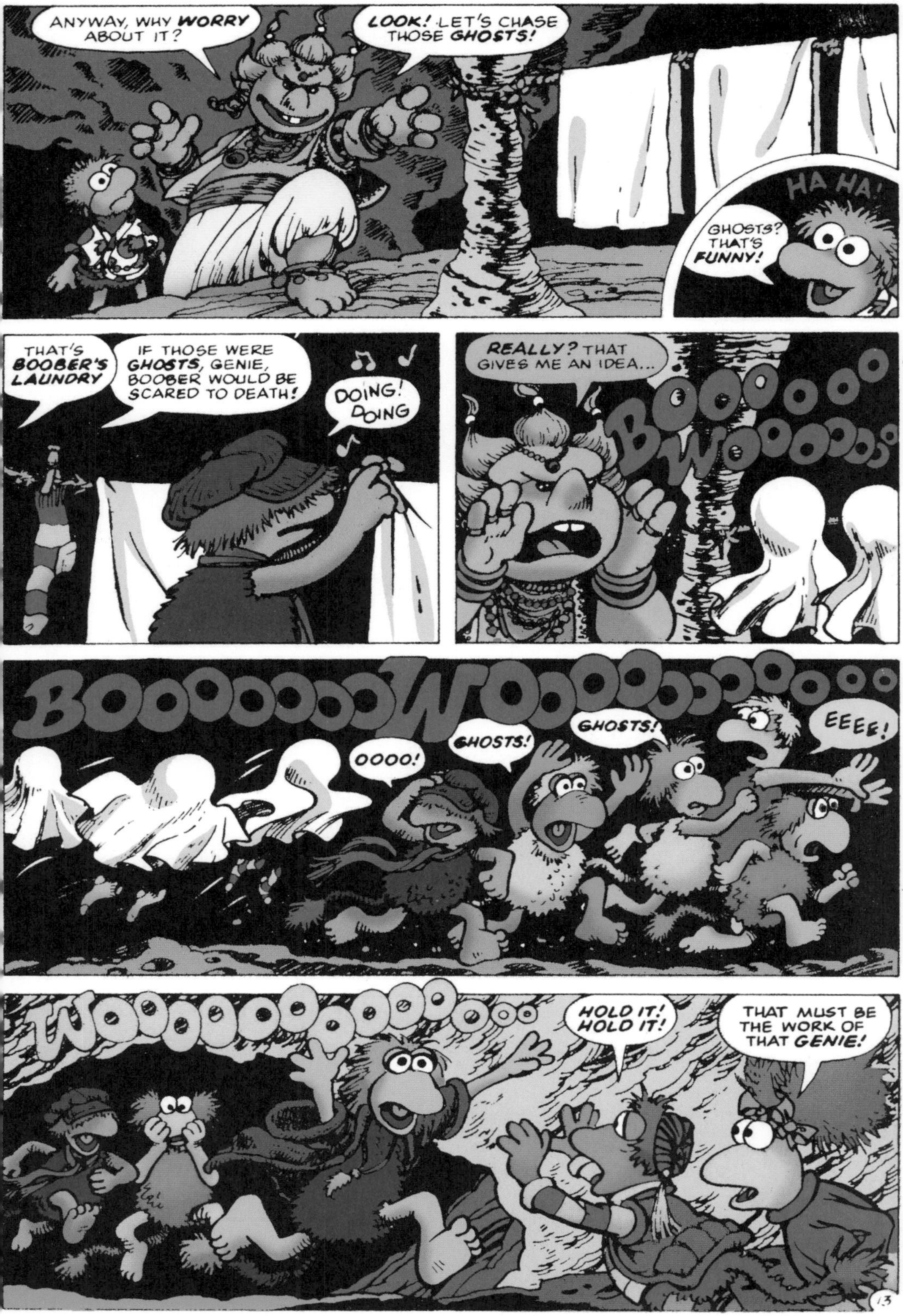

ANYWAY, WHY WORRY ABOUT IT?
LOOK! LET'S CHASE THOSE GHOSTS!
HA HA!
GHOSTS? THAT'S FUNNY!
THAT'S BOOBER'S LAUNDRY
IF THOSE WERE GHOSTS, GENIE, BOOBER WOULD BE SCARED TO DEATH!
DOING! DOING
REALLY? THAT GIVES ME AN IDEA...
BOOOOOOO WOOOOOOO
BOOOOOOOOWOOOOOOOOOOOO
OOOO!
GHOSTS!
GHOSTS!
EEEE!
WOOOOOOOOOOOOO
HOLD IT! HOLD IT!
THAT MUST BE THE WORK OF THAT GENIE!
13

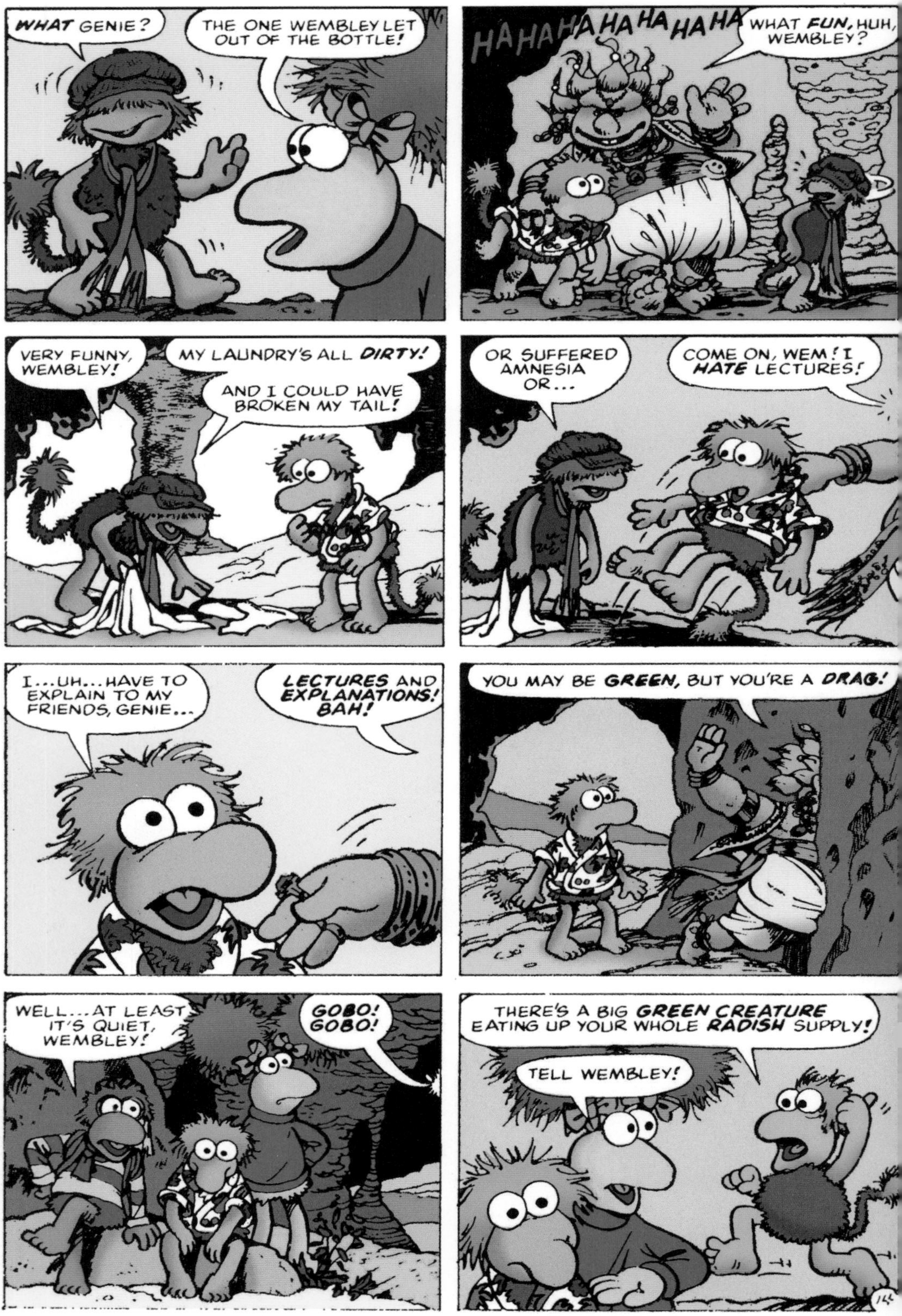
WHAT GENIE?
THE ONE WEMBLEY LET OUT OF THE BOTTLE!
HAHAHAHAHAHAHAHAHA
WHAT FUN, HUH, WEMBLEY?
VERY FUNNY, WEMBLEY!
MY LAUNDRY'S ALL DIRTY!
AND I COULD HAVE BROKEN MY TAIL!
OR SUFFERED AMNESIA OR...
COME ON, WEM! I HATE LECTURES!
I...UH...HAVE TO EXPLAIN TO MY FRIENDS, GENIE...
LECTURES AND EXPLANATIONS! BAH!
YOU MAY BE GREEN, BUT YOU'RE A DRAG!
WELL...AT LEAST IT'S QUIET, WEMBLEY!
GOBO! GOBO!
THERE'S A BIG GREEN CREATURE EATING UP YOUR WHOLE RADISH SUPPLY!
TELL WEMBLEY!

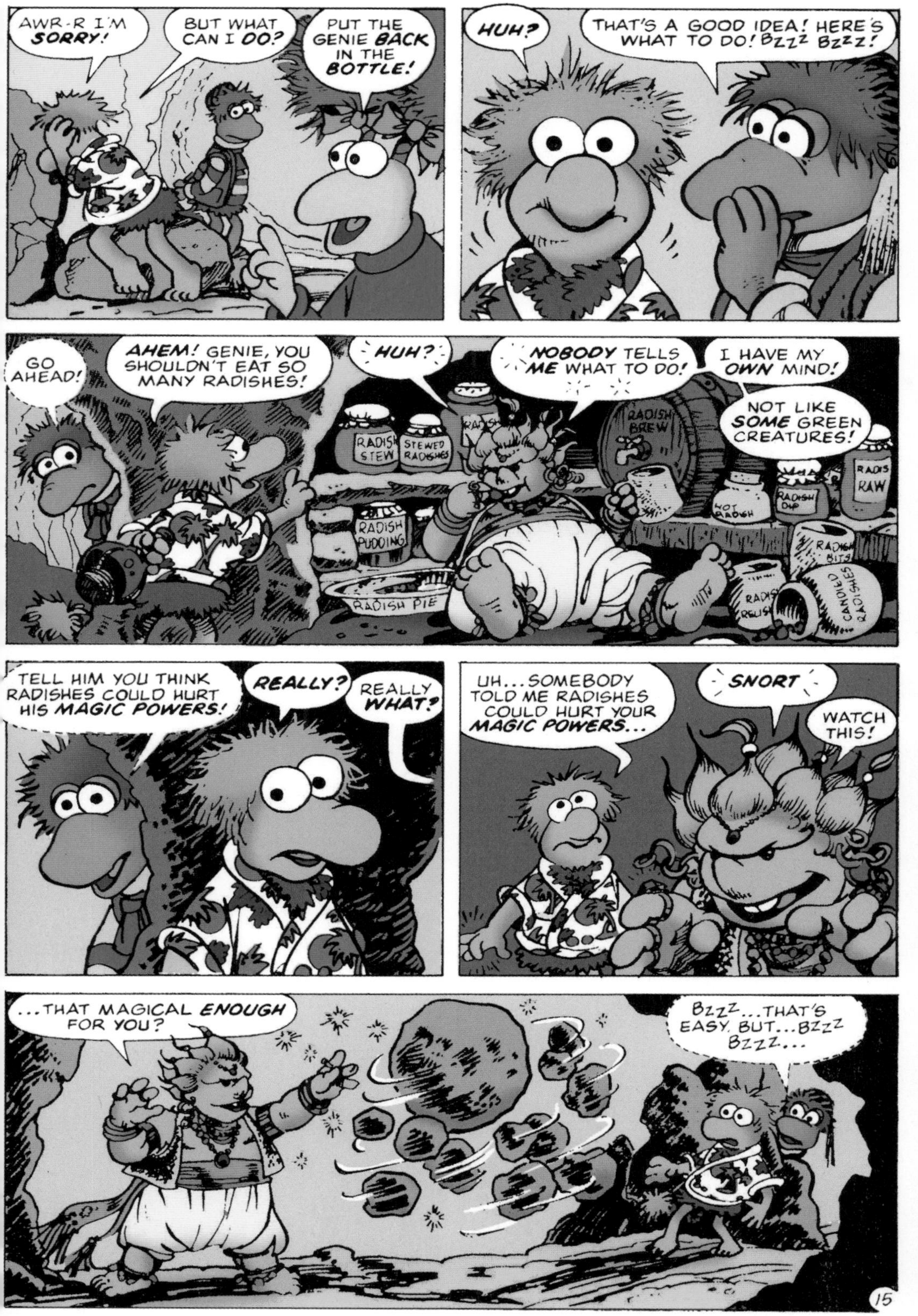
AWR-R I'M SORRY!
BUT WHAT CAN I DO?
PUT THE GENIE BACK IN THE BOTTLE!
HUH?
THAT'S A GOOD IDEA! HERE'S WHAT TO DO! Bzzz Bzzz!
GO AHEAD!
AHEM! GENIE, YOU SHOULDN'T EAT SO MANY RADISHES!
HUH?
NOBODY TELLS ME WHAT TO DO!
I HAVE MY OWN MIND!
NOT LIKE SOME GREEN CREATURES!
RADISH STEW
STEWED RADISHES
RADISH BREW
RADISH PUDDING
RADISH PIE
RADIS RAW
RADISH DIP
HOT RADISH
RADISH BITS
CANDIED RADISHES
TELL HIM YOU THINK RADISHES COULD HURT HIS MAGIC POWERS!
REALLY?
REALLY WHAT?
UH...SOMEBODY TOLD ME RADISHES COULD HURT YOUR MAGIC POWERS...
SNORT
WATCH THIS!
...THAT MAGICAL ENOUGH FOR YOU?
Bzzz...THAT'S EASY, BUT...Bzzz Bzzz...
15

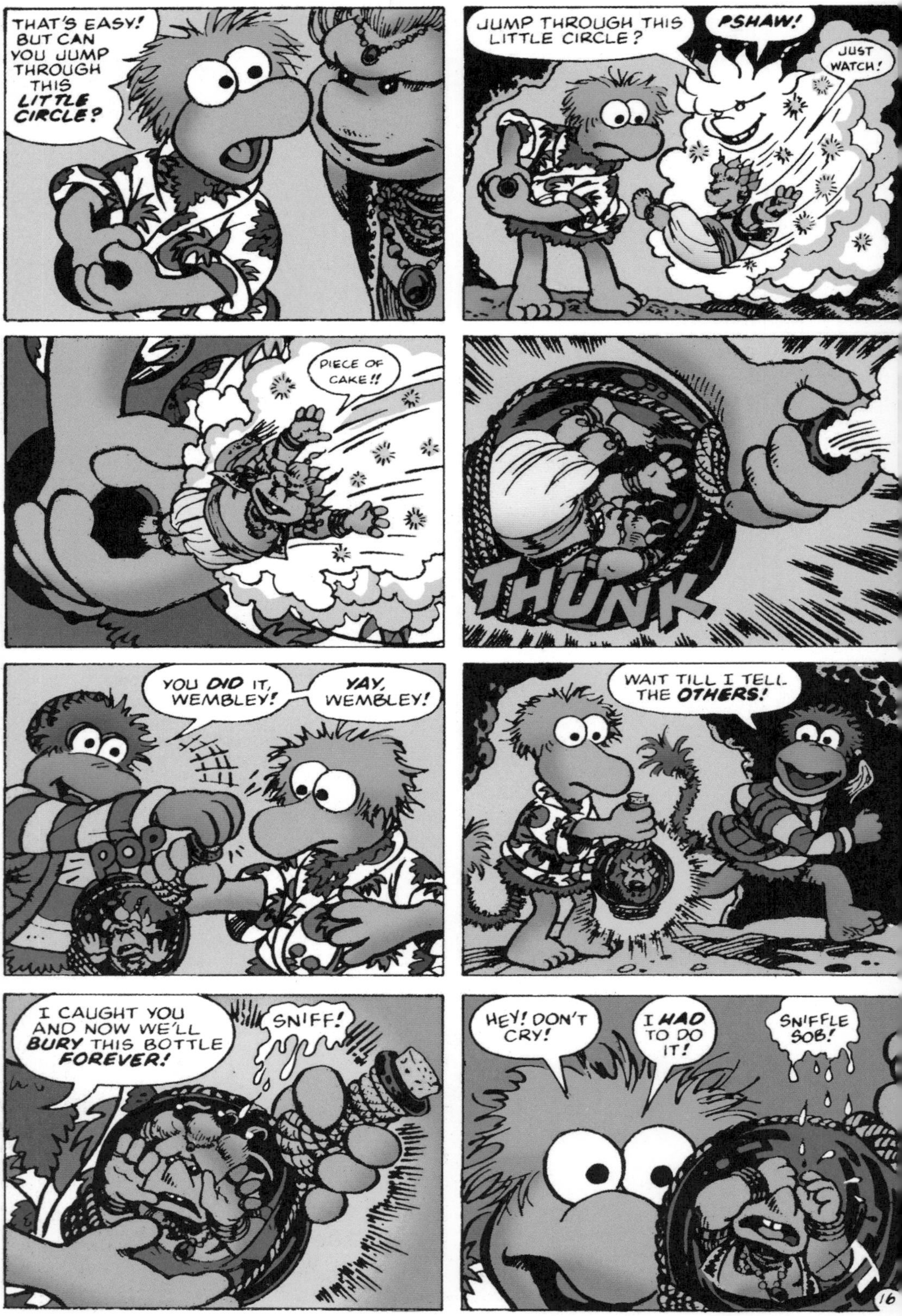
THAT'S EASY! BUT CAN YOU JUMP THROUGH THIS LITTLE CIRCLE?
JUMP THROUGH THIS LITTLE CIRCLE?
PSHAW!
JUST WATCH!
PIECE OF CAKE!!
THUNK
YOU DID IT, WEMBLEY!
YAY, WEMBLEY!
POP
WAIT TILL I TELL THE OTHERS!
I CAUGHT YOU AND NOW WE'LL BURY THIS BOTTLE FOREVER!
SNIFF!
HEY! DON'T CRY!
I HAD TO DO IT!
SNIFFLE SOB!
16

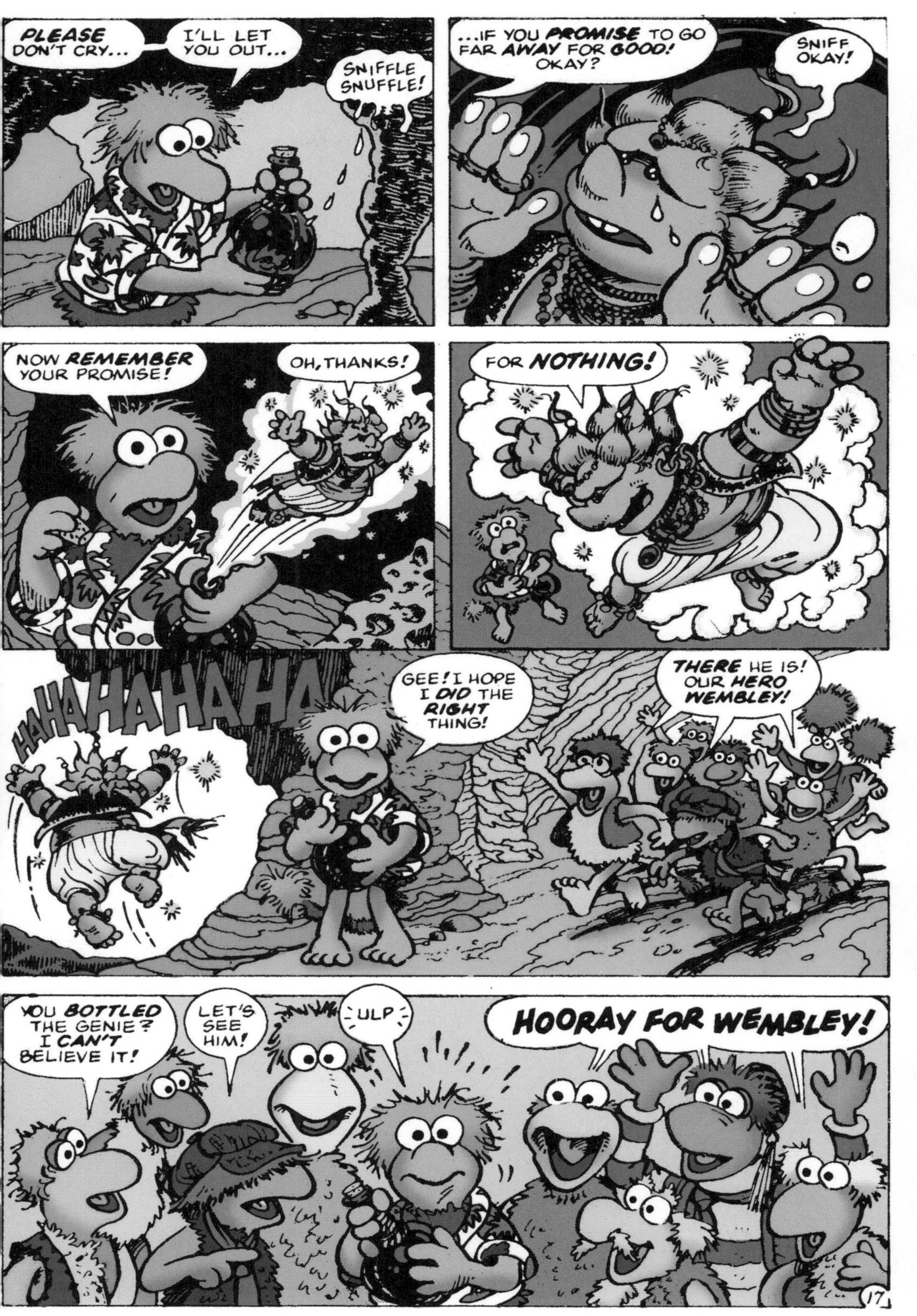
PLEASE DON'T CRY...
I'LL LET YOU OUT...
SNIFFLE SNUFFLE!
...IF YOU PROMISE TO GO FAR AWAY FOR GOOD! OKAY?
SNIFF OKAY!
NOW REMEMBER YOUR PROMISE!
OH, THANKS!
FOR NOTHING!
HAHAHAHAHAHA
GEE! I HOPE I DID THE RIGHT THING!
THERE HE IS! OUR HERO WEMBLEY!
YOU BOTTLED THE GENIE? I CAN'T BELIEVE IT!
LET'S SEE HIM!
ULP
HOORAY FOR WEMBLEY!
17

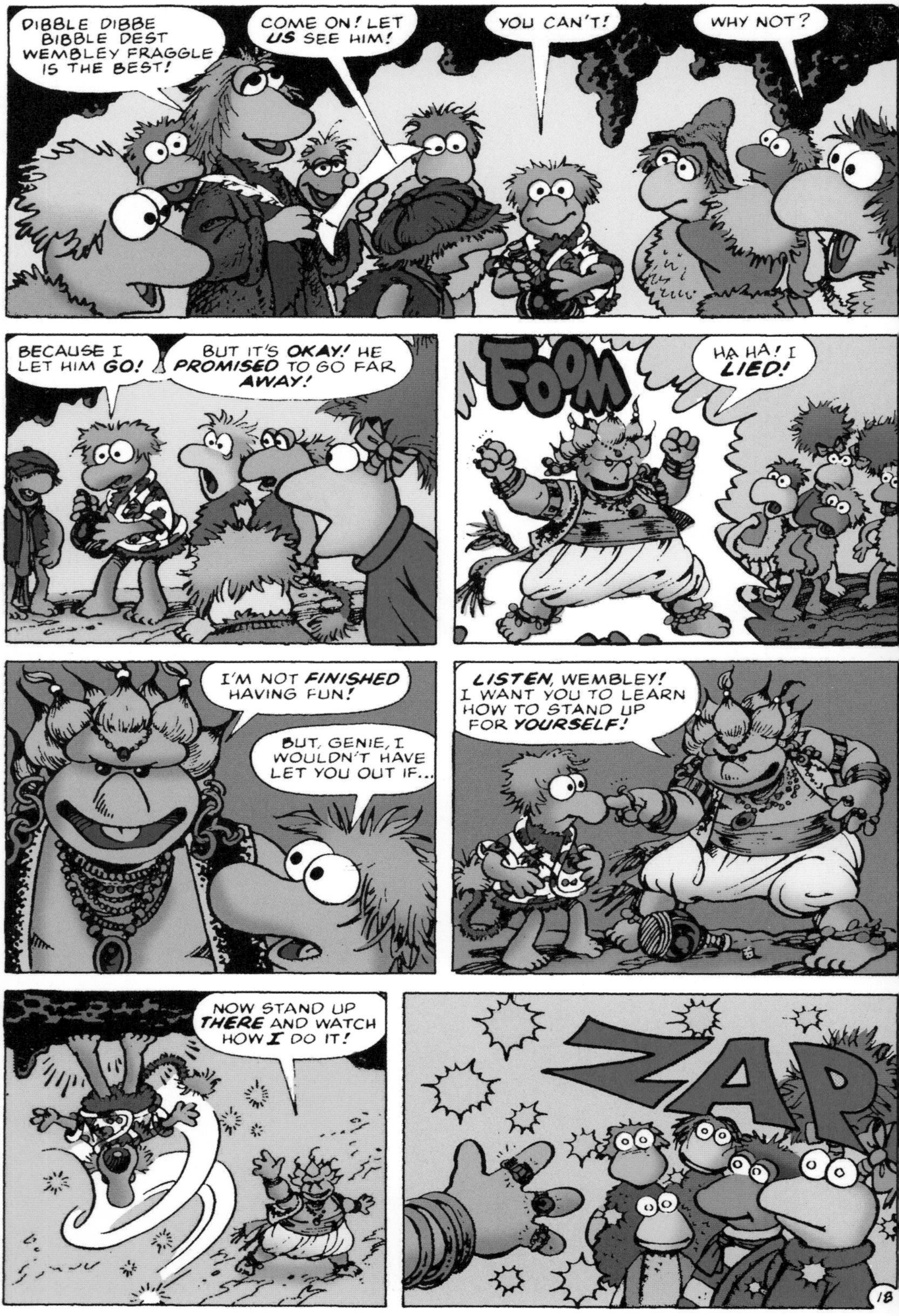
DIBBLE DIBBE BIBBLE DEST WEMBLEY FRAGGLE IS THE BEST!
COME ON! LET US SEE HIM!
YOU CAN'T!
WHY NOT?
BECAUSE I LET HIM GO!
BUT IT'S OKAY! HE PROMISED TO GO FAR AWAY!
FOOM
HA HA! I LIED!
I'M NOT FINISHED HAVING FUN!
BUT, GENIE, I WOULDN'T HAVE LET YOU OUT IF...
LISTEN, WEMBLEY! I WANT YOU TO LEARN HOW TO STAND UP FOR YOURSELF!
NOW STAND UP THERE AND WATCH HOW I DO IT!
ZAP
18

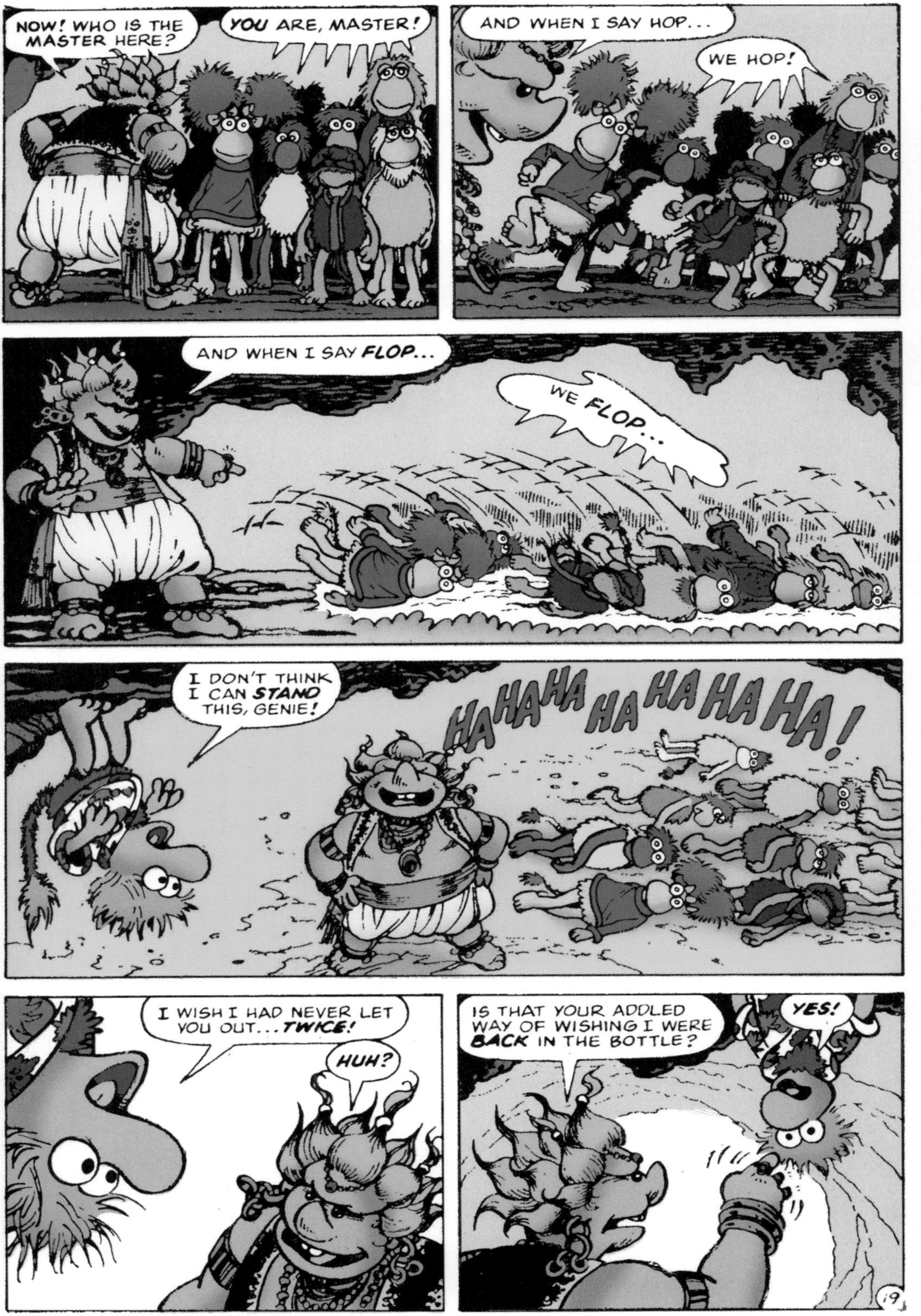
NOW! WHO IS THE MASTER HERE?
YOU ARE, MASTER!
AND WHEN I SAY HOP...
WE HOP!
AND WHEN I SAY FLOP...
WE FLOP...
I DON'T THINK I CAN STAND THIS, GENIE!
HAHAHA HAHAHAHAHA!
I WISH I HAD NEVER LET YOU OUT...TWICE!
HUH?
IS THAT YOUR ADDLED WAY OF WISHING I WERE BACK IN THE BOTTLE?
YES!
19

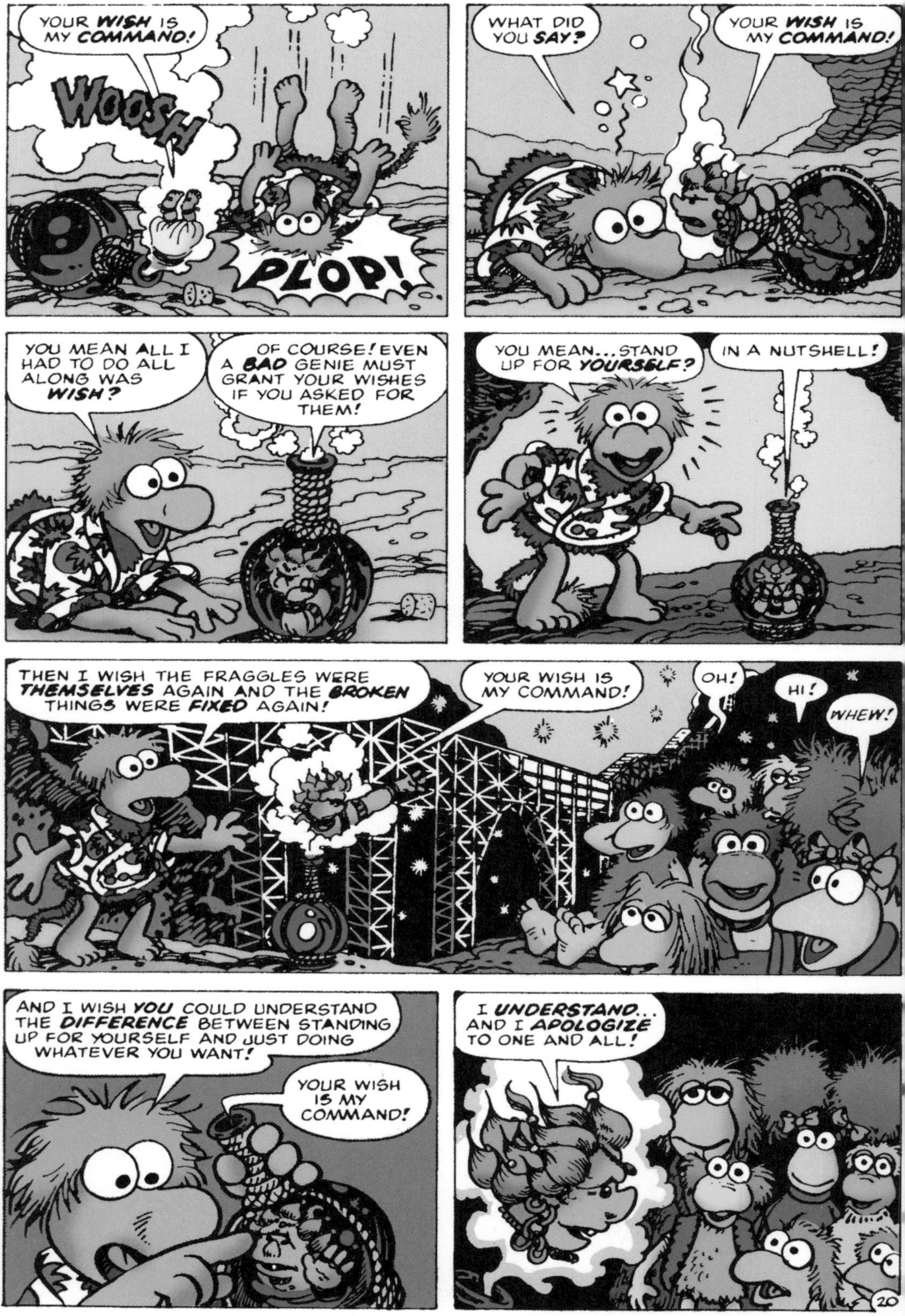
YOUR WISH IS MY COMMAND!
WOOSH
PLOP!
WHAT DID YOU SAY?
YOUR WISH IS MY COMMAND!
YOU MEAN ALL I HAD TO DO ALL ALONG WAS WISH?
OF COURSE! EVEN A BAD GENIE MUST GRANT YOUR WISHES IF YOU ASKED FOR THEM!
YOU MEAN... STAND UP FOR YOURSELF?
IN A NUTSHELL!
THEN I WISH THE FRAGGLES WERE THEMSELVES AGAIN AND THE BROKEN THINGS WERE FIXED AGAIN!
YOUR WISH IS MY COMMAND!
OH!
HI!
WHEW!
AND I WISH YOU COULD UNDERSTAND THE DIFFERENCE BETWEEN STANDING UP FOR YOURSELF AND JUST DOING WHATEVER YOU WANT!
YOUR WISH IS MY COMMAND!
I UNDERSTAND... AND I APOLOGIZE TO ONE AND ALL!
20

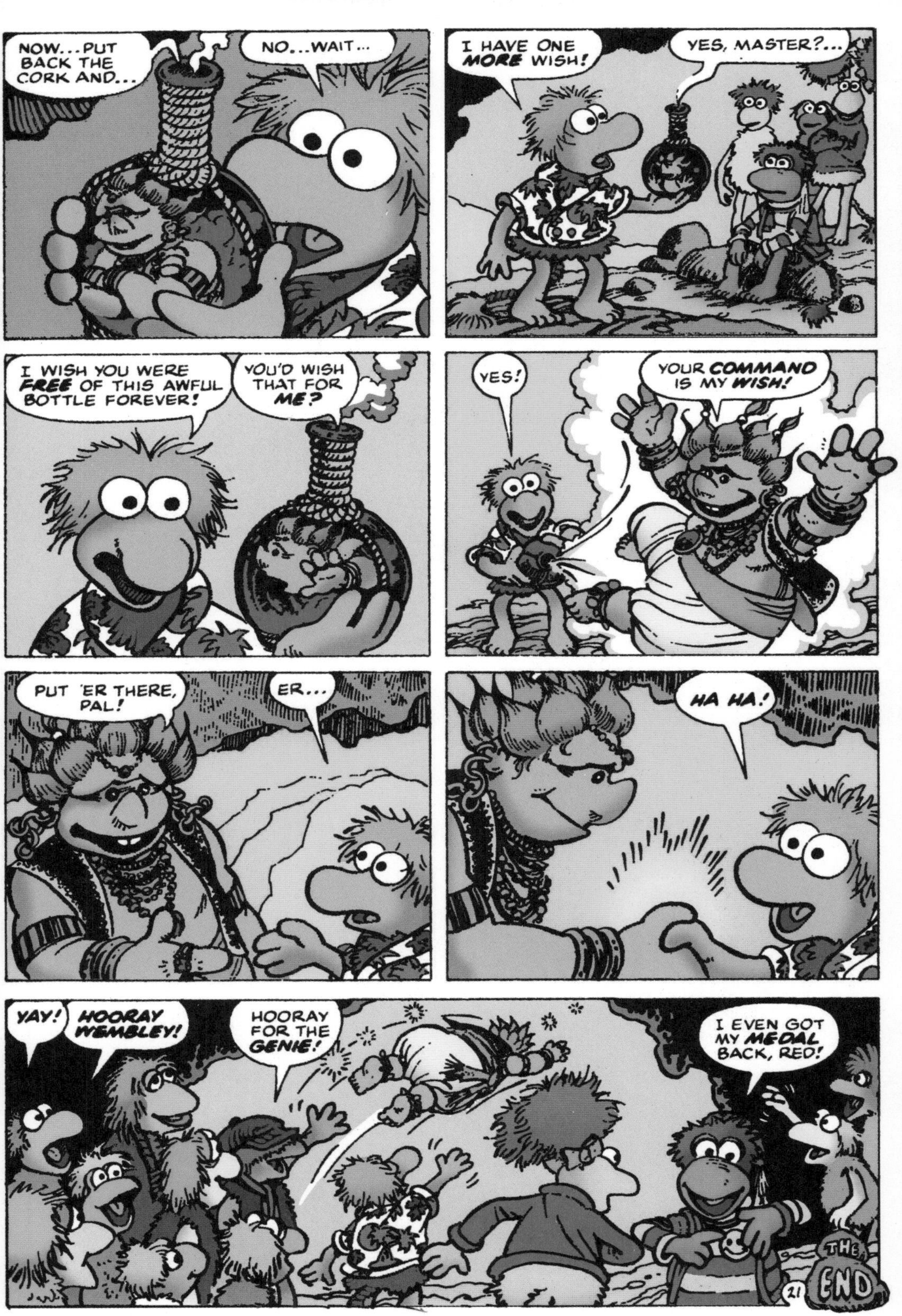
NOW...PUT BACK THE CORK AND...
NO...WAIT...
I HAVE ONE MORE WISH!
YES, MASTER?...
I WISH YOU WERE FREE OF THIS AWFUL BOTTLE FOREVER!
YOU'D WISH THAT FOR ME?
YES!
YOUR COMMAND IS MY WISH!
PUT 'ER THERE, PAL!
ER...
HA HA!
YAY!
HOORAY WEMBLEY!
HOORAY FOR THE GENIE!
I EVEN GOT MY MEDAL BACK, RED!
21
THE END

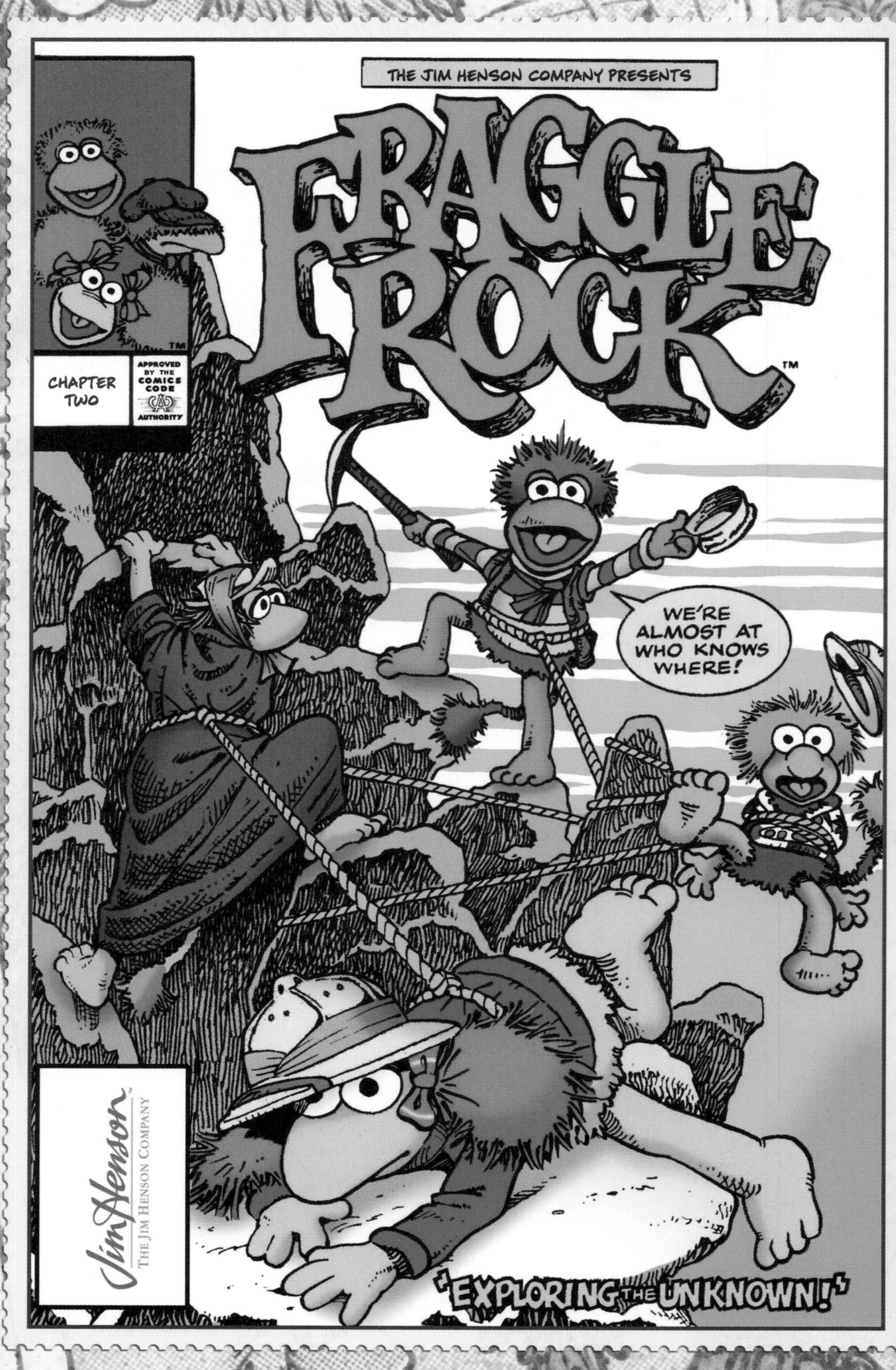
THE JIM HENSON COMPANY PRESENTS
FRAGGLE ROCK™
CHAPTER TWO
APPROVED BY THE COMICS CODE AUTHORITY
WE'RE ALMOST AT WHO KNOWS WHERE!
Jim Henson™ THE JIM HENSON COMPANY
"EXPLORING THE UNKNOWN!"

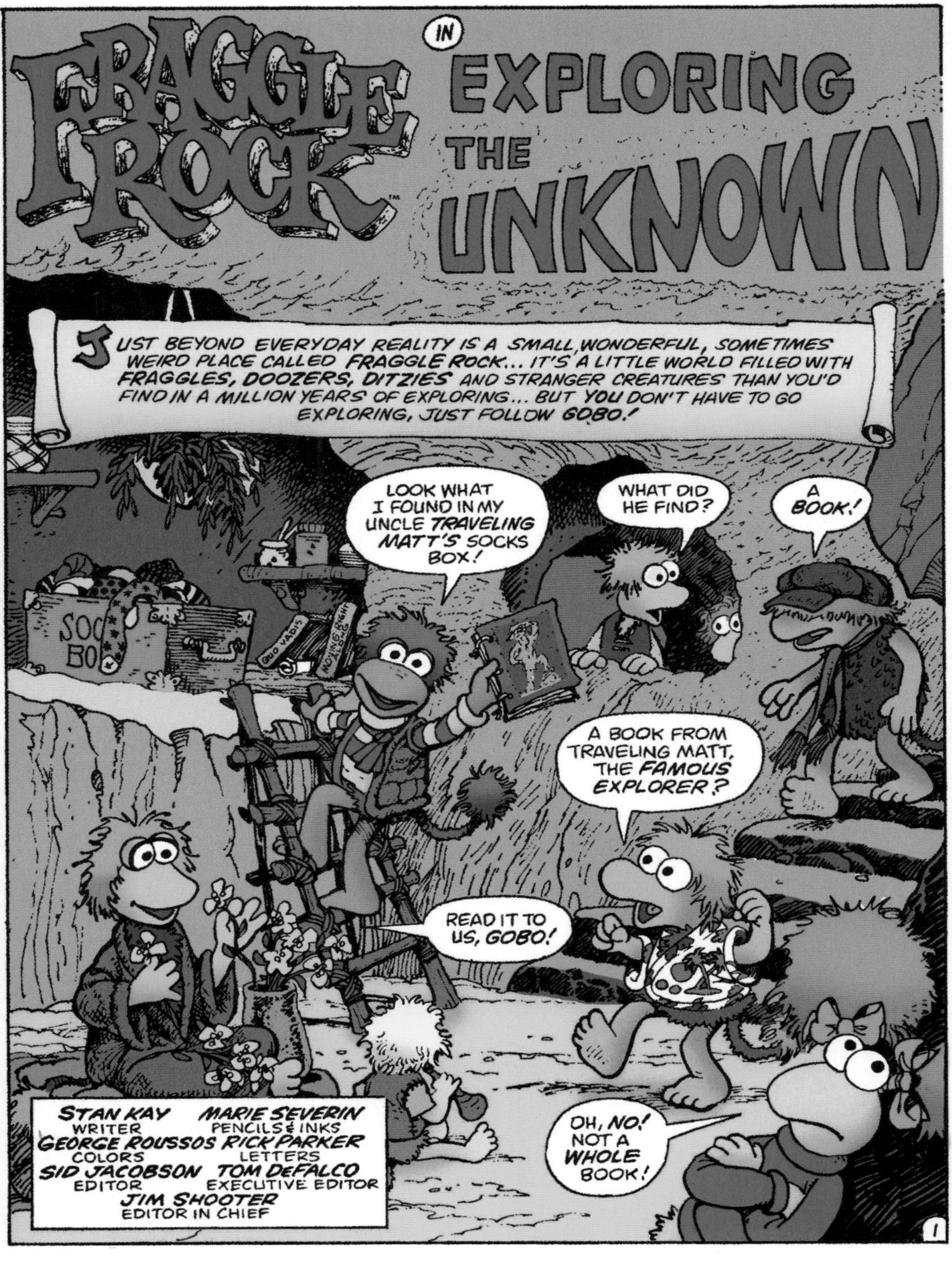

FRAGGLE ROCK™
IN
EXPLORING THE UNKNOWN
JUST BEYOND EVERYDAY REALITY IS A SMALL, WONDERFUL, SOMETIMES WEIRD PLACE CALLED FRAGGLE ROCK... IT'S A LITTLE WORLD FILLED WITH FRAGGLES, DOOZERS, DITZIES AND STRANGER CREATURES THAN YOU'D FIND IN A MILLION YEARS OF EXPLORING... BUT YOU DON'T HAVE TO GO EXPLORING, JUST FOLLOW GOBO!
LOOK WHAT I FOUND IN MY UNCLE TRAVELING MATT'S SOCKS BOX!
WHAT DID HE FIND?
A BOOK!
A BOOK FROM TRAVELING MATT, THE FAMOUS EXPLORER?
READ IT TO US, GOBO!
OH, NO! NOT A WHOLE BOOK!
STAN KAY WRITER
MARIE SEVERIN PENCILS & INKS
GEORGE ROUSSOS COLORS
RICK PARKER LETTERS
SID JACOBSON EDITOR
TOM DeFALCO EXECUTIVE EDITOR
JIM SHOOTER EDITOR IN CHIEF
1

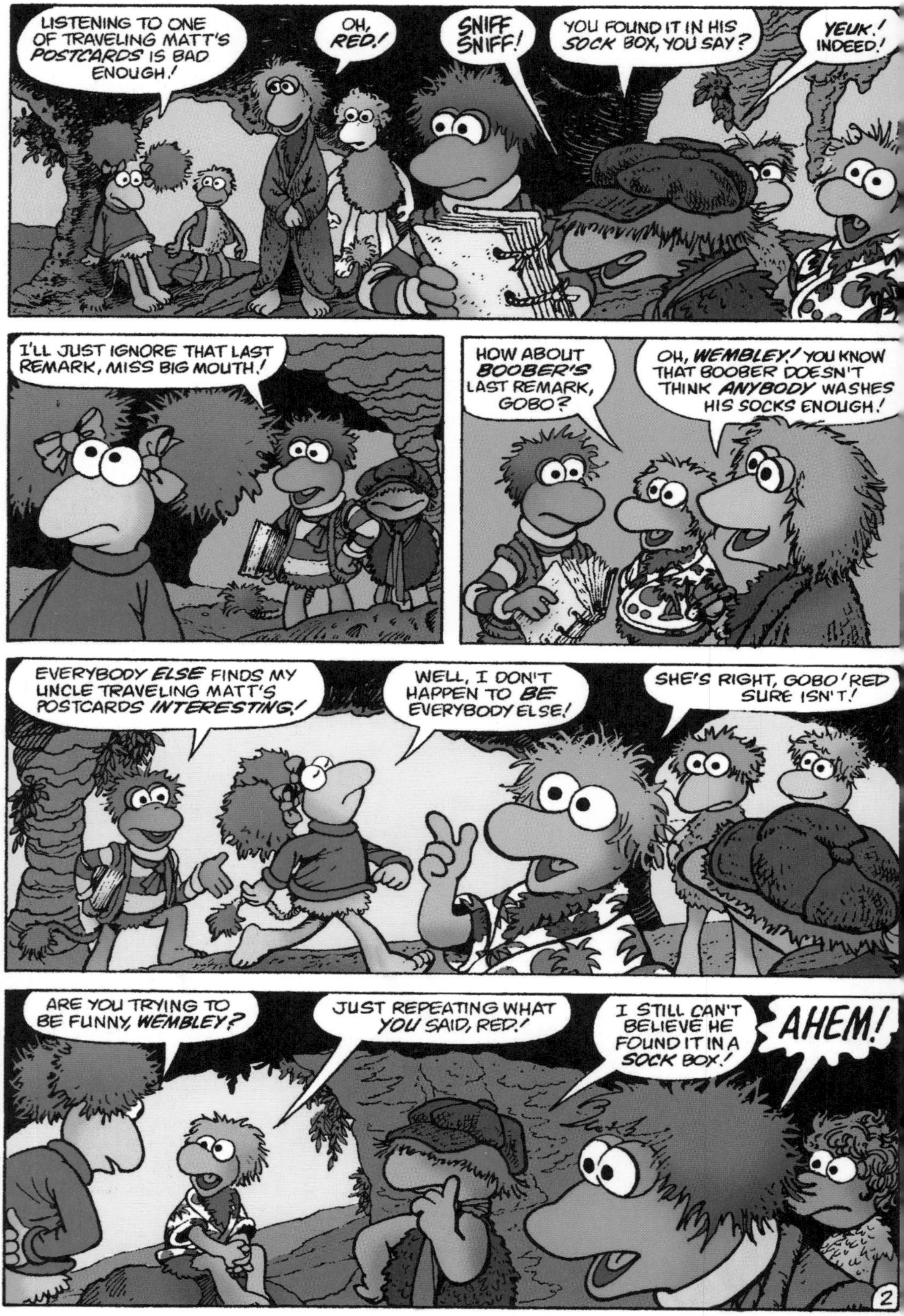
LISTENING TO ONE OF TRAVELING MATT'S POSTCARDS IS BAD ENOUGH!
OH, RED!
SNIFF SNIFF!
YOU FOUND IT IN HIS SOCK BOX, YOU SAY?
YEUK! INDEED!
I'LL JUST IGNORE THAT LAST REMARK, MISS BIG MOUTH!
HOW ABOUT BOOBER'S LAST REMARK, GOBO?
OH, WEMBLEY! YOU KNOW THAT BOOBER DOESN'T THINK ANYBODY WASHES HIS SOCKS ENOUGH!
EVERYBODY ELSE FINDS MY UNCLE TRAVELING MATT'S POSTCARDS INTERESTING!
WELL, I DON'T HAPPEN TO BE EVERYBODY ELSE!
SHE'S RIGHT, GOBO! RED SURE ISN'T!
ARE YOU TRYING TO BE FUNNY, WEMBLEY?
JUST REPEATING WHAT YOU SAID, RED!
I STILL CAN'T BELIEVE HE FOUND IT IN A SOCK BOX!
AHEM!
2

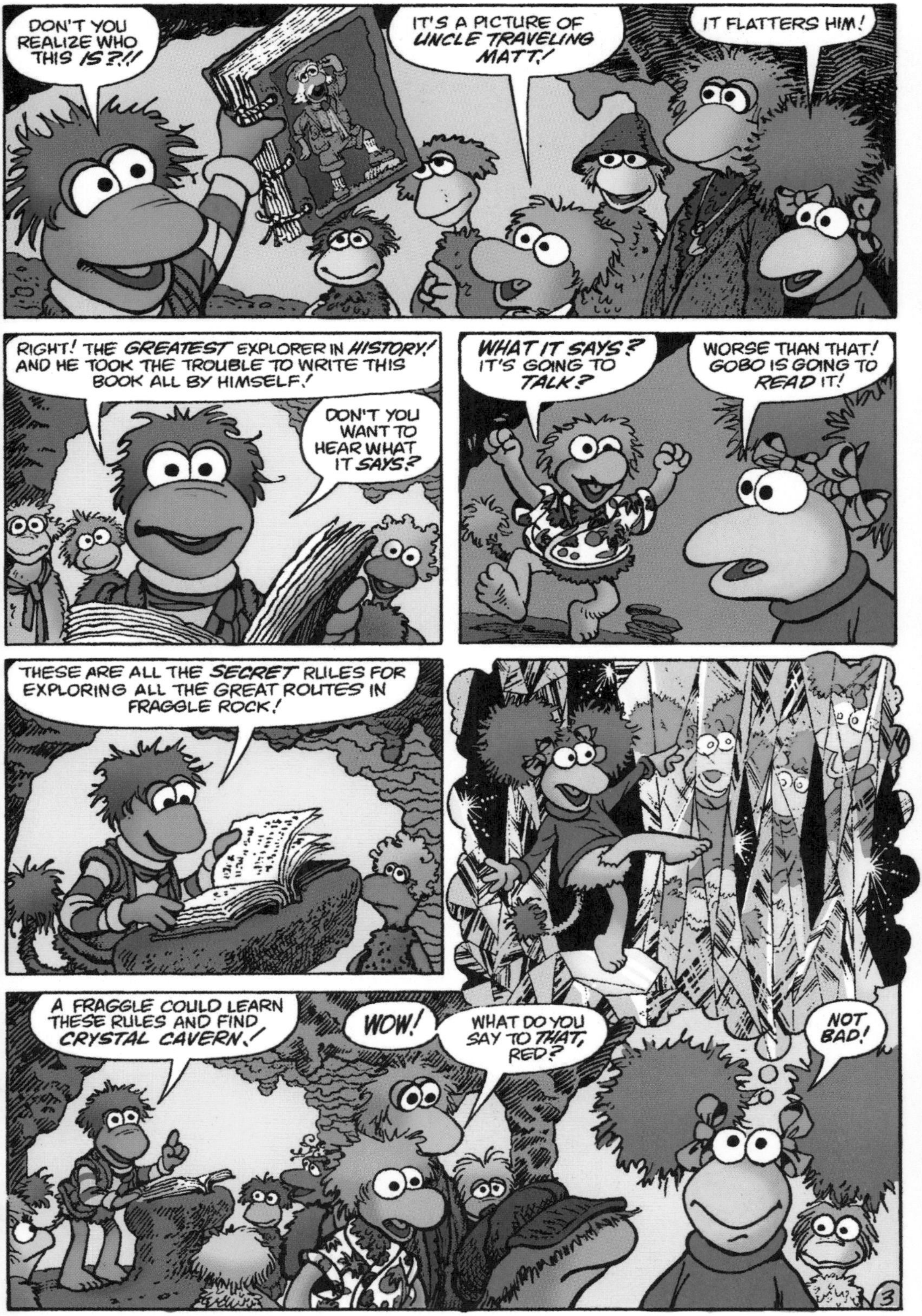
DON'T YOU REALIZE WHO THIS *IS*?!!
IT'S A PICTURE OF *UNCLE TRAVELING MATT!*
IT FLATTERS HIM!
RIGHT! THE *GREATEST* EXPLORER IN *HISTORY!* AND HE TOOK THE TROUBLE TO WRITE THIS BOOK ALL BY HIMSELF!
DON'T YOU WANT TO HEAR WHAT IT *SAYS?*
WHAT IT SAYS? IT'S GOING TO *TALK?*
WORSE THAN THAT! *GOBO* IS GOING TO *READ* IT!
THESE ARE ALL THE *SECRET* RULES FOR EXPLORING ALL THE GREAT ROUTES IN FRAGGLE ROCK!
A FRAGGLE COULD LEARN THESE RULES AND FIND *CRYSTAL CAVERN!*
WOW!
WHAT DO YOU SAY TO *THAT,* RED?
NOT BAD!
3

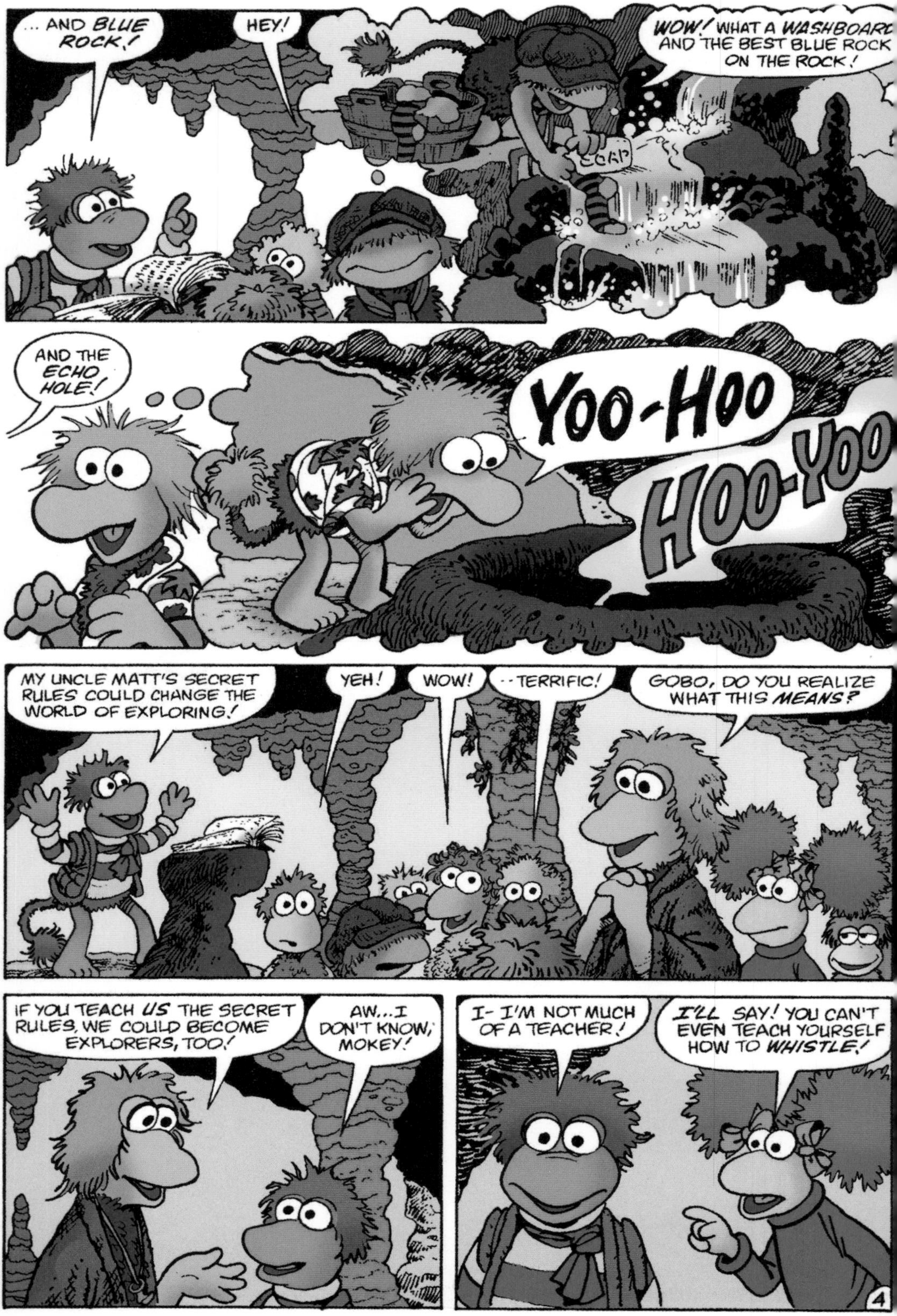

... AND BLUE ROCK!
HEY!
WOW! WHAT A WASHBOARD AND THE BEST BLUE ROCK ON THE ROCK!
SOAP
AND THE ECHO HOLE!
YOO-HOO
HOO-YOO
MY UNCLE MATT'S SECRET RULES COULD CHANGE THE WORLD OF EXPLORING!
YEH!
WOW!
--TERRIFIC!
GOBO, DO YOU REALIZE WHAT THIS MEANS?
IF YOU TEACH US THE SECRET RULES, WE COULD BECOME EXPLORERS, TOO!
AW...I DON'T KNOW, MOKEY!
I- I'M NOT MUCH OF A TEACHER!
I'LL SAY! YOU CAN'T EVEN TEACH YOURSELF HOW TO WHISTLE!
4

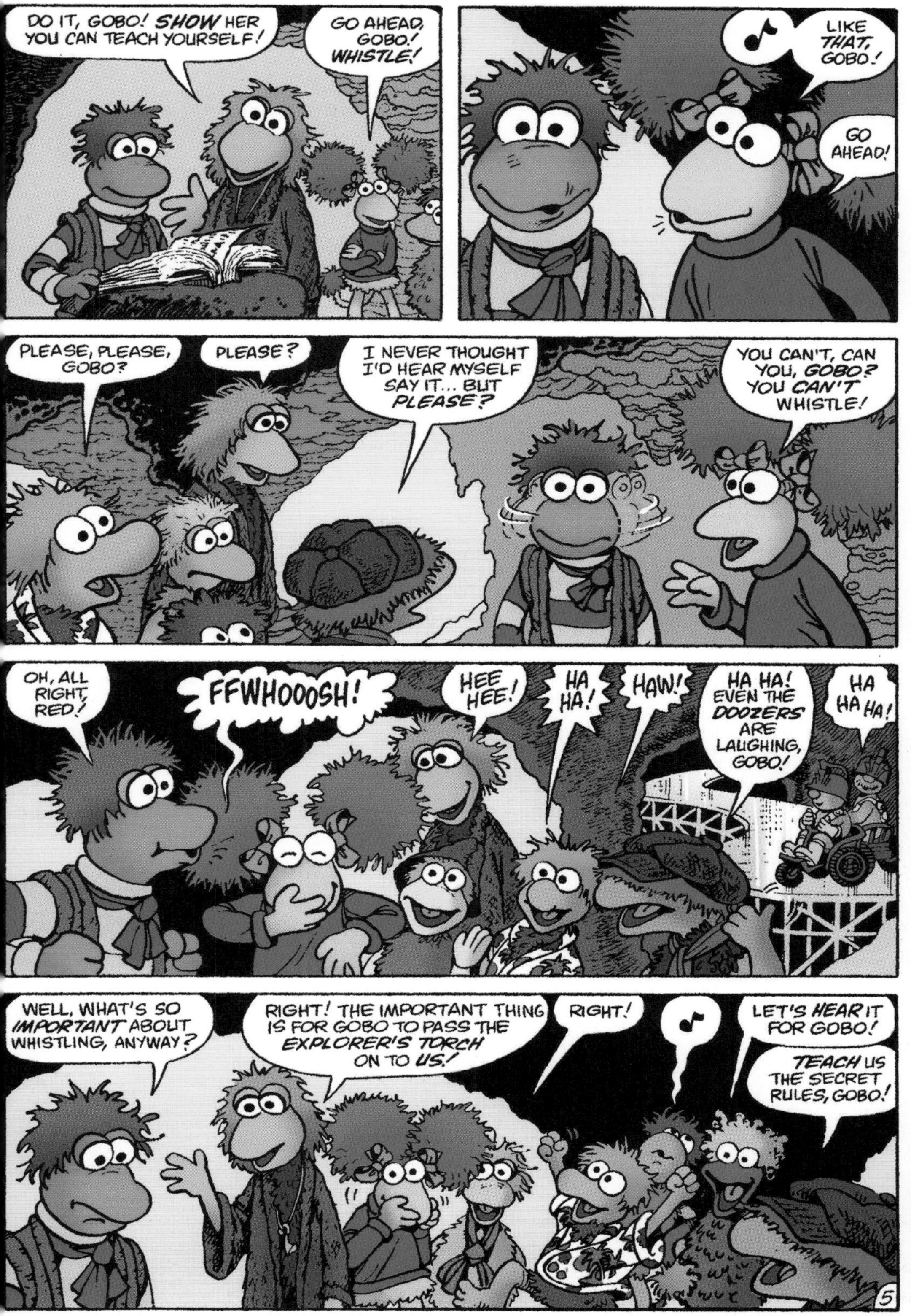

DO IT, GOBO! SHOW HER YOU CAN TEACH YOURSELF!
GO AHEAD, GOBO! WHISTLE!
♪
LIKE THAT, GOBO!
GO AHEAD!
PLEASE, PLEASE, GOBO?
PLEASE?
I NEVER THOUGHT I'D HEAR MYSELF SAY IT... BUT PLEASE?
YOU CAN'T, CAN YOU, GOBO? YOU CAN'T WHISTLE!
OH, ALL RIGHT, RED!
FFWHOOOSH!
HEE HEE!
HA HA!
HAW!
HA HA! EVEN THE DOOZERS ARE LAUGHING, GOBO!
HA HA HA!
WELL, WHAT'S SO IMPORTANT ABOUT WHISTLING, ANYWAY?
RIGHT! THE IMPORTANT THING IS FOR GOBO TO PASS THE EXPLORER'S TORCH ON TO US!
RIGHT!
♪
LET'S HEAR IT FOR GOBO!
TEACH US THE SECRET RULES, GOBO!
5

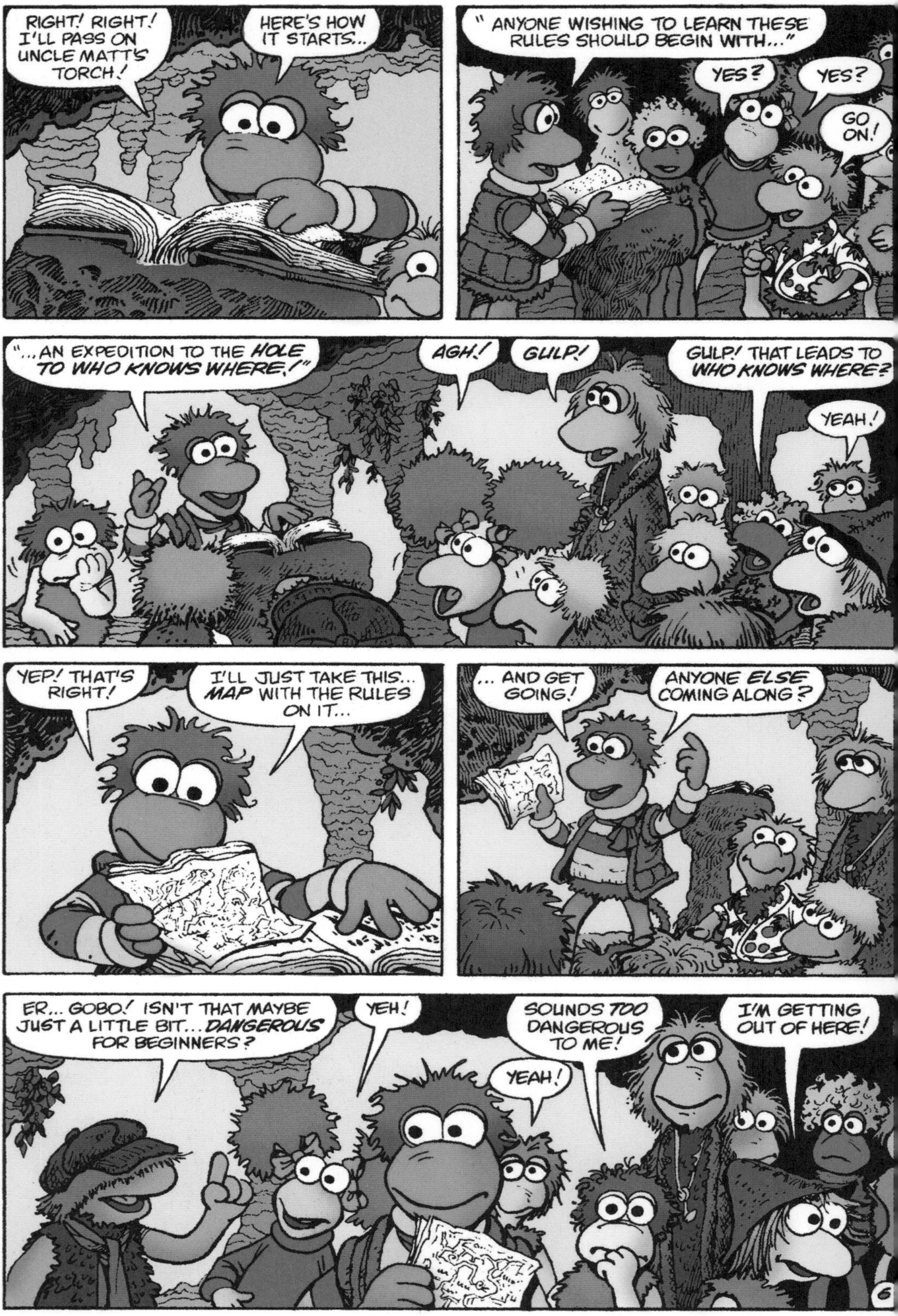
RIGHT! RIGHT! I'LL PASS ON UNCLE MATT'S TORCH!
HERE'S HOW IT STARTS...
" ANYONE WISHING TO LEARN THESE RULES SHOULD BEGIN WITH..."
YES?
YES?
GO ON!
"...AN EXPEDITION TO THE HOLE TO WHO KNOWS WHERE!"
AGH!
GULP!
GULP! THAT LEADS TO WHO KNOWS WHERE?
YEAH!
YEP! THAT'S RIGHT!
I'LL JUST TAKE THIS... MAP WITH THE RULES ON IT...
... AND GET GOING!
ANYONE ELSE COMING ALONG?
ER... GOBO! ISN'T THAT MAYBE JUST A LITTLE BIT... DANGEROUS FOR BEGINNERS?
YEH!
SOUNDS TOO DANGEROUS TO ME!
YEAH!
I'M GETTING OUT OF HERE!
6

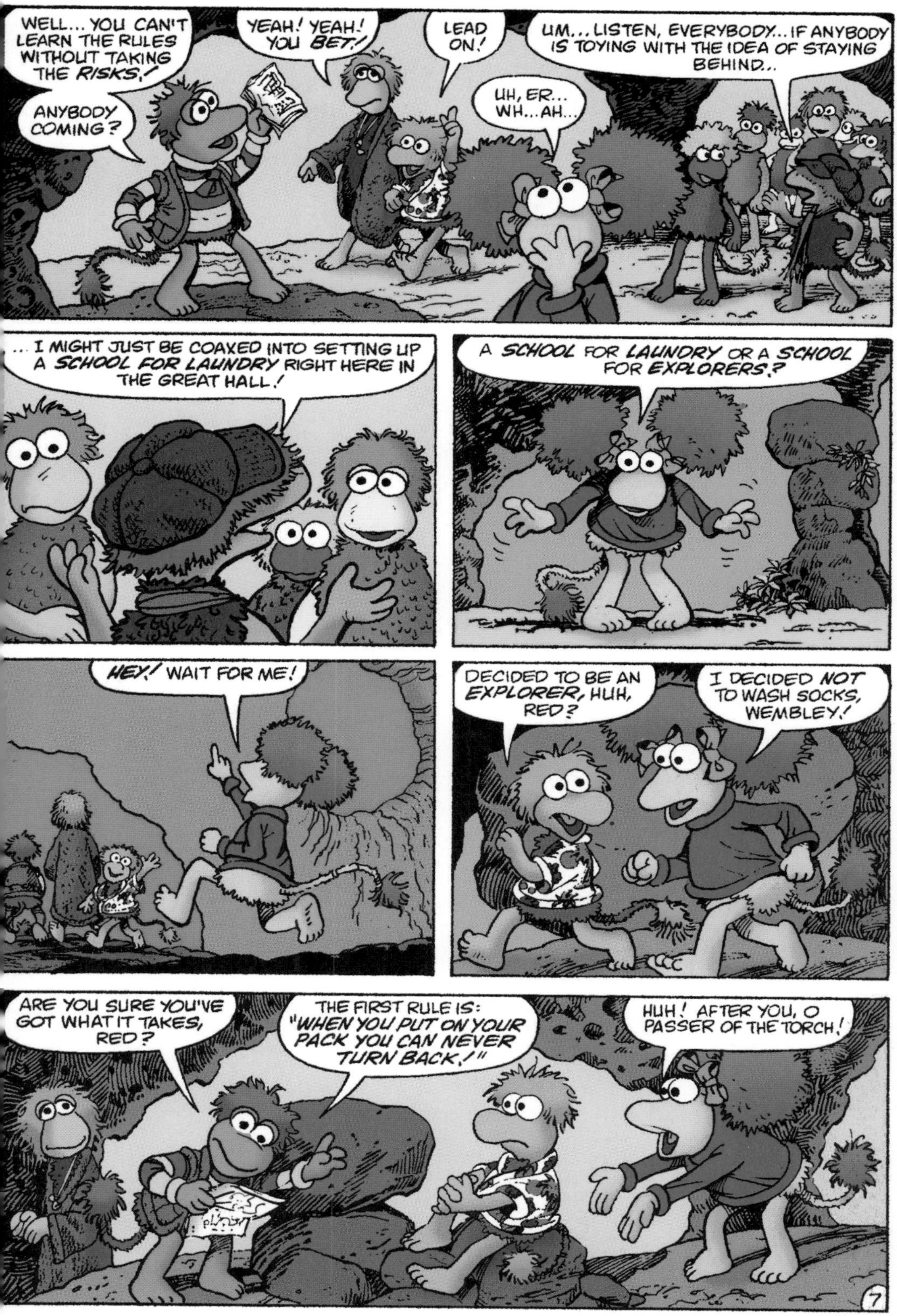

WELL... YOU CAN'T LEARN THE RULES WITHOUT TAKING THE *RISKS*!
ANYBODY COMING?
YEAH! YEAH! YOU *BET*!
LEAD ON!
UH, ER... WH...AH...
UM... LISTEN, EVERYBODY... IF ANYBODY IS TOYING WITH THE IDEA OF STAYING BEHIND...
... I MIGHT JUST BE COAXED INTO SETTING UP A *SCHOOL FOR LAUNDRY* RIGHT HERE IN THE GREAT HALL!
A *SCHOOL* FOR *LAUNDRY* OR A *SCHOOL* FOR *EXPLORERS*?
HEY! WAIT FOR ME!
DECIDED TO BE AN *EXPLORER*, HUH, RED?
I DECIDED *NOT* TO WASH SOCKS, WEMBLEY!
ARE YOU SURE YOU'VE GOT WHAT IT TAKES, RED?
THE FIRST RULE IS: *"WHEN YOU PUT ON YOUR PACK YOU CAN NEVER TURN BACK!"*
HUH! AFTER YOU, O PASSER OF THE TORCH!
7

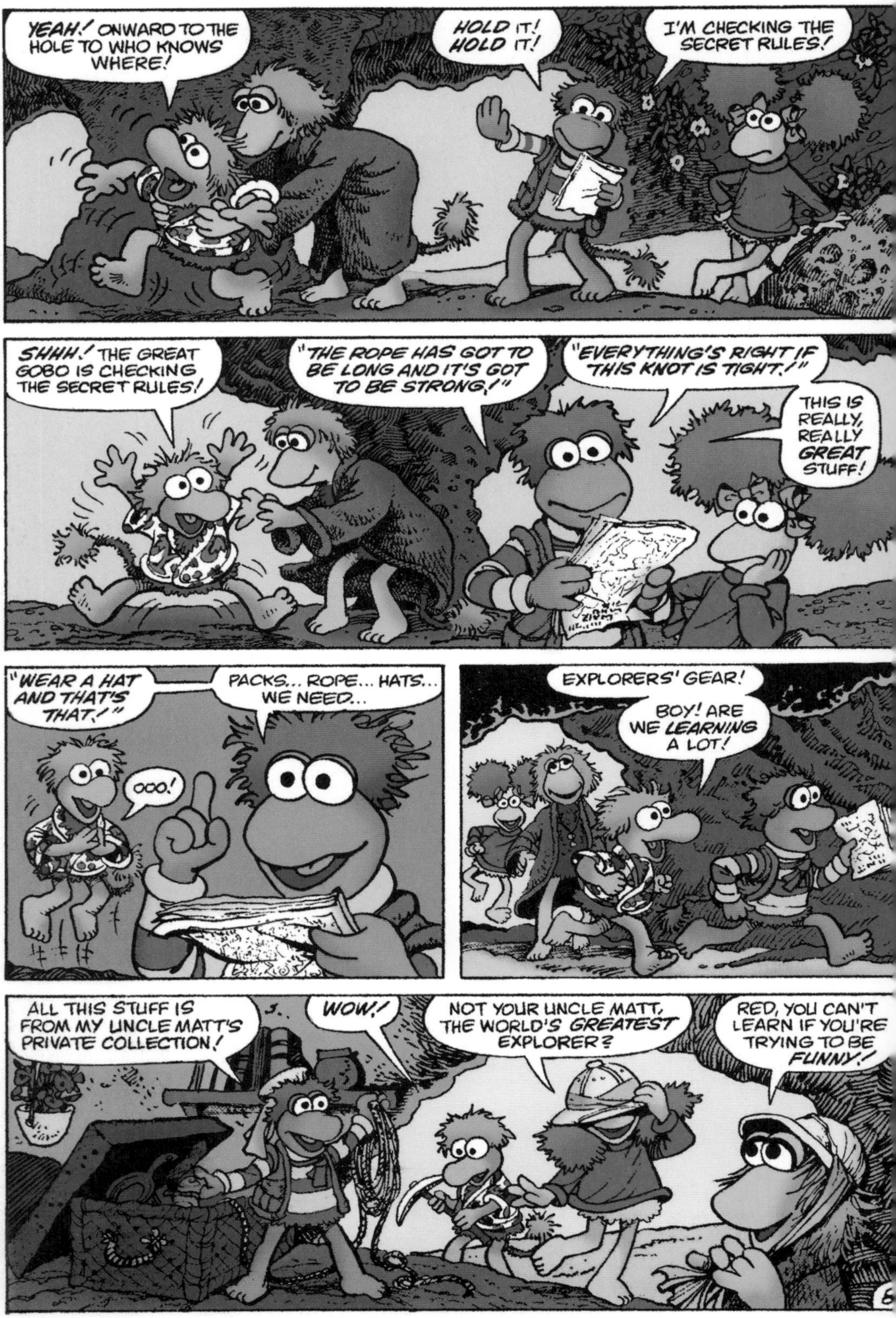
YEAH! ONWARD TO THE HOLE TO WHO KNOWS WHERE!
HOLD IT! HOLD IT!
I'M CHECKING THE SECRET RULES!
SHHH! THE GREAT GOBO IS CHECKING THE SECRET RULES!
"THE ROPE HAS GOT TO BE LONG AND IT'S GOT TO BE STRONG!"
"EVERYTHING'S RIGHT IF THIS KNOT IS TIGHT!"
THIS IS REALLY, REALLY GREAT STUFF!
"WEAR A HAT AND THAT'S THAT!"
PACKS... ROPE... HATS... WE NEED...
OOO!
EXPLORERS' GEAR!
BOY! ARE WE LEARNING A LOT!
ALL THIS STUFF IS FROM MY UNCLE MATT'S PRIVATE COLLECTION!
WOW!
NOT YOUR UNCLE MATT, THE WORLD'S GREATEST EXPLORER?
RED, YOU CAN'T LEARN IF YOU'RE TRYING TO BE FUNNY!

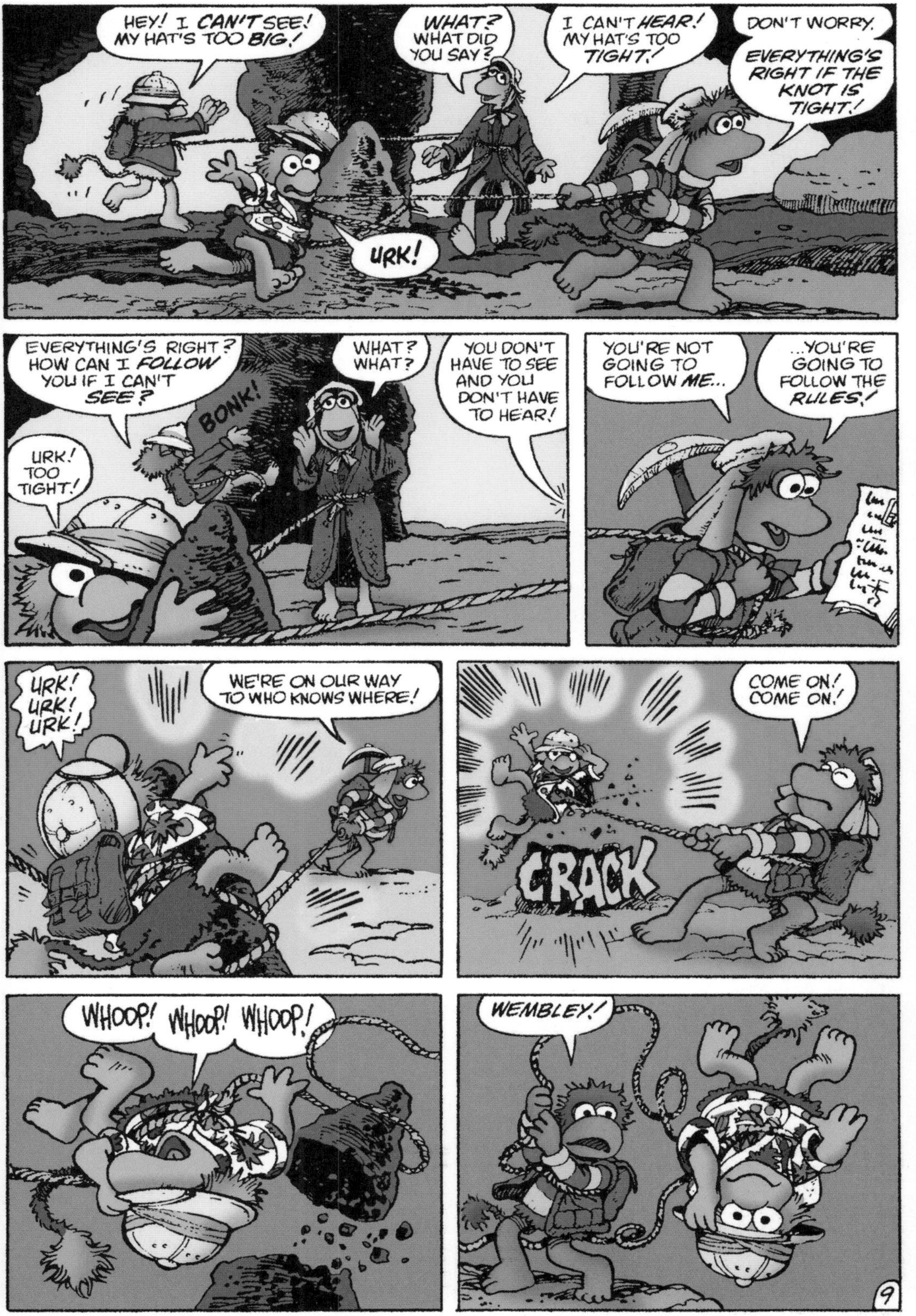
HEY! I CAN'T SEE! MY HAT'S TOO BIG!
WHAT? WHAT DID YOU SAY?
I CAN'T HEAR! MY HAT'S TOO TIGHT!
DON'T WORRY.
EVERYTHING'S RIGHT IF THE KNOT IS TIGHT!
URK!
EVERYTHING'S RIGHT? HOW CAN I FOLLOW YOU IF I CAN'T SEE?
BONK!
URK! TOO TIGHT!
WHAT? WHAT?
YOU DON'T HAVE TO SEE AND YOU DON'T HAVE TO HEAR!
YOU'RE NOT GOING TO FOLLOW ME...
...YOU'RE GOING TO FOLLOW THE RULES!
URK! URK! URK!
WE'RE ON OUR WAY TO WHO KNOWS WHERE!
COME ON! COME ON!
CRACK
WHOOP! WHOOP! WHOOP!
WEMBLEY!
9

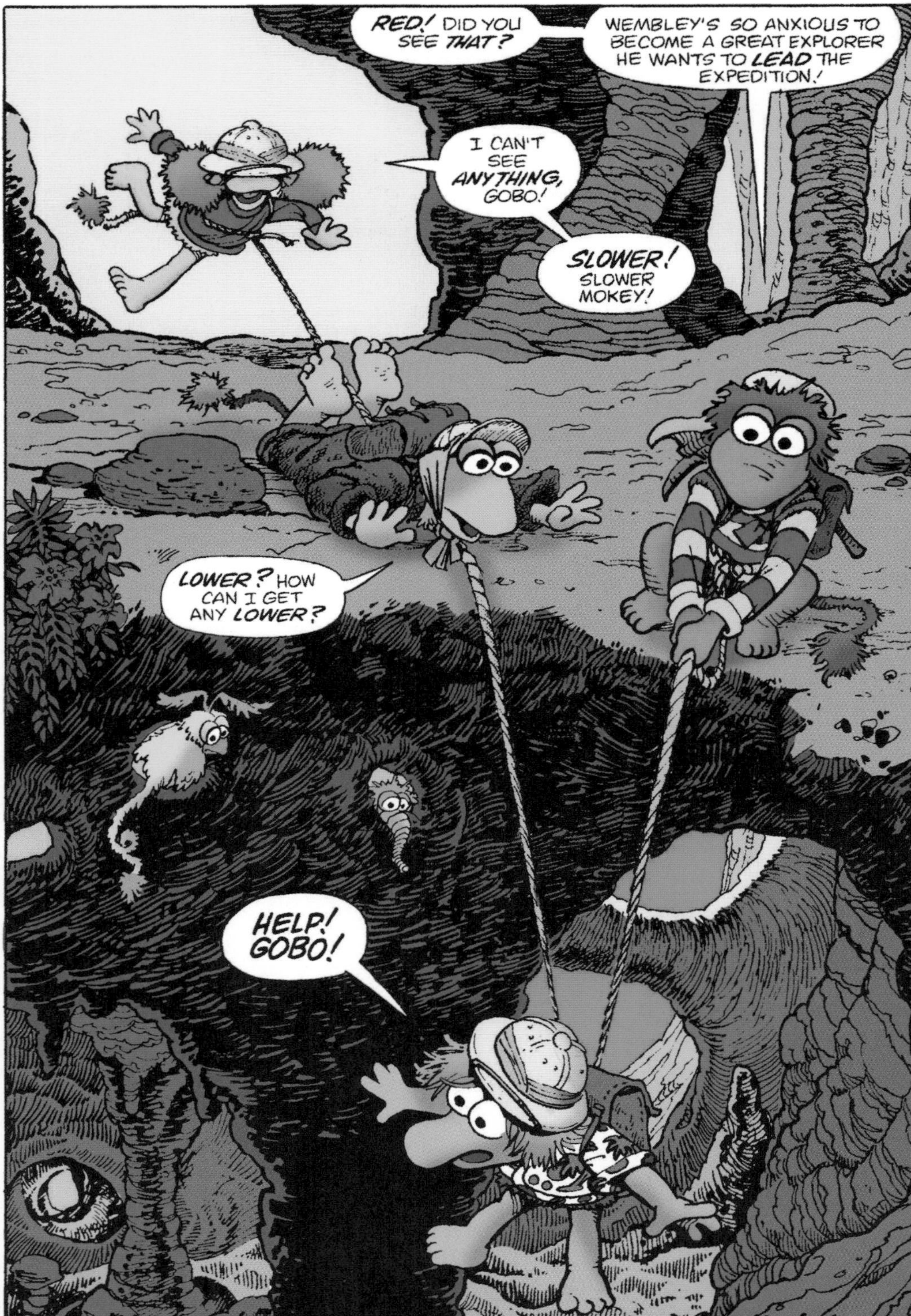

RED! DID YOU SEE THAT?
WEMBLEY'S SO ANXIOUS TO BECOME A GREAT EXPLORER HE WANTS TO LEAD THE EXPEDITION!
I CAN'T SEE ANYTHING, GOBO!
SLOWER! SLOWER MOKEY!
LOWER? HOW CAN I GET ANY LOWER?
HELP! GOBO!
10

CONTINUED IN THIS ISSUE...

FRAGGLE ROCK in EXPLORING THE UNKNOWN PART II "THE HOLE TO WHO KNOWS WHERE"

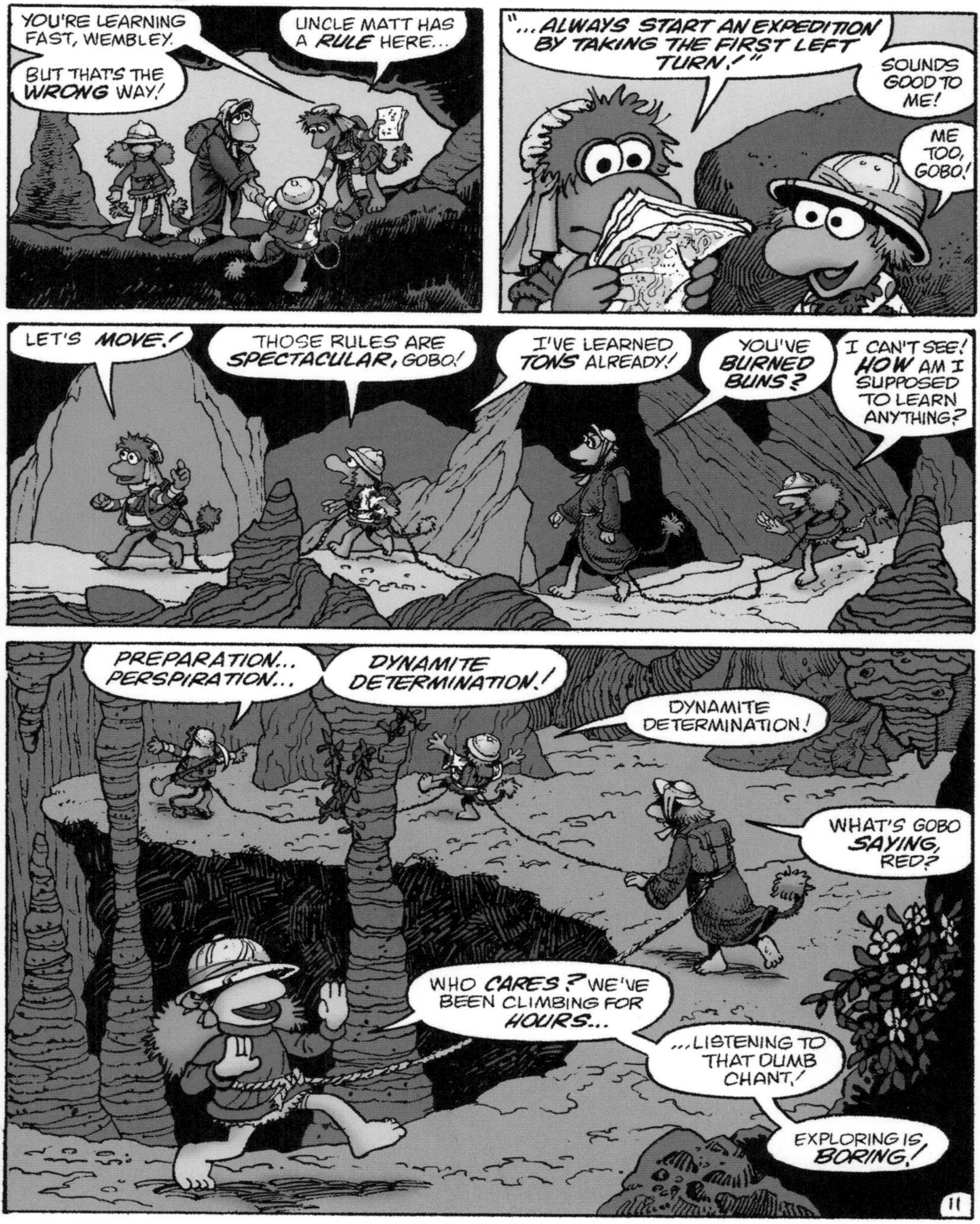

YOU'RE LEARNING FAST, WEMBLEY.
BUT THAT'S THE WRONG WAY!
UNCLE MATT HAS A RULE HERE...
"...ALWAYS START AN EXPEDITION BY TAKING THE FIRST LEFT TURN!"
SOUNDS GOOD TO ME!
ME TOO, GOBO!
LET'S MOVE!
THOSE RULES ARE SPECTACULAR, GOBO!
I'VE LEARNED TONS ALREADY!
YOU'VE BURNED BUNS?
I CAN'T SEE! HOW AM I SUPPOSED TO LEARN ANYTHING?
PREPARATION... PERSPIRATION...
DYNAMITE DETERMINATION!
DYNAMITE DETERMINATION!
WHAT'S GOBO SAYING, RED?
WHO CARES? WE'VE BEEN CLIMBING FOR HOURS...
...LISTENING TO THAT DUMB CHANT!
EXPLORING IS BORING!
11

ALL I CAN SEE...

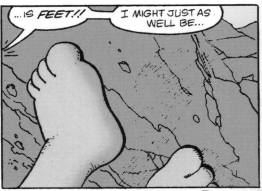

...IS *FEET!!* I MIGHT JUST AS WELL BE...

..." LEARNING TO *WASH SOCKS!*"

NO, NO, TOSH! ELBOWS HIGHER!

HIGH ELBOWS GIVE THAT *SCRUBBING POWER!*

REMEMBER THAT RULE, MORRIS!

ON THE OTHER HAND, *BOOBER* IS A *RULE NUT,* TOO!

WHO'S A *FOOL, MUTT?*

MOKEY! GET RID OF THAT DUMB HAT!

BOING!

POP

OH! I *CAN HEAR!* I CAN HEAR!

JUST THINK, WEMBLEY! EXCEPT FOR UNCLE MATT...

...WE'RE THE *FIRST* LIVING CREATURES WHO EVER SET FOOT...

12

38

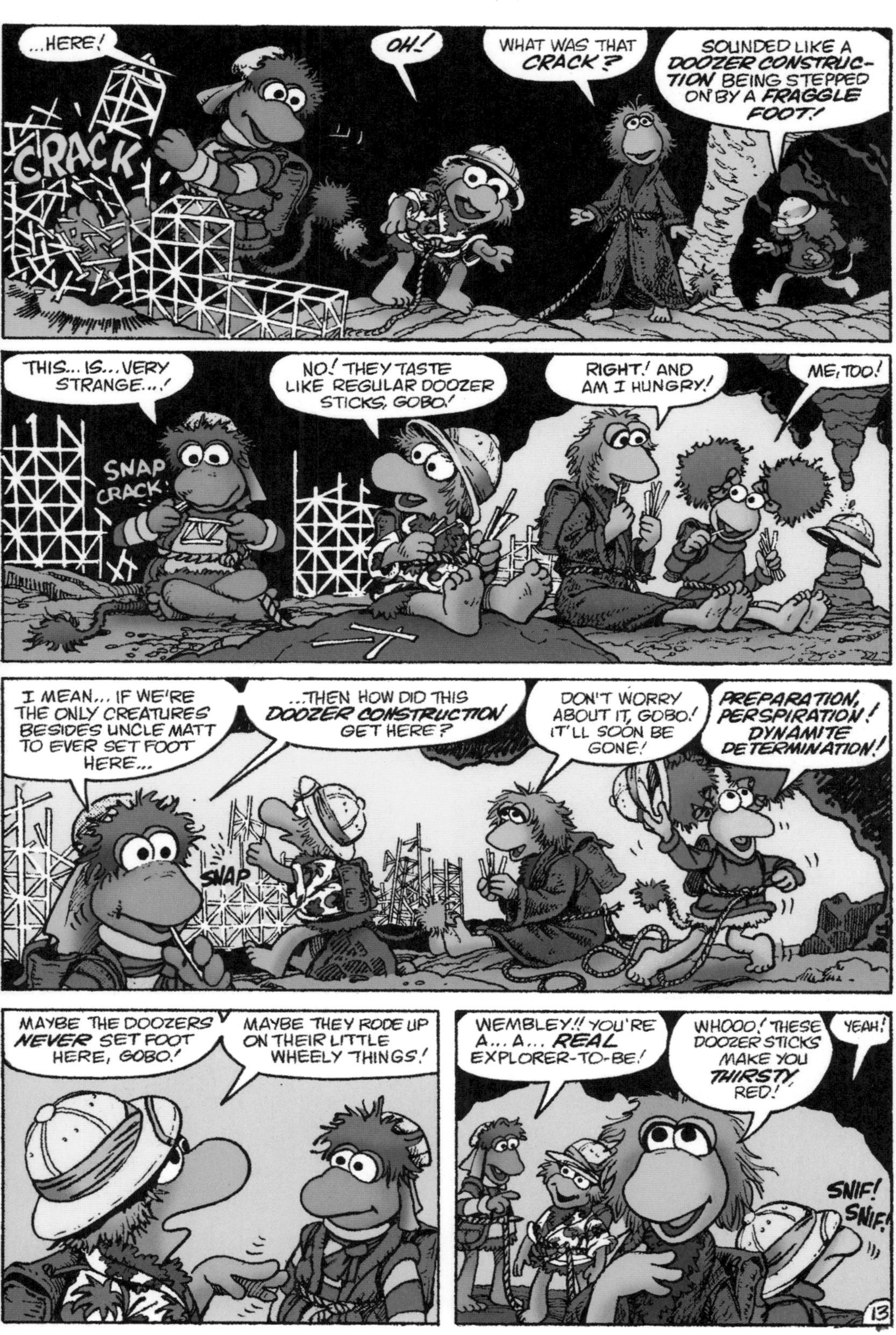
...HERE!
CRACK
OH!
WHAT WAS THAT CRACK?
SOUNDED LIKE A DOOZER CONSTRUCTION BEING STEPPED ON BY A FRAGGLE FOOT!
THIS... IS... VERY STRANGE...!
SNAP CRACK
NO! THEY TASTE LIKE REGULAR DOOZER STICKS, GOBO!
RIGHT! AND AM I HUNGRY!
ME, TOO!
I MEAN... IF WE'RE THE ONLY CREATURES BESIDES UNCLE MATT TO EVER SET FOOT HERE...
...THEN HOW DID THIS DOOZER CONSTRUCTION GET HERE?
SNAP
DON'T WORRY ABOUT IT, GOBO! IT'LL SOON BE GONE!
PREPARATION, PERSPIRATION! DYNAMITE DETERMINATION!
MAYBE THE DOOZERS NEVER SET FOOT HERE, GOBO!
MAYBE THEY RODE UP ON THEIR LITTLE WHEELY THINGS!
WEMBLEY!! YOU'RE A... A... REAL EXPLORER-TO-BE!
WHOOO! THESE DOOZER STICKS MAKE YOU THIRSTY, RED!
YEAH!
SNIF! SNIF!
13

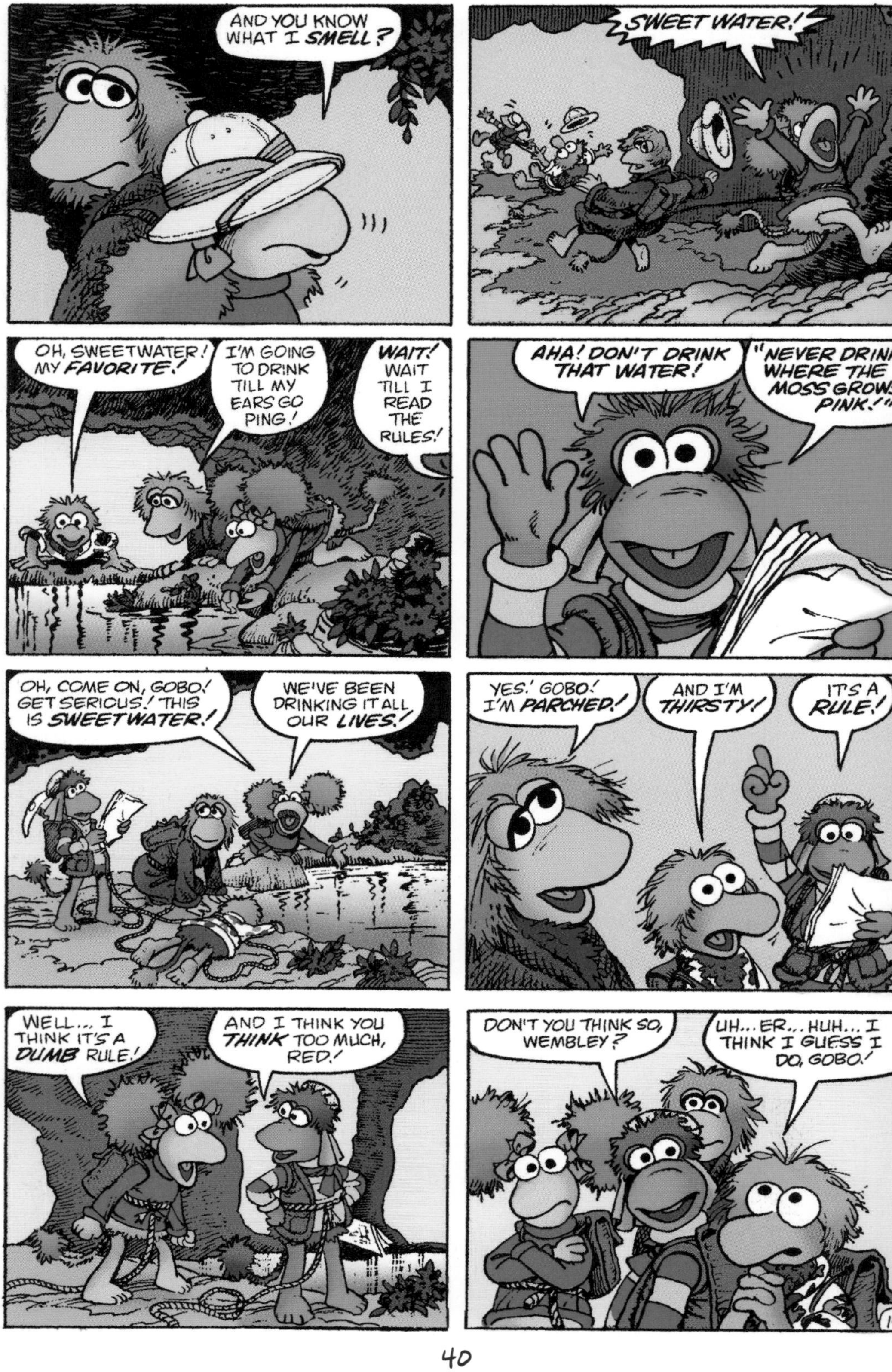
AND YOU KNOW WHAT I SMELL?
SWEET WATER!
OH, SWEETWATER! MY FAVORITE!
I'M GOING TO DRINK TILL MY EARS GO PING!
WAIT! WAIT TILL I READ THE RULES!
AHA! DON'T DRINK THAT WATER!
"NEVER DRINK WHERE THE MOSS GROWS PINK!"
OH, COME ON, GOBO! GET SERIOUS! THIS IS SWEETWATER!
WE'VE BEEN DRINKING IT ALL OUR LIVES!
YES! GOBO! I'M PARCHED!
AND I'M THIRSTY!
IT'S A RULE!
WELL... I THINK IT'S A DUMB RULE!
AND I THINK YOU THINK TOO MUCH, RED!
DON'T YOU THINK SO, WEMBLEY?
UH... ER... HUH... I THINK I GUESS I DO, GOBO!
14

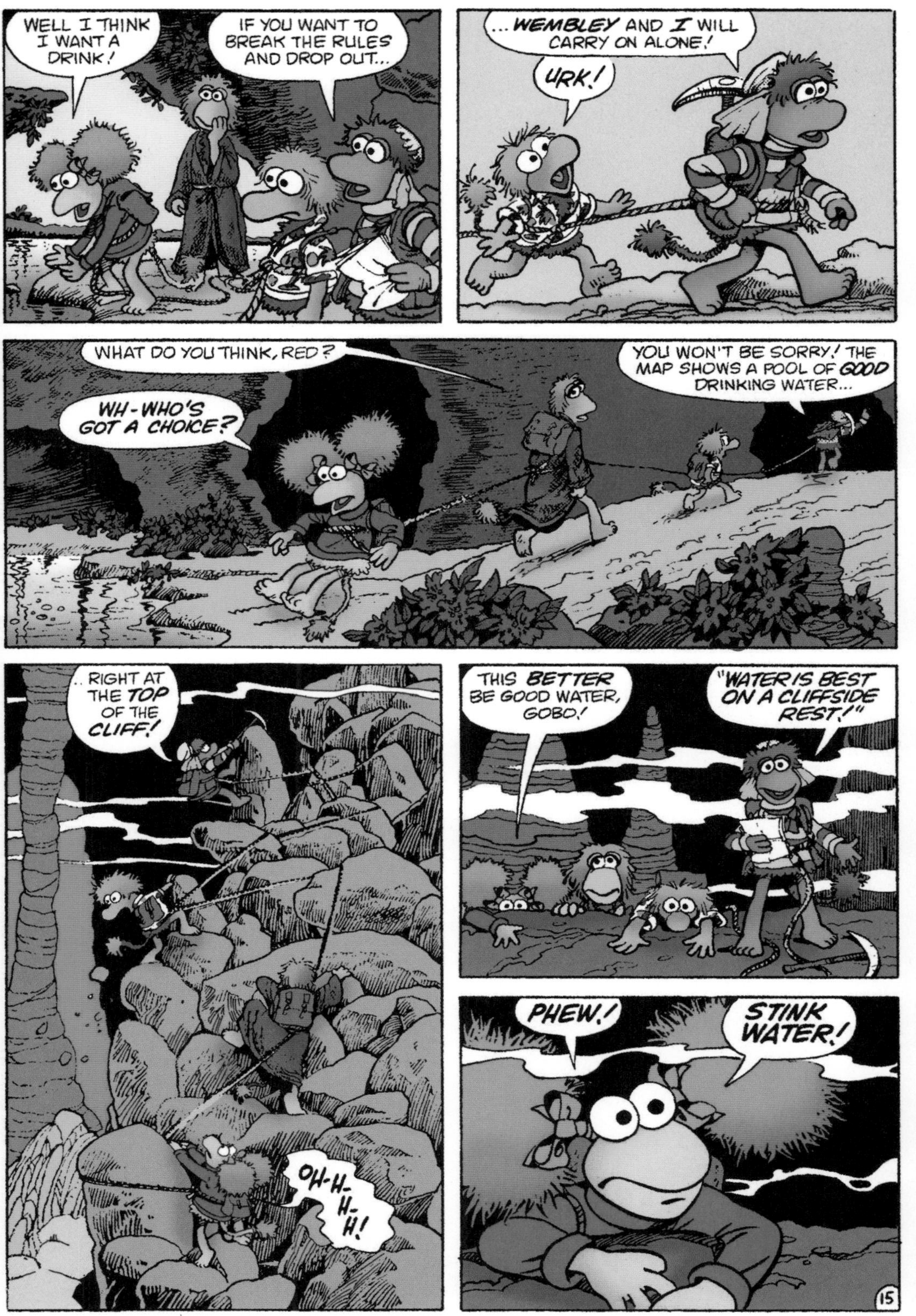

WELL I THINK I WANT A DRINK!
IF YOU WANT TO BREAK THE RULES AND DROP OUT...
...WEMBLEY AND I WILL CARRY ON ALONE!
URK!
WHAT DO YOU THINK, RED?
WH-WHO'S GOT A CHOICE?
YOU WON'T BE SORRY! THE MAP SHOWS A POOL OF GOOD DRINKING WATER...
..RIGHT AT THE TOP OF THE CLIFF!
OH-H-H-H!
THIS BETTER BE GOOD WATER, GOBO!
"WATER IS BEST ON A CLIFFSIDE REST!"
PHEW!
STINK WATER!
15

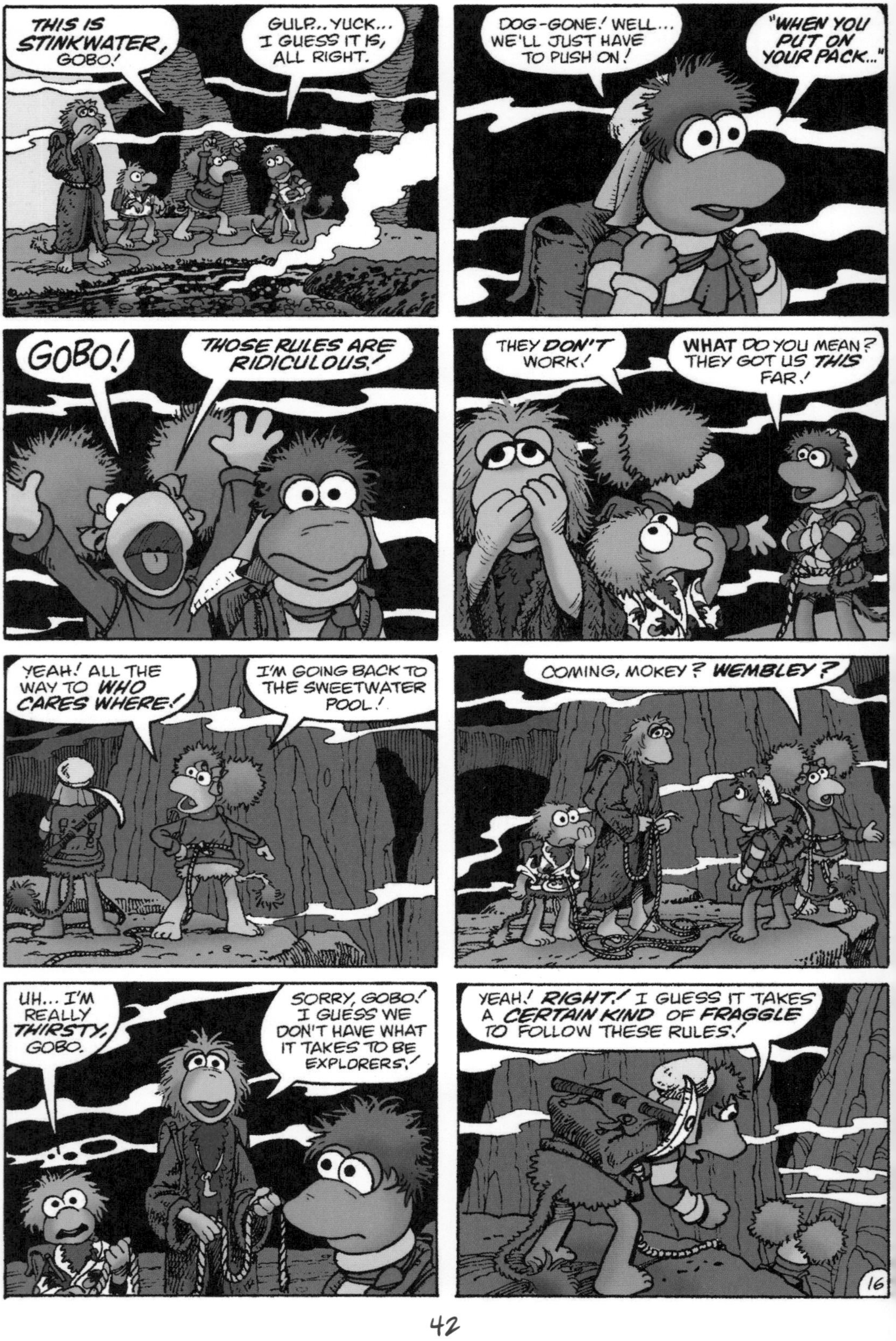
THIS IS STINKWATER, GOBO!
GULP... YUCK... I GUESS IT IS, ALL RIGHT.
DOG-GONE! WELL... WE'LL JUST HAVE TO PUSH ON!
"WHEN YOU PUT ON YOUR PACK..."
GOBO!
THOSE RULES ARE RIDICULOUS!
THEY DON'T WORK!
WHAT DO YOU MEAN? THEY GOT US THIS FAR!
YEAH! ALL THE WAY TO WHO CARES WHERE!
I'M GOING BACK TO THE SWEETWATER POOL!
COMING, MOKEY? WEMBLEY?
UH... I'M REALLY THIRSTY, GOBO.
SORRY, GOBO! I GUESS WE DON'T HAVE WHAT IT TAKES TO BE EXPLORERS!
YEAH! RIGHT! I GUESS IT TAKES A CERTAIN KIND OF FRAGGLE TO FOLLOW THESE RULES!
16

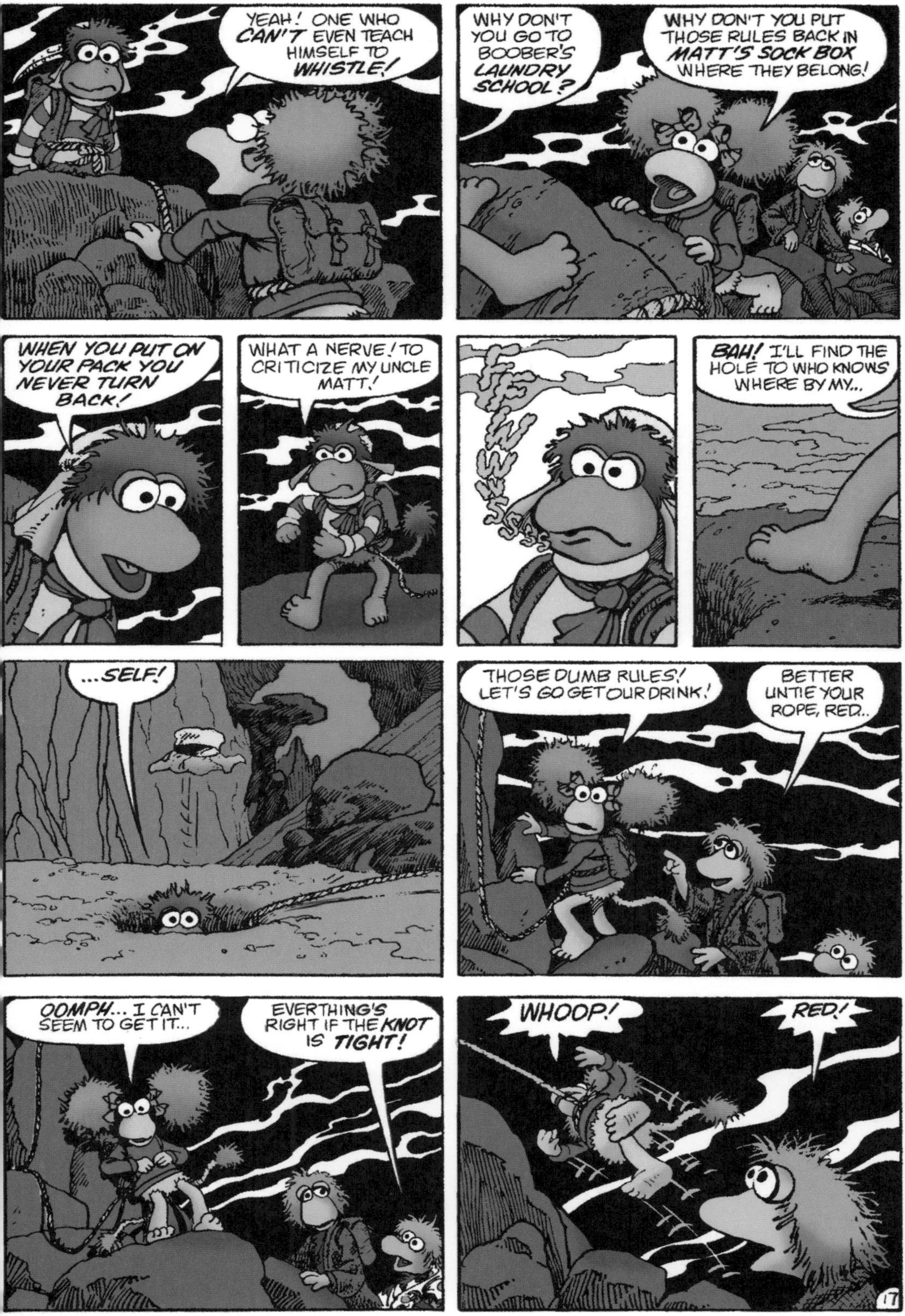
YEAH! ONE WHO CAN'T EVEN TEACH HIMSELF TO WHISTLE!
WHY DON'T YOU GO TO BOOBER'S LAUNDRY SCHOOL?
WHY DON'T YOU PUT THOSE RULES BACK IN MATT'S SOCK BOX WHERE THEY BELONG!
WHEN YOU PUT ON YOUR PACK YOU NEVER TURN BACK!
WHAT A NERVE! TO CRITICIZE MY UNCLE MATT!
FFEWWWSSSS
BAH! I'LL FIND THE HOLE TO WHO KNOWS WHERE BY MY...
...SELF!
THOSE DUMB RULES! LET'S GO GET OUR DRINK!
BETTER UNTIE YOUR ROPE, RED..
OOMPH... I CAN'T SEEM TO GET IT...
EVERTHING'S RIGHT IF THE KNOT IS TIGHT!
WHOOP!
RED!
17

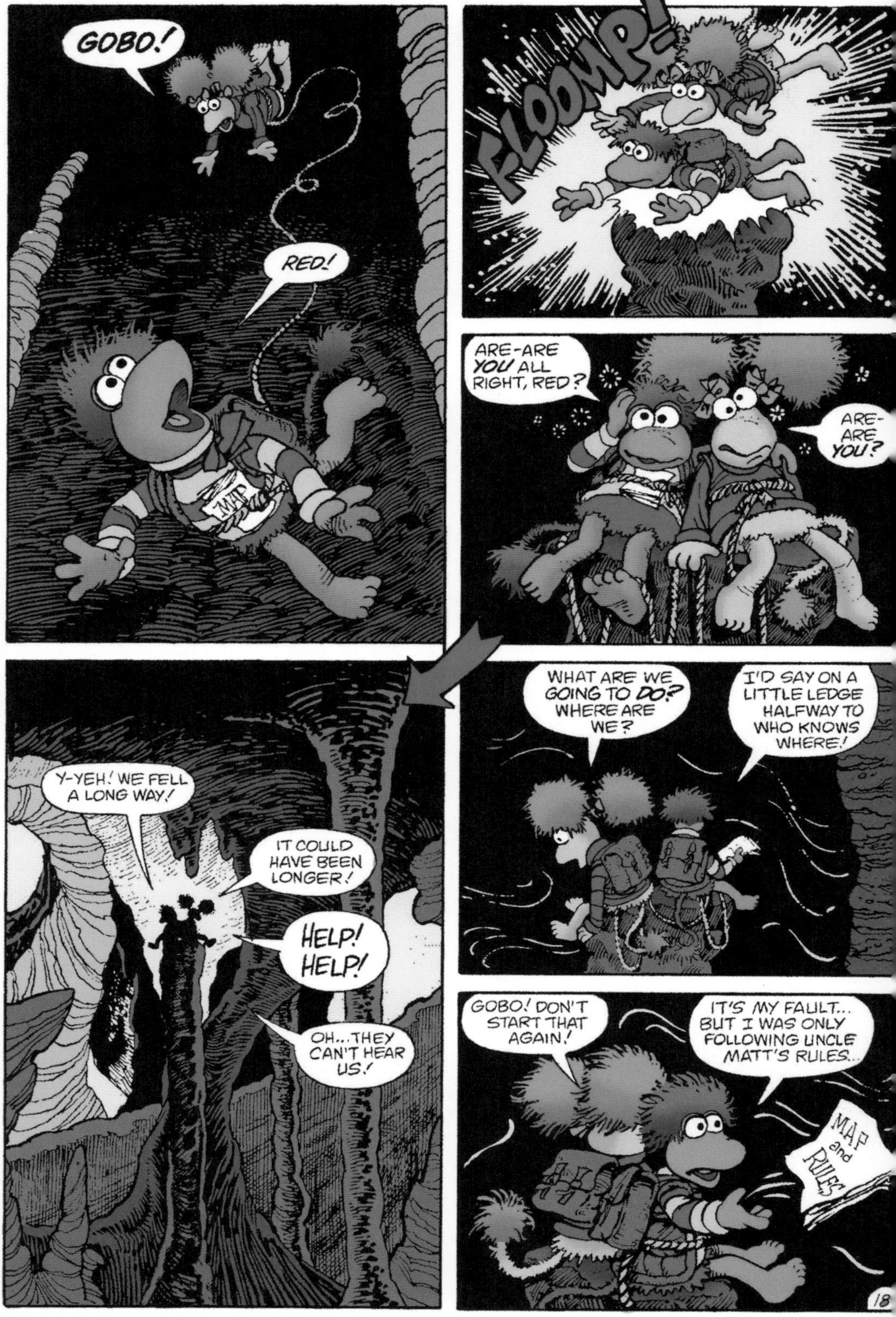
GOBO!
RED!
FLOOMP!
ARE-ARE YOU ALL RIGHT, RED?
ARE-ARE YOU?
Y-YEH! WE FELL A LONG WAY!
IT COULD HAVE BEEN LONGER!
HELP! HELP!
OH... THEY CAN'T HEAR US!
WHAT ARE WE GOING TO DO? WHERE ARE WE?
I'D SAY ON A LITTLE LEDGE HALFWAY TO WHO KNOWS WHERE!
GOBO! DON'T START THAT AGAIN!
IT'S MY FAULT... BUT I WAS ONLY FOLLOWING UNCLE MATT'S RULES...
MAP and RULES
18

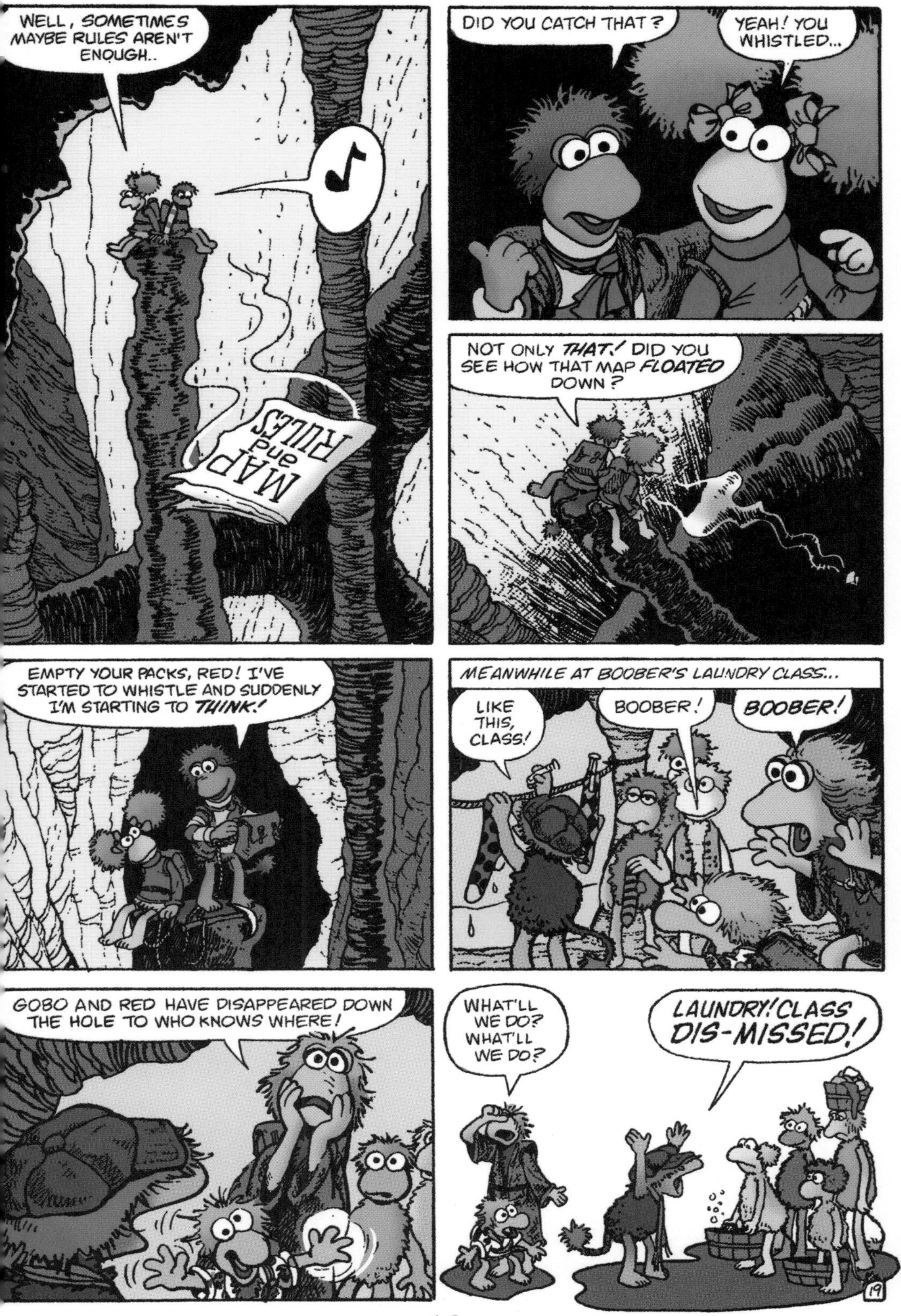
WELL, SOMETIMES MAYBE RULES AREN'T ENOUGH..
♪
MAP and RULES
DID YOU CATCH THAT?
YEAH! YOU WHISTLED...
NOT ONLY THAT! DID YOU SEE HOW THAT MAP FLOATED DOWN?
EMPTY YOUR PACKS, RED! I'VE STARTED TO WHISTLE AND SUDDENLY I'M STARTING TO THINK!
MEANWHILE AT BOOBER'S LAUNDRY CLASS...
LIKE THIS, CLASS!
BOOBER!
BOOBER!
GOBO AND RED HAVE DISAPPEARED DOWN THE HOLE TO WHO KNOWS WHERE!
WHAT'LL WE DO? WHAT'LL WE DO?
LAUNDRY! CLASS DIS-MISSED!
19

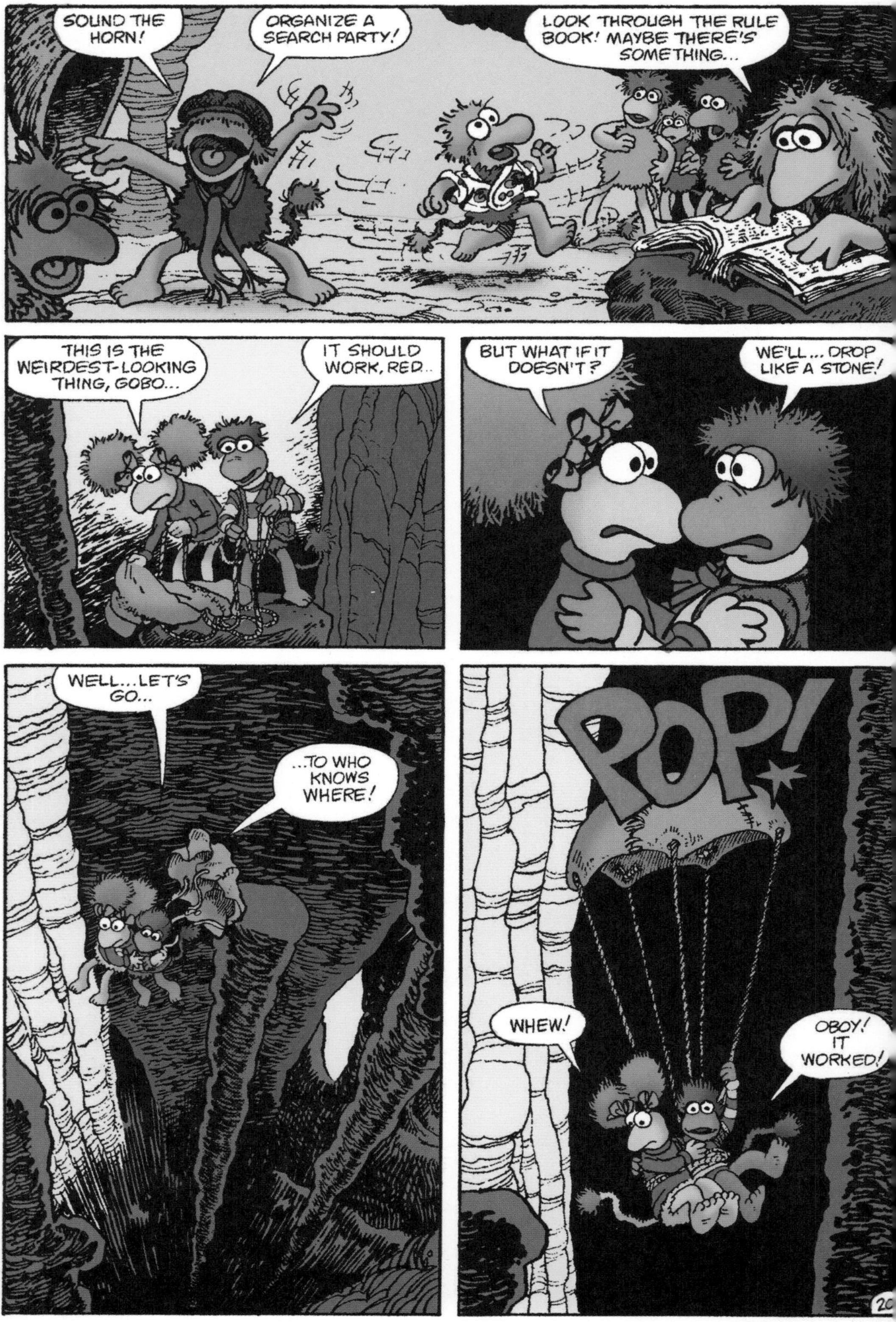
SOUND THE HORN!
ORGANIZE A SEARCH PARTY!
LOOK THROUGH THE RULE BOOK! MAYBE THERE'S SOMETHING...
THIS IS THE WEIRDEST-LOOKING THING, GOBO...
IT SHOULD WORK, RED..
BUT WHAT IF IT DOESN'T?
WE'LL... DROP LIKE A STONE!
WELL...LET'S GO...
...TO WHO KNOWS WHERE!
POP!
WHEW!
OBOY! IT WORKED!
20

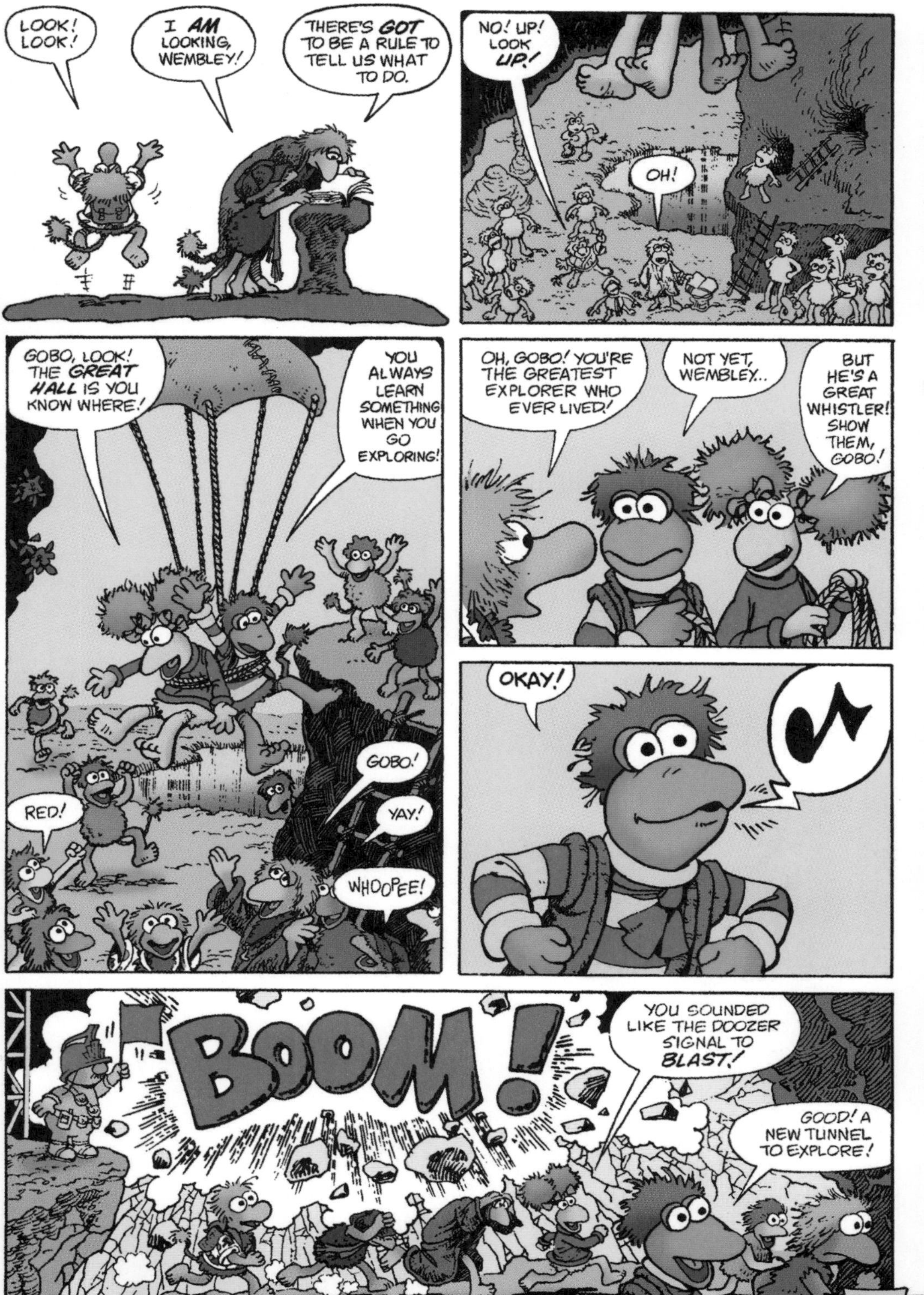
LOOK! LOOK!
I AM LOOKING, WEMBLEY!
THERE'S GOT TO BE A RULE TO TELL US WHAT TO DO.
NO! UP! LOOK UP!
OH!
GOBO, LOOK! THE GREAT HALL IS YOU KNOW WHERE!
YOU ALWAYS LEARN SOMETHING WHEN YOU GO EXPLORING!
RED!
GOBO!
YAY!
WHOOPEE!
OH, GOBO! YOU'RE THE GREATEST EXPLORER WHO EVER LIVED!
NOT YET, WEMBLEY...
BUT HE'S A GREAT WHISTLER! SHOW THEM, GOBO!
OKAY!
BOOM!
YOU SOUNDED LIKE THE DOOZER SIGNAL TO BLAST!
GOOD! A NEW TUNNEL TO EXPLORE!
END

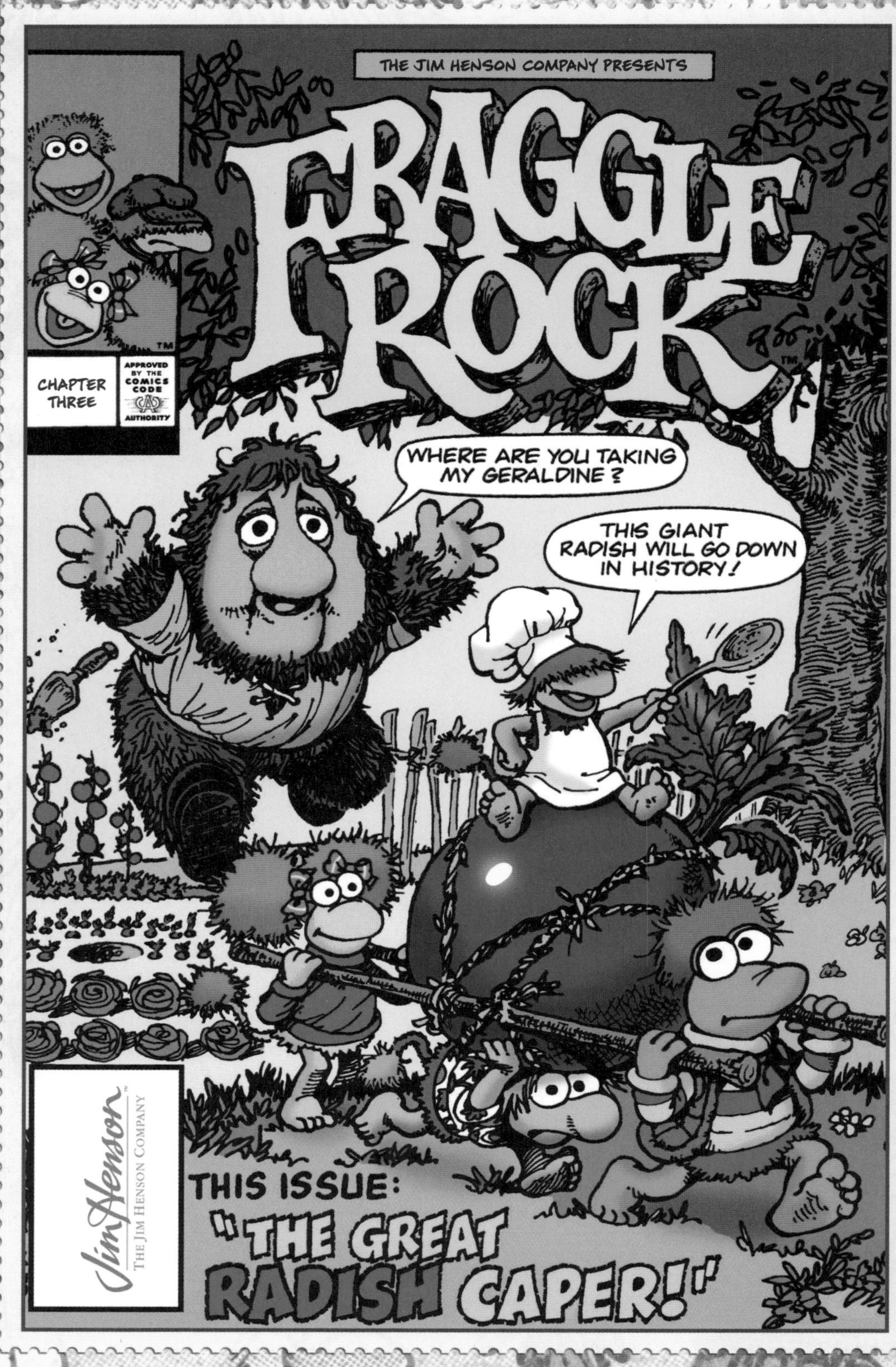

THE JIM HENSON COMPANY PRESENTS
FRAGGLE ROCK™
CHAPTER THREE
APPROVED BY THE COMICS CODE AUTHORITY
WHERE ARE YOU TAKING MY GERALDINE?
THIS GIANT RADISH WILL GO DOWN IN HISTORY!
Jim Henson™ THE JIM HENSON COMPANY
THIS ISSUE:
"THE GREAT RADISH CAPER!"

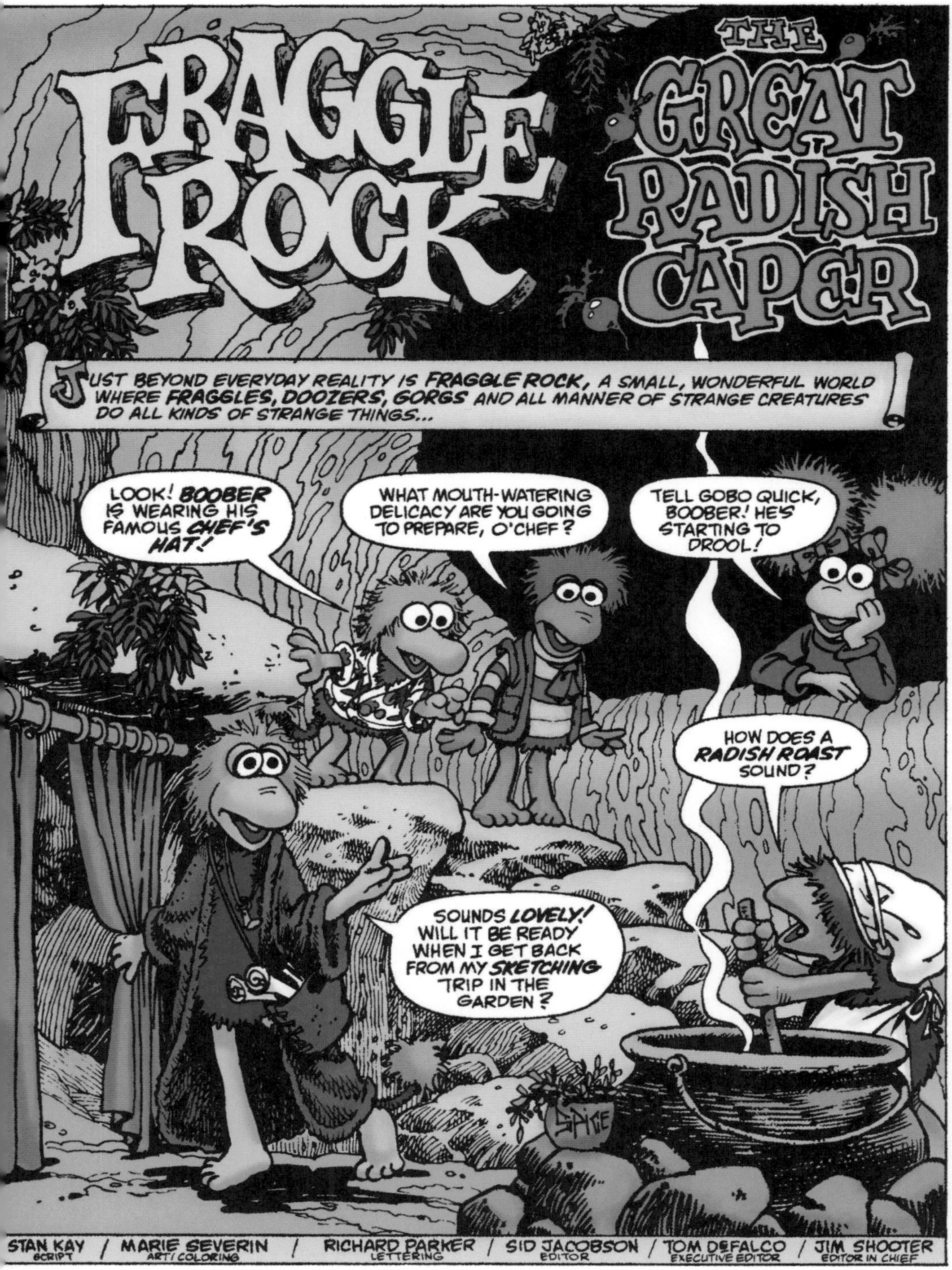
FRAGGLE ROCK
THE GREAT RADISH CAPER
JUST BEYOND EVERYDAY REALITY IS FRAGGLE ROCK, A SMALL, WONDERFUL WORLD WHERE FRAGGLES, DOOZERS, GORGS AND ALL MANNER OF STRANGE CREATURES DO ALL KINDS OF STRANGE THINGS...
LOOK! BOOBER IS WEARING HIS FAMOUS CHEF'S HAT!
WHAT MOUTH-WATERING DELICACY ARE YOU GOING TO PREPARE, O'CHEF?
TELL GOBO QUICK, BOOBER! HE'S STARTING TO DROOL!
HOW DOES A RADISH ROAST SOUND?
SOUNDS LOVELY! WILL IT BE READY WHEN I GET BACK FROM MY SKETCHING TRIP IN THE GARDEN?
SPICE

STAN KAY SCRIPT / MARIE SEVERIN ART/COLORING / RICHARD PARKER LETTERING / SID JACOBSON EDITOR / TOM DeFALCO EXECUTIVE EDITOR / JIM SHOOTER EDITOR IN CHIEF

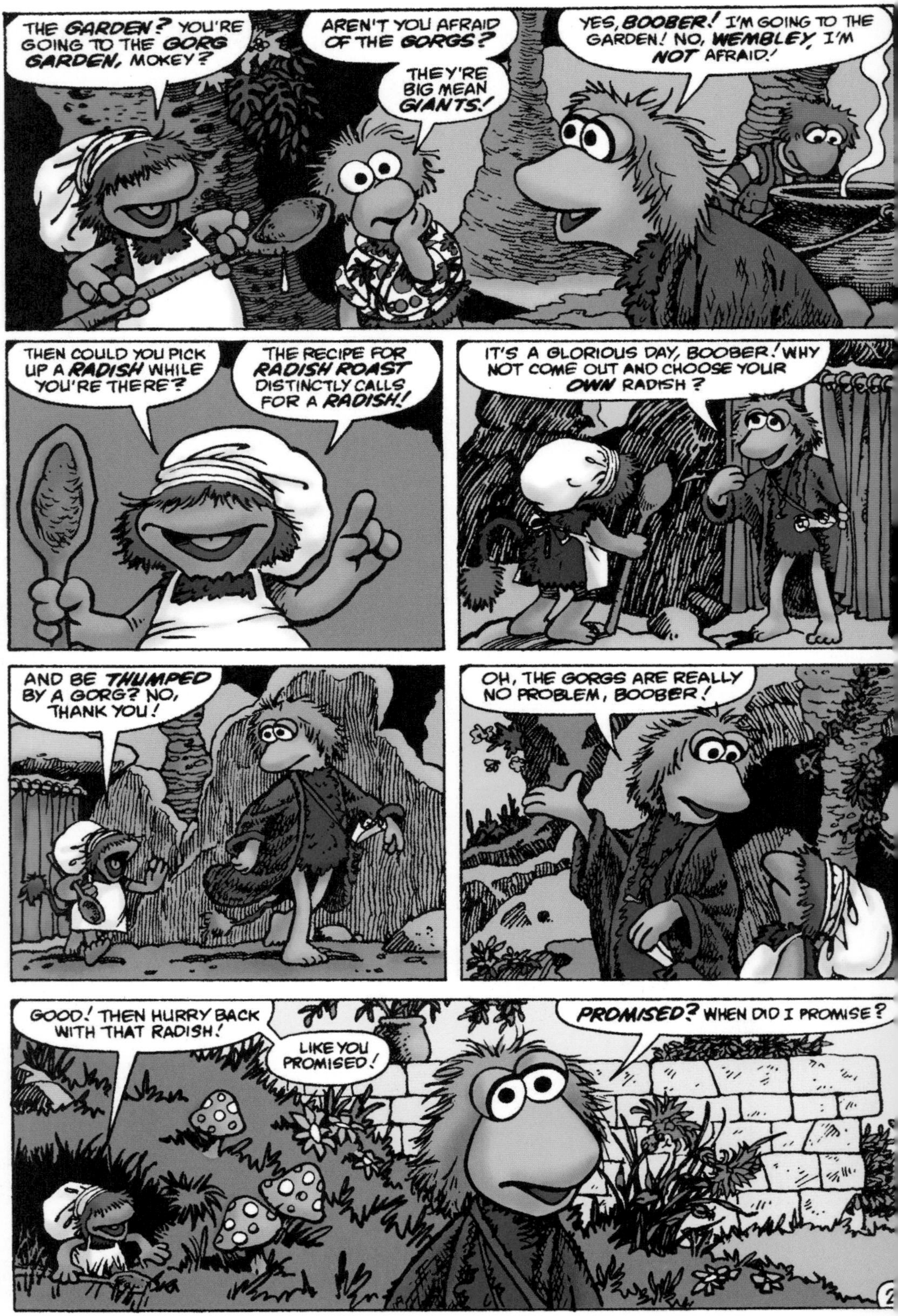
THE GARDEN? YOU'RE GOING TO THE GORG GARDEN, MOKEY?
AREN'T YOU AFRAID OF THE GORGS?
THEY'RE BIG MEAN GIANTS!
YES, BOOBER! I'M GOING TO THE GARDEN! NO, WEMBLEY, I'M NOT AFRAID!
THEN COULD YOU PICK UP A RADISH WHILE YOU'RE THERE?
THE RECIPE FOR RADISH ROAST DISTINCTLY CALLS FOR A RADISH!
IT'S A GLORIOUS DAY, BOOBER! WHY NOT COME OUT AND CHOOSE YOUR OWN RADISH?
AND BE THUMPED BY A GORG? NO, THANK YOU!
OH, THE GORGS ARE REALLY NO PROBLEM, BOOBER!
GOOD! THEN HURRY BACK WITH THAT RADISH!
LIKE YOU PROMISED!
PROMISED? WHEN DID I PROMISE?

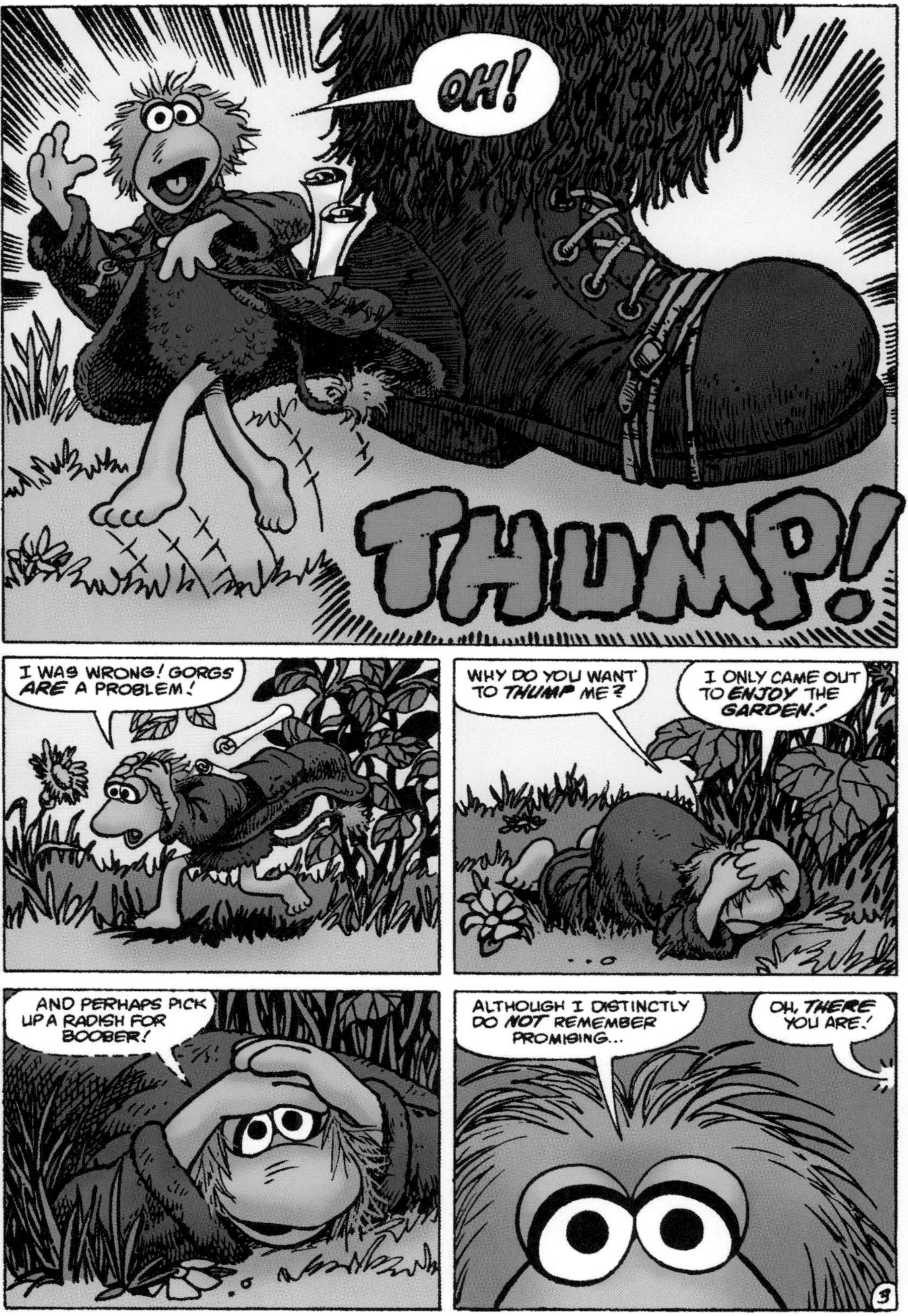
OH!
THUMP!
I WAS WRONG! GORGS ARE A PROBLEM!
WHY DO YOU WANT TO THUMP ME?
I ONLY CAME OUT TO ENJOY THE GARDEN!
AND PERHAPS PICK UP A RADISH FOR BOOBER!
ALTHOUGH I DISTINCTLY DO NOT REMEMBER PROMISING...
OH, THERE YOU ARE!
3

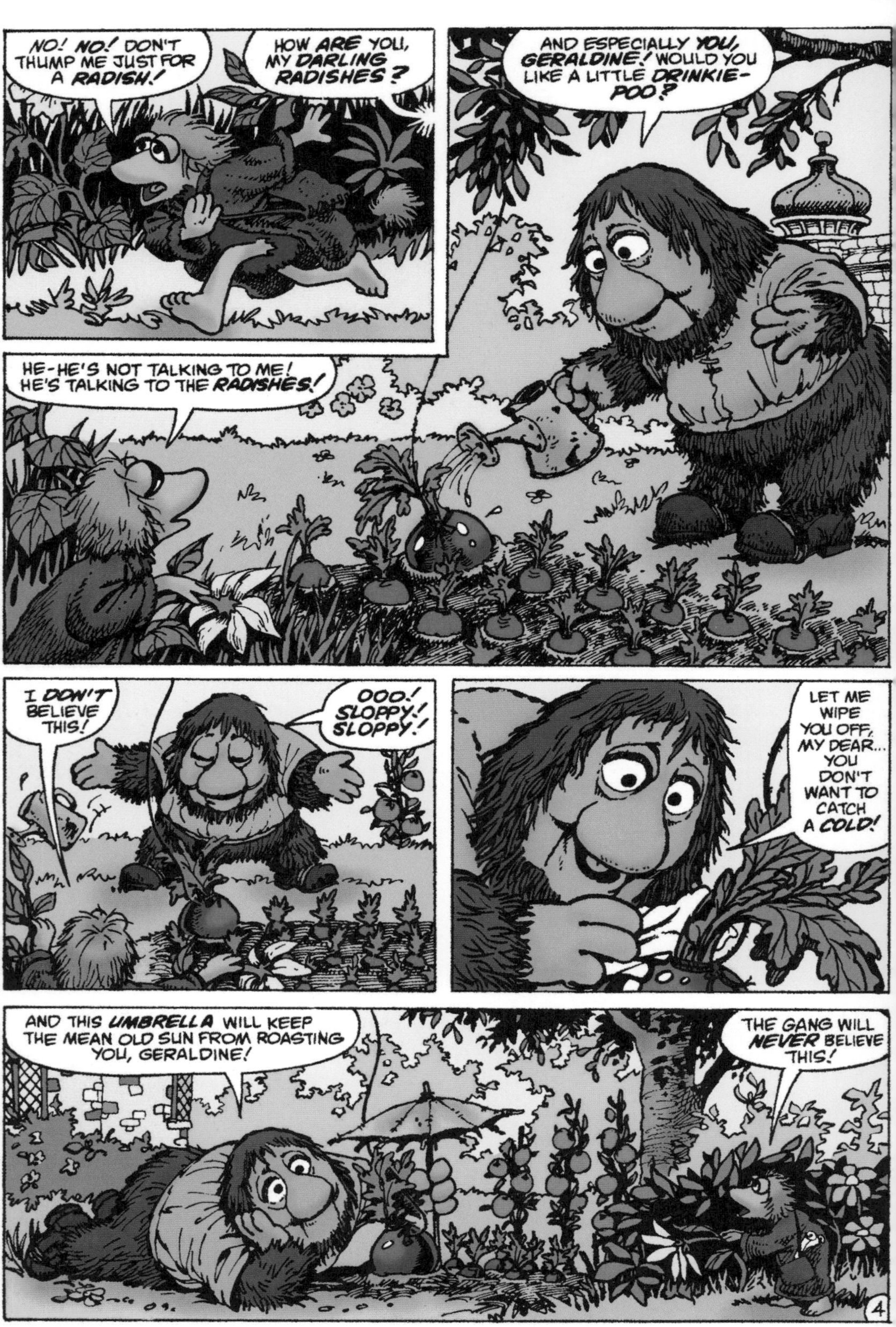
NO! NO! DON'T THUMP ME JUST FOR A RADISH!
HOW ARE YOU, MY DARLING RADISHES?
AND ESPECIALLY YOU, GERALDINE! WOULD YOU LIKE A LITTLE DRINKIE-POO?
HE-HE'S NOT TALKING TO ME! HE'S TALKING TO THE RADISHES!
I DON'T BELIEVE THIS!
OOO! SLOPPY! SLOPPY!
LET ME WIPE YOU OFF, MY DEAR... YOU DON'T WANT TO CATCH A COLD!
AND THIS UMBRELLA WILL KEEP THE MEAN OLD SUN FROM ROASTING YOU, GERALDINE!
THE GANG WILL NEVER BELIEVE THIS!
4

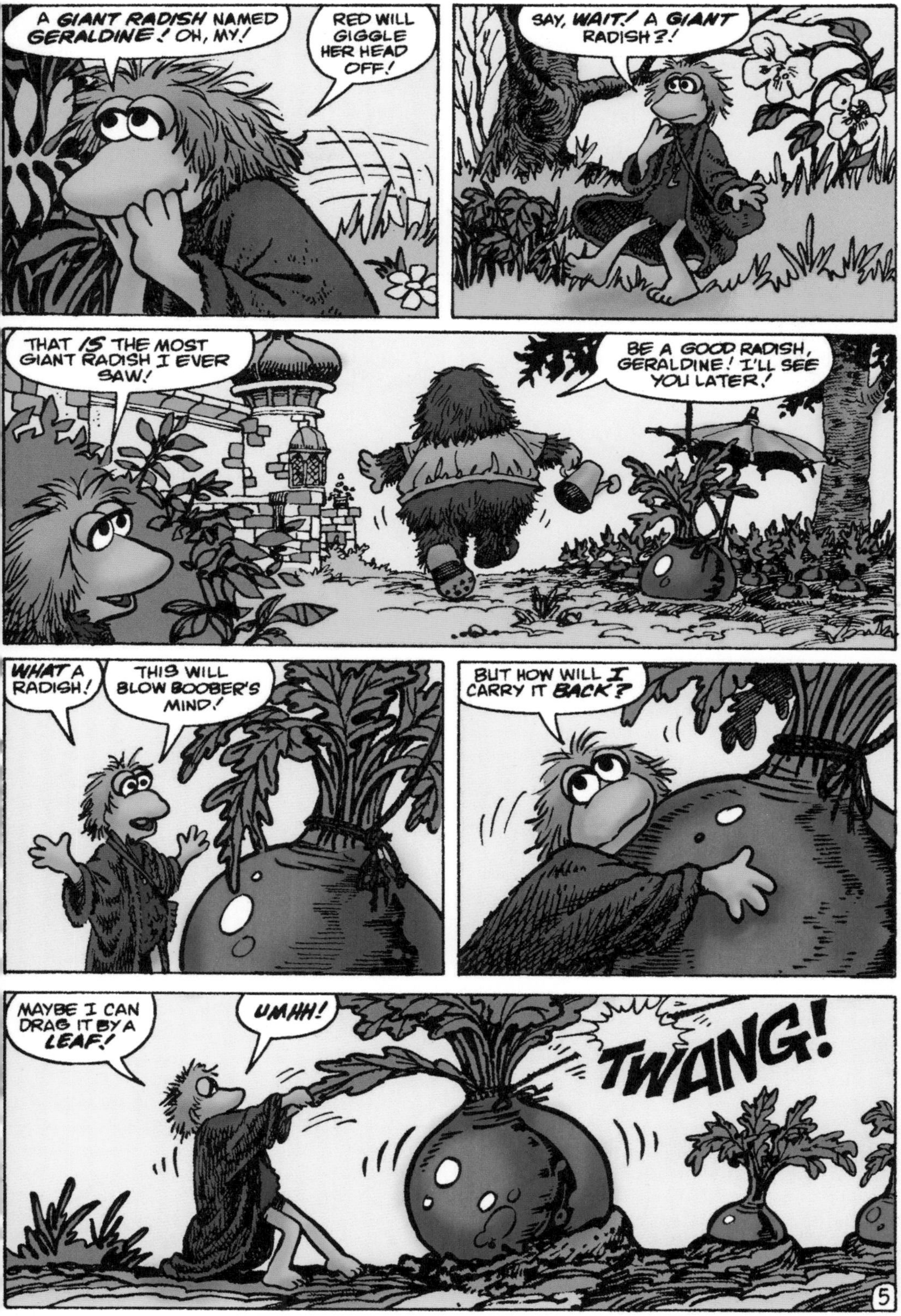
A GIANT RADISH NAMED GERALDINE! OH, MY!
RED WILL GIGGLE HER HEAD OFF!
SAY, WAIT! A GIANT RADISH?!
THAT IS THE MOST GIANT RADISH I EVER SAW!
BE A GOOD RADISH, GERALDINE! I'LL SEE YOU LATER!
WHAT A RADISH!
THIS WILL BLOW BOOBER'S MIND!
BUT HOW WILL I CARRY IT BACK?
MAYBE I CAN DRAG IT BY A LEAF!
UMHH!
TWANG!
5

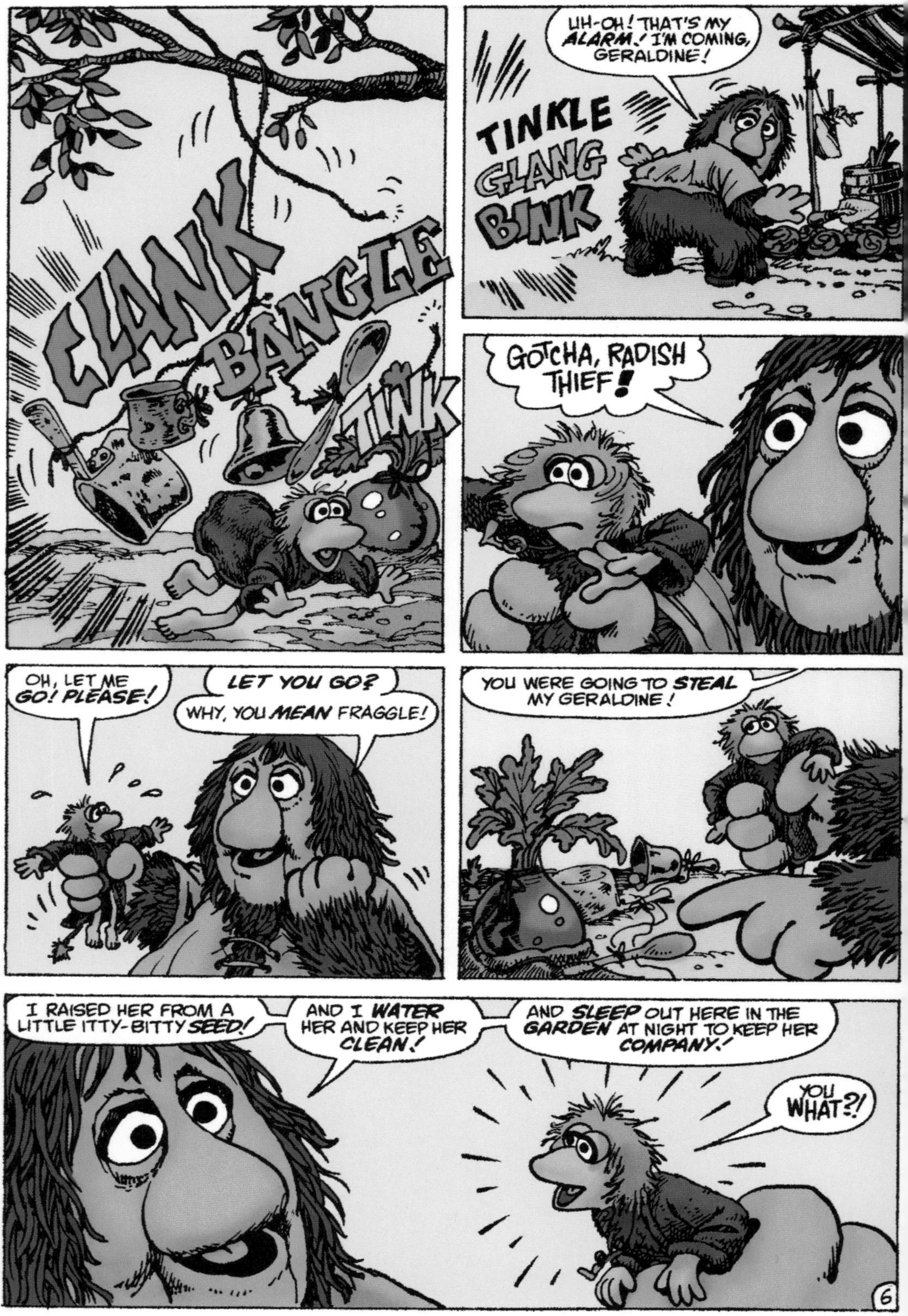
CLANK
BANGLE
TINK
UH-OH! THAT'S MY ALARM! I'M COMING, GERALDINE!
TINKLE
CLANG
BINK
GOTCHA, RADISH THIEF!
OH, LET ME GO! PLEASE!
LET YOU GO?
WHY, YOU MEAN FRAGGLE!
YOU WERE GOING TO STEAL MY GERALDINE!
I RAISED HER FROM A LITTLE ITTY-BITTY SEED!
AND I WATER HER AND KEEP HER CLEAN!
AND SLEEP OUT HERE IN THE GARDEN AT NIGHT TO KEEP HER COMPANY!
YOU WHAT?!
6

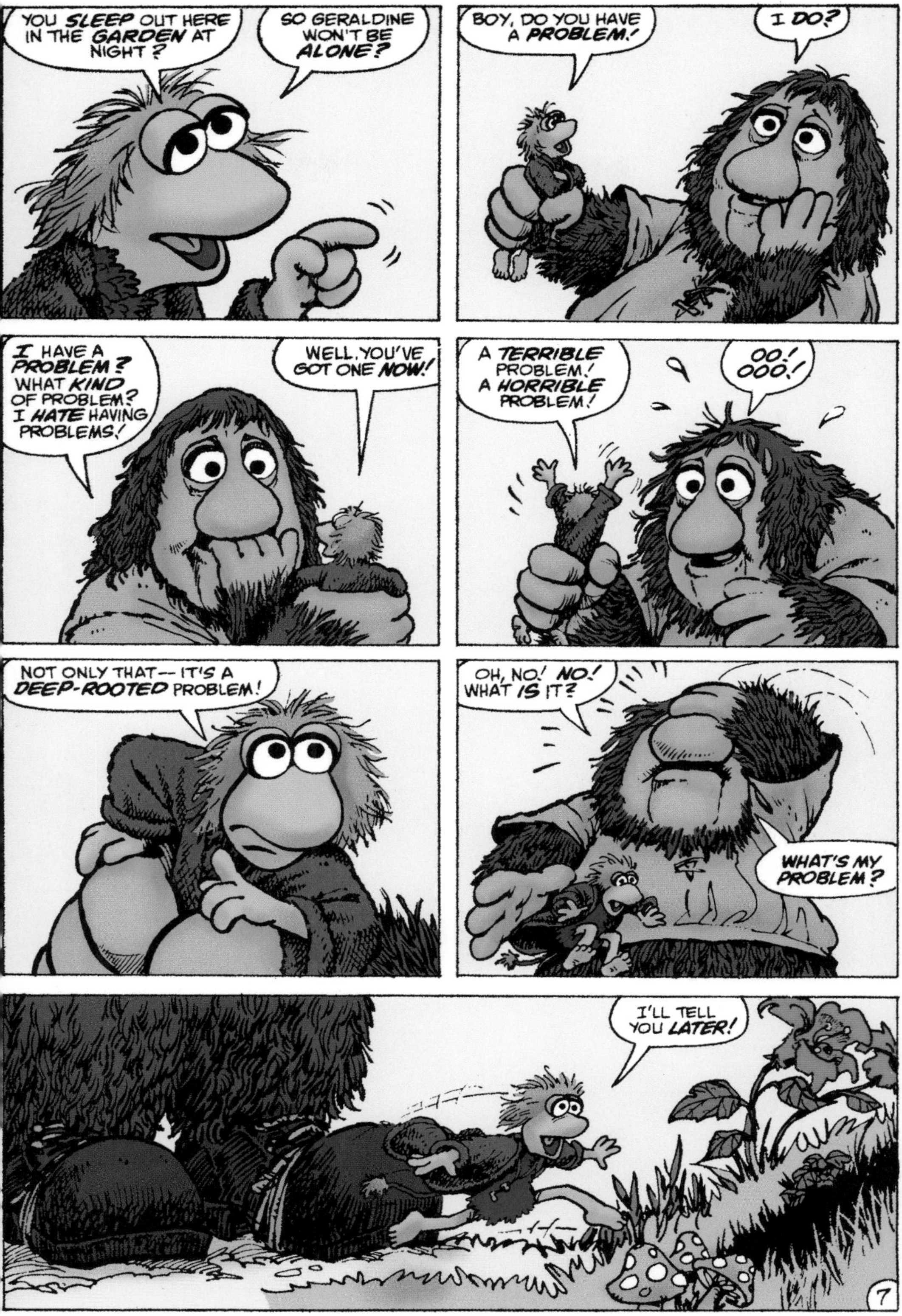
YOU SLEEP OUT HERE IN THE GARDEN AT NIGHT?
SO GERALDINE WON'T BE ALONE?
BOY, DO YOU HAVE A PROBLEM!
I DO?
I HAVE A PROBLEM? WHAT KIND OF PROBLEM? I HATE HAVING PROBLEMS!
WELL, YOU'VE GOT ONE NOW!
A TERRIBLE PROBLEM! A HORRIBLE PROBLEM!
OO! OOO!
NOT ONLY THAT-- IT'S A DEEP-ROOTED PROBLEM!
OH, NO! NO! WHAT IS IT?
WHAT'S MY PROBLEM?
I'LL TELL YOU LATER!
7

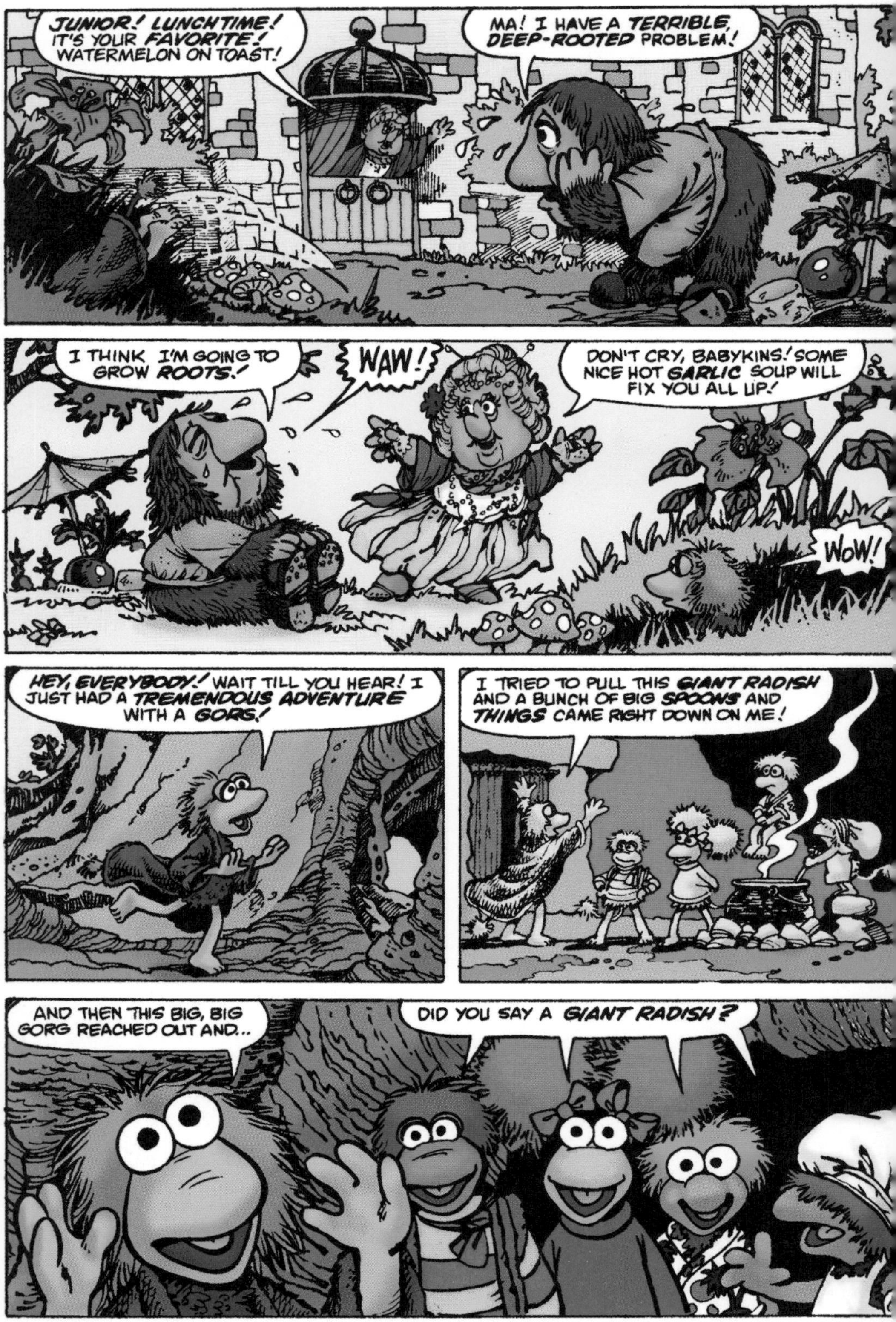
JUNIOR! LUNCHTIME! IT'S YOUR FAVORITE! WATERMELON ON TOAST!
MA! I HAVE A TERRIBLE, DEEP-ROOTED PROBLEM!
I THINK I'M GOING TO GROW ROOTS!
WAW!
DON'T CRY, BABYKINS! SOME NICE HOT GARLIC SOUP WILL FIX YOU ALL UP!
WOW!
HEY, EVERYBODY! WAIT TILL YOU HEAR! I JUST HAD A TREMENDOUS ADVENTURE WITH A GORG!
I TRIED TO PULL THIS GIANT RADISH AND A BUNCH OF BIG SPOONS AND THINGS CAME RIGHT DOWN ON ME!
AND THEN THIS BIG, BIG GORG REACHED OUT AND...
DID YOU SAY A GIANT RADISH?

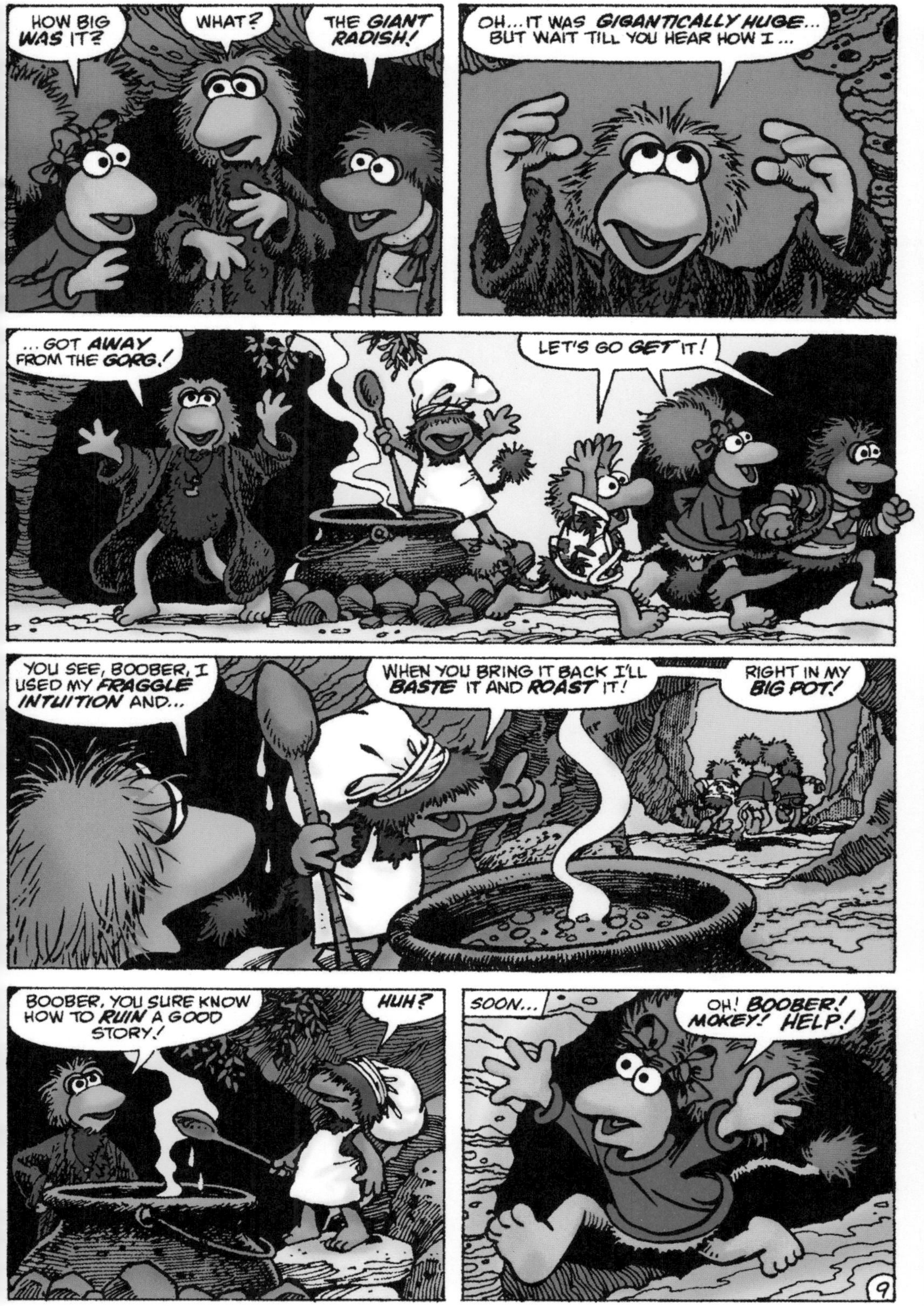
HOW BIG WAS IT?
WHAT?
THE GIANT RADISH!
OH... IT WAS GIGANTICALLY HUGE... BUT WAIT TILL YOU HEAR HOW I ...
... GOT AWAY FROM THE GORG!
LET'S GO GET IT!
YOU SEE, BOOBER, I USED MY FRAGGLE INTUITION AND...
WHEN YOU BRING IT BACK I'LL BASTE IT AND ROAST IT!
RIGHT IN MY BIG POT!
BOOBER, YOU SURE KNOW HOW TO RUIN A GOOD STORY!
HUH?
SOON...
OH! BOOBER! MOKEY! HELP!
9

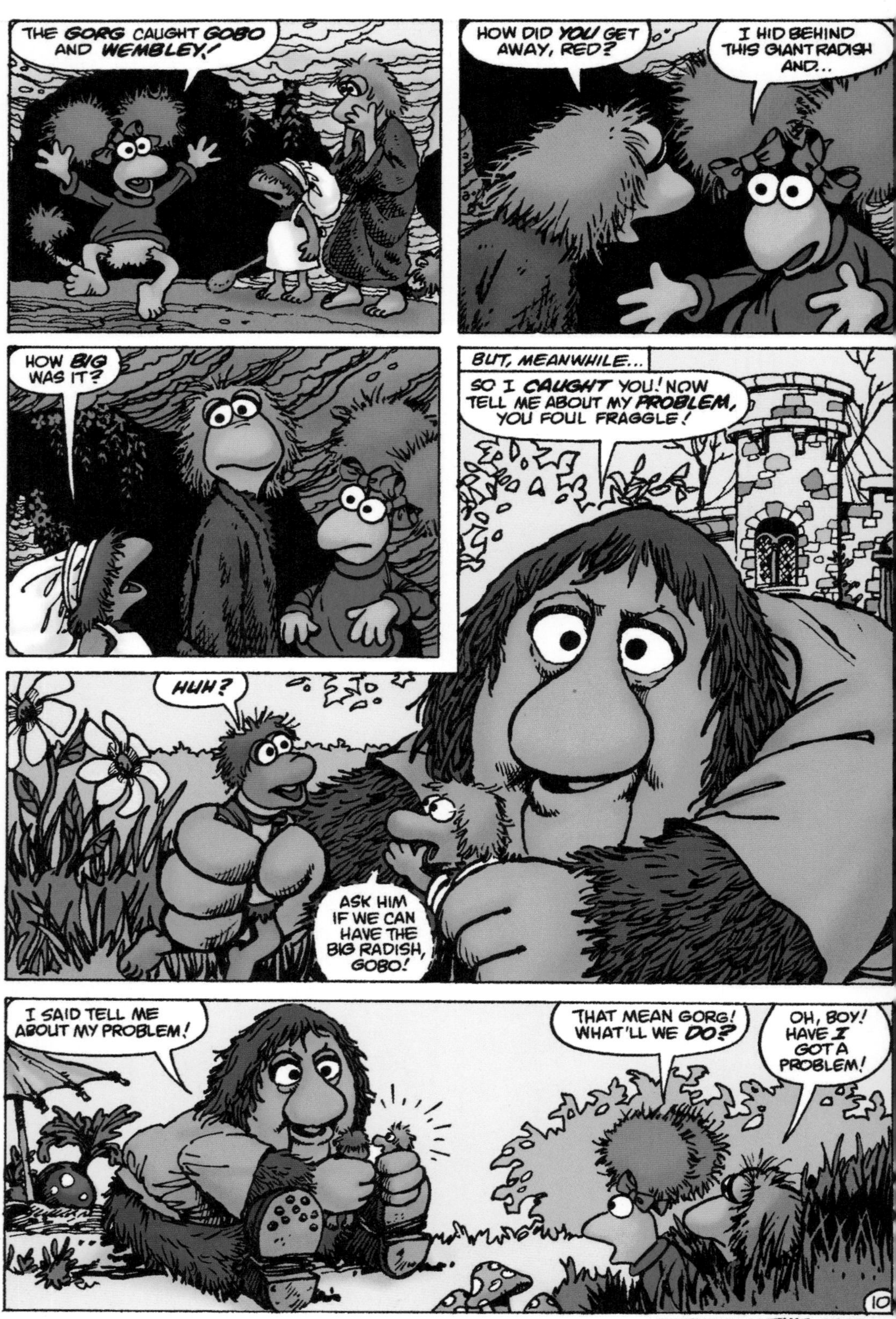

THE GORG CAUGHT GOBO AND WEMBLEY!
HOW DID YOU GET AWAY, RED?
I HID BEHIND THIS GIANT RADISH AND...
HOW BIG WAS IT?
BUT, MEANWHILE...
SO I CAUGHT YOU! NOW TELL ME ABOUT MY PROBLEM, YOU FOUL FRAGGLE!
HUH?
ASK HIM IF WE CAN HAVE THE BIG RADISH, GOBO!
I SAID TELL ME ABOUT MY PROBLEM!
THAT MEAN GORG! WHAT'LL WE DO?
OH, BOY! HAVE I GOT A PROBLEM!
10

CONTINUED IN THIS ISSUE...

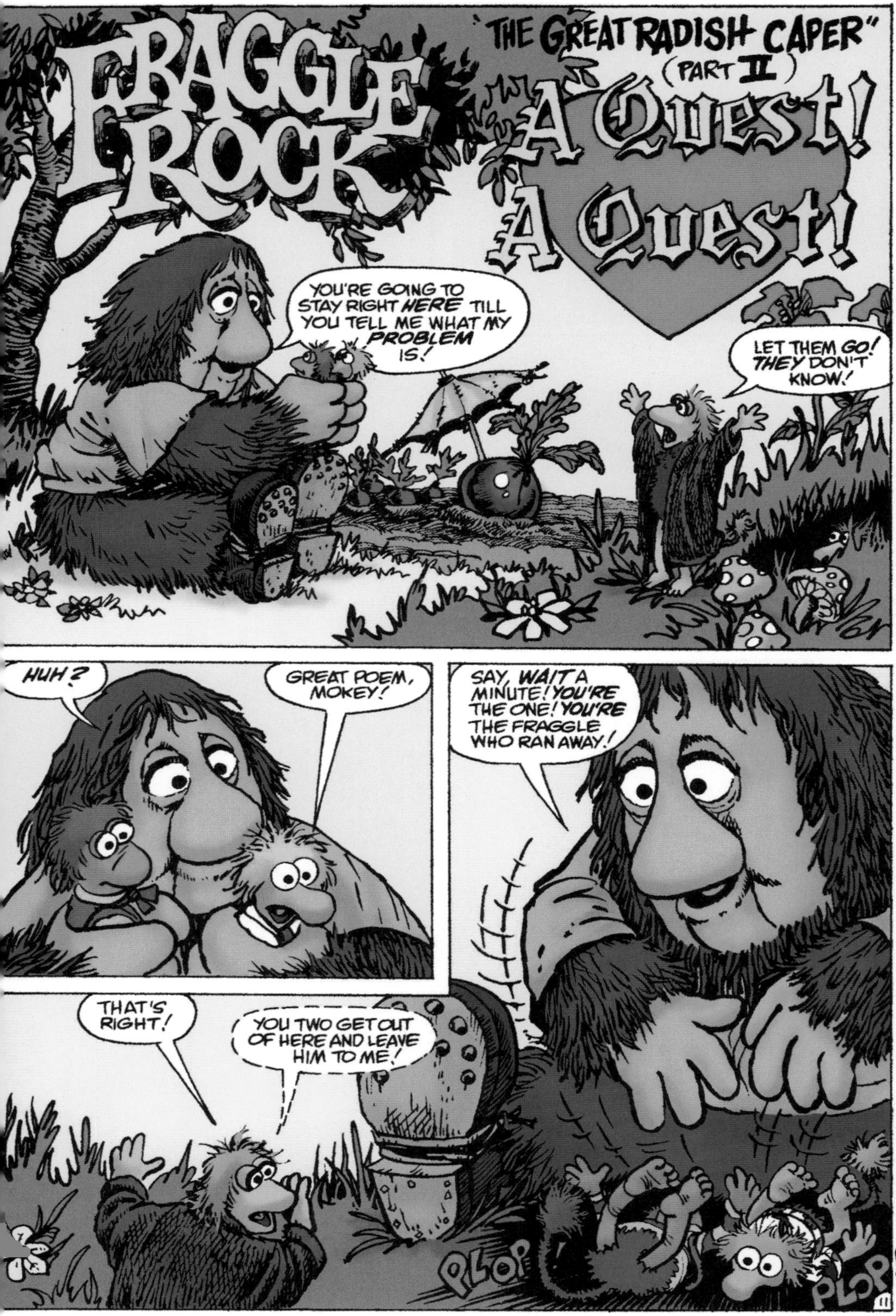
FRAGGLE ROCK
"THE GREAT RADISH CAPER" (PART II)
A Quest! A Quest!
YOU'RE GOING TO STAY RIGHT HERE TILL YOU TELL ME WHAT MY PROBLEM IS!
LET THEM GO! THEY DON'T KNOW!
HUH?
GREAT POEM, MOKEY!
SAY, WAIT A MINUTE! YOU'RE THE ONE! YOU'RE THE FRAGGLE WHO RAN AWAY!
THAT'S RIGHT!
YOU TWO GET OUT OF HERE AND LEAVE HIM TO ME!
PLOP
PLOP!
11

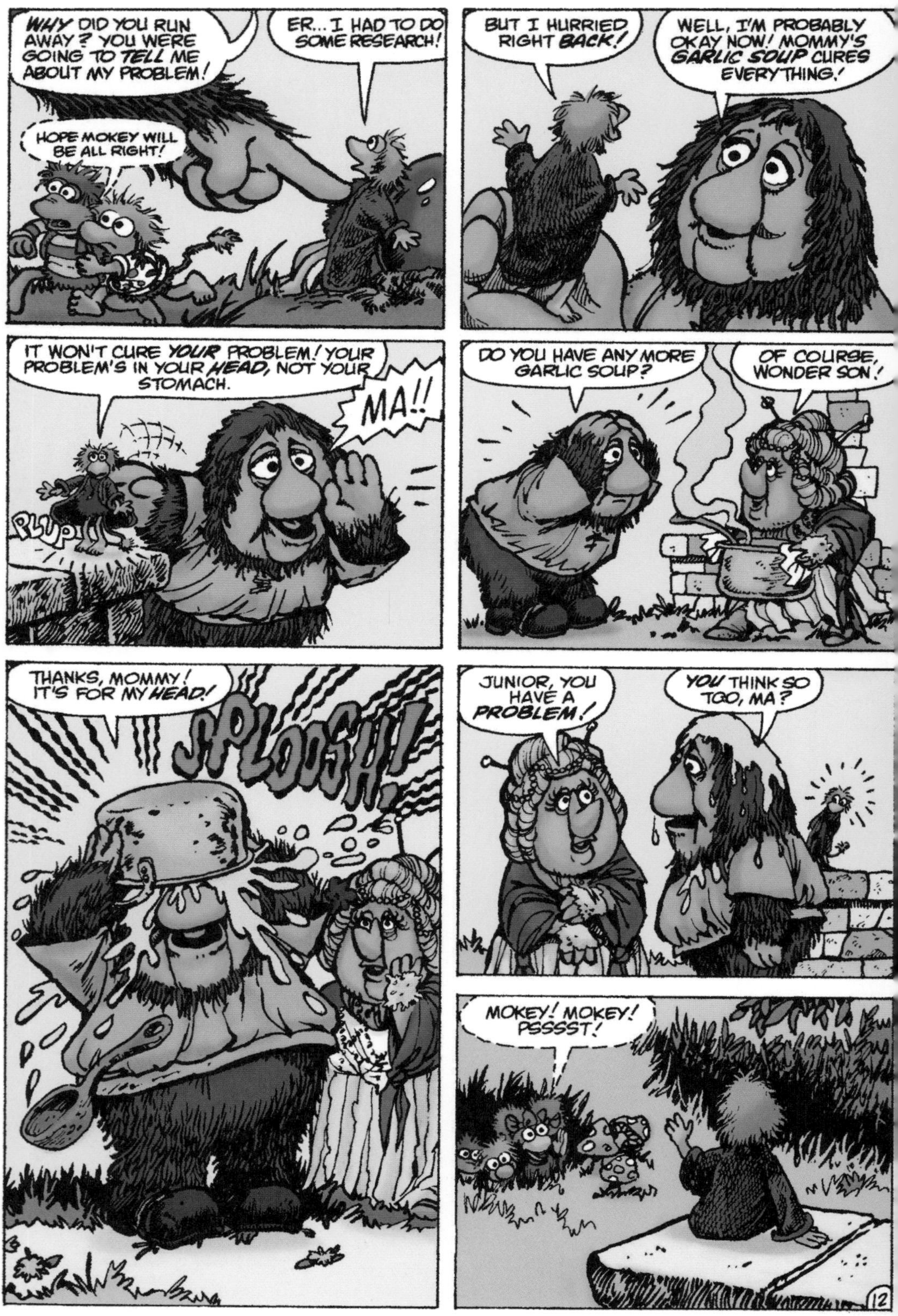
WHY DID YOU RUN AWAY? YOU WERE GOING TO TELL ME ABOUT MY PROBLEM!
ER... I HAD TO DO SOME RESEARCH!
HOPE MOKEY WILL BE ALL RIGHT!
BUT I HURRIED RIGHT BACK!
WELL, I'M PROBABLY OKAY NOW! MOMMY'S GARLIC SOUP CURES EVERYTHING!
IT WON'T CURE YOUR PROBLEM! YOUR PROBLEM'S IN YOUR HEAD, NOT YOUR STOMACH.
MA!!
PLUP!
DO YOU HAVE ANY MORE GARLIC SOUP?
OF COURSE, WONDER SON!
THANKS, MOMMY! IT'S FOR MY HEAD!
SPLOOSH!
JUNIOR, YOU HAVE A PROBLEM!
YOU THINK SO TOO, MA?
MOKEY! MOKEY! PSSSST!
12

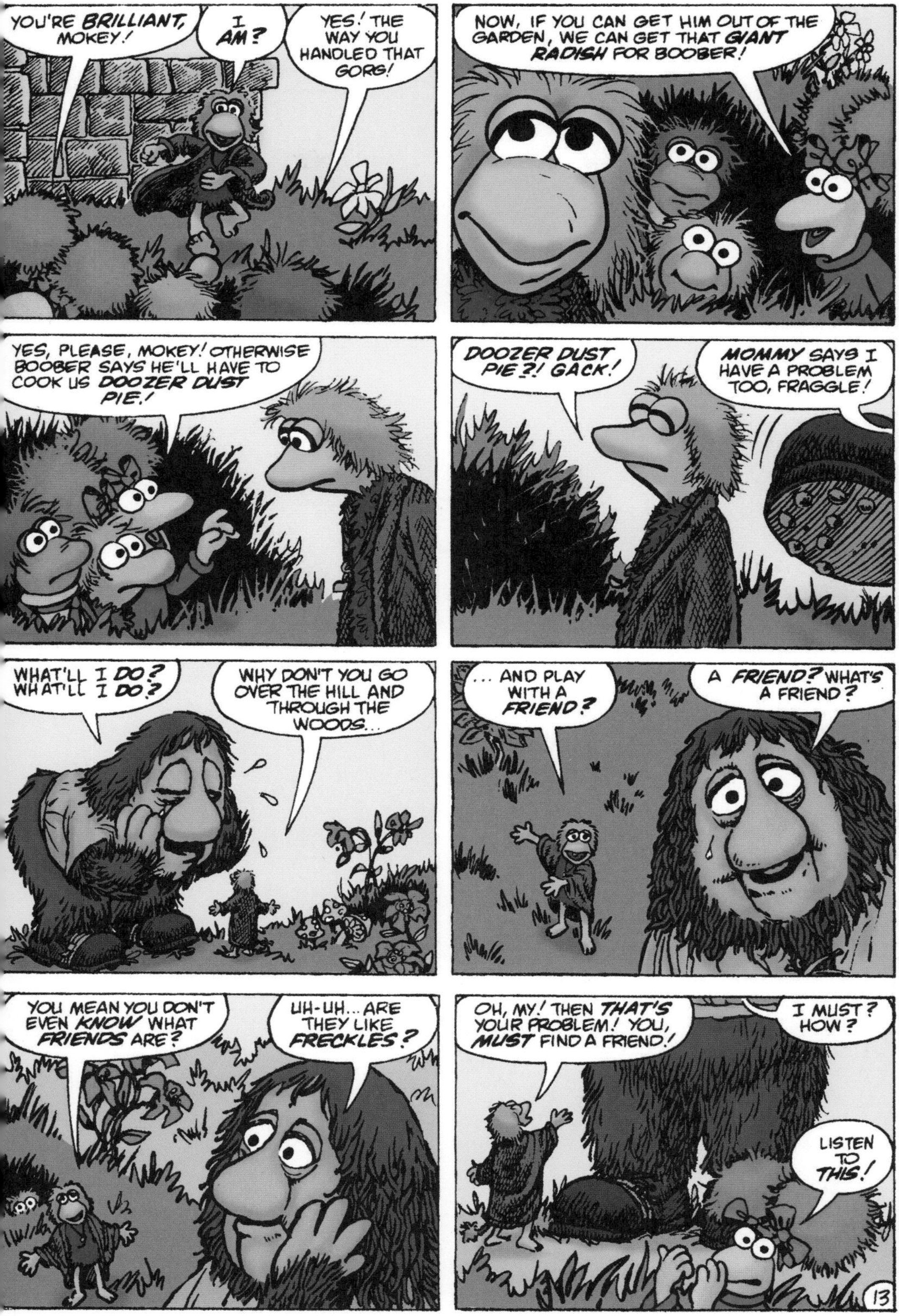
YOU'RE BRILLIANT, MOKEY!
I AM?
YES! THE WAY YOU HANDLED THAT GORG!
NOW, IF YOU CAN GET HIM OUT OF THE GARDEN, WE CAN GET THAT GIANT RADISH FOR BOOBER!
YES, PLEASE, MOKEY! OTHERWISE BOOBER SAYS HE'LL HAVE TO COOK US DOOZER DUST PIE!
DOOZER DUST PIE?! GACK!
MOMMY SAYS I HAVE A PROBLEM TOO, FRAGGLE!
WHAT'LL I DO? WHAT'LL I DO?
WHY DON'T YOU GO OVER THE HILL AND THROUGH THE WOODS...
... AND PLAY WITH A FRIEND?
A FRIEND? WHAT'S A FRIEND?
YOU MEAN YOU DON'T EVEN KNOW WHAT FRIENDS ARE?
UH-UH... ARE THEY LIKE FRECKLES?
OH, MY! THEN THAT'S YOUR PROBLEM! YOU, MUST FIND A FRIEND!
I MUST? HOW?
LISTEN TO THIS!
13

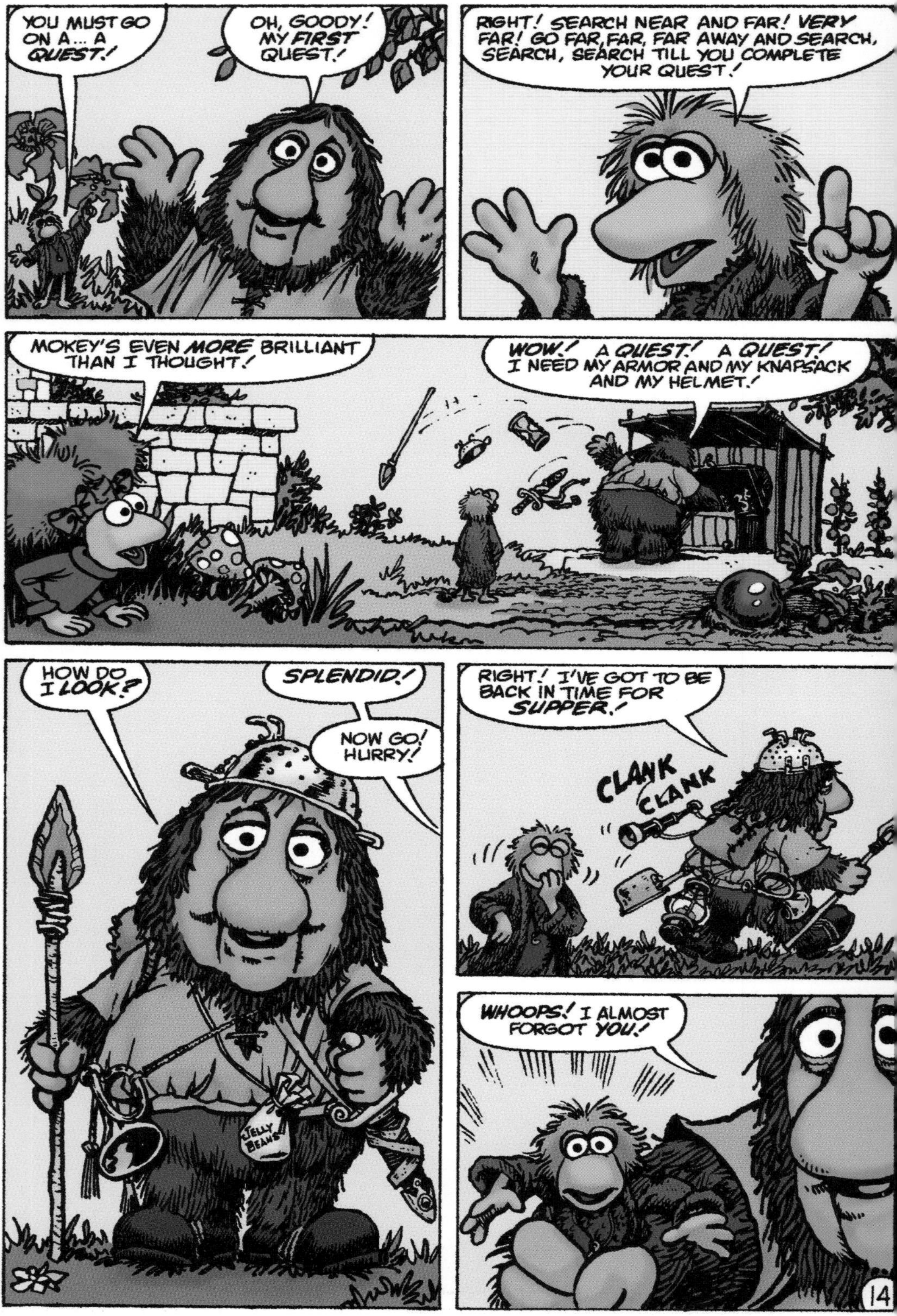
YOU MUST GO ON A... A QUEST!
OH, GOODY! MY FIRST QUEST!
RIGHT! SEARCH NEAR AND FAR! VERY FAR! GO FAR, FAR, FAR AWAY AND SEARCH, SEARCH, SEARCH TILL YOU COMPLETE YOUR QUEST!
MOKEY'S EVEN MORE BRILLIANT THAN I THOUGHT!
WOW! A QUEST! A QUEST! I NEED MY ARMOR AND MY KNAPSACK AND MY HELMET!
HOW DO I LOOK?
SPLENDID!
NOW GO! HURRY!
JELLY BEANS
RIGHT! I'VE GOT TO BE BACK IN TIME FOR SUPPER!
CLANK
CLANK
WHOOPS! I ALMOST FORGOT YOU!
14

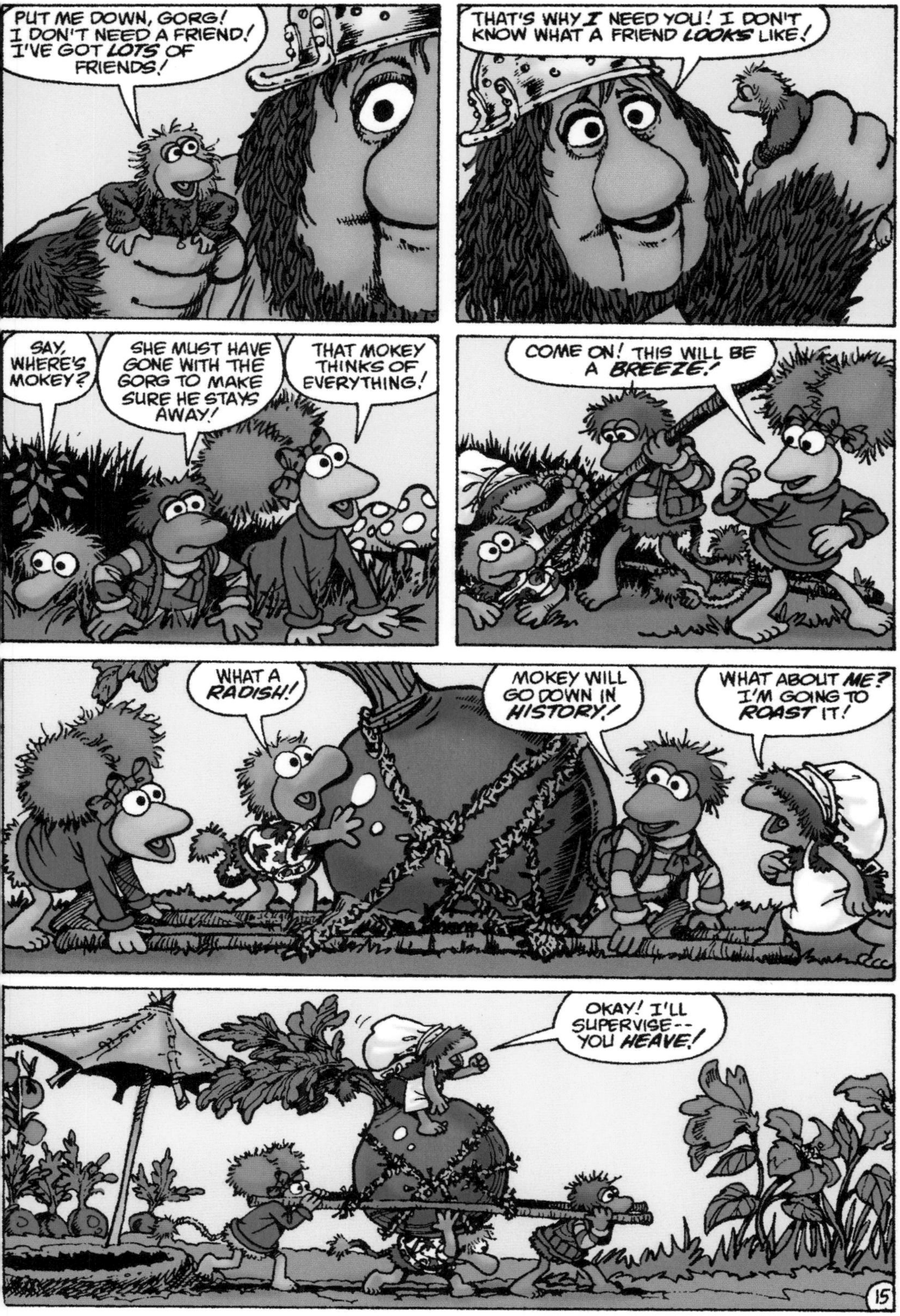
PUT ME DOWN, GORG! I DON'T NEED A FRIEND! I'VE GOT LOTS OF FRIENDS!
THAT'S WHY I NEED YOU! I DON'T KNOW WHAT A FRIEND LOOKS LIKE!
SAY, WHERE'S MOKEY?
SHE MUST HAVE GONE WITH THE GORG TO MAKE SURE HE STAYS AWAY!
THAT MOKEY THINKS OF EVERYTHING!
COME ON! THIS WILL BE A BREEZE!
WHAT A RADISH!
MOKEY WILL GO DOWN IN HISTORY!
WHAT ABOUT ME? I'M GOING TO ROAST IT!
OKAY! I'LL SUPERVISE-- YOU HEAVE!
15

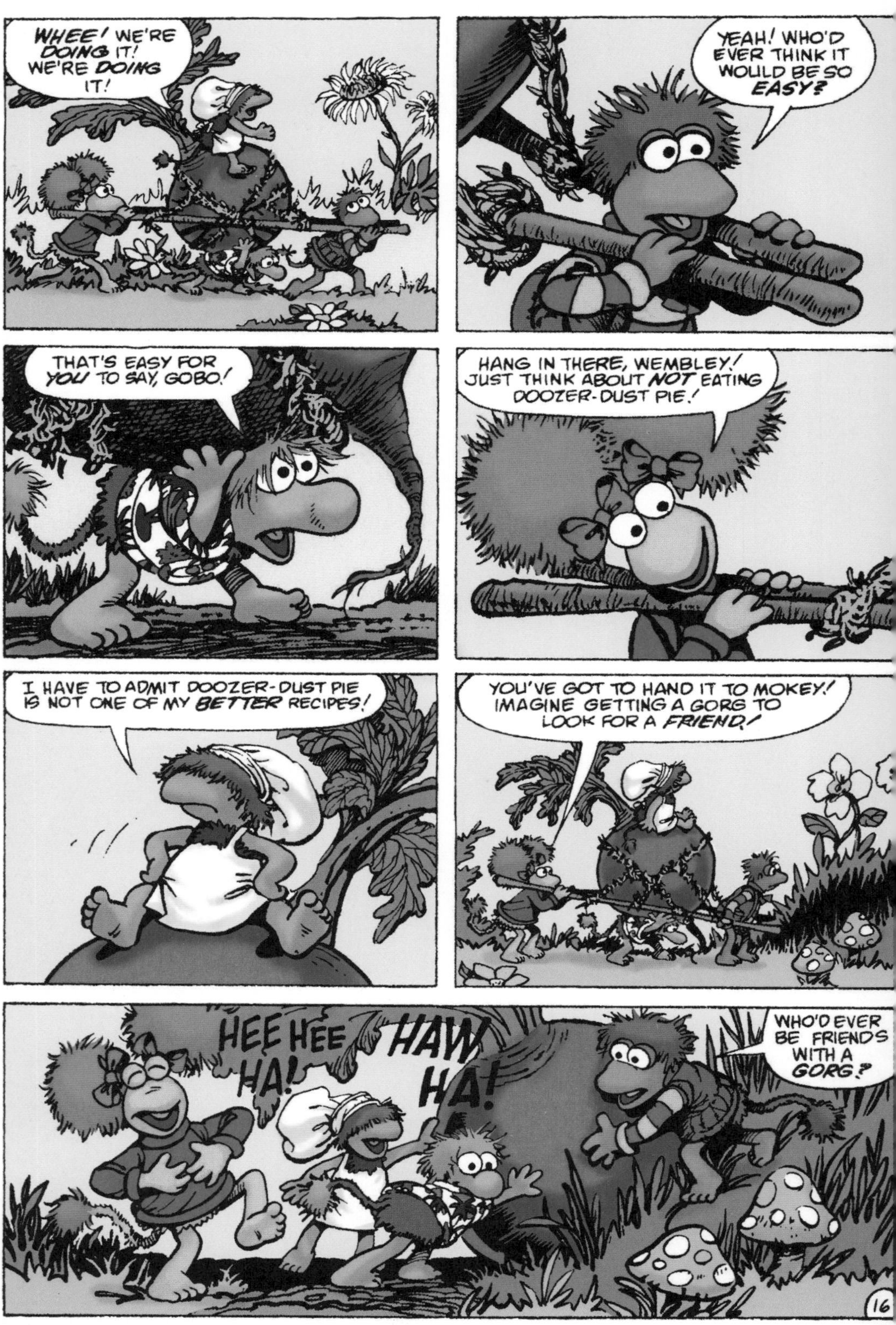
WHEE! WE'RE DOING IT! WE'RE DOING IT!
YEAH! WHO'D EVER THINK IT WOULD BE SO EASY?
THAT'S EASY FOR YOU TO SAY, GOBO!
HANG IN THERE, WEMBLEY! JUST THINK ABOUT NOT EATING DOOZER-DUST PIE!
I HAVE TO ADMIT DOOZER-DUST PIE IS NOT ONE OF MY BETTER RECIPES!
YOU'VE GOT TO HAND IT TO MOKEY! IMAGINE GETTING A GORG TO LOOK FOR A FRIEND!
HEE HEE HA!
HAW HA!
WHO'D EVER BE FRIENDS WITH A GORG?
16

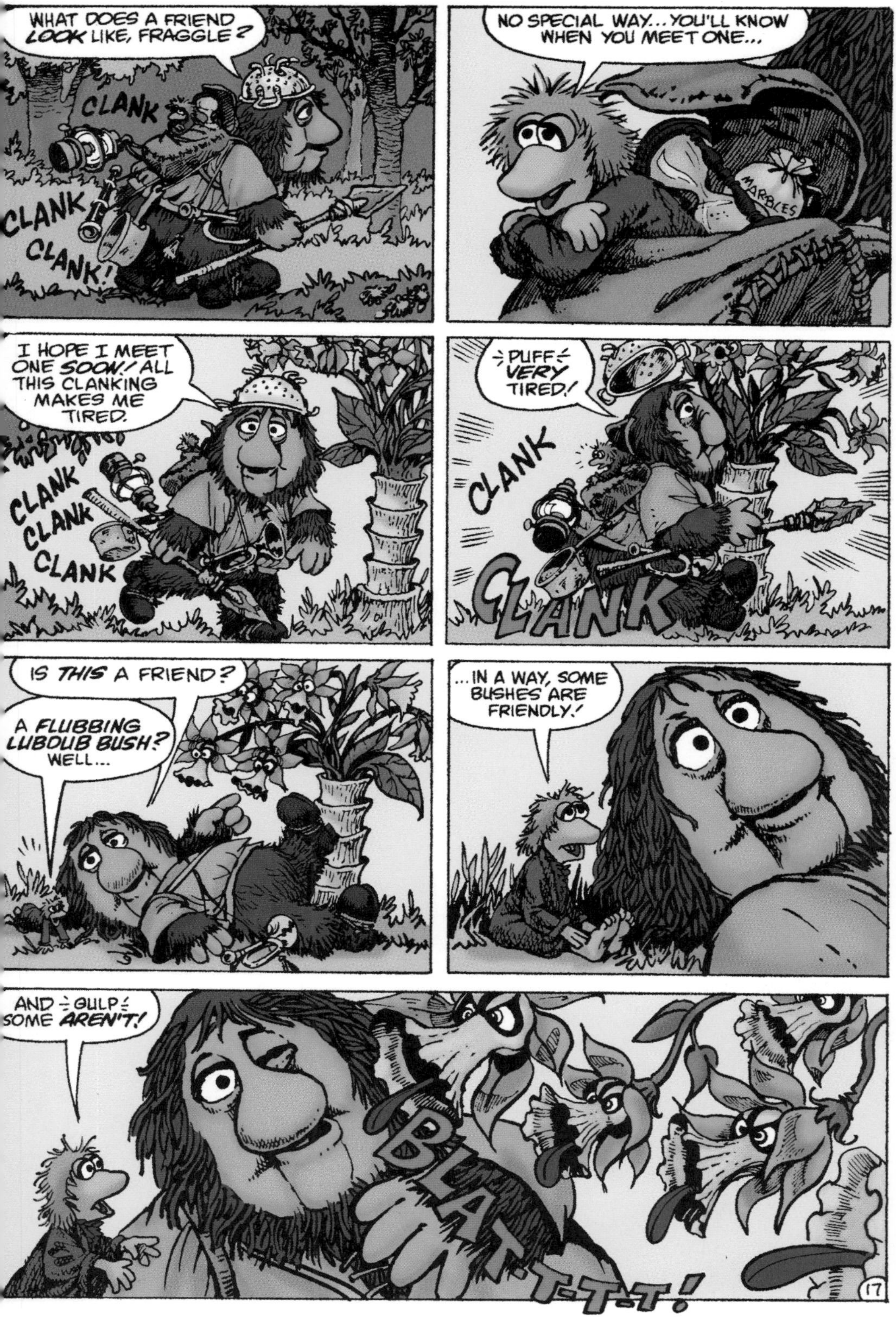

WHAT DOES A FRIEND *LOOK* LIKE, FRAGGLE?
CLANK
CLANK
CLANK!
NO SPECIAL WAY... YOU'LL KNOW WHEN YOU MEET ONE...
MARBLES
I HOPE I MEET ONE *SOON!* ALL THIS CLANKING MAKES ME TIRED.
CLANK
CLANK
CLANK
PUFF *VERY* TIRED!
CLANK
CLANK
IS *THIS* A FRIEND?
A *FLUBBING LUBDUB BUSH?* WELL...
...IN A WAY, SOME BUSHES ARE FRIENDLY!
AND GULP SOME *AREN'T!*
BLAT-T-T-T!
17

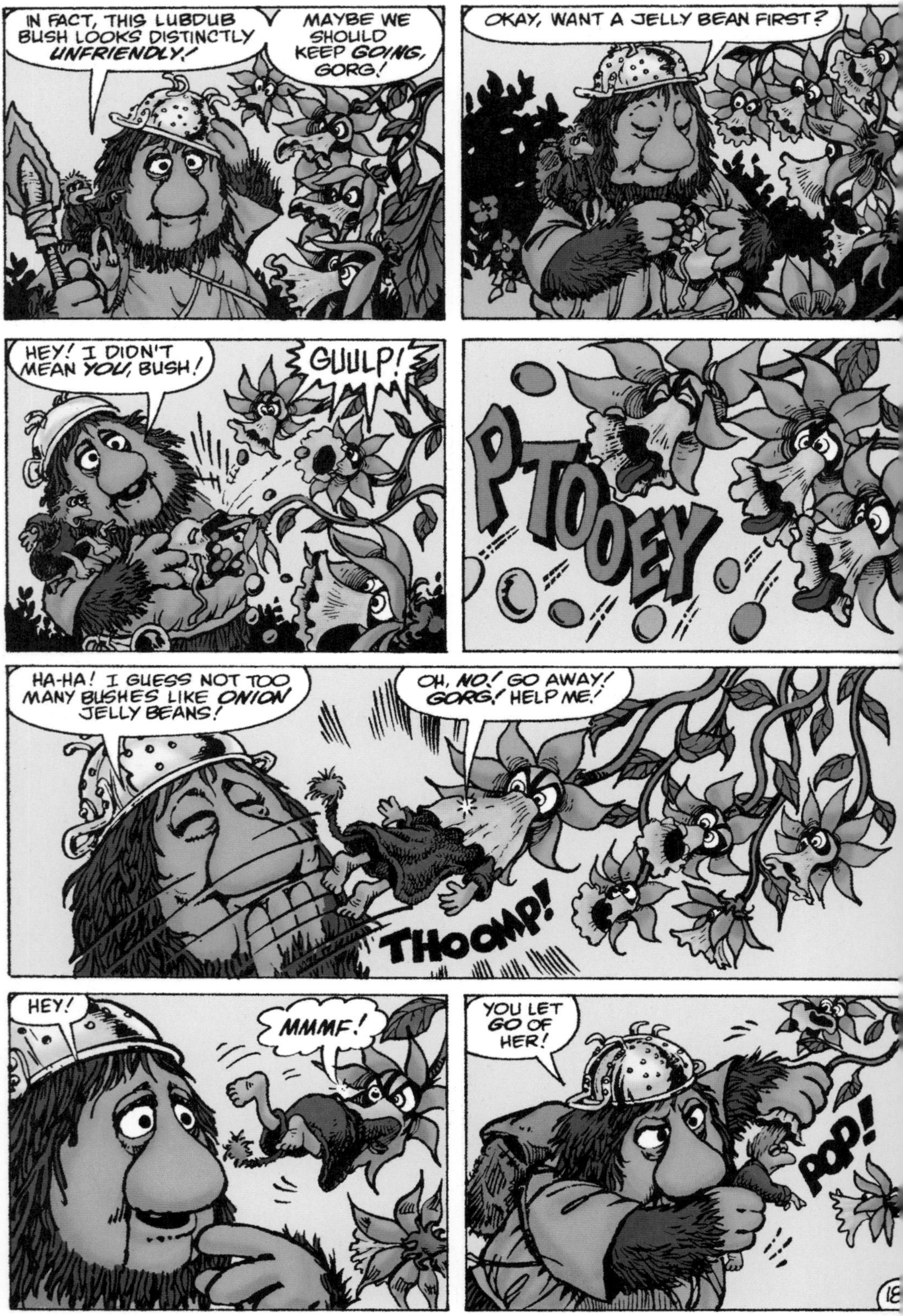
IN FACT, THIS LUBDUB BUSH LOOKS DISTINCTLY UNFRIENDLY!
MAYBE WE SHOULD KEEP GOING, GORG!
OKAY, WANT A JELLY BEAN FIRST?
HEY! I DIDN'T MEAN YOU, BUSH!
GUULP!
PTOOEY
HA-HA! I GUESS NOT TOO MANY BUSHES LIKE ONION JELLY BEANS!
OH, NO! GO AWAY! GORG! HELP ME!
THOOMP!
HEY!
MMMF!
YOU LET GO OF HER!
POP!
18

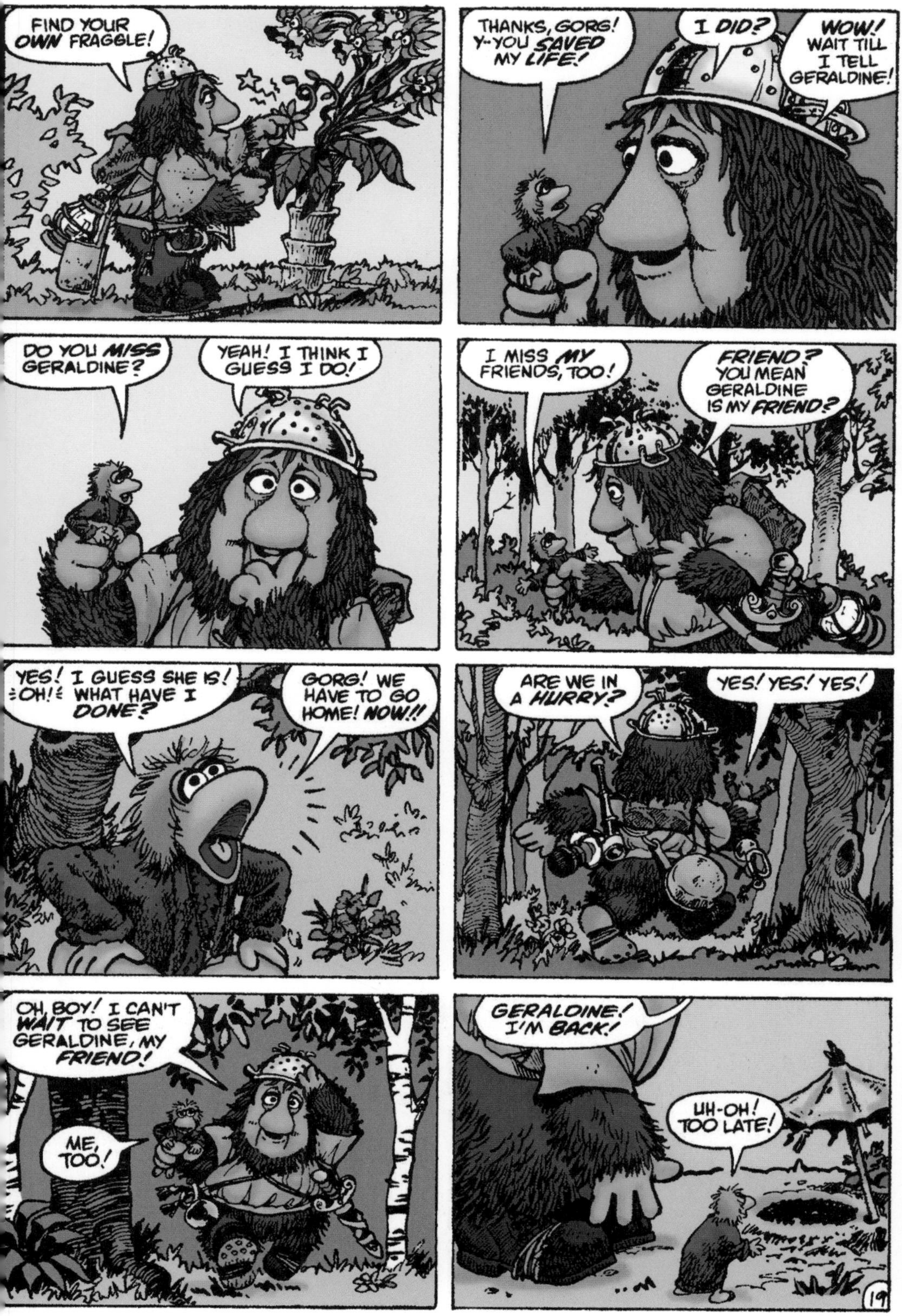
FIND YOUR OWN FRAGGLE!
THANKS, GORG! Y-YOU SAVED MY LIFE!
I DID?
WOW! WAIT TILL I TELL GERALDINE!
DO YOU MISS GERALDINE?
YEAH! I THINK I GUESS I DO!
I MISS MY FRIENDS, TOO!
FRIEND? YOU MEAN GERALDINE IS MY FRIEND?
YES! I GUESS SHE IS! OH! WHAT HAVE I DONE?
GORG! WE HAVE TO GO HOME! NOW!!
ARE WE IN A HURRY?
YES! YES! YES!
OH, BOY! I CAN'T WAIT TO SEE GERALDINE, MY FRIEND!
ME, TOO!
GERALDINE! I'M BACK!
UH-OH! TOO LATE!
19

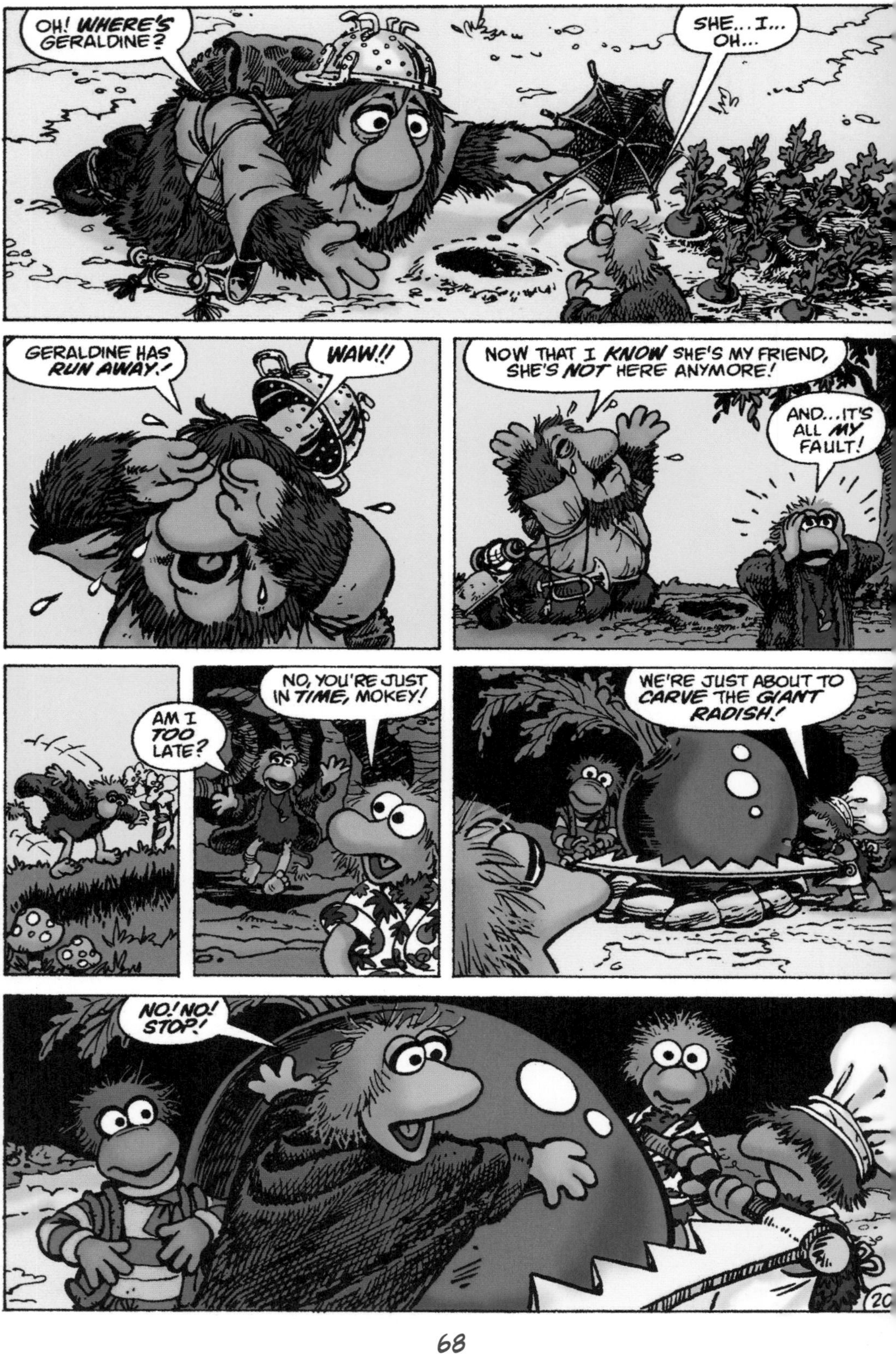
OH! WHERE'S GERALDINE?
SHE... I... OH...
GERALDINE HAS RUN AWAY!
WAW!!
NOW THAT I KNOW SHE'S MY FRIEND, SHE'S NOT HERE ANYMORE!
AND...IT'S ALL MY FAULT!
AM I TOO LATE?
NO, YOU'RE JUST IN TIME, MOKEY!
WE'RE JUST ABOUT TO CARVE THE GIANT RADISH!
NO! NO! STOP!

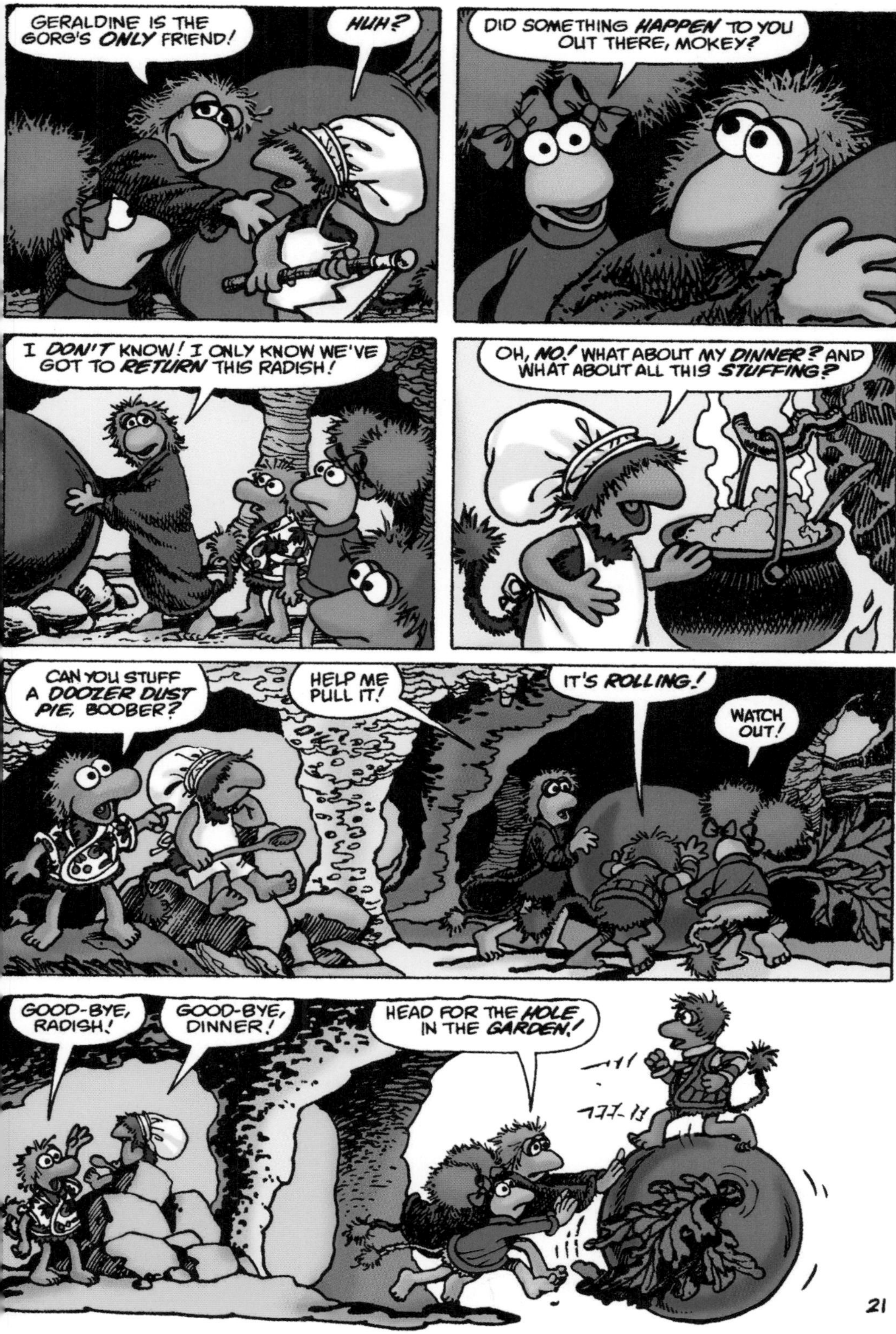
GERALDINE IS THE GORG'S ONLY FRIEND!
HUH?
DID SOMETHING HAPPEN TO YOU OUT THERE, MOKEY?
I DON'T KNOW! I ONLY KNOW WE'VE GOT TO RETURN THIS RADISH!
OH, NO! WHAT ABOUT MY DINNER? AND WHAT ABOUT ALL THIS STUFFING?
CAN YOU STUFF A DOOZER DUST PIE, BOOBER?
HELP ME PULL IT!
IT'S ROLLING!
WATCH OUT!
GOOD-BYE, RADISH!
GOOD-BYE, DINNER!
HEAD FOR THE HOLE IN THE GARDEN!
21

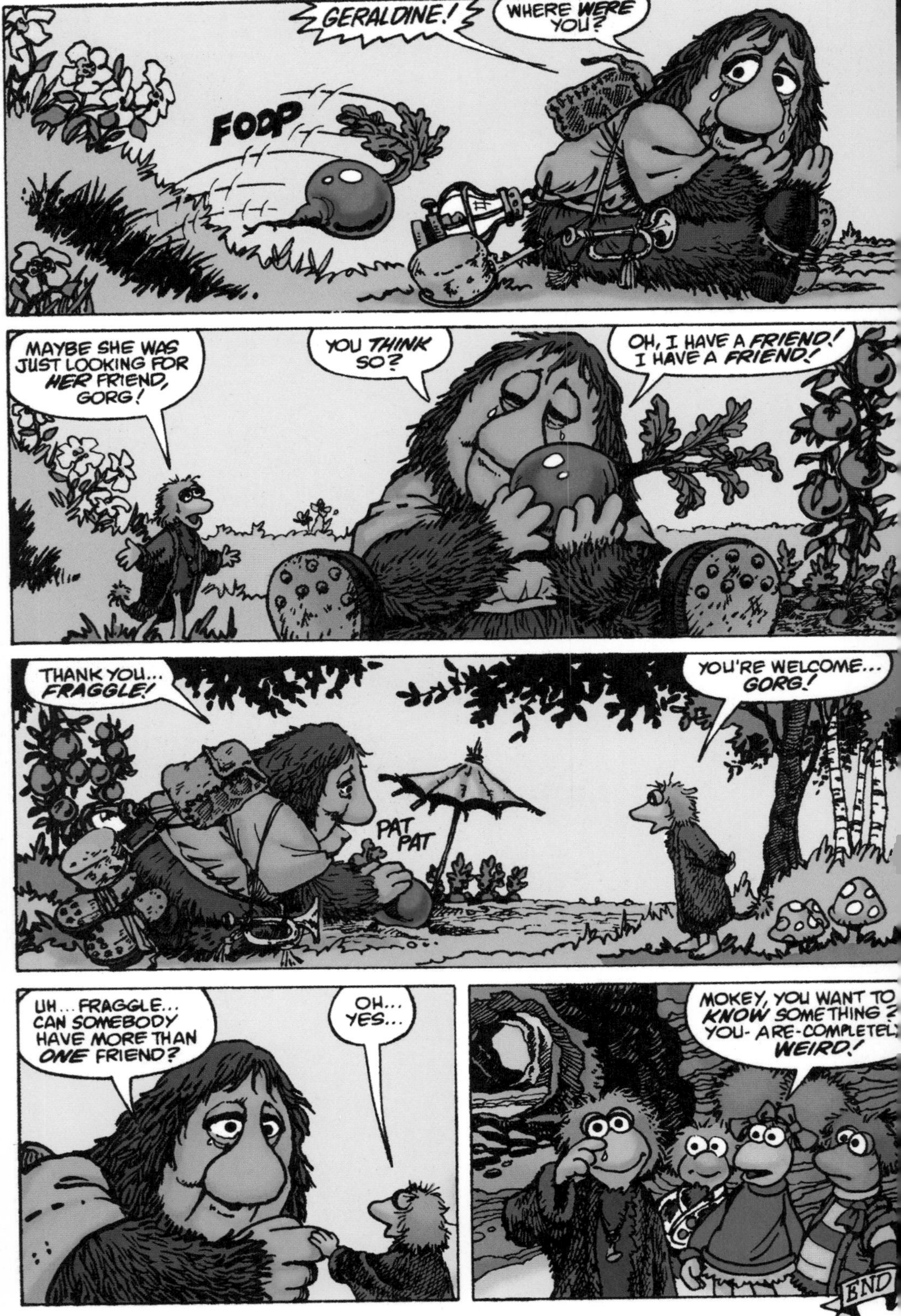
GERALDINE!
WHERE WERE YOU?
FOOP
MAYBE SHE WAS JUST LOOKING FOR HER FRIEND, GORG!
YOU THINK SO?
OH, I HAVE A FRIEND! I HAVE A FRIEND!
THANK YOU... FRAGGLE!
PAT PAT
YOU'RE WELCOME... GORG!
UH... FRAGGLE... CAN SOMEBODY HAVE MORE THAN ONE FRIEND?
OH... YES...
MOKEY, YOU WANT TO KNOW SOMETHING? YOU- ARE-COMPLETEL WEIRD!
END

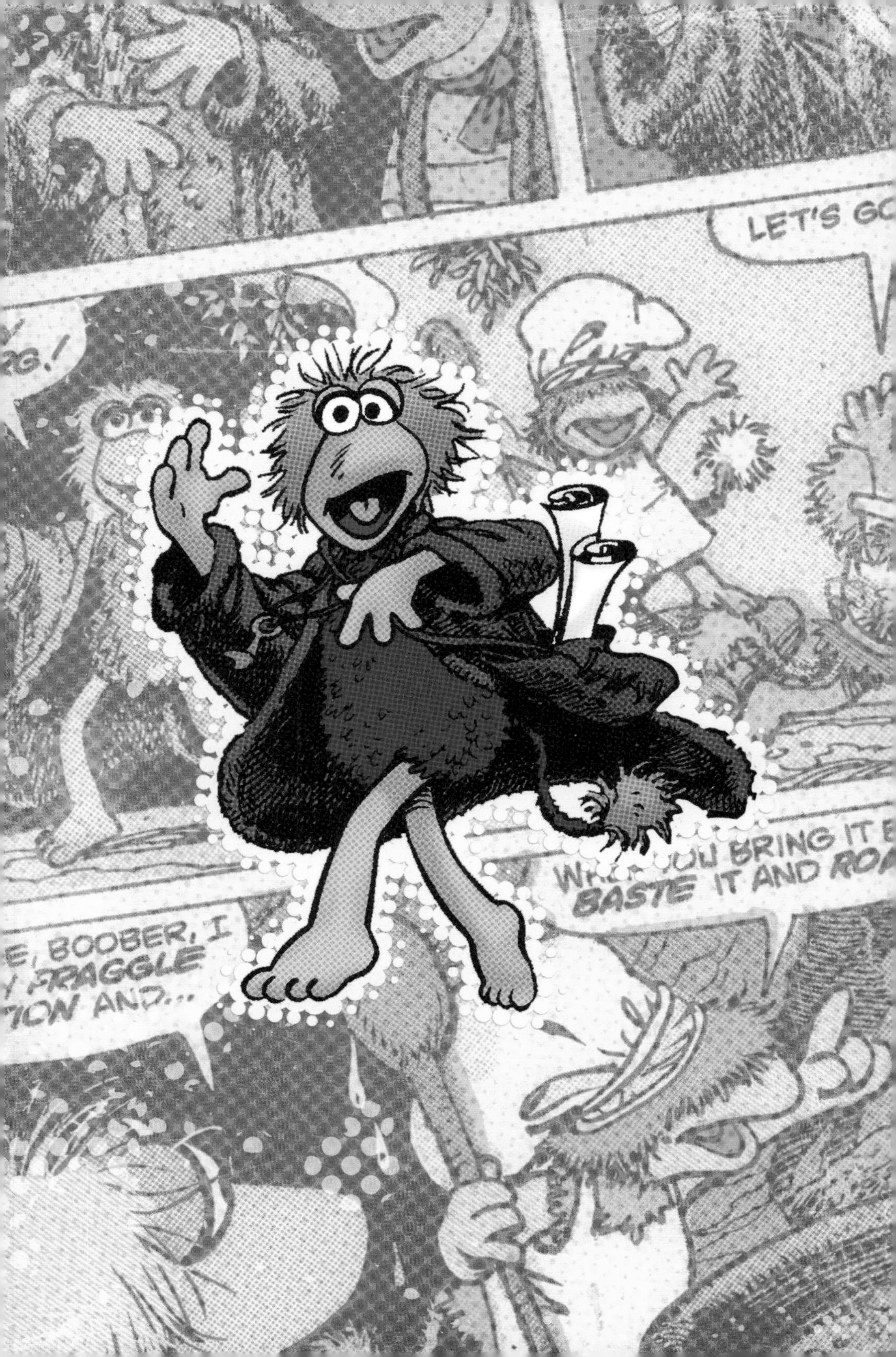

LET'S
BOOBER, I
FRAGGLE
AND...
BRING IT
BASTE IT AND

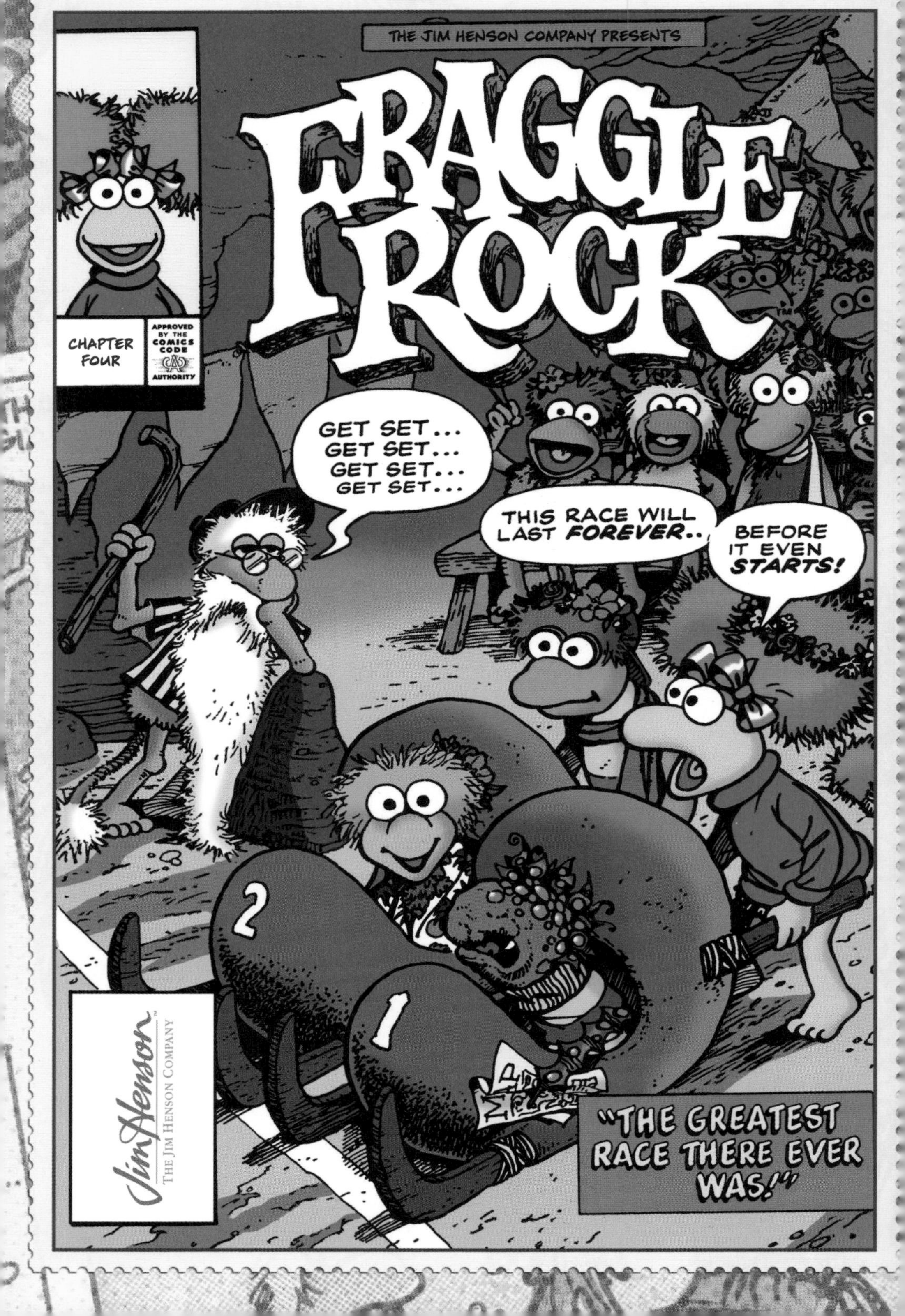
THE JIM HENSON COMPANY PRESENTS
FRAGGLE ROCK
CHAPTER FOUR
APPROVED BY THE COMICS CODE AUTHORITY
GET SET... GET SET... GET SET... GET SET...
THIS RACE WILL LAST FOREVER..
BEFORE IT EVEN STARTS!
2
1
Jim Henson THE JIM HENSON COMPANY
"THE GREATEST RACE THERE EVER WAS!"

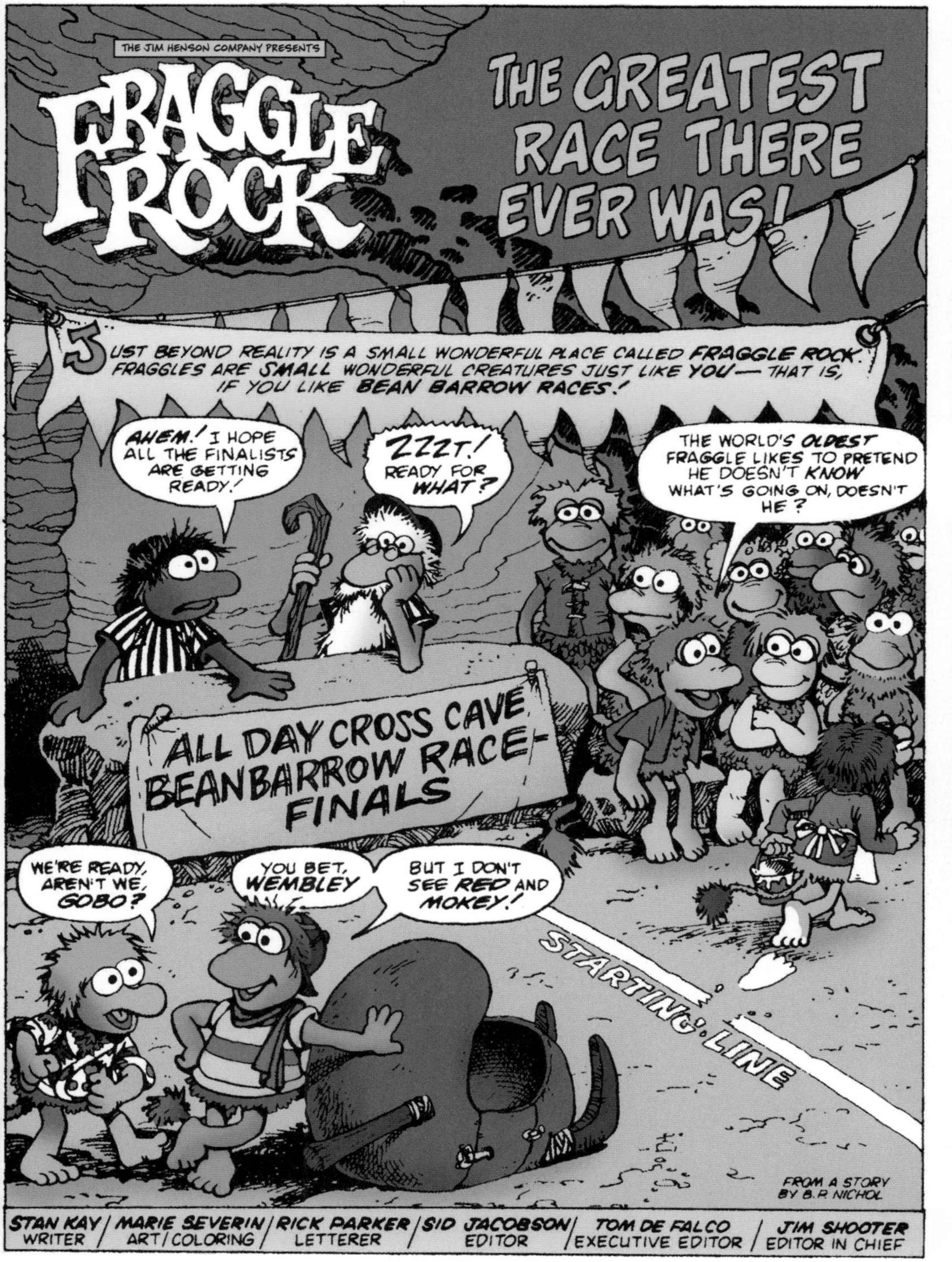
THE JIM HENSON COMPANY PRESENTS
FRAGGLE ROCK
THE GREATEST RACE THERE EVER WAS!
JUST BEYOND REALITY IS A SMALL WONDERFUL PLACE CALLED FRAGGLE ROCK. FRAGGLES ARE SMALL WONDERFUL CREATURES JUST LIKE YOU— THAT IS, IF YOU LIKE BEAN BARROW RACES!
AHEM! I HOPE ALL THE FINALISTS ARE GETTING READY!
ZZZT! READY FOR WHAT?
THE WORLD'S OLDEST FRAGGLE LIKES TO PRETEND HE DOESN'T KNOW WHAT'S GOING ON, DOESN'T HE?
ALL DAY CROSS CAVE BEANBARROW RACE- FINALS
WE'RE READY, AREN'T WE, GOBO?
YOU BET, WEMBLEY
BUT I DON'T SEE RED AND MOKEY!
STARTING LINE
FROM A STORY BY B.R. NICHOL
STAN KAY / WRITER
MARIE SEVERIN / ART/COLORING
RICK PARKER / LETTERER
SID JACOBSON / EDITOR
TOM DE FALCO / EXECUTIVE EDITOR
JIM SHOOTER / EDITOR IN CHIEF

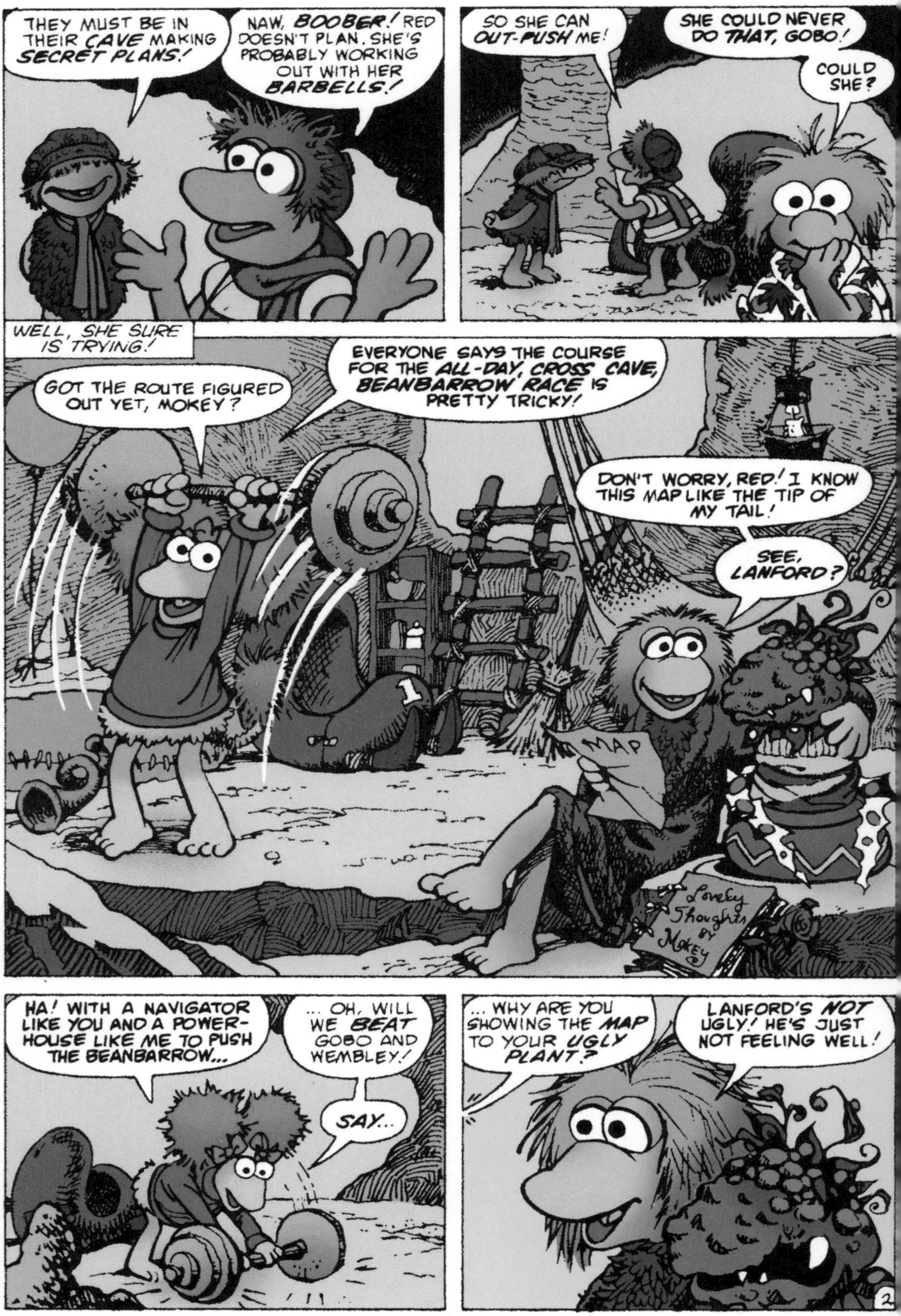
THEY MUST BE IN THEIR CAVE MAKING SECRET PLANS!
NAW, BOOBER! RED DOESN'T PLAN. SHE'S PROBABLY WORKING OUT WITH HER BARBELLS!
SO SHE CAN OUT-PUSH ME!
SHE COULD NEVER DO THAT, GOBO!
COULD SHE?
WELL, SHE SURE IS TRYING!
GOT THE ROUTE FIGURED OUT YET, MOKEY?
EVERYONE SAYS THE COURSE FOR THE ALL-DAY, CROSS CAVE, BEANBARROW RACE IS PRETTY TRICKY!
DON'T WORRY, RED! I KNOW THIS MAP LIKE THE TIP OF MY TAIL!
SEE, LANFORD?
MAP
Lovely Thoughts by Mokey
HA! WITH A NAVIGATOR LIKE YOU AND A POWER-HOUSE LIKE ME TO PUSH THE BEANBARROW...
... OH, WILL WE BEAT GOBO AND WEMBLEY!
SAY...
... WHY ARE YOU SHOWING THE MAP TO YOUR UGLY PLANT?
LANFORD'S NOT UGLY! HE'S JUST NOT FEELING WELL!
2

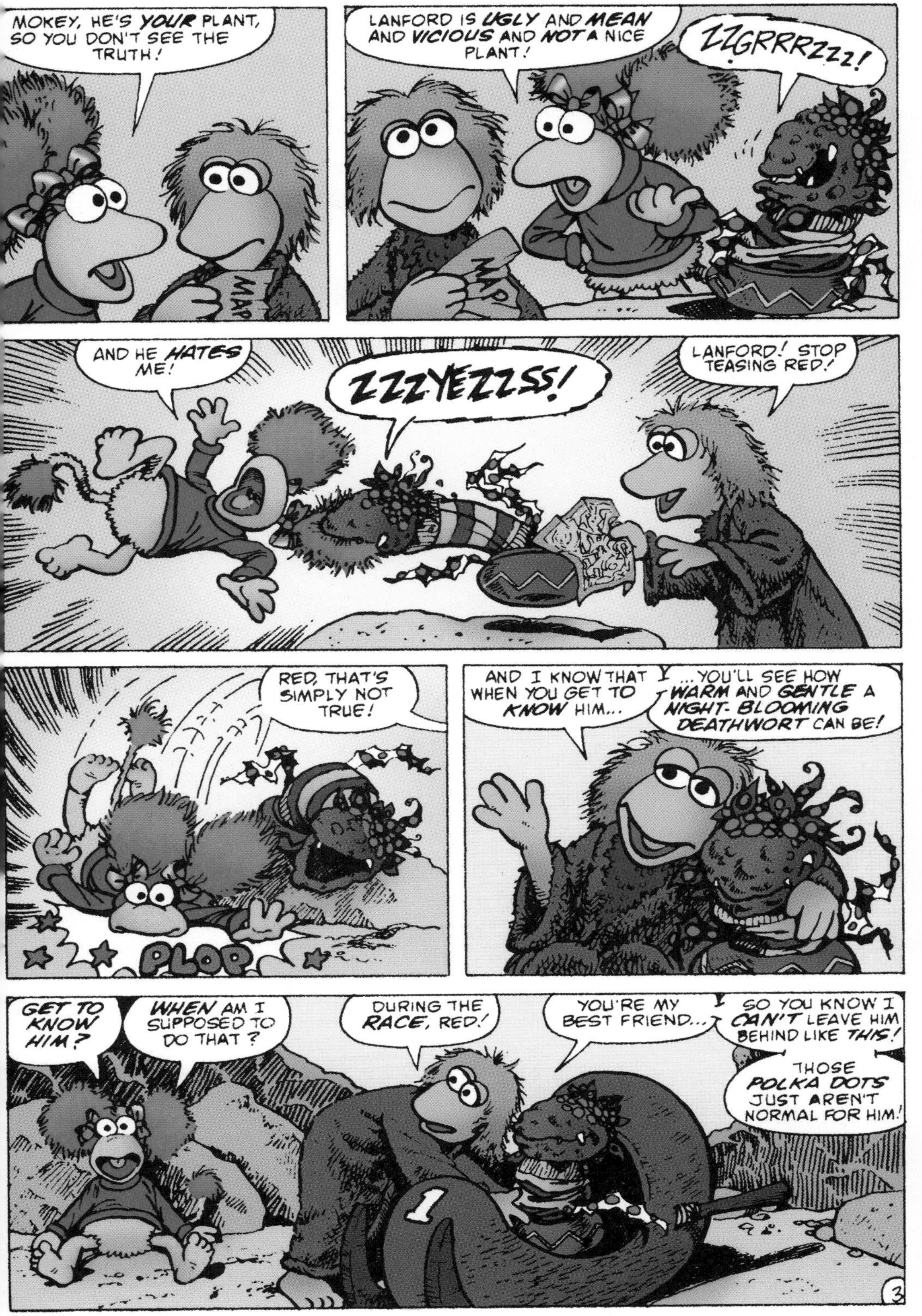
MOKEY, HE'S YOUR PLANT, SO YOU DON'T SEE THE TRUTH!
MAP
LANFORD IS UGLY AND MEAN AND VICIOUS AND NOT A NICE PLANT!
ZZGRRRZzzz!
MAP
AND HE HATES ME!
ZZZYEZZZSS!
LANFORD! STOP TEASING RED!
RED, THAT'S SIMPLY NOT TRUE!
PLOP
AND I KNOW THAT WHEN YOU GET TO KNOW HIM...
...YOU'LL SEE HOW WARM AND GENTLE A NIGHT-BLOOMING DEATHWORT CAN BE!
GET TO KNOW HIM?
WHEN AM I SUPPOSED TO DO THAT?
DURING THE RACE, RED!
YOU'RE MY BEST FRIEND...
SO YOU KNOW I CAN'T LEAVE HIM BEHIND LIKE THIS!
THOSE POLKA DOTS JUST AREN'T NORMAL FOR HIM!
1
3

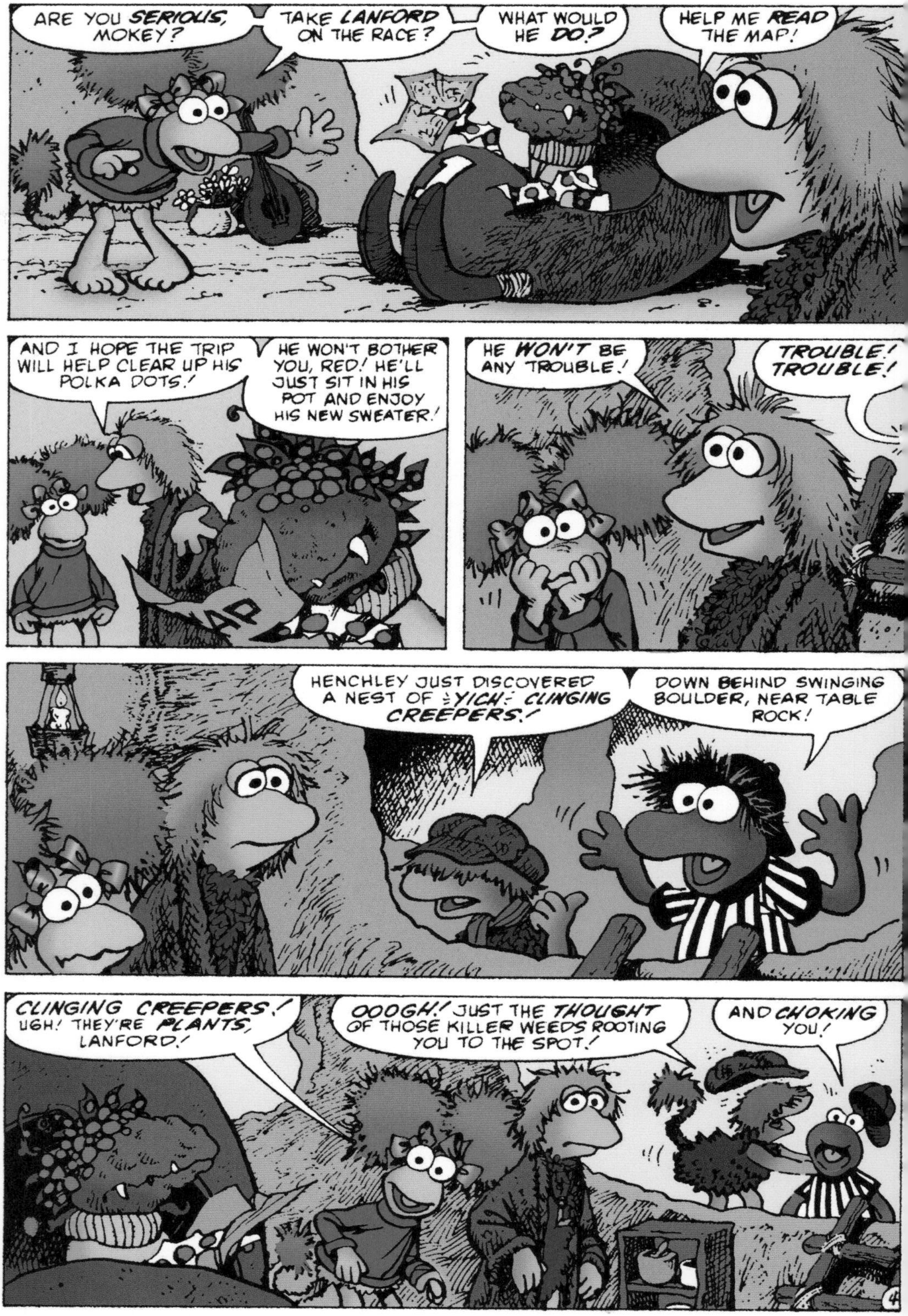
ARE YOU SERIOUS, MOKEY?
TAKE LANFORD ON THE RACE?
WHAT WOULD HE DO?
HELP ME READ THE MAP!
AND I HOPE THE TRIP WILL HELP CLEAR UP HIS POLKA DOTS!
HE WON'T BOTHER YOU, RED! HE'LL JUST SIT IN HIS POT AND ENJOY HIS NEW SWEATER!
MAP
HE WON'T BE ANY TROUBLE!
TROUBLE! TROUBLE!
HENCHLEY JUST DISCOVERED A NEST OF -YICH- CLINGING CREEPERS!
DOWN BEHIND SWINGING BOULDER, NEAR TABLE ROCK!
CLINGING CREEPERS! UGH! THEY'RE PLANTS, LANFORD!
OOOGH! JUST THE THOUGHT OF THOSE KILLER WEEDS ROOTING YOU TO THE SPOT!
AND CHOKING YOU!
4

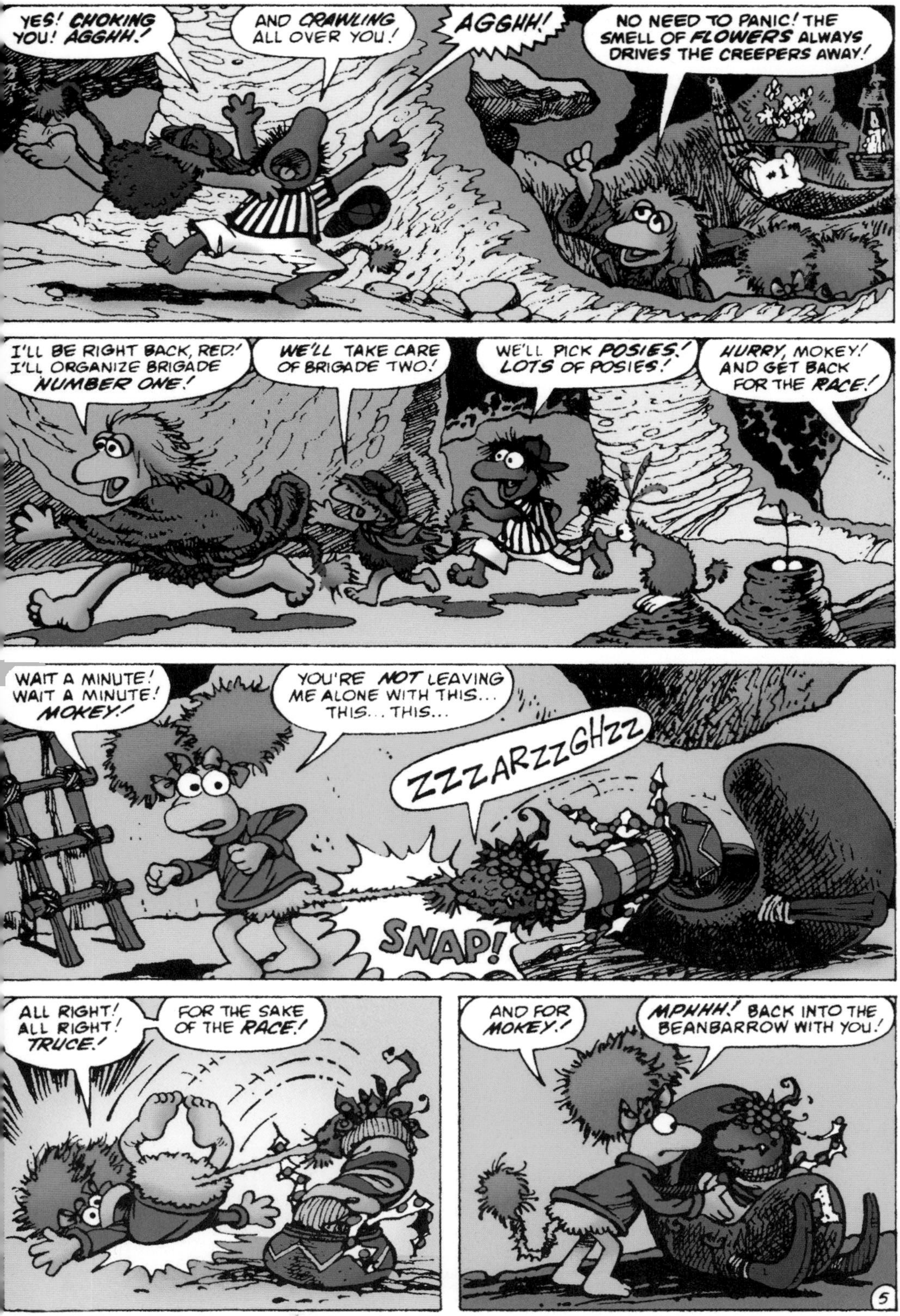
YES! CHOKING YOU! AGGHH!
AND CRAWLING ALL OVER YOU!
AGGHH!
NO NEED TO PANIC! THE SMELL OF FLOWERS ALWAYS DRIVES THE CREEPERS AWAY!
I'LL BE RIGHT BACK, RED! I'LL ORGANIZE BRIGADE NUMBER ONE!
WE'LL TAKE CARE OF BRIGADE TWO!
WE'LL PICK POSIES! LOTS OF POSIES!
HURRY, MOKEY! AND GET BACK FOR THE RACE!
WAIT A MINUTE! WAIT A MINUTE! MOKEY!
YOU'RE NOT LEAVING ME ALONE WITH THIS... THIS... THIS...
ZZZARZZGHZZ
SNAP!
ALL RIGHT! ALL RIGHT! TRUCE!
FOR THE SAKE OF THE RACE!
AND FOR MOKEY!
MPHHH! BACK INTO THE BEANBARROW WITH YOU!
5

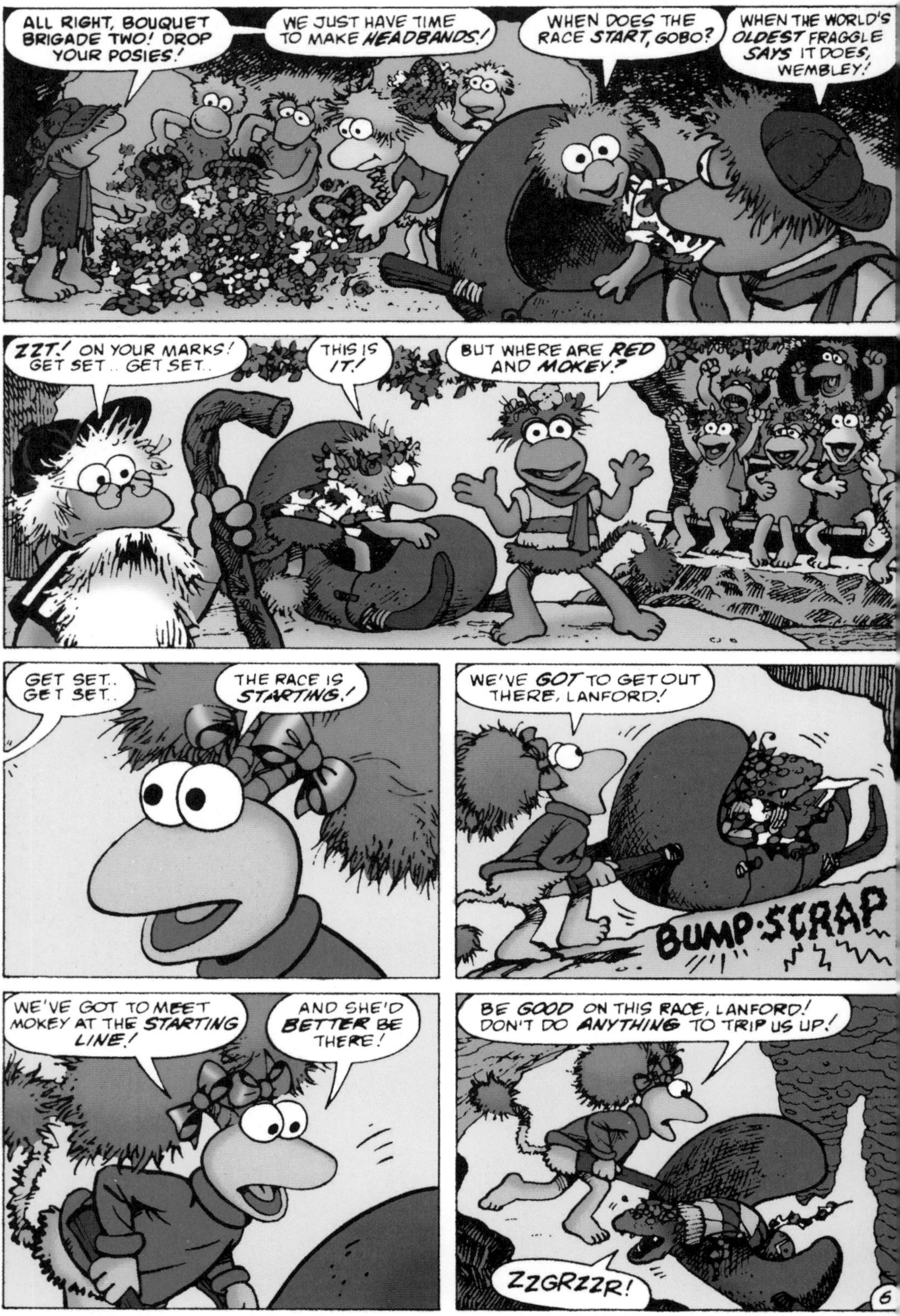
ALL RIGHT, BOUQUET BRIGADE TWO! DROP YOUR POSIES!
WE JUST HAVE TIME TO MAKE HEADBANDS!
WHEN DOES THE RACE START, GOBO?
WHEN THE WORLD'S OLDEST FRAGGLE SAYS IT DOES, WEMBLEY!
ZZT! ON YOUR MARKS! GET SET.. GET SET..
THIS IS IT!
BUT WHERE ARE RED AND MOKEY?
GET SET.. GET SET..
THE RACE IS STARTING!
WE'VE GOT TO GET OUT THERE, LANFORD!
BUMP·SCRAP
WE'VE GOT TO MEET MOKEY AT THE STARTING LINE!
AND SHE'D BETTER BE THERE!
BE GOOD ON THIS RACE, LANFORD! DON'T DO ANYTHING TO TRIP US UP!
ZZGRZZR!
6

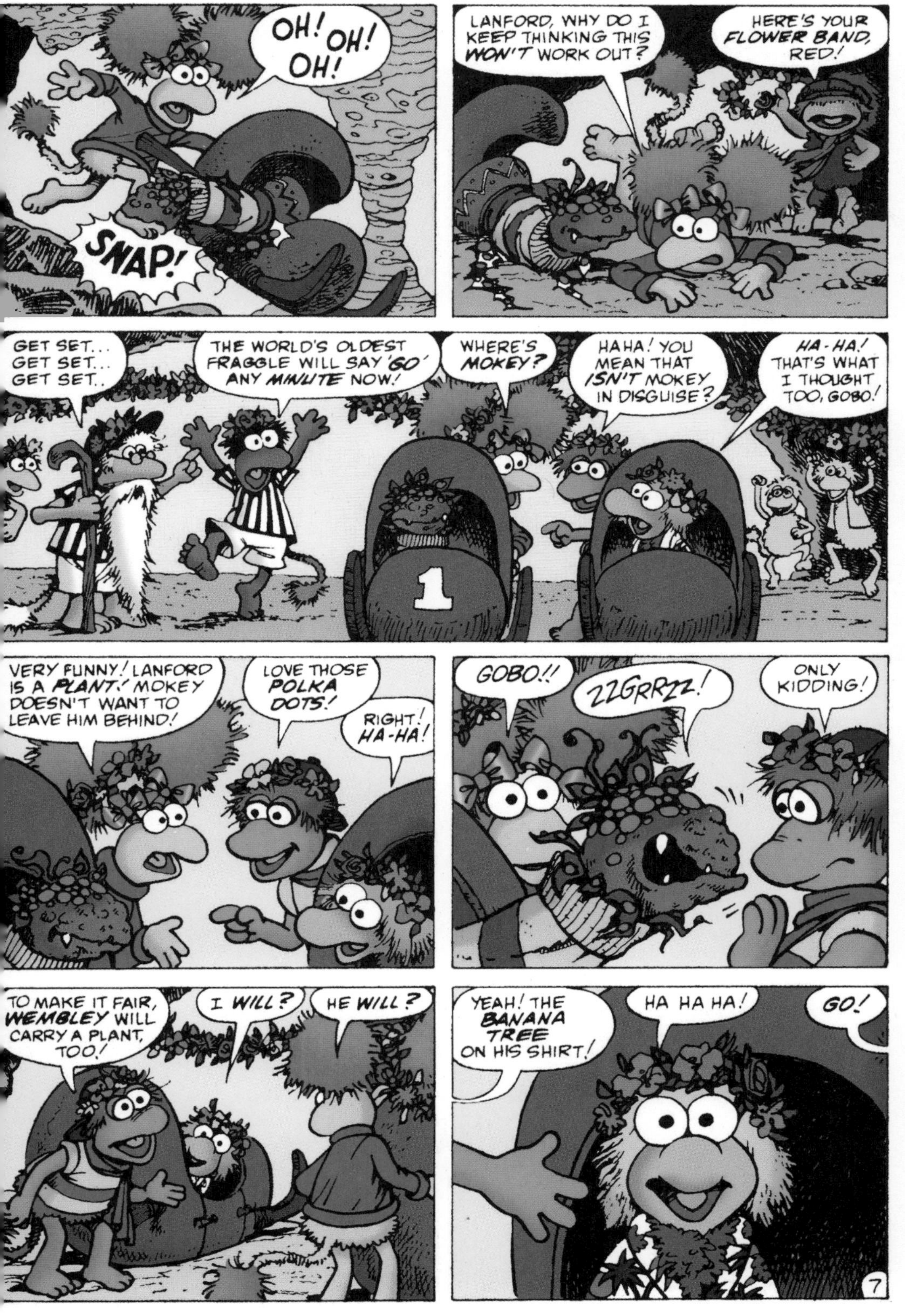

OH! OH! OH!
SNAP!
LANFORD, WHY DO I KEEP THINKING THIS WON'T WORK OUT?
HERE'S YOUR FLOWER BAND, RED!
GET SET... GET SET... GET SET..
THE WORLD'S OLDEST FRAGGLE WILL SAY 'GO' ANY MINUTE NOW!
WHERE'S MOKEY?
HA HA! YOU MEAN THAT ISN'T MOKEY IN DISGUISE?
HA-HA! THAT'S WHAT I THOUGHT TOO, GOBO!
1
VERY FUNNY! LANFORD IS A PLANT! MOKEY DOESN'T WANT TO LEAVE HIM BEHIND!
LOVE THOSE POLKA DOTS!
RIGHT! HA-HA!
GOBO!!
ZZGRRZZ!
ONLY KIDDING!
TO MAKE IT FAIR, WEMBLEY WILL CARRY A PLANT, TOO!
I WILL?
HE WILL?
YEAH! THE BANANA TREE ON HIS SHIRT!
HA HA HA!
GO!
7

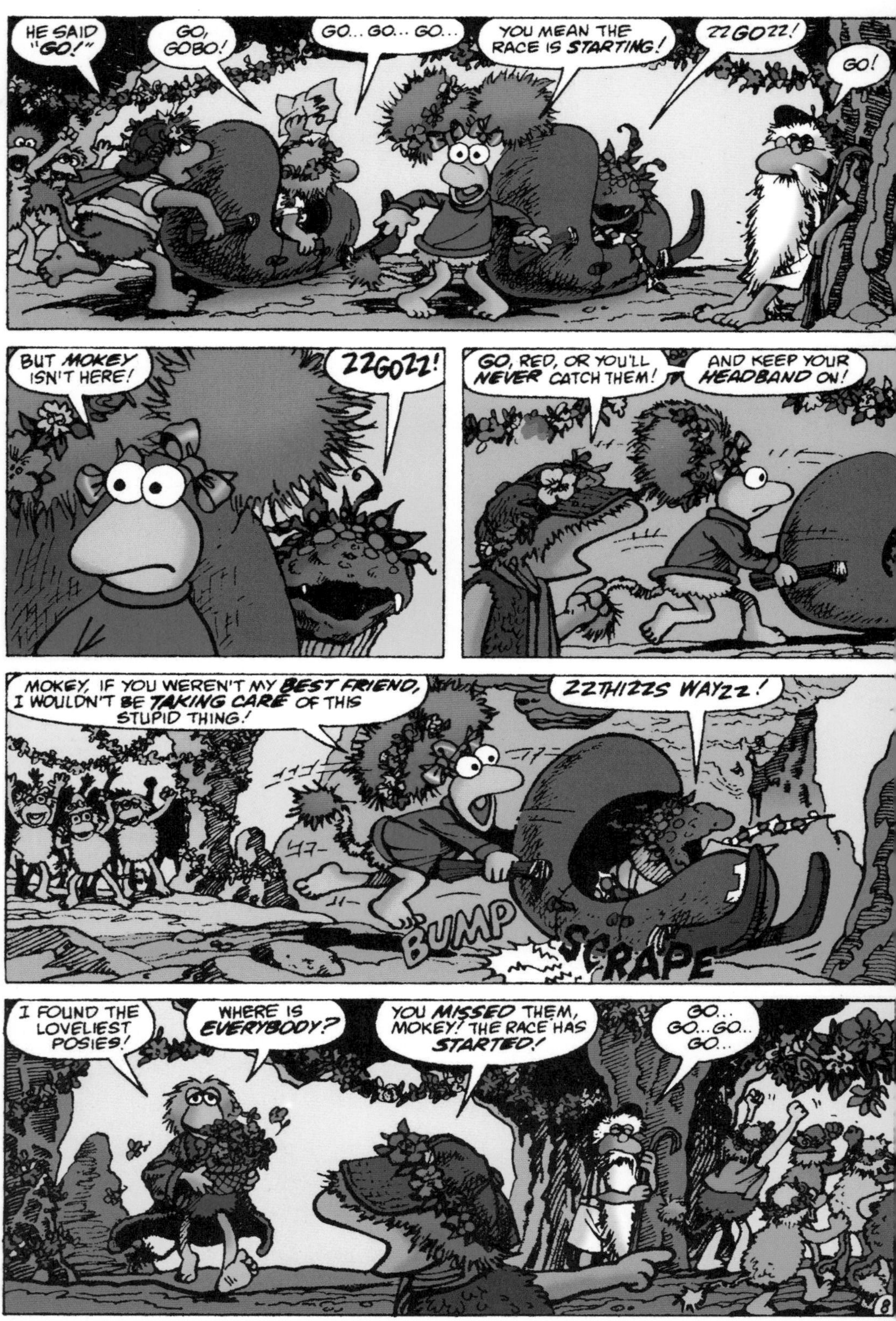
HE SAID "GO!"
GO, GOBO!
GO... GO... GO...
YOU MEAN THE RACE IS STARTING!
ZZGOZZ!
GO!
BUT MOKEY ISN'T HERE!
ZZGOZZ!
GO, RED, OR YOU'LL NEVER CATCH THEM!
AND KEEP YOUR HEADBAND ON!
MOKEY, IF YOU WEREN'T MY BEST FRIEND, I WOULDN'T BE TAKING CARE OF THIS STUPID THING!
ZZTHIZZS WAYZZ!
BUMP
SCRAPE
I FOUND THE LOVELIEST POSIES!
WHERE IS EVERYBODY?
YOU MISSED THEM, MOKEY! THE RACE HAS STARTED!
GO... GO...GO.. GO...

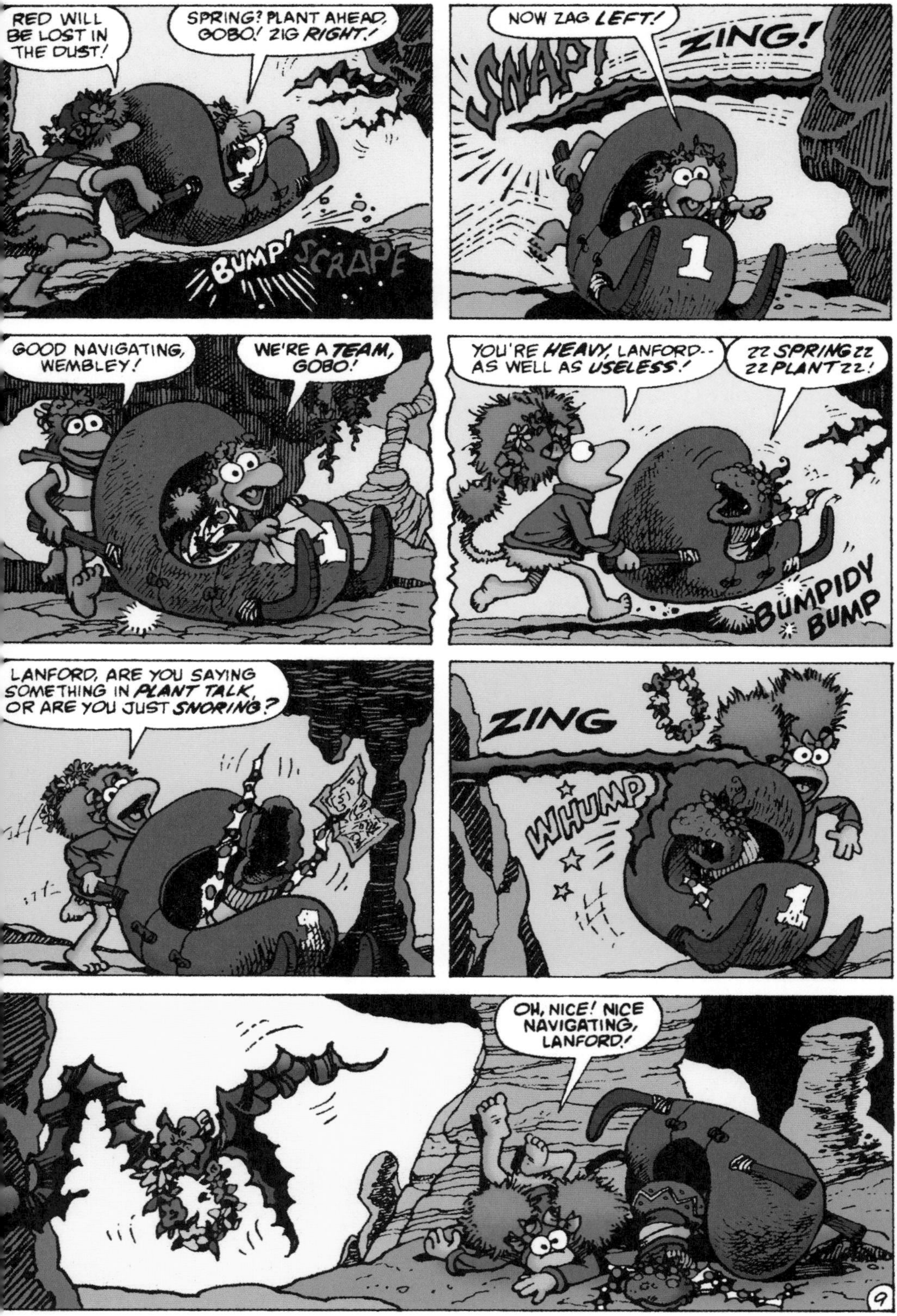
RED WILL BE LOST IN THE DUST!
SPRING? PLANT AHEAD, GOBO! ZIG RIGHT!
BUMP! SCRAPE
NOW ZAG LEFT!
SNAP!
ZING!
1
GOOD NAVIGATING, WEMBLEY!
WE'RE A TEAM, GOBO!
YOU'RE HEAVY, LANFORD-- AS WELL AS USELESS!
ZZ SPRING ZZ ZZ PLANT ZZ!
BUMPIDY BUMP
LANFORD, ARE YOU SAYING SOMETHING IN PLANT TALK, OR ARE YOU JUST SNORING?
ZING
WHUMP
OH, NICE! NICE NAVIGATING, LANFORD!
9

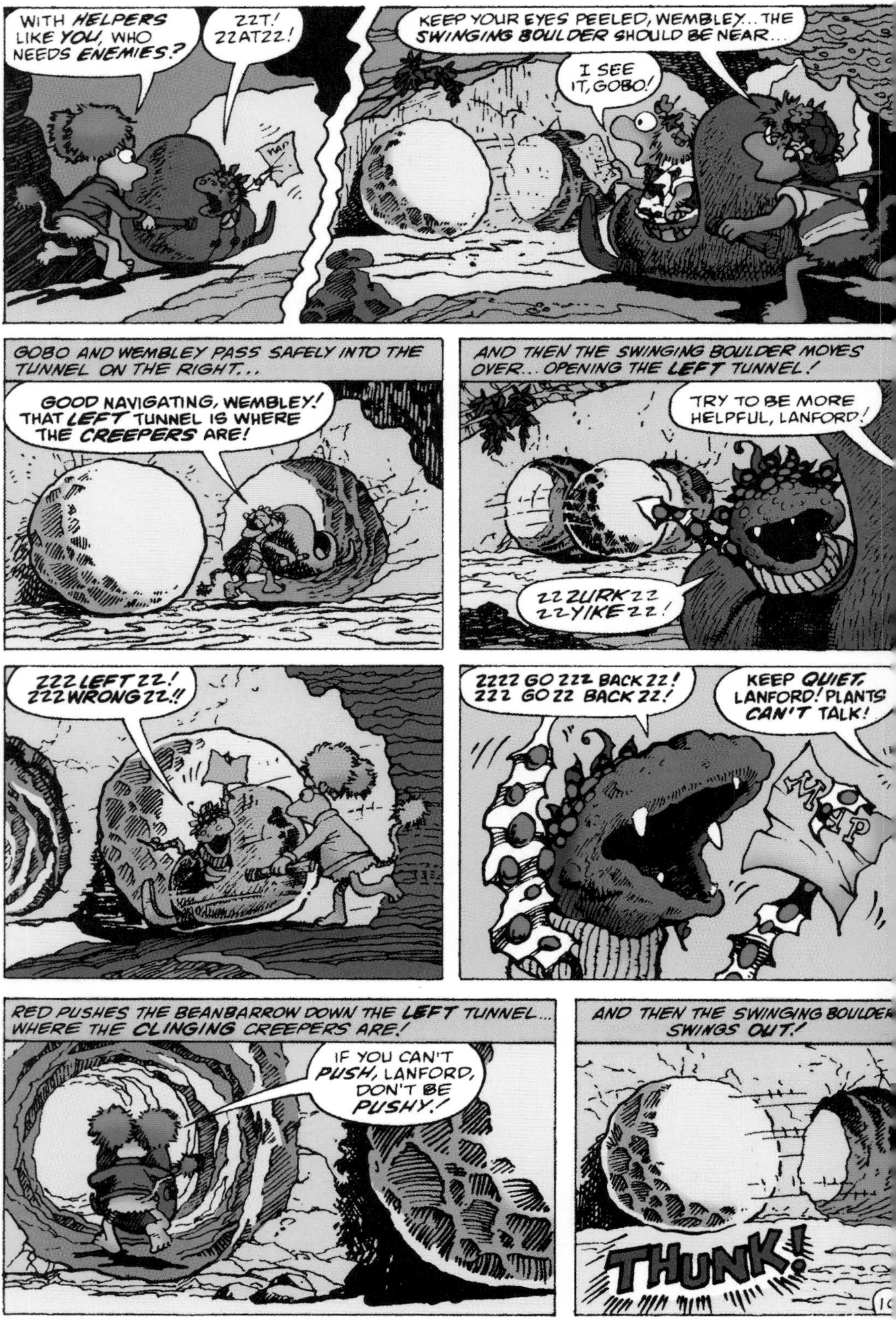
WITH HELPERS LIKE YOU, WHO NEEDS ENEMIES?
ZZT! ZZATZZ!
KEEP YOUR EYES PEELED, WEMBLEY... THE SWINGING BOULDER SHOULD BE NEAR...
I SEE IT, GOBO!
GOBO AND WEMBLEY PASS SAFELY INTO THE TUNNEL ON THE RIGHT...
GOOD NAVIGATING, WEMBLEY! THAT LEFT TUNNEL IS WHERE THE CREEPERS ARE!
AND THEN THE SWINGING BOULDER MOVES OVER... OPENING THE LEFT TUNNEL!
TRY TO BE MORE HELPFUL, LANFORD!
ZZZURKZZ ZZYIKEZZ!
ZZZLEFTZZ! ZZZWRONGZZ!!
ZZZZ GO ZZZ BACK ZZ! ZZZ GO ZZ BACK ZZ!
KEEP QUIET, LANFORD! PLANTS CAN'T TALK!
RED PUSHES THE BEANBARROW DOWN THE LEFT TUNNEL... WHERE THE CLINGING CREEPERS ARE!
IF YOU CAN'T PUSH, LANFORD, DON'T BE PUSHY!
AND THEN THE SWINGING BOULDER SWINGS OUT!
THUNK!

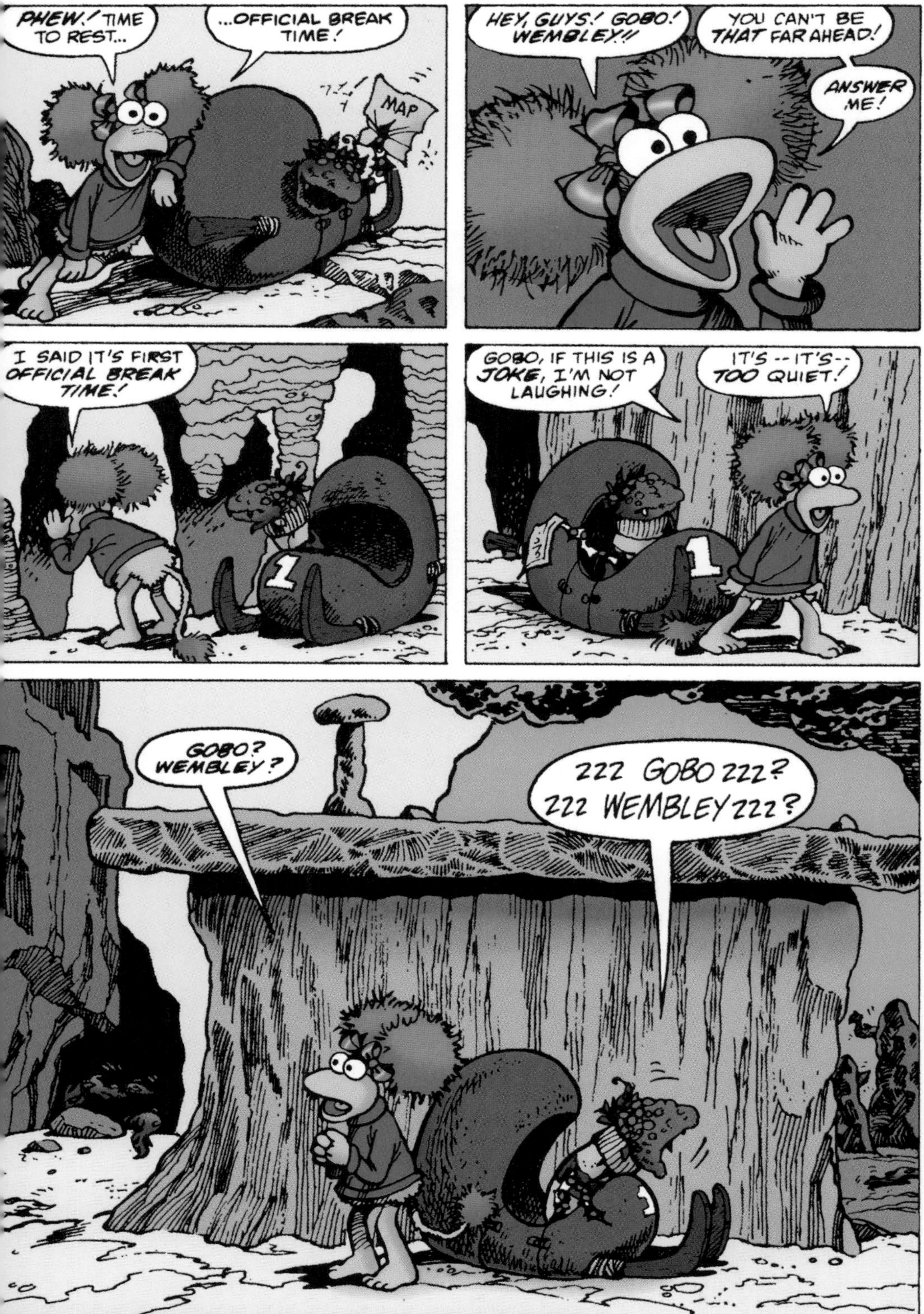
PHEW! TIME TO REST...
...OFFICIAL BREAK TIME!
MAP
HEY, GUYS! GOBO! WEMBLEY!!
YOU CAN'T BE THAT FAR AHEAD!
ANSWER ME!
I SAID IT'S FIRST OFFICIAL BREAK TIME!
GOBO, IF THIS IS A JOKE, I'M NOT LAUGHING!
IT'S -- IT'S -- TOO QUIET!
GOBO? WEMBLEY?
ZZZ GOBO ZZZ? ZZZ WEMBLEY ZZZ?
AND SILENTLY, OMINOUS GREEN VINES BEGIN TO APPEAR!
11

CONTINUED IN THIS ISSUE...

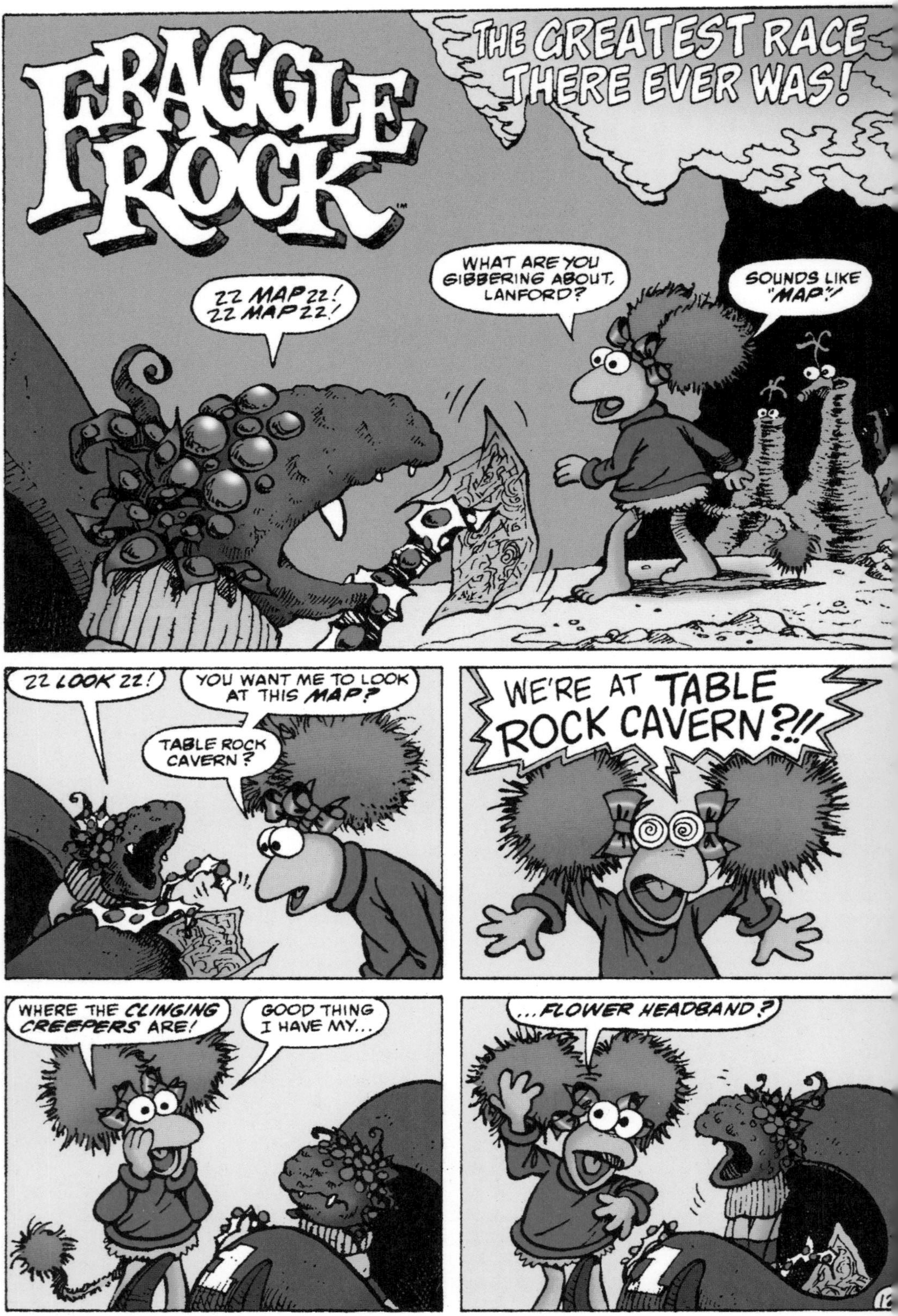

FRAGGLE ROCK™
THE GREATEST RACE THERE EVER WAS!
ZZ MAP ZZ! ZZ MAP ZZ!
WHAT ARE YOU GIBBERING ABOUT, LANFORD?
SOUNDS LIKE "MAP"!
ZZ LOOK ZZ!
YOU WANT ME TO LOOK AT THIS MAP?
TABLE ROCK CAVERN?
WE'RE AT TABLE ROCK CAVERN?!!
WHERE THE CLINGING CREEPERS ARE!
GOOD THING I HAVE MY...
...FLOWER HEADBAND?

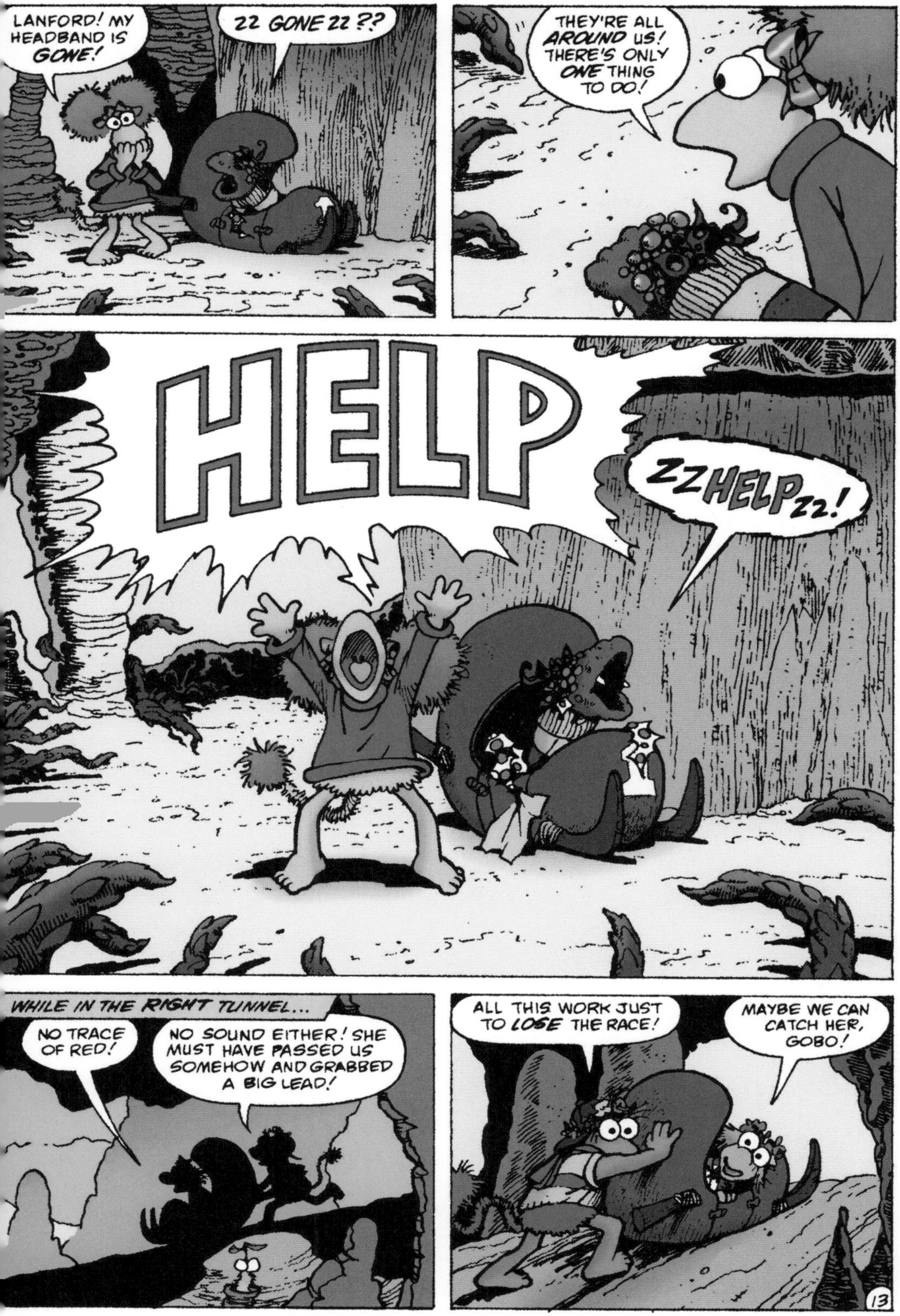

LANFORD! MY HEADBAND IS GONE!
ZZ GONE ZZ ??
THEY'RE ALL AROUND US! THERE'S ONLY ONE THING TO DO!
HELP
ZZ HELP ZZ!
WHILE IN THE RIGHT TUNNEL...
NO TRACE OF RED!
NO SOUND EITHER! SHE MUST HAVE PASSED US SOMEHOW AND GRABBED A BIG LEAD!
ALL THIS WORK JUST TO LOSE THE RACE!
MAYBE WE CAN CATCH HER, GOBO!
13

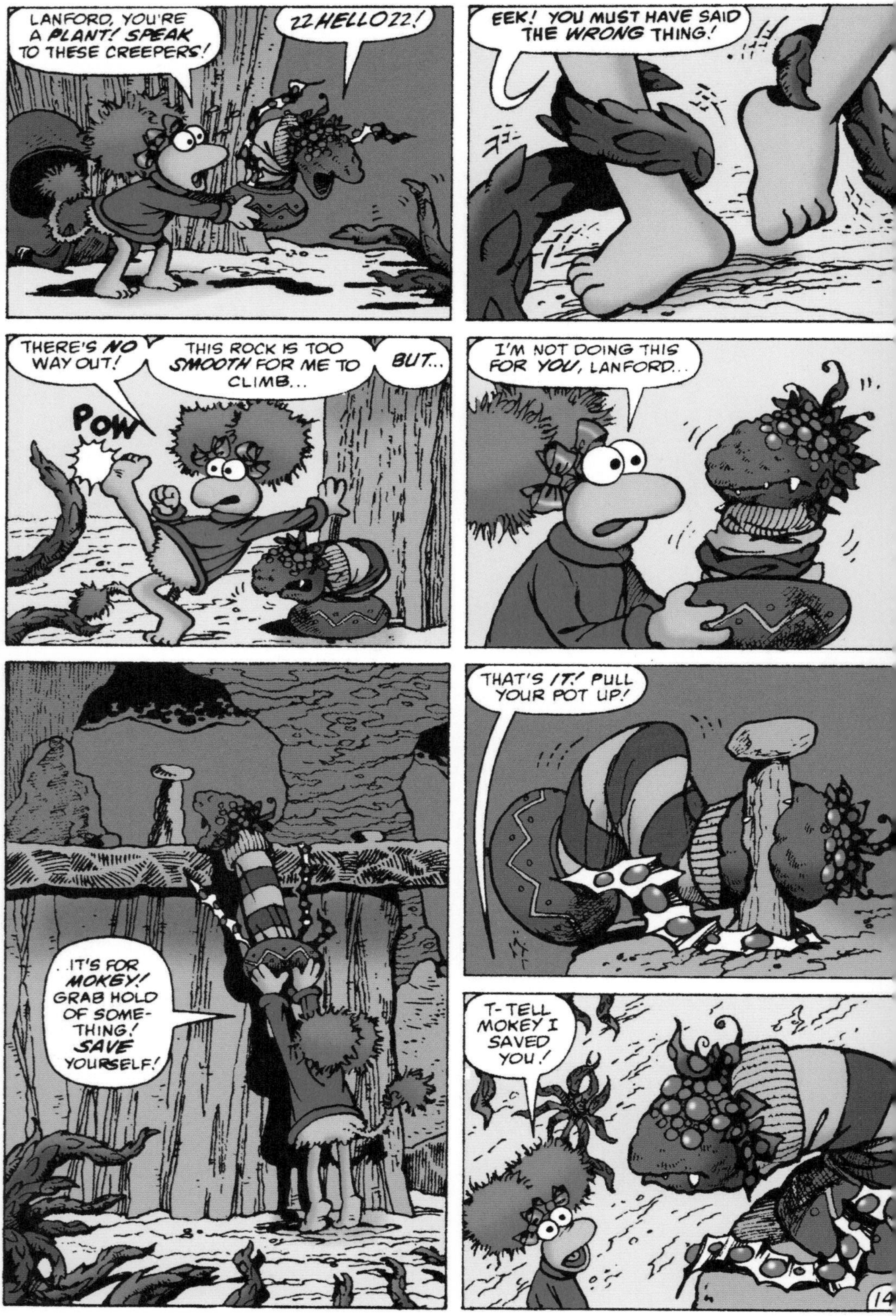
LANFORD, YOU'RE A PLANT! SPEAK TO THESE CREEPERS!
ZZ HELLO ZZ!
EEK! YOU MUST HAVE SAID THE WRONG THING!
THERE'S NO WAY OUT!
THIS ROCK IS TOO SMOOTH FOR ME TO CLIMB...
BUT...
POW
I'M NOT DOING THIS FOR YOU, LANFORD...
...IT'S FOR MOKEY! GRAB HOLD OF SOME-THING! SAVE YOURSELF!
THAT'S IT! PULL YOUR POT UP!
T-TELL MOKEY I SAVED YOU!
14

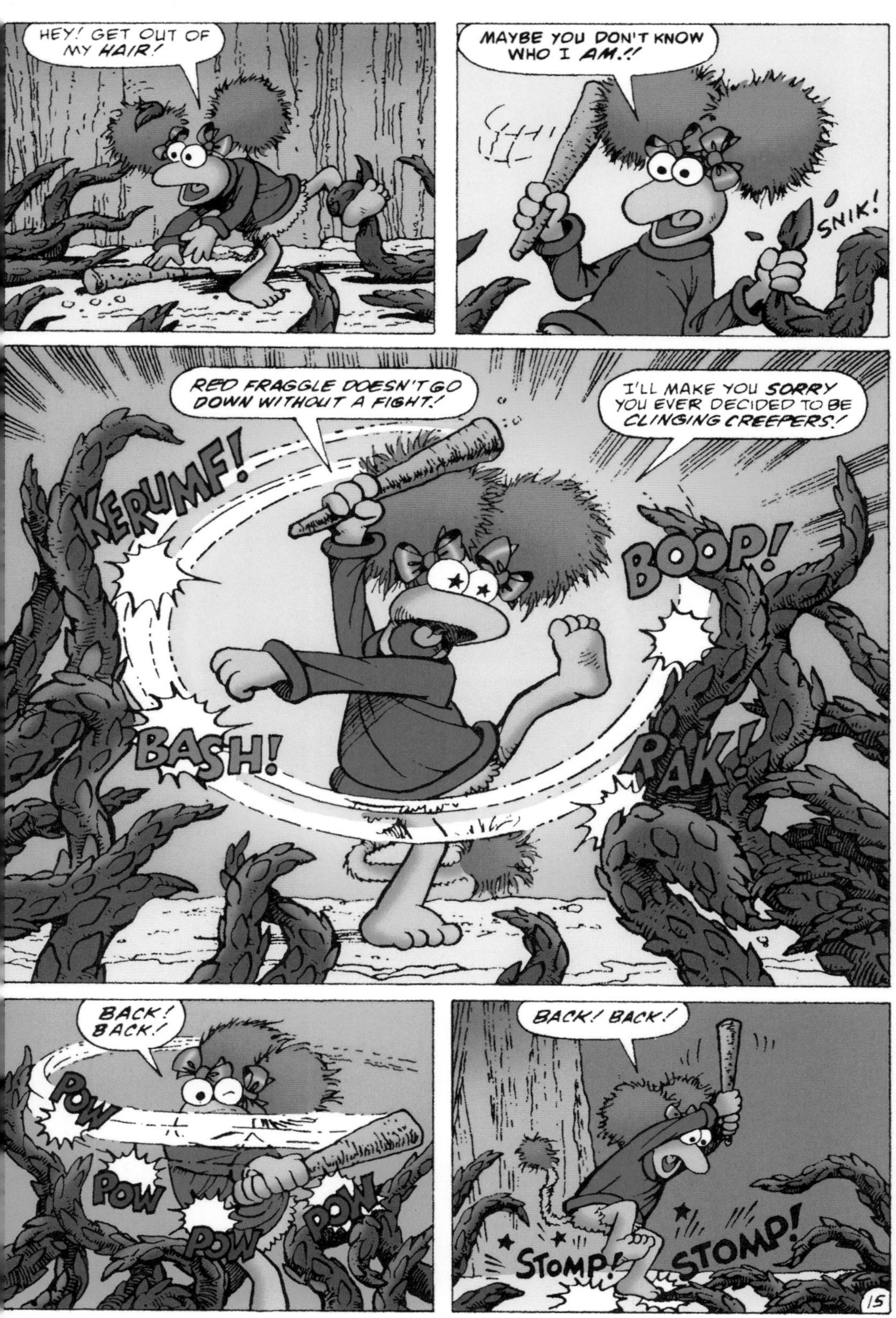
HEY! GET OUT OF MY HAIR!
MAYBE YOU DON'T KNOW WHO I AM.!!
SNIK!
RED FRAGGLE DOESN'T GO DOWN WITHOUT A FIGHT!
I'LL MAKE YOU SORRY YOU EVER DECIDED TO BE CLINGING CREEPERS!
KERUMF!
BOOP!
BASH!
RAK!
BACK! BACK!
POW
POW
POW
POW
BACK! BACK!
STOMP!
STOMP!
15

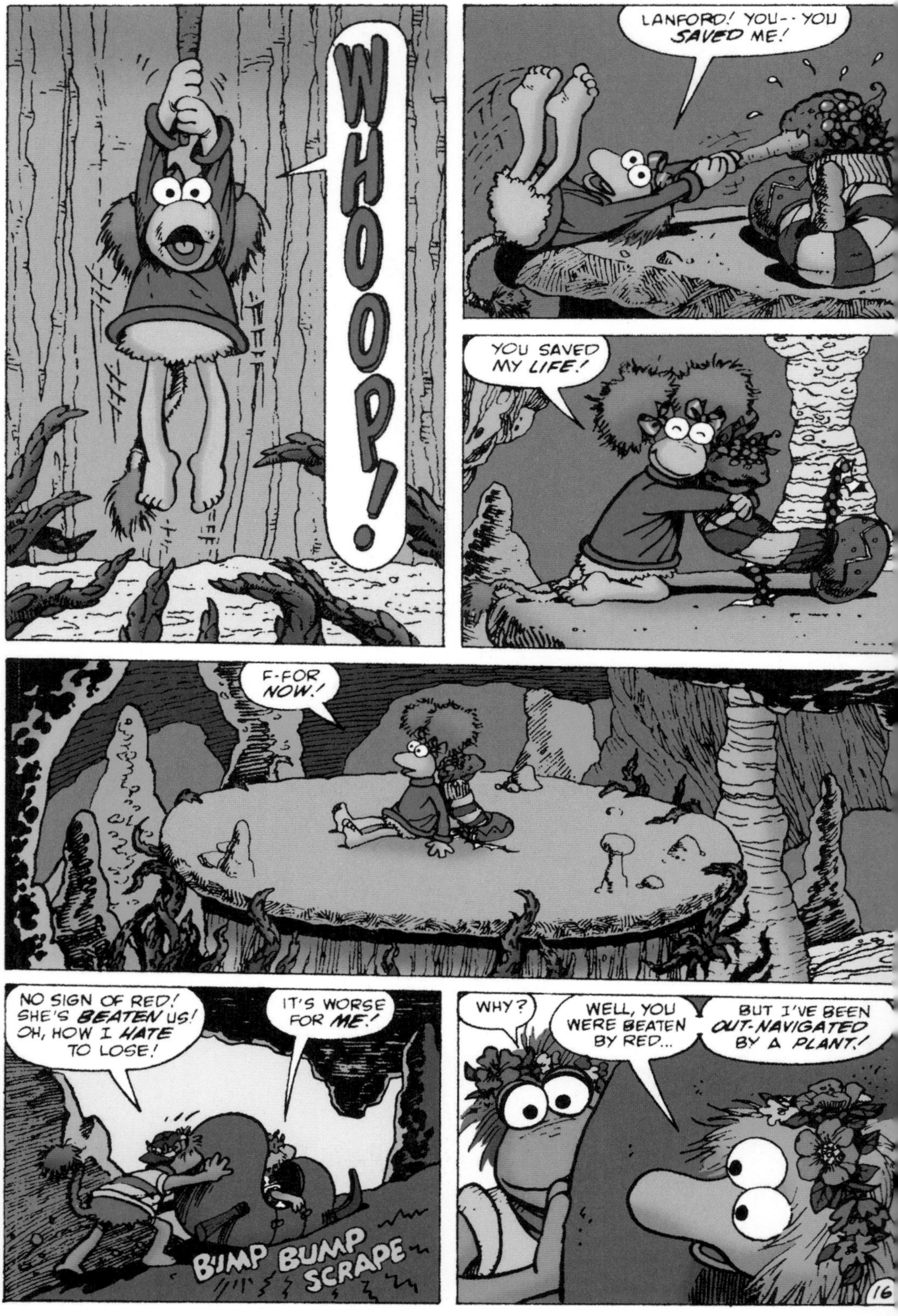
WHOOOP!
LANFORD! YOU-- YOU SAVED ME!
YOU SAVED MY LIFE!
F-FOR NOW!
NO SIGN OF RED! SHE'S BEATEN US! OH, HOW I HATE TO LOSE!
IT'S WORSE FOR ME!
BUMP BUMP SCRAPE
WHY?
WELL, YOU WERE BEATEN BY RED...
BUT I'VE BEEN OUT-NAVIGATED BY A PLANT!
16

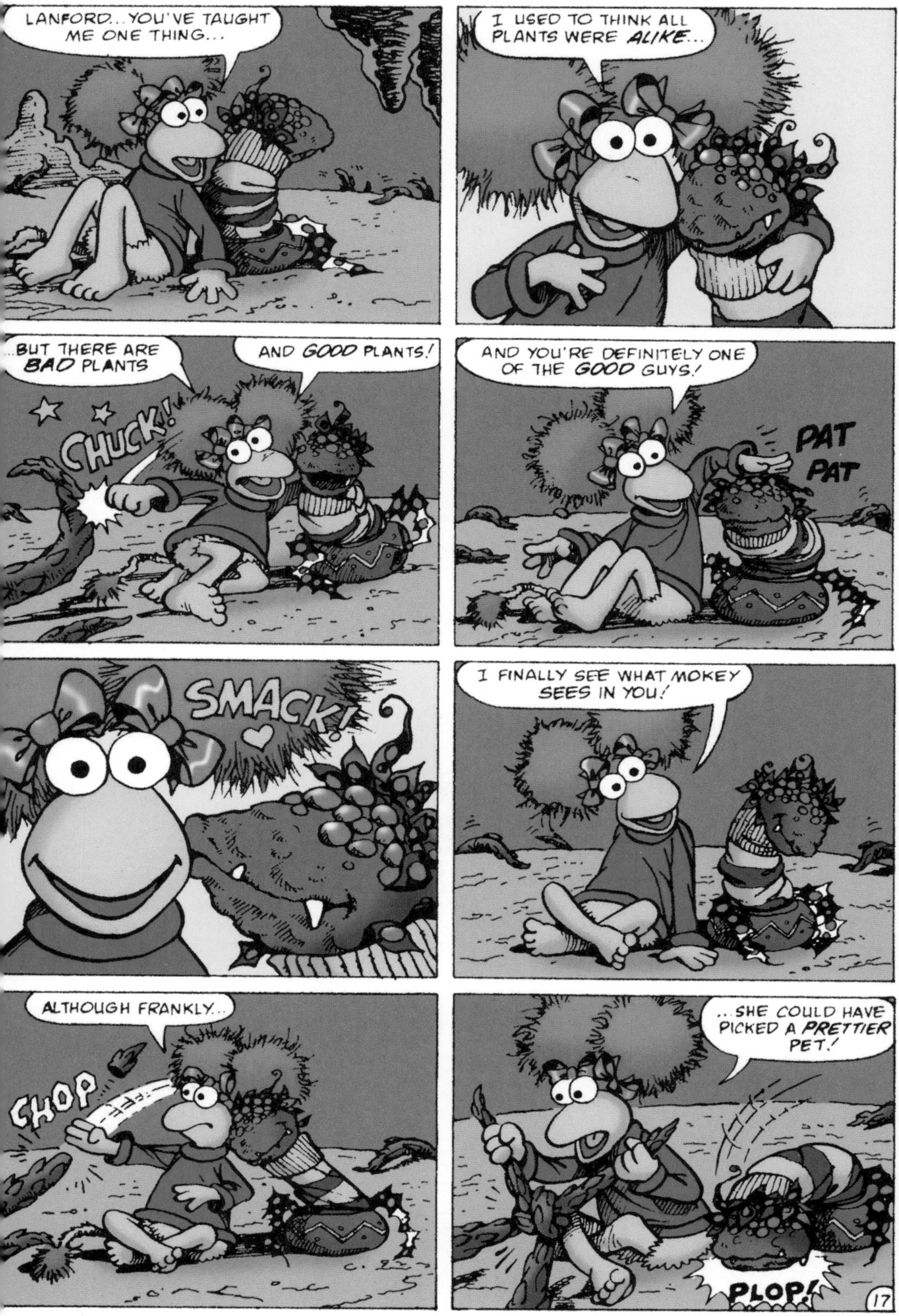
LANFORD...YOU'VE TAUGHT ME ONE THING...
I USED TO THINK ALL PLANTS WERE ALIKE...
...BUT THERE ARE BAD PLANTS
AND GOOD PLANTS!
CHUCK!
AND YOU'RE DEFINITELY ONE OF THE GOOD GUYS!
PAT PAT
SMACK!
I FINALLY SEE WHAT MOKEY SEES IN YOU!
ALTHOUGH FRANKLY...
CHOP
...SHE COULD HAVE PICKED A PRETTIER PET!
PLOP!
17

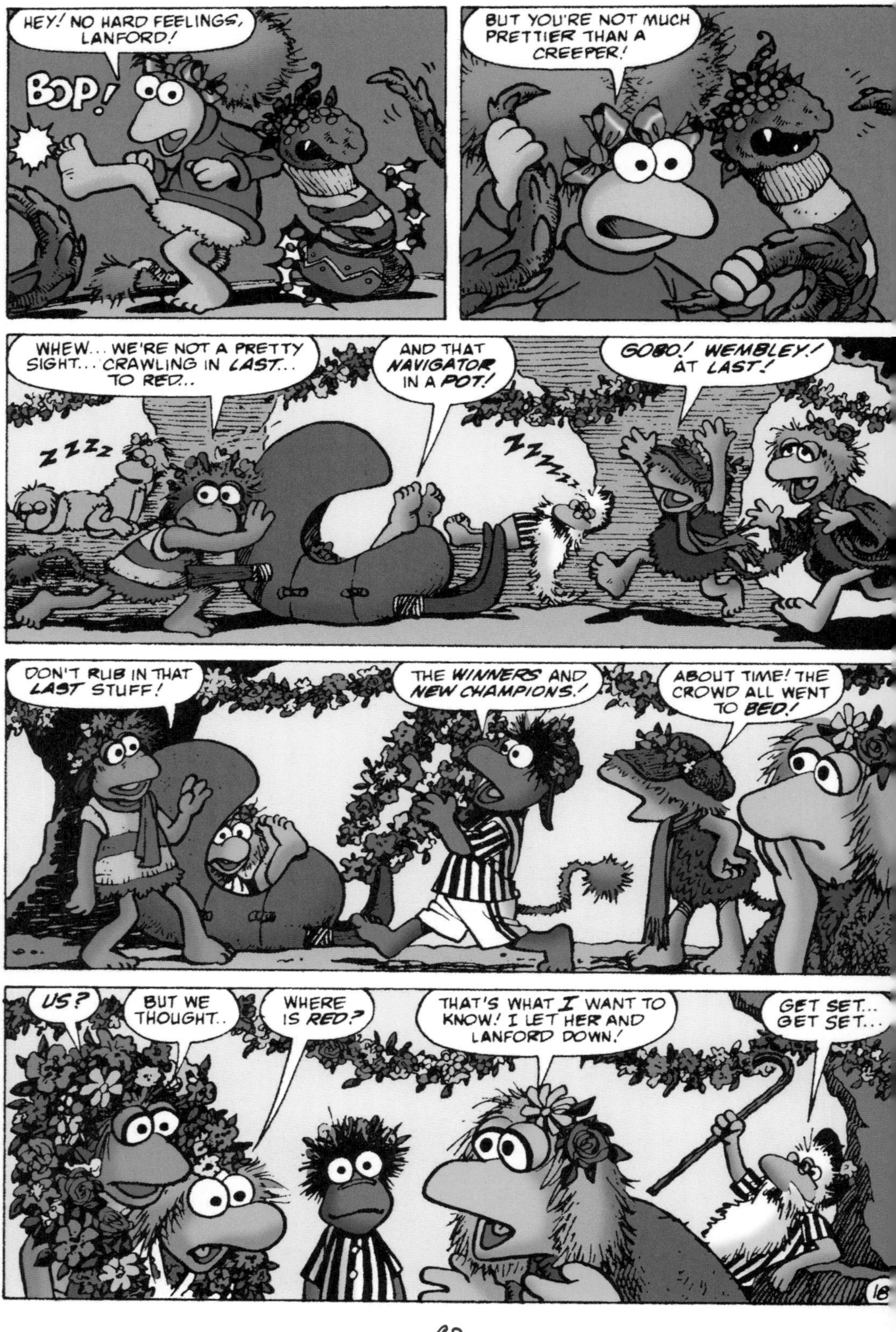
HEY! NO HARD FEELINGS, LANFORD!
BOP!
BUT YOU'RE NOT MUCH PRETTIER THAN A CREEPER!
WHEW... WE'RE NOT A PRETTY SIGHT... CRAWLING IN LAST... TO RED...
AND THAT NAVIGATOR IN A POT!
GOBO! WEMBLEY! AT LAST!
ZZZZ
ZZZZZZ
DON'T RUB IN THAT LAST STUFF!
THE WINNERS AND NEW CHAMPIONS!
ABOUT TIME! THE CROWD ALL WENT TO BED!
US?
BUT WE THOUGHT..
WHERE IS RED?
THAT'S WHAT I WANT TO KNOW! I LET HER AND LANFORD DOWN!
GET SET... GET SET...
18

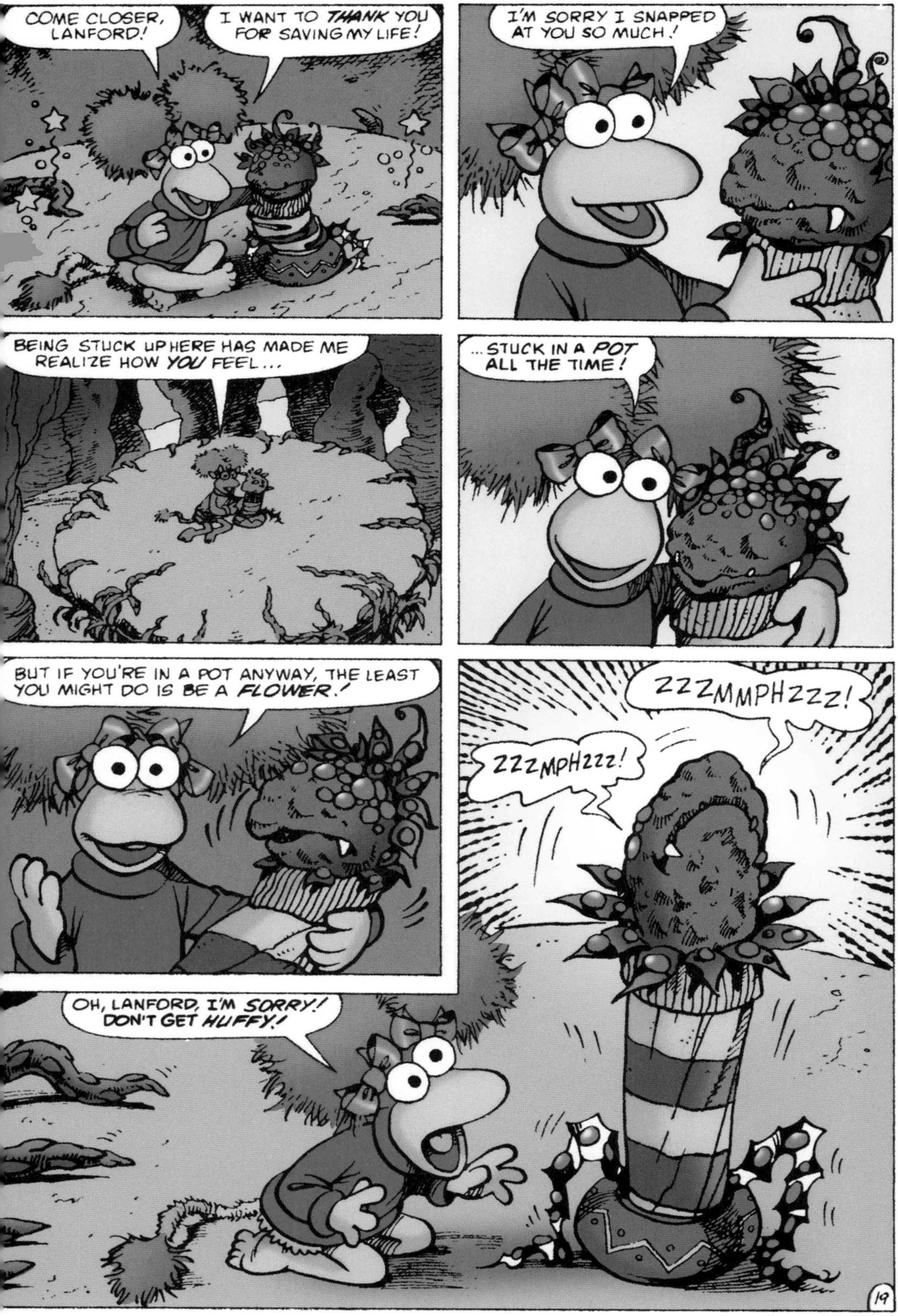
COME CLOSER, LANFORD!
I WANT TO THANK YOU FOR SAVING MY LIFE!
I'M SORRY I SNAPPED AT YOU SO MUCH!
BEING STUCK UP HERE HAS MADE ME REALIZE HOW YOU FEEL...
...STUCK IN A POT ALL THE TIME!
BUT IF YOU'RE IN A POT ANYWAY, THE LEAST YOU MIGHT DO IS BE A FLOWER!
ZZZMMPHZZZ!
ZZZMPHZZZ!
OH, LANFORD, I'M SORRY! DON'T GET HUFFY!
19

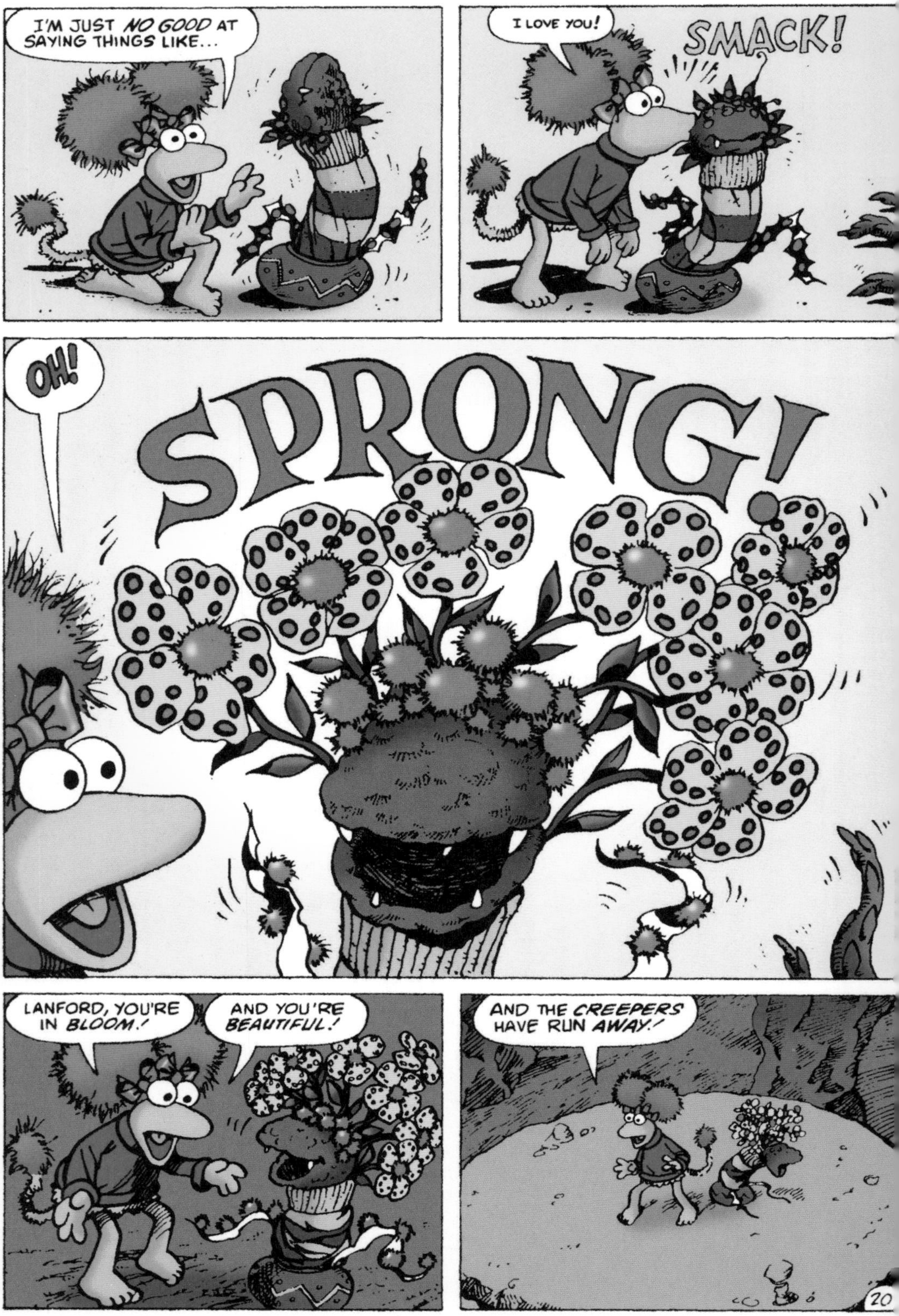
I'M JUST NO GOOD AT SAYING THINGS LIKE...
I LOVE YOU!
SMACK!
OH!
SPRONG!
LANFORD, YOU'RE IN BLOOM!
AND YOU'RE BEAUTIFUL!
AND THE CREEPERS HAVE RUN AWAY!
20

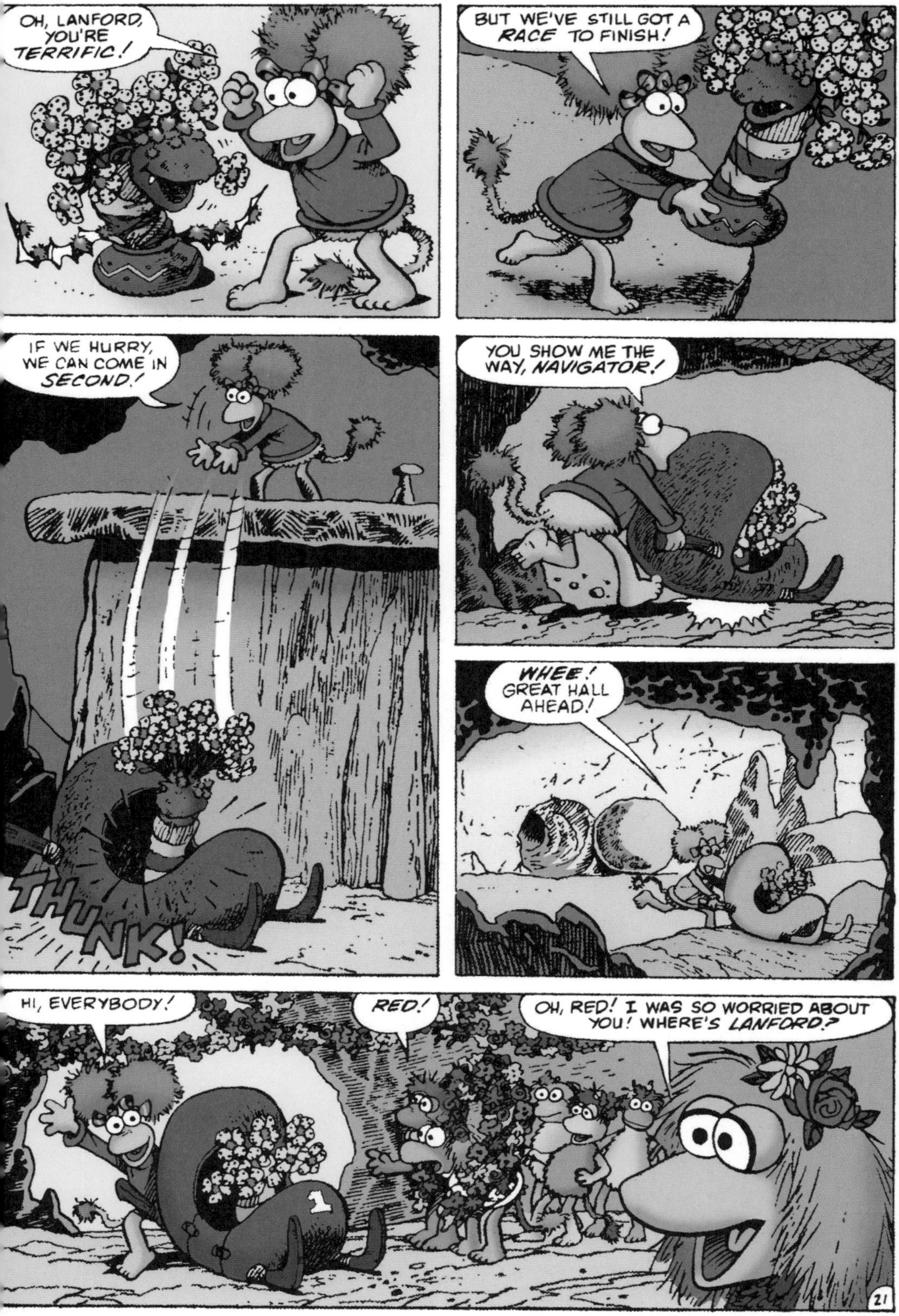
OH, LANFORD, YOU'RE TERRIFIC!
BUT WE'VE STILL GOT A RACE TO FINISH!
IF WE HURRY, WE CAN COME IN SECOND!
THUNK!
YOU SHOW ME THE WAY, NAVIGATOR!
WHEE! GREAT HALL AHEAD!
HI, EVERYBODY!
RED!
OH, RED! I WAS SO WORRIED ABOUT YOU! WHERE'S LANFORD?
21

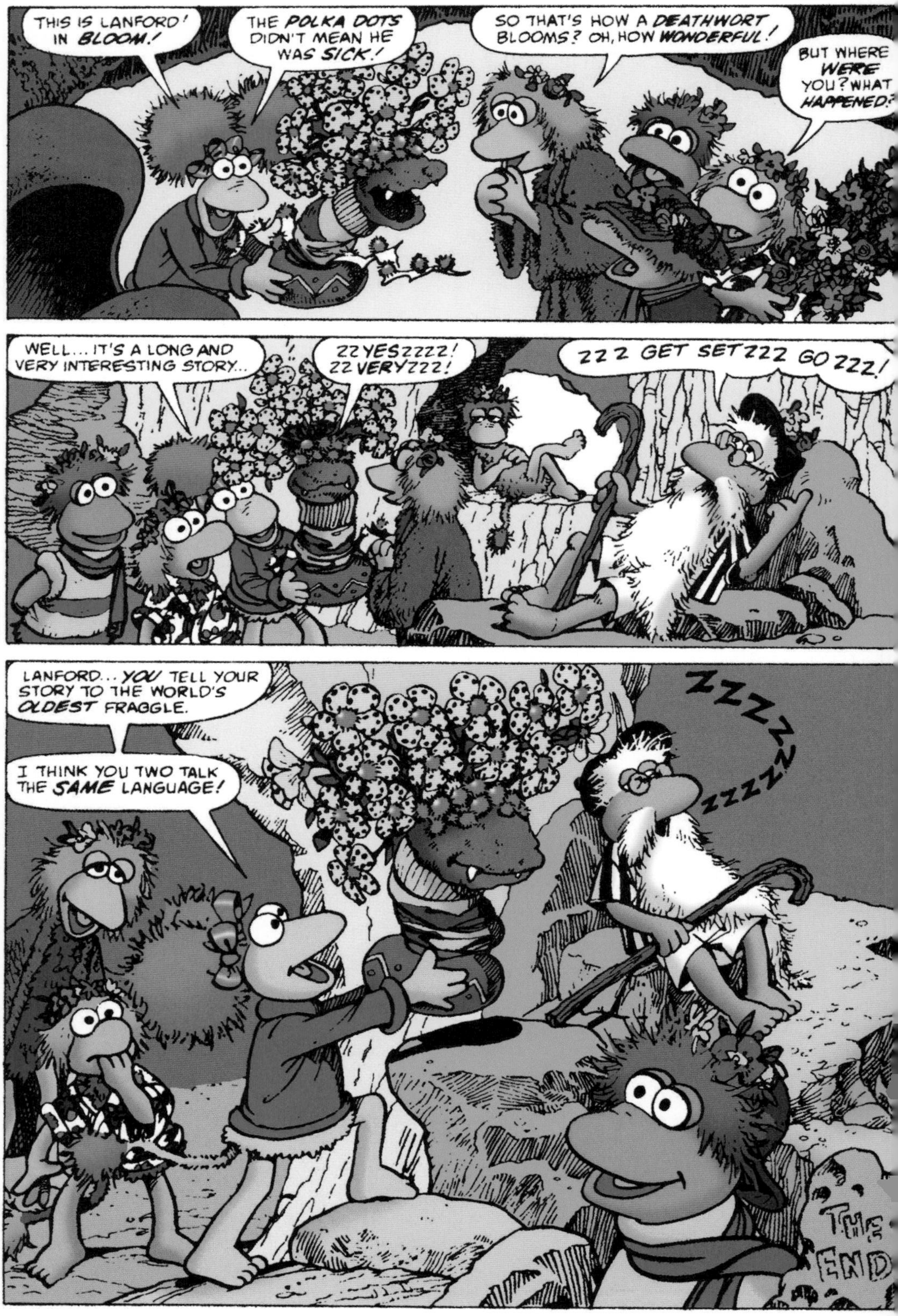
THIS IS LANFORD! IN BLOOM!
THE POLKA DOTS DIDN'T MEAN HE WAS SICK!
SO THAT'S HOW A DEATHWORT BLOOMS? OH, HOW WONDERFUL!
BUT WHERE WERE YOU? WHAT HAPPENED?
WELL... IT'S A LONG AND VERY INTERESTING STORY...
ZZ YES ZZZZ! ZZ VERY ZZZ!
ZZZ GET SET ZZZ GO ZZZ!
LANFORD... YOU TELL YOUR STORY TO THE WORLD'S OLDEST FRAGGLE.
I THINK YOU TWO TALK THE SAME LANGUAGE!
ZZZZZ ZZZZZ
THE END

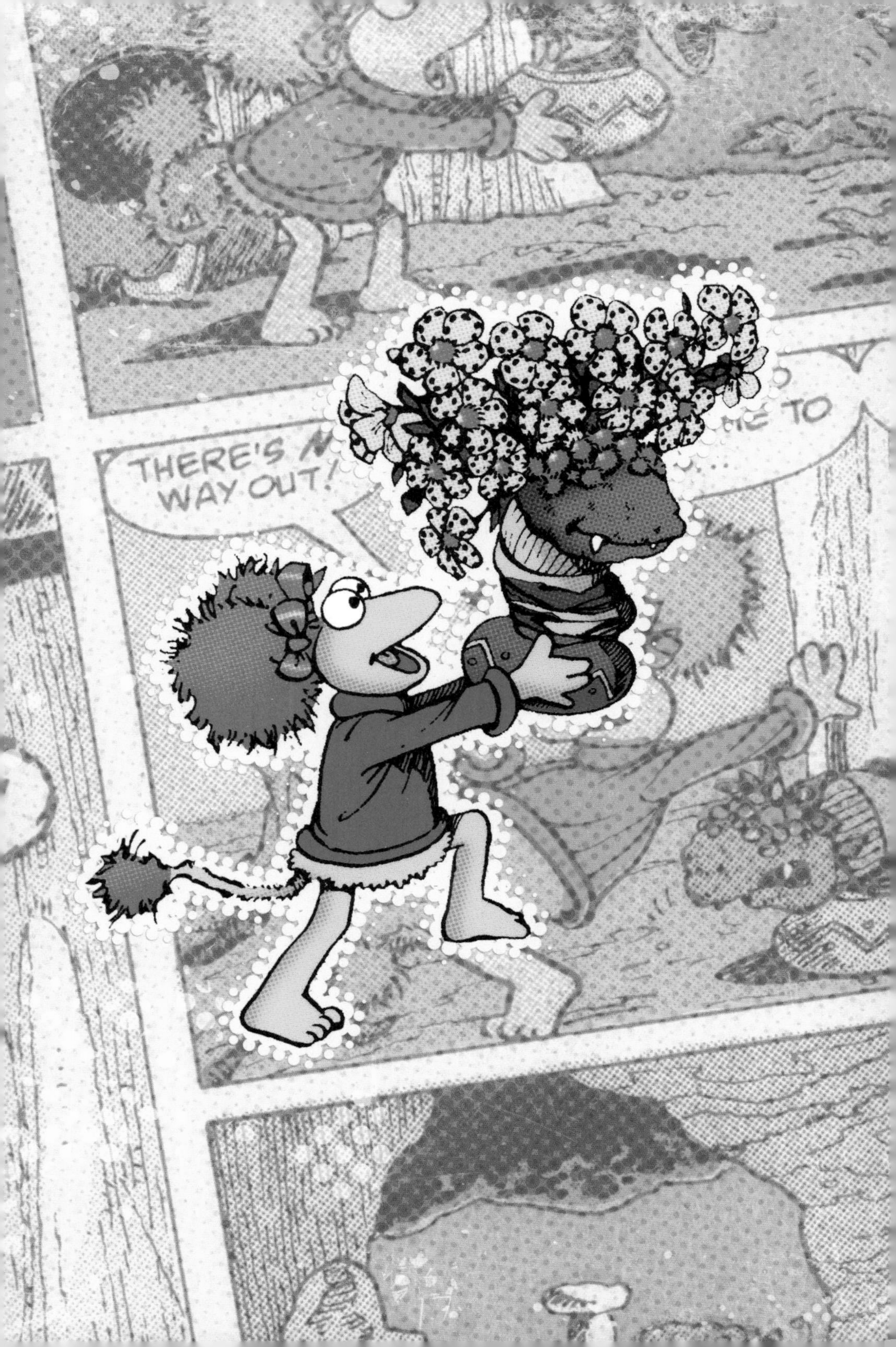
THERE'S
WAY OUT!
TO

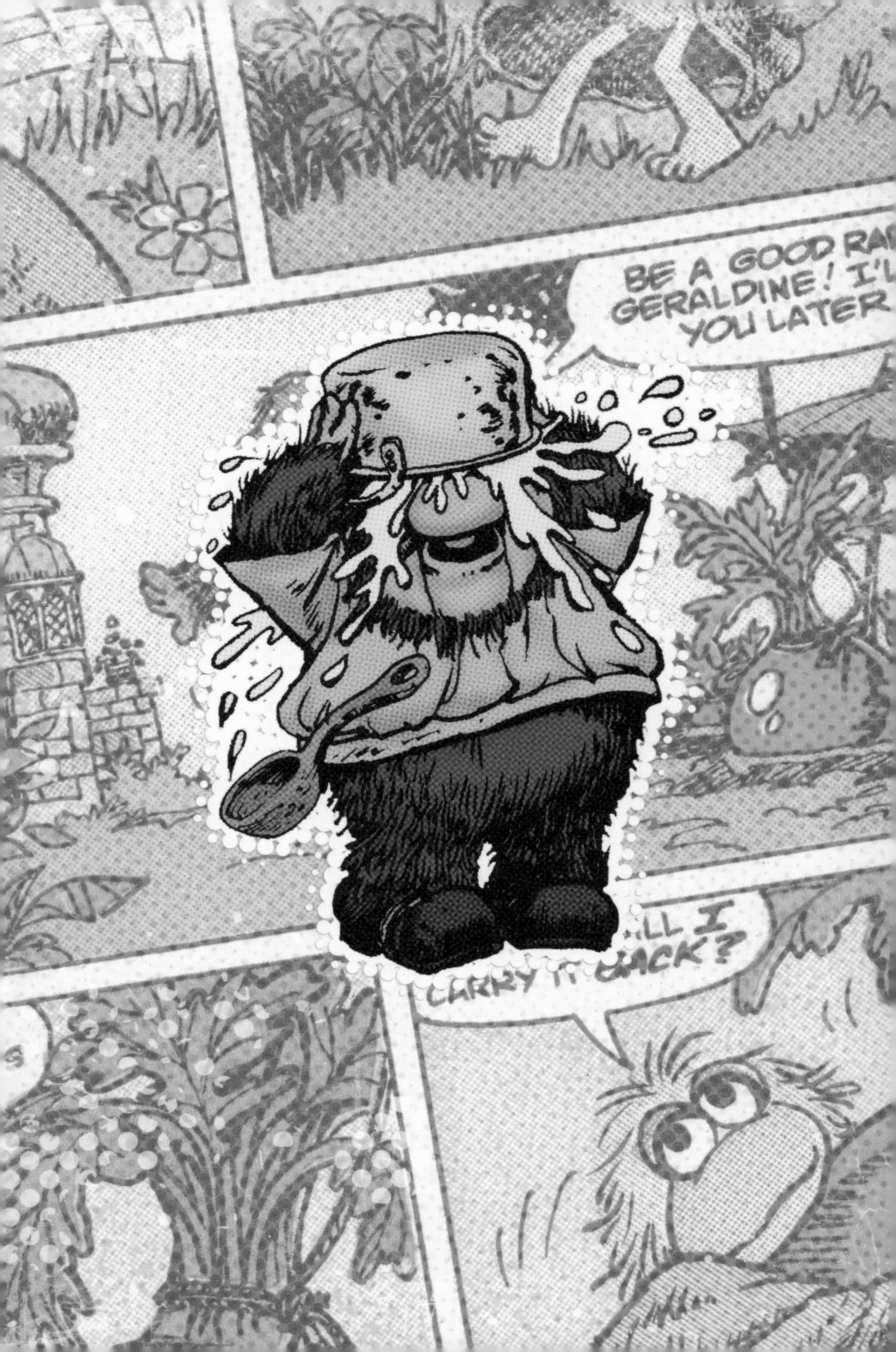
BE A GOOD
GERALDINE!
YOU LATER

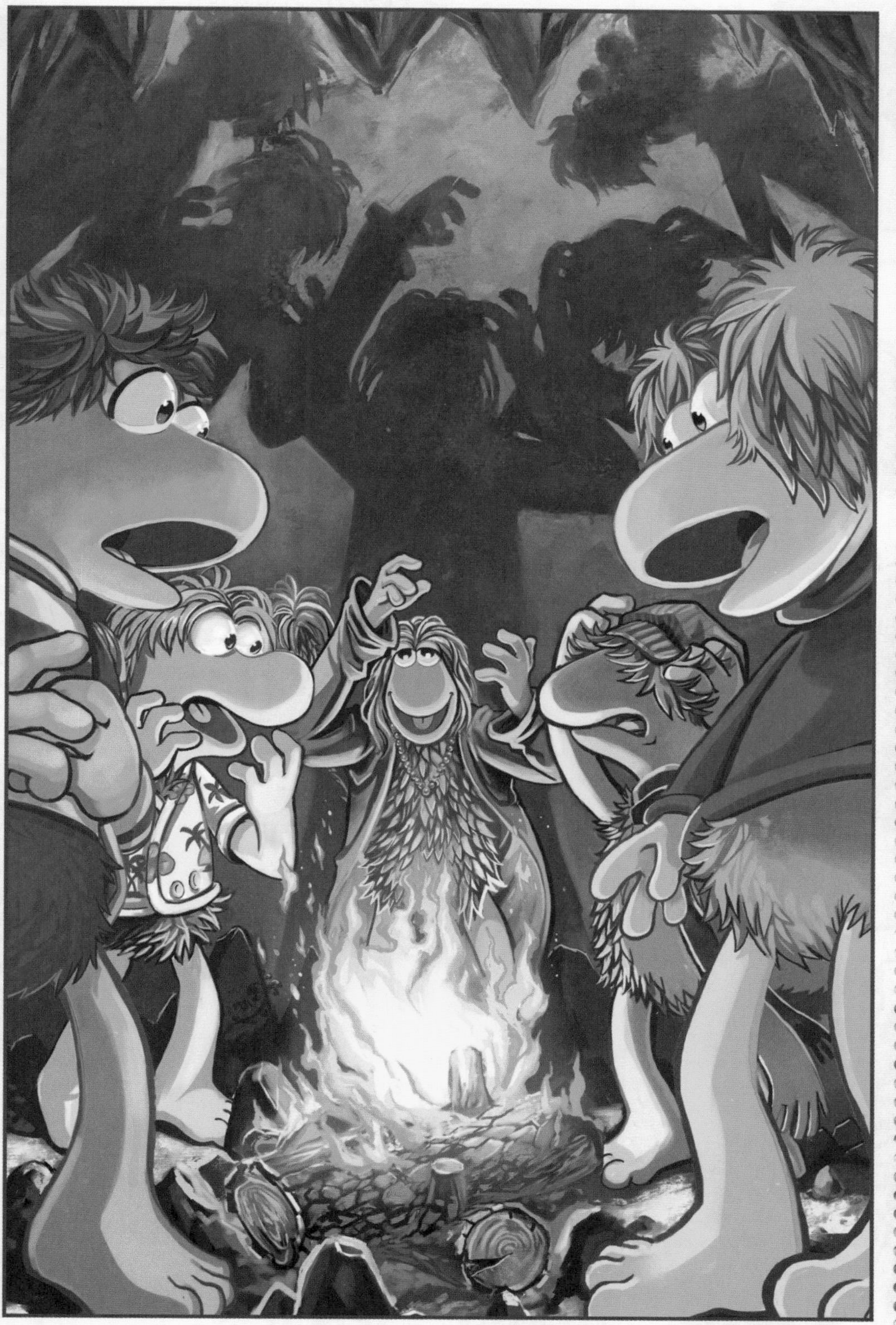

FRAGGLE ROCK™

Monsters from Outer Space!

FIRST PRINTED FOR ARCHAIA'S 2011 DIAMOND HALLOWEEN ASHCAN

Story by
**MEL CAYLO, HEATHER NUHFER,
& KATIE STRICKLAND**

Written by
**HEATHER NUHFER
& KATIE STRICKLAND**

Illustrated by
JAKE MYLER

Lettered by
DERON BENNETT

Cover by
JAKE MYLER

Edited by
**TIM BEEDLE &
PAUL MORRISSEY**

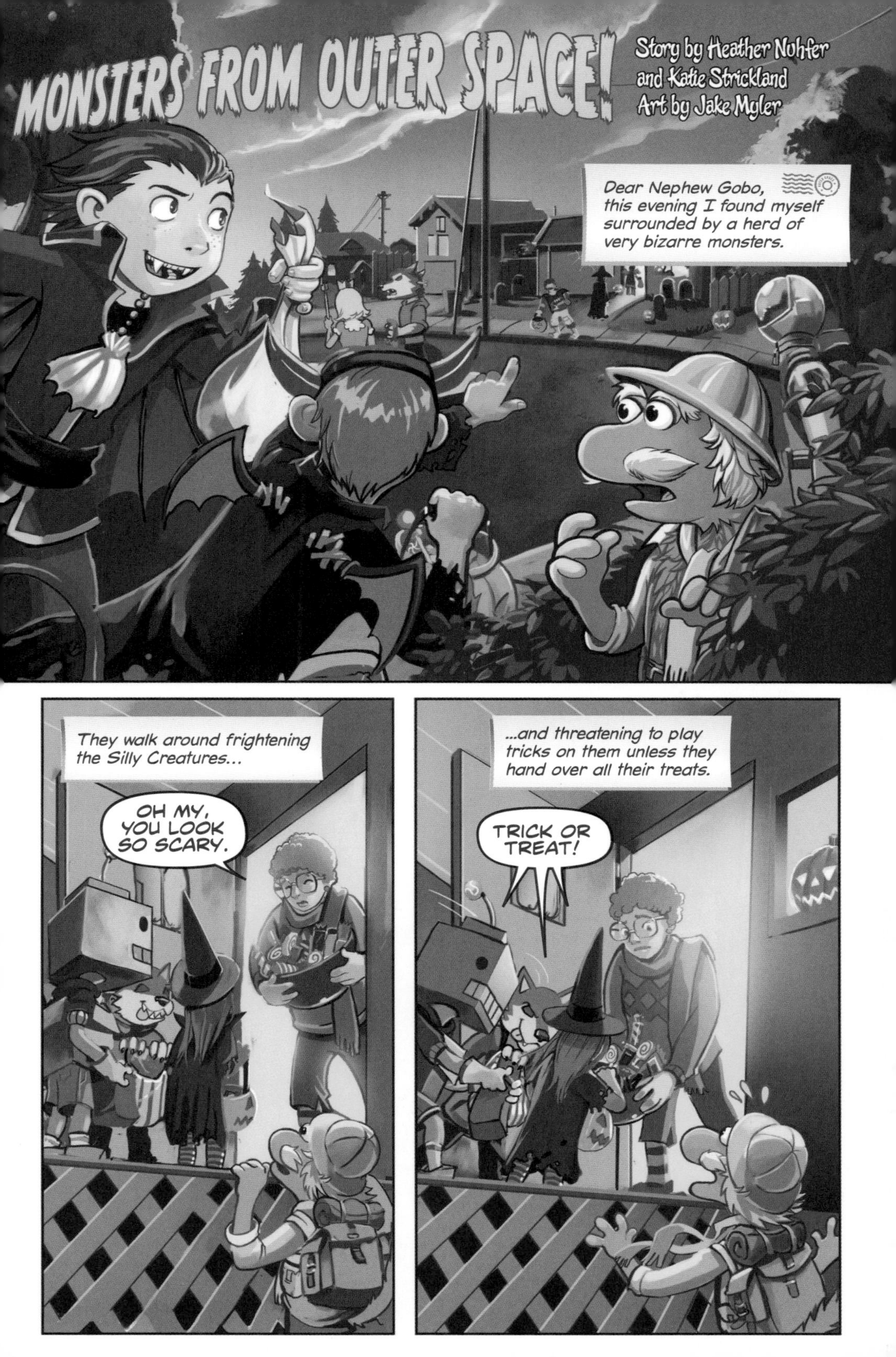
MONSTERS FROM OUTER SPACE!
Story by Heather Nuhfer and Katie Strickland
Art by Jake Myler
Dear Nephew Gobo, this evening I found myself surrounded by a herd of very bizarre monsters.
They walk around frightening the Silly Creatures...
OH MY, YOU LOOK SO SCARY.
...and threatening to play tricks on them unless they hand over all their treats.
TRICK OR TREAT!

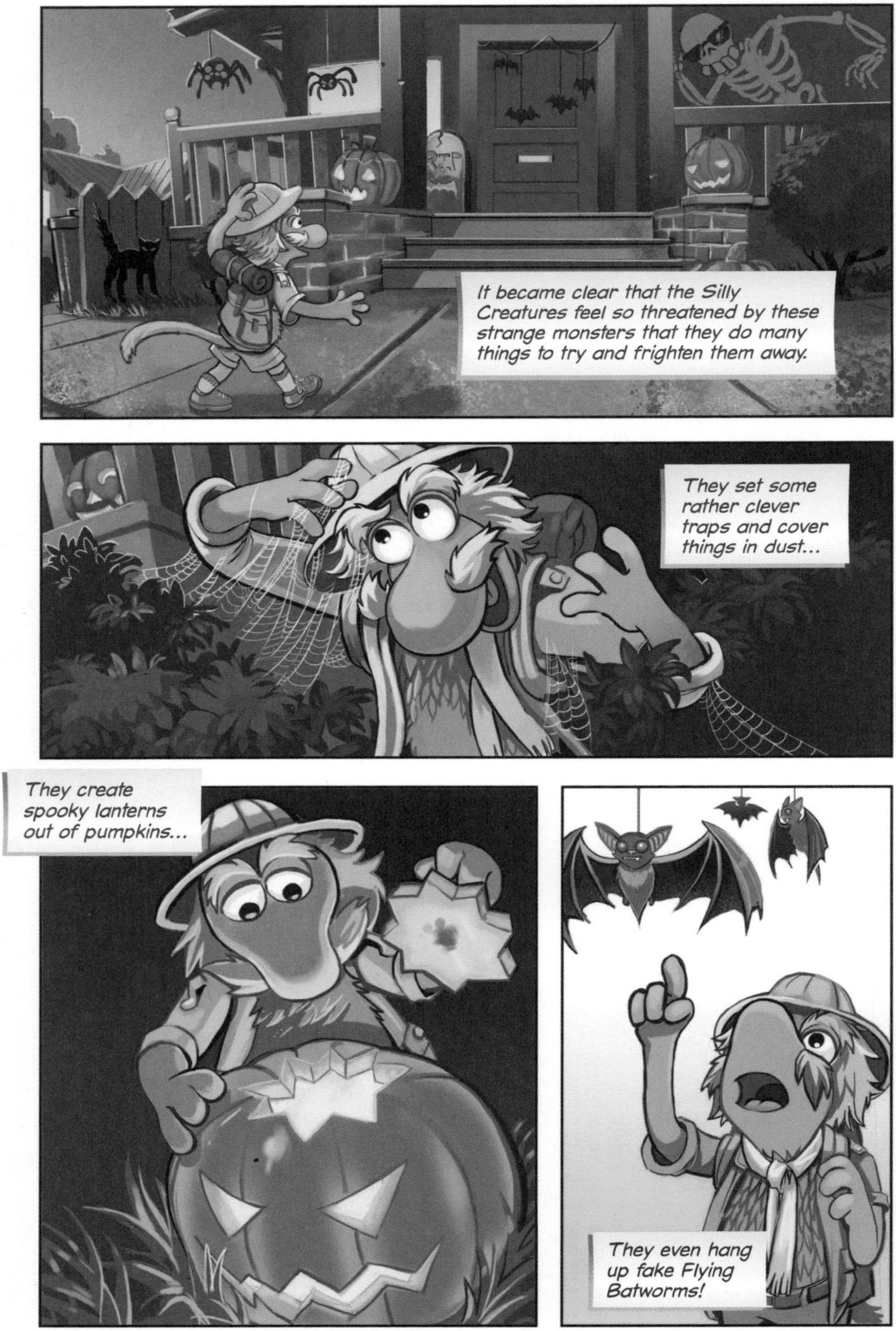

It became clear that the Silly Creatures feel so threatened by these strange monsters that they do many things to try and frighten them away.
They set some rather clever traps and cover things in dust...
They create spooky lanterns out of pumpkins...
They even hang up fake Flying Batworms!

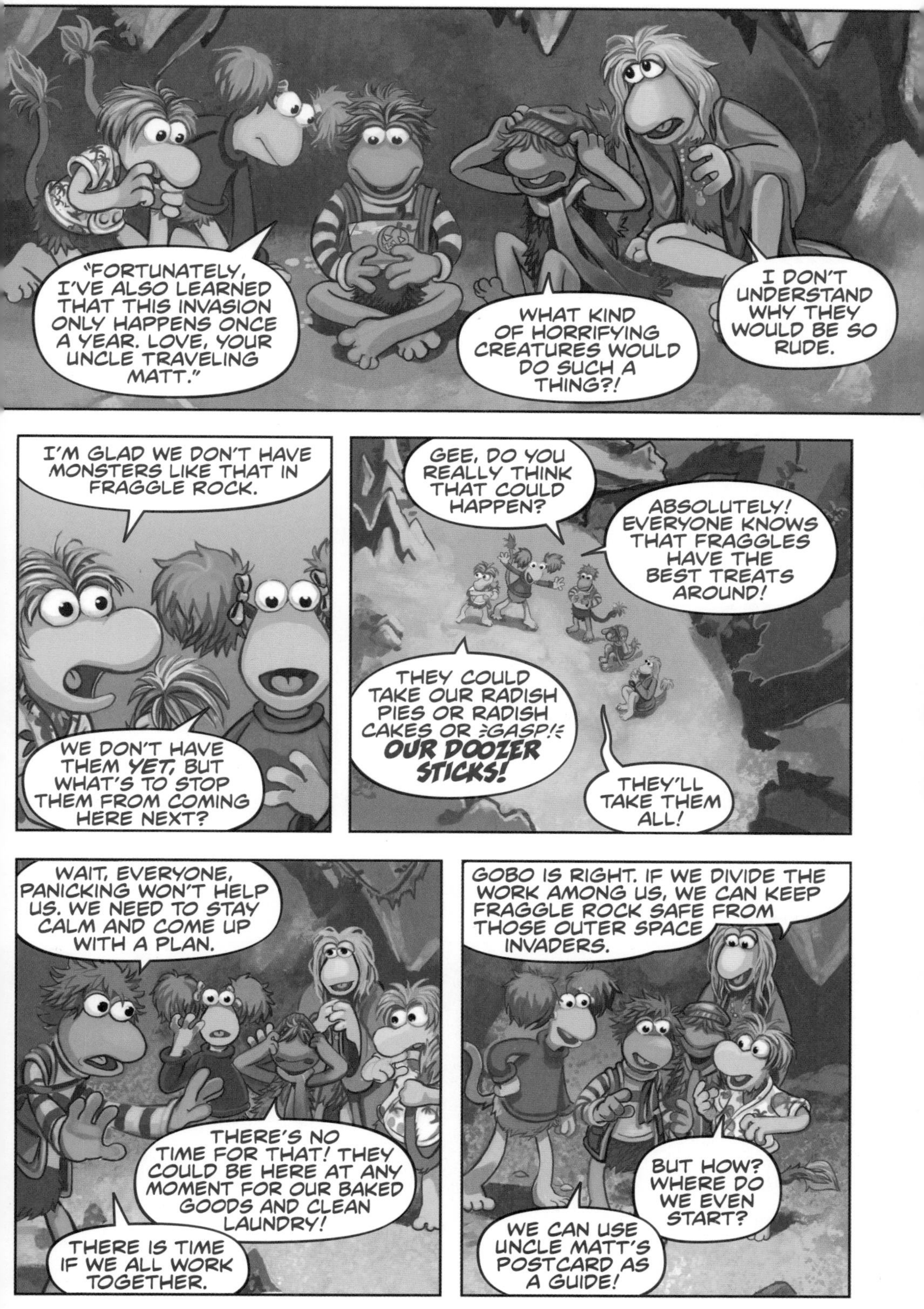

"FORTUNATELY, I'VE ALSO LEARNED THAT THIS INVASION ONLY HAPPENS ONCE A YEAR. LOVE, YOUR UNCLE TRAVELING MATT."
WHAT KIND OF HORRIFYING CREATURES WOULD DO SUCH A THING?!
I DON'T UNDERSTAND WHY THEY WOULD BE SO RUDE.
I'M GLAD WE DON'T HAVE MONSTERS LIKE THAT IN FRAGGLE ROCK.
WE DON'T HAVE THEM *YET*, BUT WHAT'S TO STOP THEM FROM COMING HERE NEXT?
GEE, DO YOU REALLY THINK THAT COULD HAPPEN?
ABSOLUTELY! EVERYONE KNOWS THAT FRAGGLES HAVE THE BEST TREATS AROUND!
THEY COULD TAKE OUR RADISH PIES OR RADISH CAKES OR GASP! **OUR DOOZER STICKS!**
THEY'LL TAKE THEM ALL!
WAIT, EVERYONE, PANICKING WON'T HELP US. WE NEED TO STAY CALM AND COME UP WITH A PLAN.
THERE'S NO TIME FOR THAT! THEY COULD BE HERE AT ANY MOMENT FOR OUR BAKED GOODS AND CLEAN LAUNDRY!
THERE IS TIME IF WE ALL WORK TOGETHER.
GOBO IS RIGHT. IF WE DIVIDE THE WORK AMONG US, WE CAN KEEP FRAGGLE ROCK SAFE FROM THOSE OUTER SPACE INVADERS.
BUT HOW? WHERE DO WE EVEN START?
WE CAN USE UNCLE MATT'S POSTCARD AS A GUIDE!

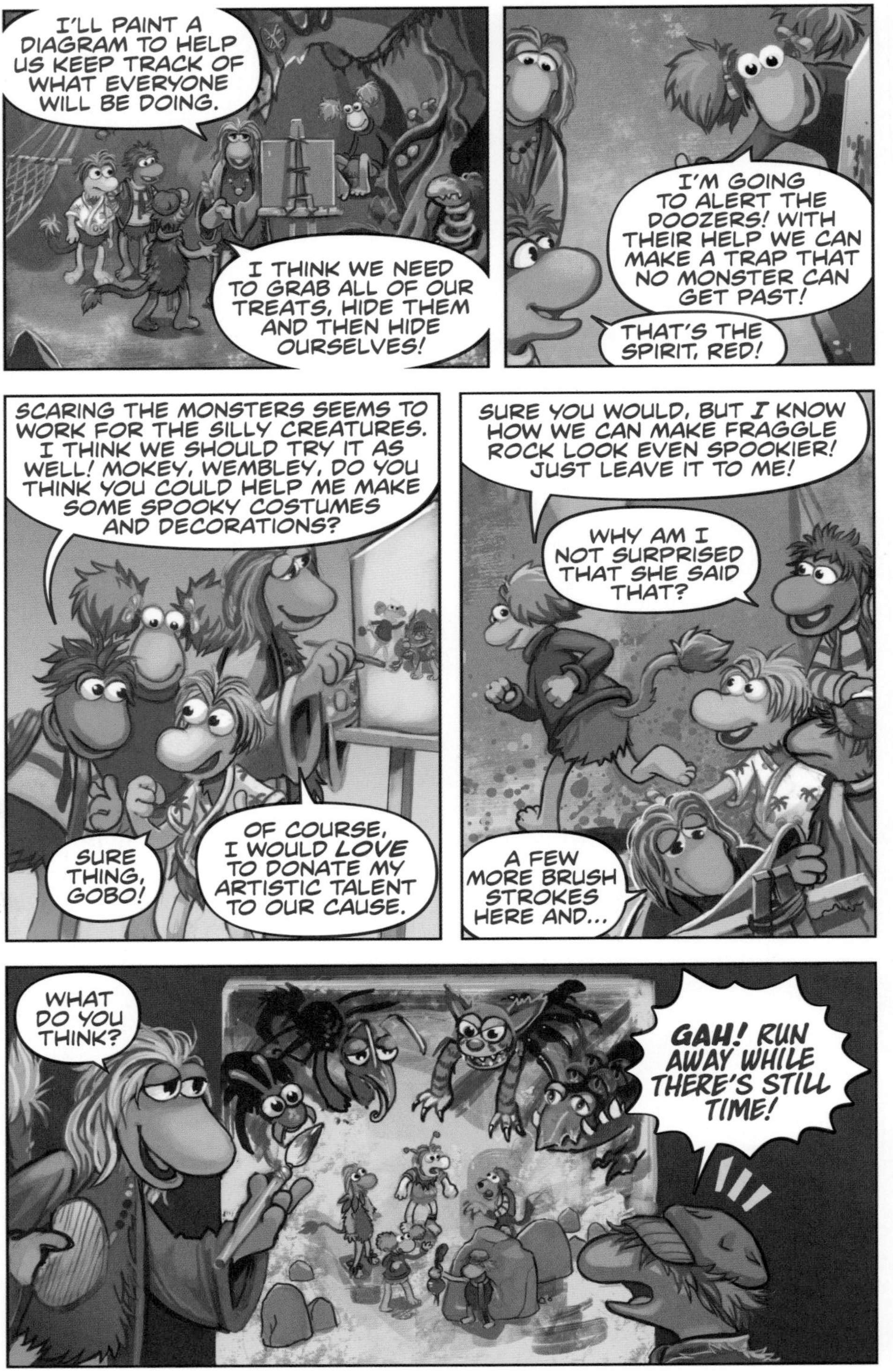
I'LL PAINT A DIAGRAM TO HELP US KEEP TRACK OF WHAT EVERYONE WILL BE DOING.
I THINK WE NEED TO GRAB ALL OF OUR TREATS, HIDE THEM AND THEN HIDE OURSELVES!
I'M GOING TO ALERT THE DOOZERS! WITH THEIR HELP WE CAN MAKE A TRAP THAT NO MONSTER CAN GET PAST!
THAT'S THE SPIRIT, RED!
SCARING THE MONSTERS SEEMS TO WORK FOR THE SILLY CREATURES. I THINK WE SHOULD TRY IT AS WELL! MOKEY, WEMBLEY, DO YOU THINK YOU COULD HELP ME MAKE SOME SPOOKY COSTUMES AND DECORATIONS?
SURE THING, GOBO!
OF COURSE, I WOULD LOVE TO DONATE MY ARTISTIC TALENT TO OUR CAUSE.
SURE YOU WOULD, BUT I KNOW HOW WE CAN MAKE FRAGGLE ROCK LOOK EVEN SPOOKIER! JUST LEAVE IT TO ME!
WHY AM I NOT SURPRISED THAT SHE SAID THAT?
A FEW MORE BRUSH STROKES HERE AND...
WHAT DO YOU THINK?
GAH! RUN AWAY WHILE THERE'S STILL TIME!

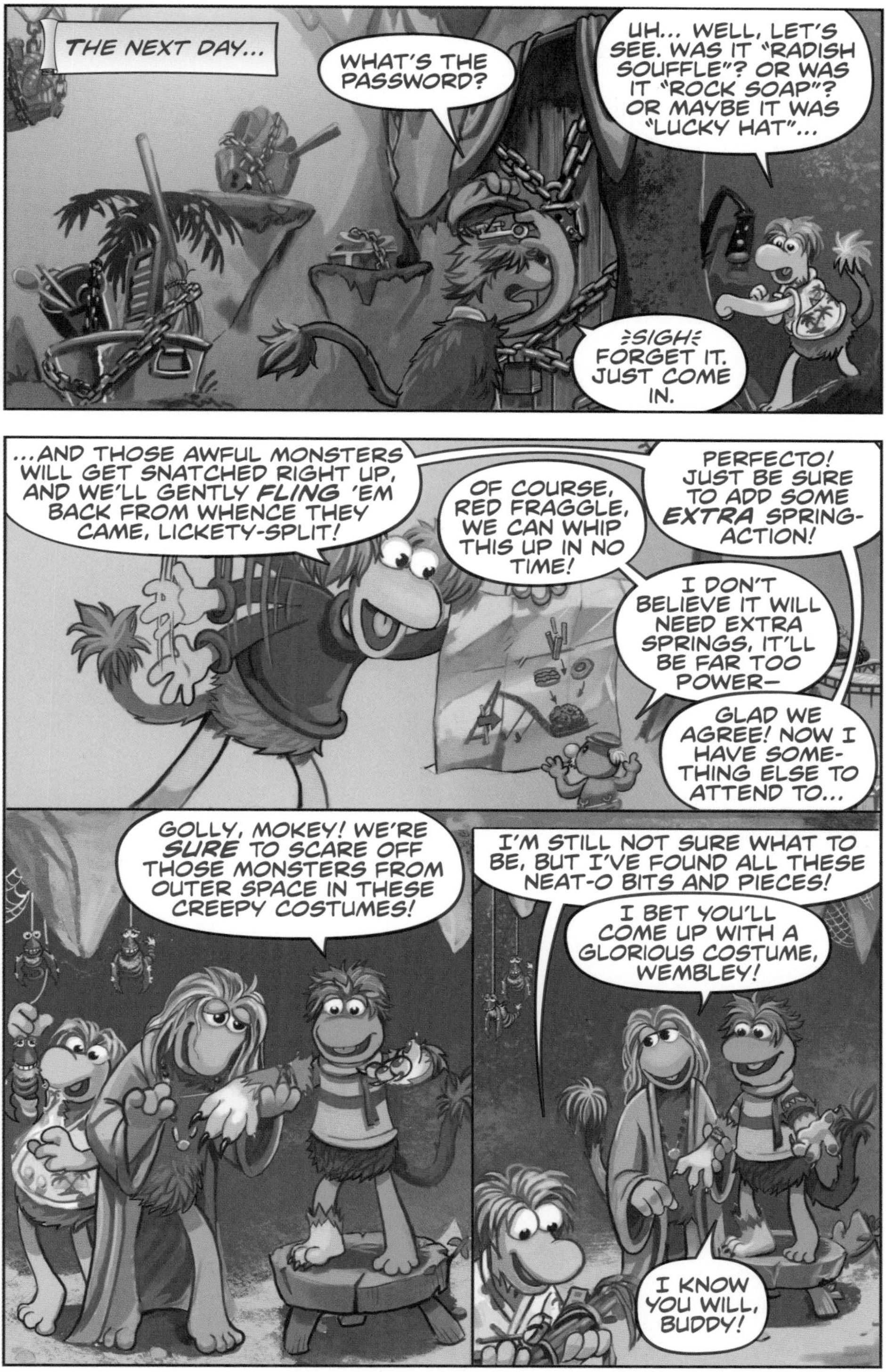
THE NEXT DAY...
WHAT'S THE PASSWORD?
UH... WELL, LET'S SEE. WAS IT "RADISH SOUFFLE"? OR WAS IT "ROCK SOAP"? OR MAYBE IT WAS "LUCKY HAT"...
SIGH FORGET IT. JUST COME IN.
...AND THOSE AWFUL MONSTERS WILL GET SNATCHED RIGHT UP, AND WE'LL GENTLY FLING 'EM BACK FROM WHENCE THEY CAME, LICKETY-SPLIT!
OF COURSE, RED FRAGGLE, WE CAN WHIP THIS UP IN NO TIME!
PERFECTO! JUST BE SURE TO ADD SOME EXTRA SPRING-ACTION!
I DON'T BELIEVE IT WILL NEED EXTRA SPRINGS, IT'LL BE FAR TOO POWER—
GLAD WE AGREE! NOW I HAVE SOME-THING ELSE TO ATTEND TO...
GOLLY, MOKEY! WE'RE SURE TO SCARE OFF THOSE MONSTERS FROM OUTER SPACE IN THESE CREEPY COSTUMES!
I'M STILL NOT SURE WHAT TO BE, BUT I'VE FOUND ALL THESE NEAT-O BITS AND PIECES!
I BET YOU'LL COME UP WITH A GLORIOUS COSTUME, WEMBLEY!
I KNOW YOU WILL, BUDDY!

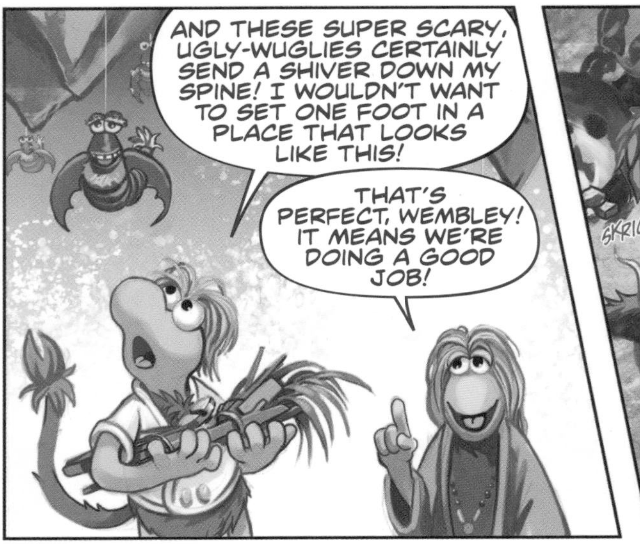
AND THESE SUPER SCARY, UGLY-WUGLIES CERTAINLY SEND A SHIVER DOWN MY SPINE! I WOULDN'T WANT TO SET ONE FOOT IN A PLACE THAT LOOKS LIKE THIS!
THAT'S PERFECT, WEMBLEY! IT MEANS WE'RE DOING A GOOD JOB!

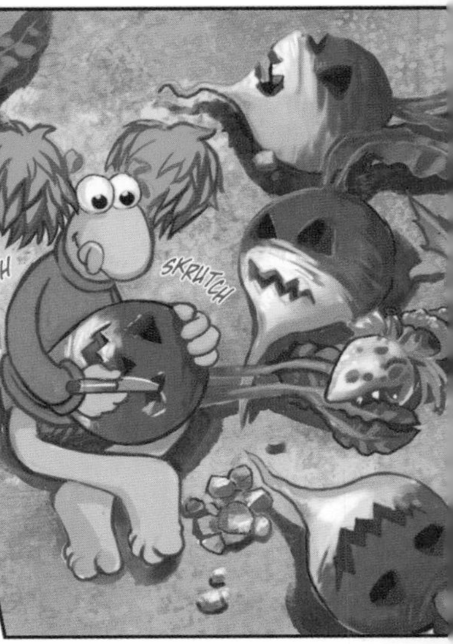
SKRICH
SKRUTCH

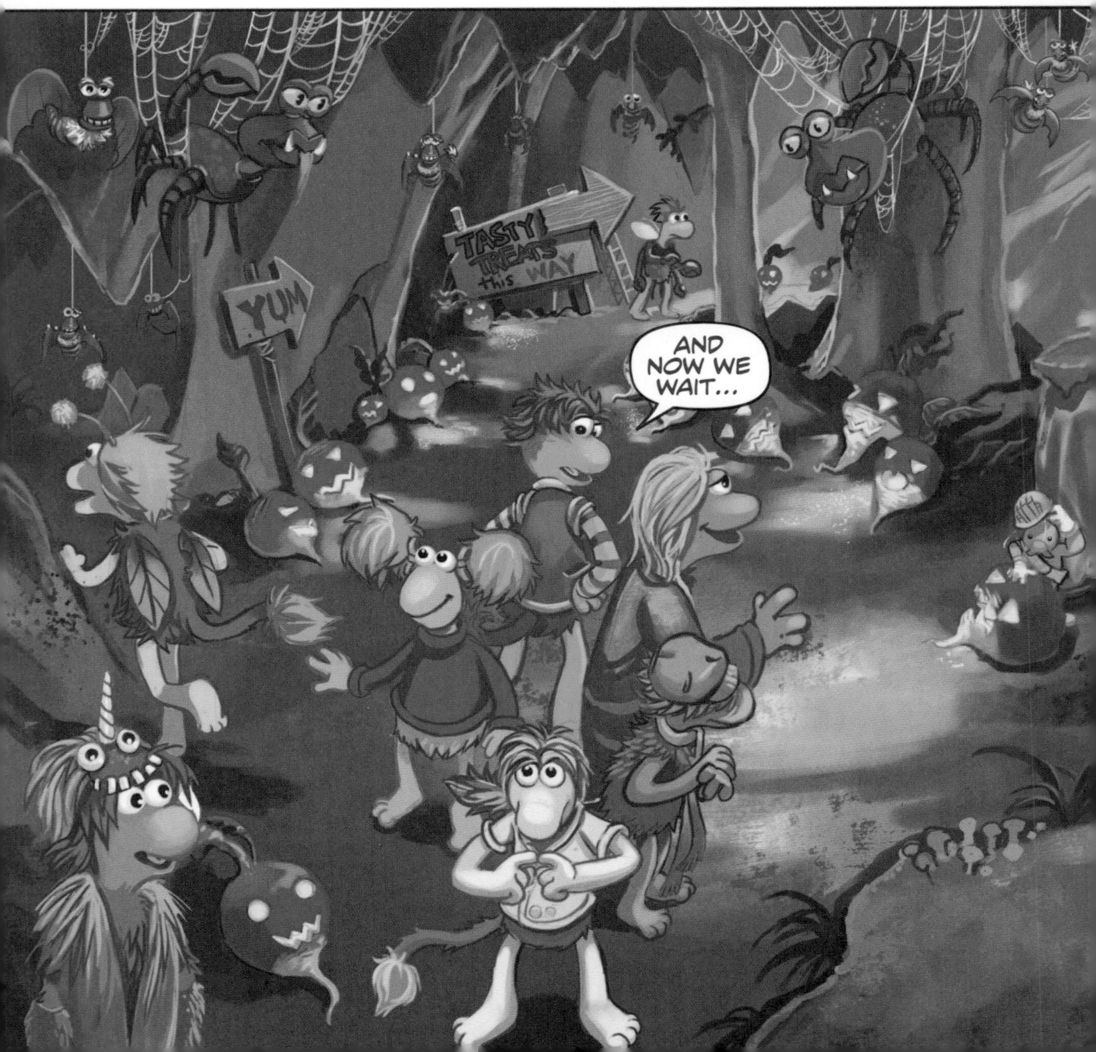
TASTY TREATS this WAY
YUM
AND NOW WE WAIT...

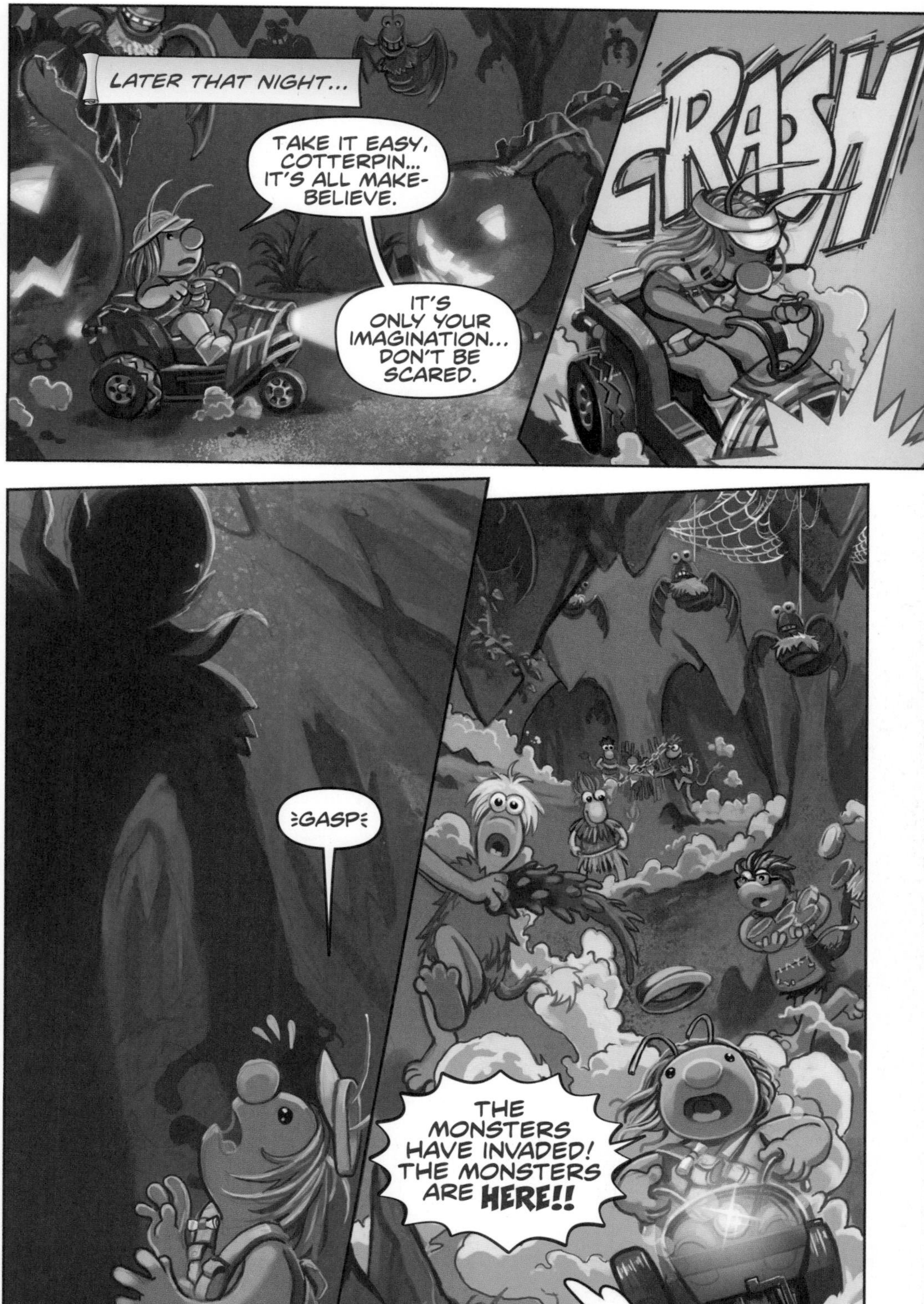

LATER THAT NIGHT...
TAKE IT EASY, COTTERPIN... IT'S ALL MAKE-BELIEVE.
IT'S ONLY YOUR IMAGINATION... DON'T BE SCARED.
CRASH
GASP
THE MONSTERS HAVE INVADED! THE MONSTERS ARE HERE!!

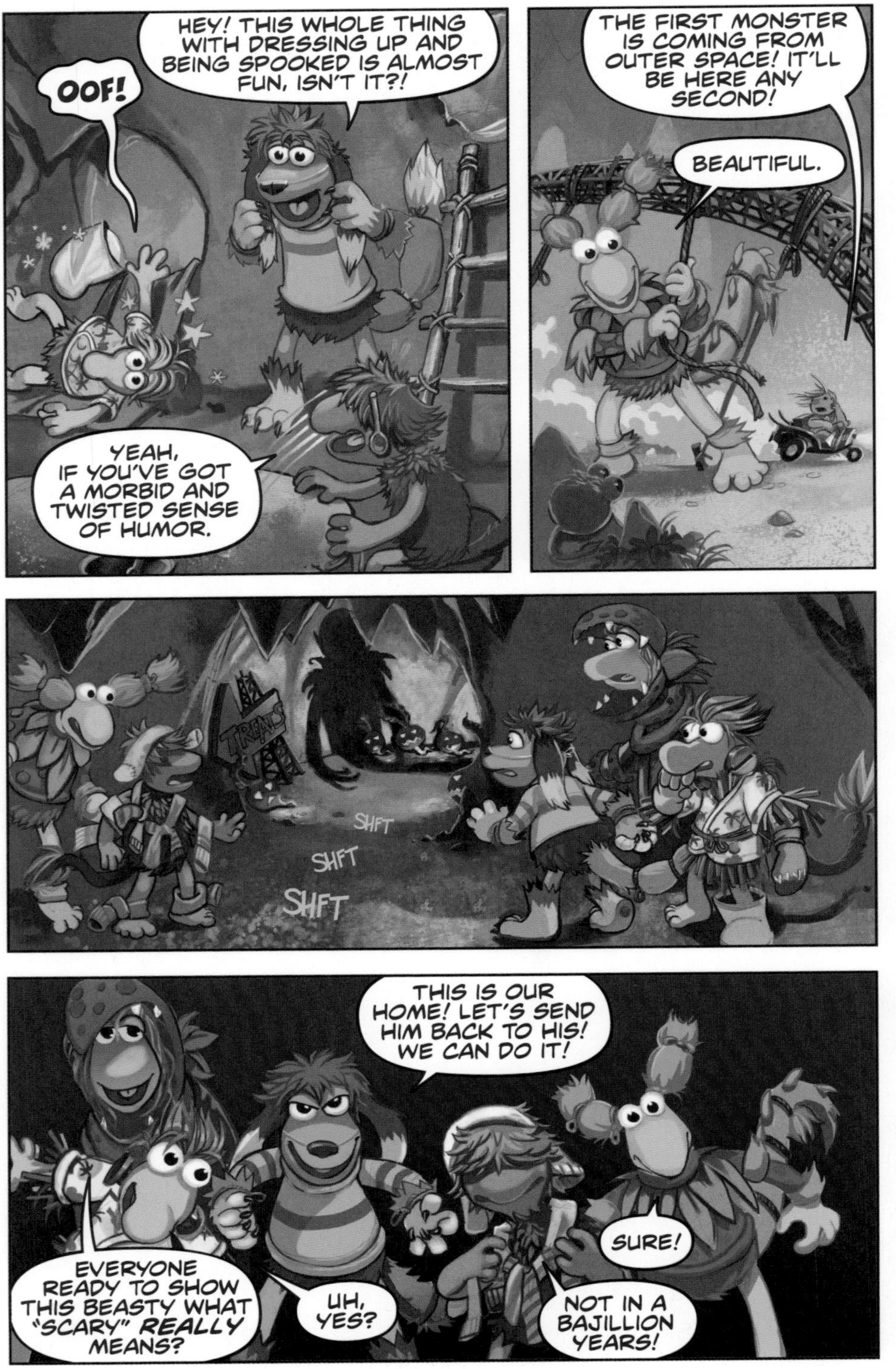
OOF!
HEY! THIS WHOLE THING WITH DRESSING UP AND BEING SPOOKED IS ALMOST FUN, ISN'T IT?!
YEAH, IF YOU'VE GOT A MORBID AND TWISTED SENSE OF HUMOR.
THE FIRST MONSTER IS COMING FROM OUTER SPACE! IT'LL BE HERE ANY SECOND!
BEAUTIFUL.
TREATS
SHFT
SHFT
SHFT
THIS IS OUR HOME! LET'S SEND HIM BACK TO HIS! WE CAN DO IT!
EVERYONE READY TO SHOW THIS BEASTY WHAT "SCARY" REALLY MEANS?
UH, YES?
SURE!
NOT IN A BAJILLION YEARS!

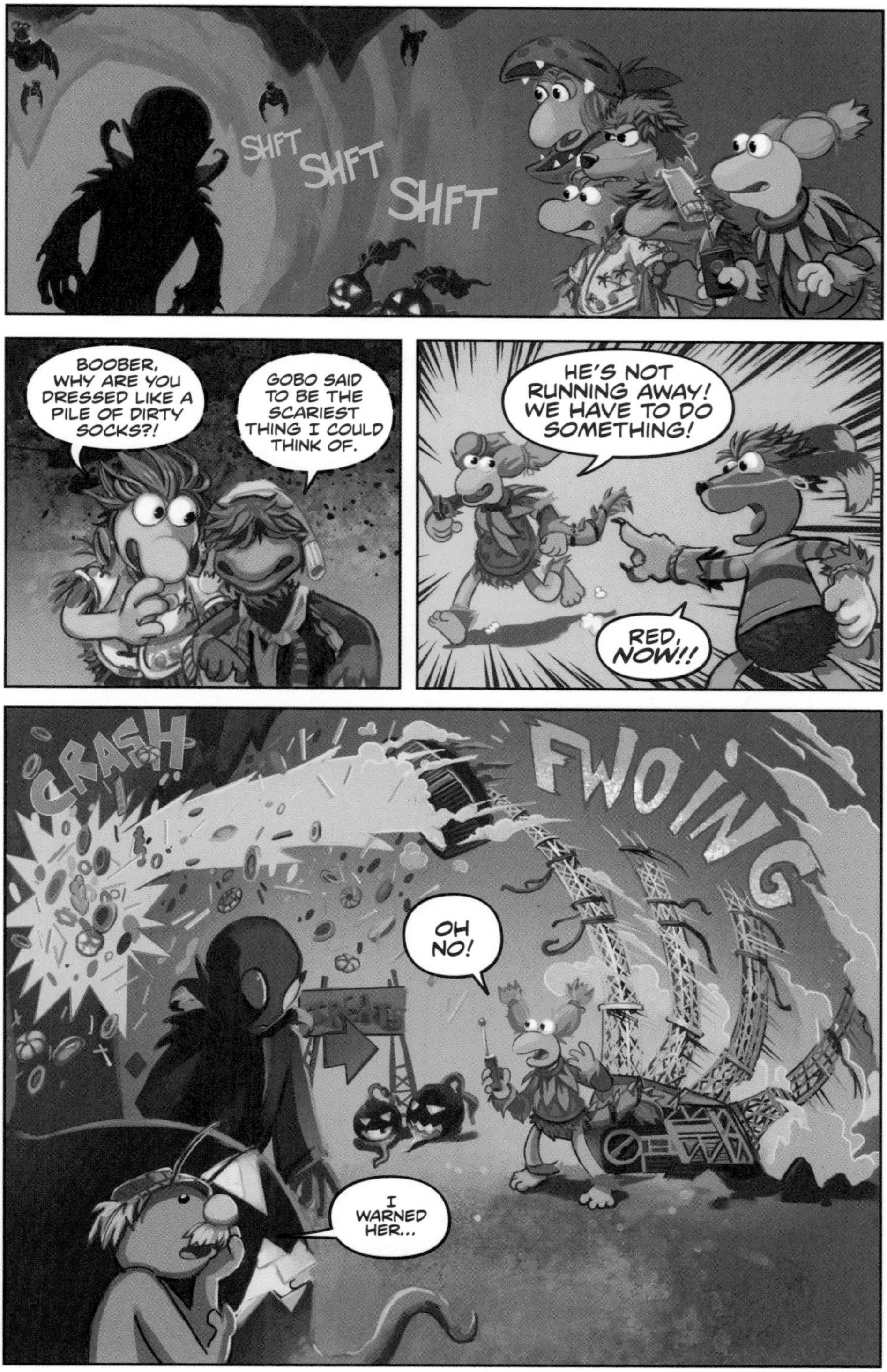
SHFT SHFT SHFT
BOOBER, WHY ARE YOU DRESSED LIKE A PILE OF DIRTY SOCKS?!
GOBO SAID TO BE THE SCARIEST THING I COULD THINK OF.
HE'S NOT RUNNING AWAY! WE HAVE TO DO SOMETHING!
RED, NOW!!
CRASH
FWOING
OH NO!
I WARNED HER...

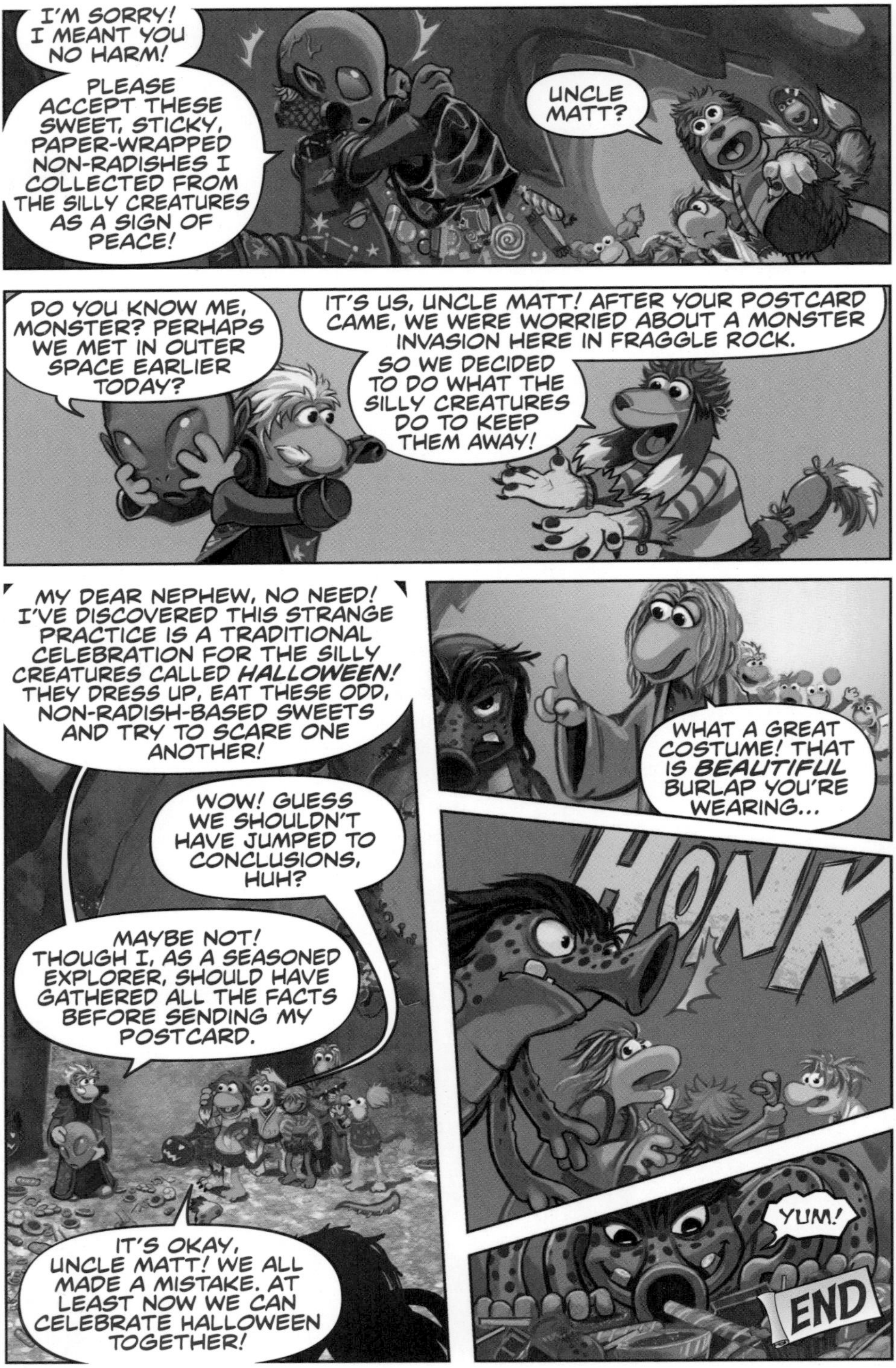
I'M SORRY! I MEANT YOU NO HARM!
PLEASE ACCEPT THESE SWEET, STICKY, PAPER-WRAPPED NON-RADISHES I COLLECTED FROM THE SILLY CREATURES AS A SIGN OF PEACE!
UNCLE MATT?
DO YOU KNOW ME, MONSTER? PERHAPS WE MET IN OUTER SPACE EARLIER TODAY?
IT'S US, UNCLE MATT! AFTER YOUR POSTCARD CAME, WE WERE WORRIED ABOUT A MONSTER INVASION HERE IN FRAGGLE ROCK.
SO WE DECIDED TO DO WHAT THE SILLY CREATURES DO TO KEEP THEM AWAY!
MY DEAR NEPHEW, NO NEED! I'VE DISCOVERED THIS STRANGE PRACTICE IS A TRADITIONAL CELEBRATION FOR THE SILLY CREATURES CALLED *HALLOWEEN!* THEY DRESS UP, EAT THESE ODD, NON-RADISH-BASED SWEETS AND TRY TO SCARE ONE ANOTHER!
WOW! GUESS WE SHOULDN'T HAVE JUMPED TO CONCLUSIONS, HUH?
MAYBE NOT! THOUGH I, AS A SEASONED EXPLORER, SHOULD HAVE GATHERED ALL THE FACTS BEFORE SENDING MY POSTCARD.
IT'S OKAY, UNCLE MATT! WE ALL MADE A MISTAKE. AT LEAST NOW WE CAN CELEBRATE HALLOWEEN TOGETHER!
WHAT A GREAT COSTUME! THAT IS ***BEAUTIFUL*** BURLAP YOU'RE WEARING...
HONK
YUM!
END

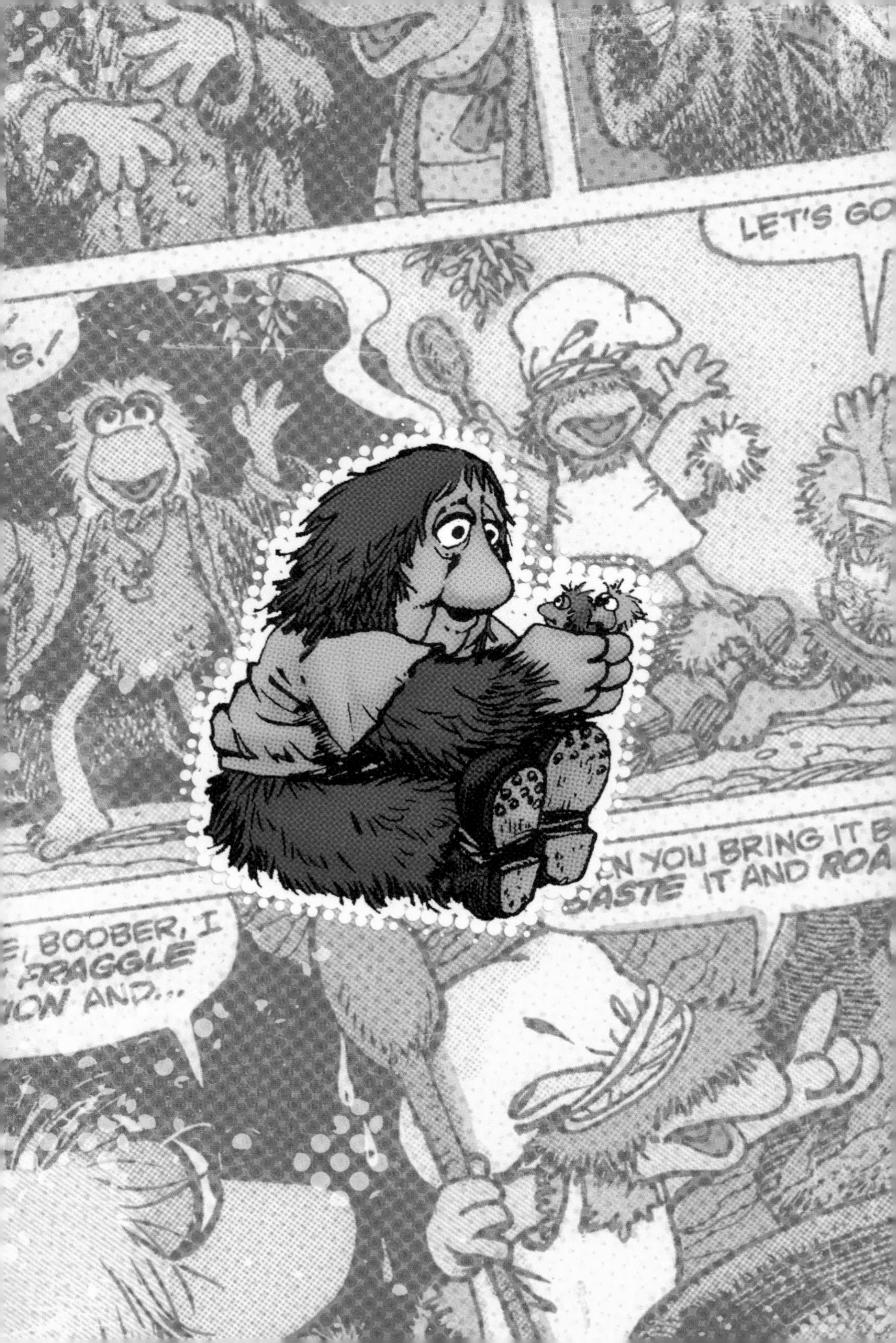

LET'S GO
G!
EN YOU BRING IT B
BASTE IT AND ROA
E, BOOBER, I
FRAGGLE
ION AND...

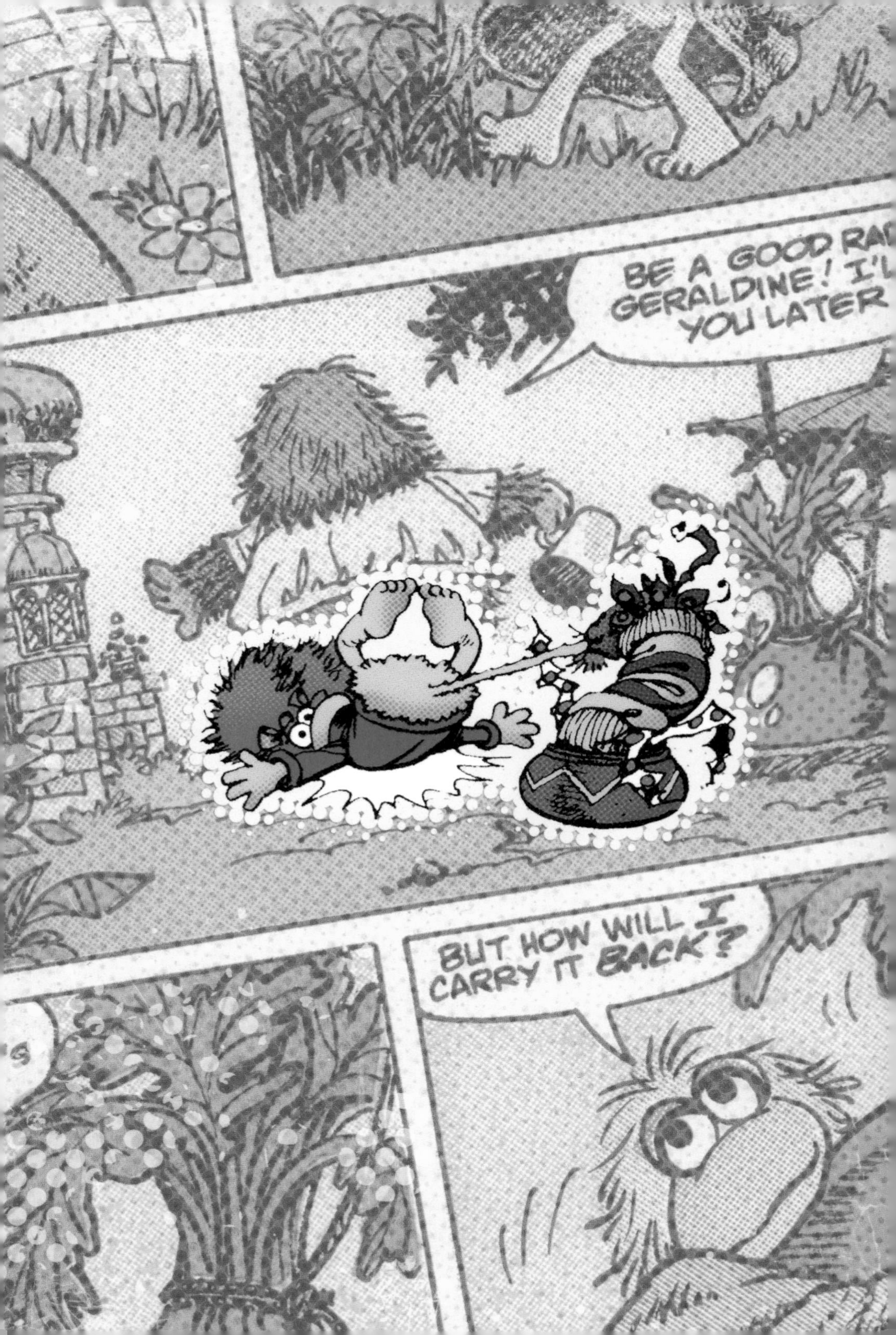
BE A GOOD RA
GERALDINE! I'L
YOU LATER
BUT HOW WILL I CARRY IT BACK?

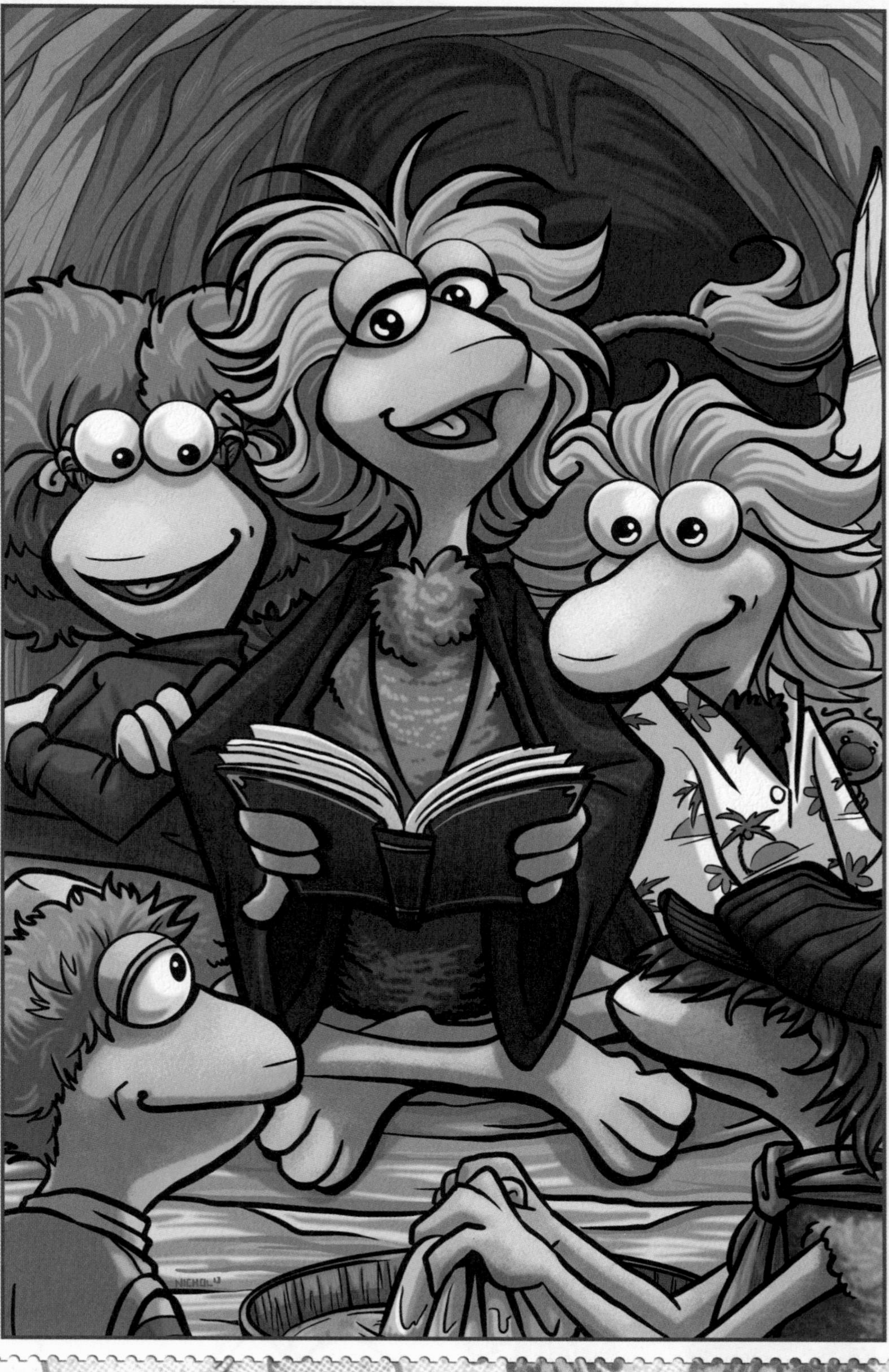

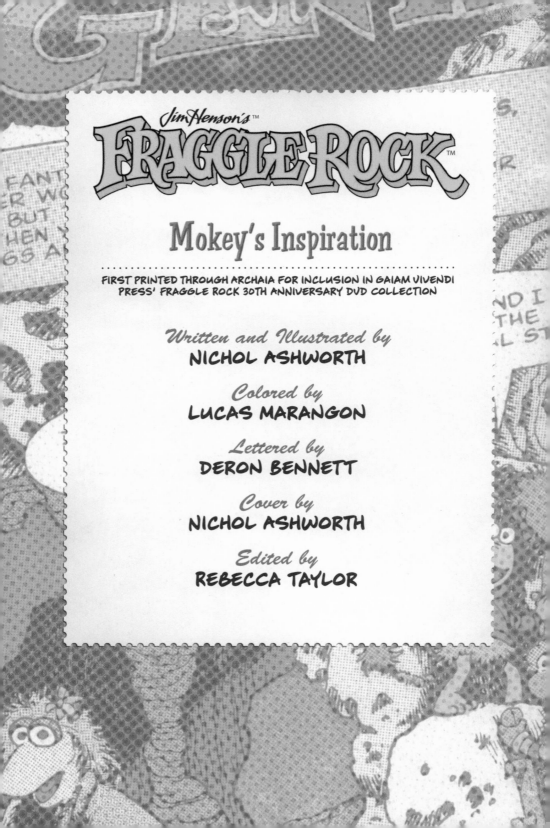

Jim Henson's™ FRAGGLE ROCK™

Mokey's Inspiration

FIRST PRINTED THROUGH ARCHAIA FOR INCLUSION IN GAIAM VIVENDI PRESS' FRAGGLE ROCK 30TH ANNIVERSARY DVD COLLECTION

Written and Illustrated by
NICHOL ASHWORTH

Colored by
LUCAS MARANGON

Lettered by
DERON BENNETT

Cover by
NICHOL ASHWORTH

Edited by
REBECCA TAYLOR

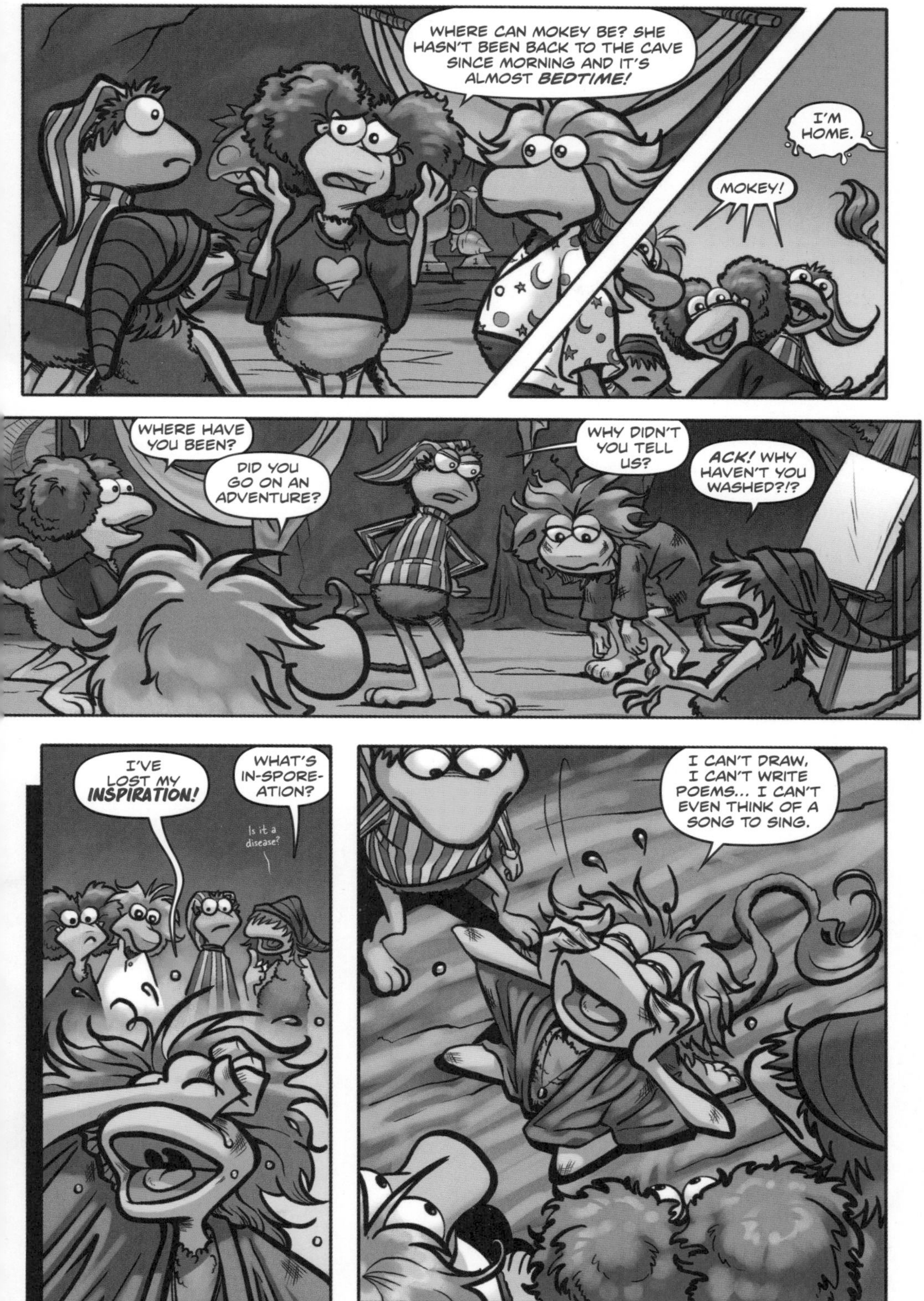
WHERE CAN MOKEY BE? SHE HASN'T BEEN BACK TO THE CAVE SINCE MORNING AND IT'S ALMOST BEDTIME!
I'M HOME.
MOKEY!
WHERE HAVE YOU BEEN?
DID YOU GO ON AN ADVENTURE?
WHY DIDN'T YOU TELL US?
ACK! WHY HAVEN'T YOU WASHED?!?
I'VE LOST MY INSPIRATION!
WHAT'S IN-SPORE-ATION?
Is it a disease?
I CAN'T DRAW, I CAN'T WRITE POEMS... I CAN'T EVEN THINK OF A SONG TO SING.

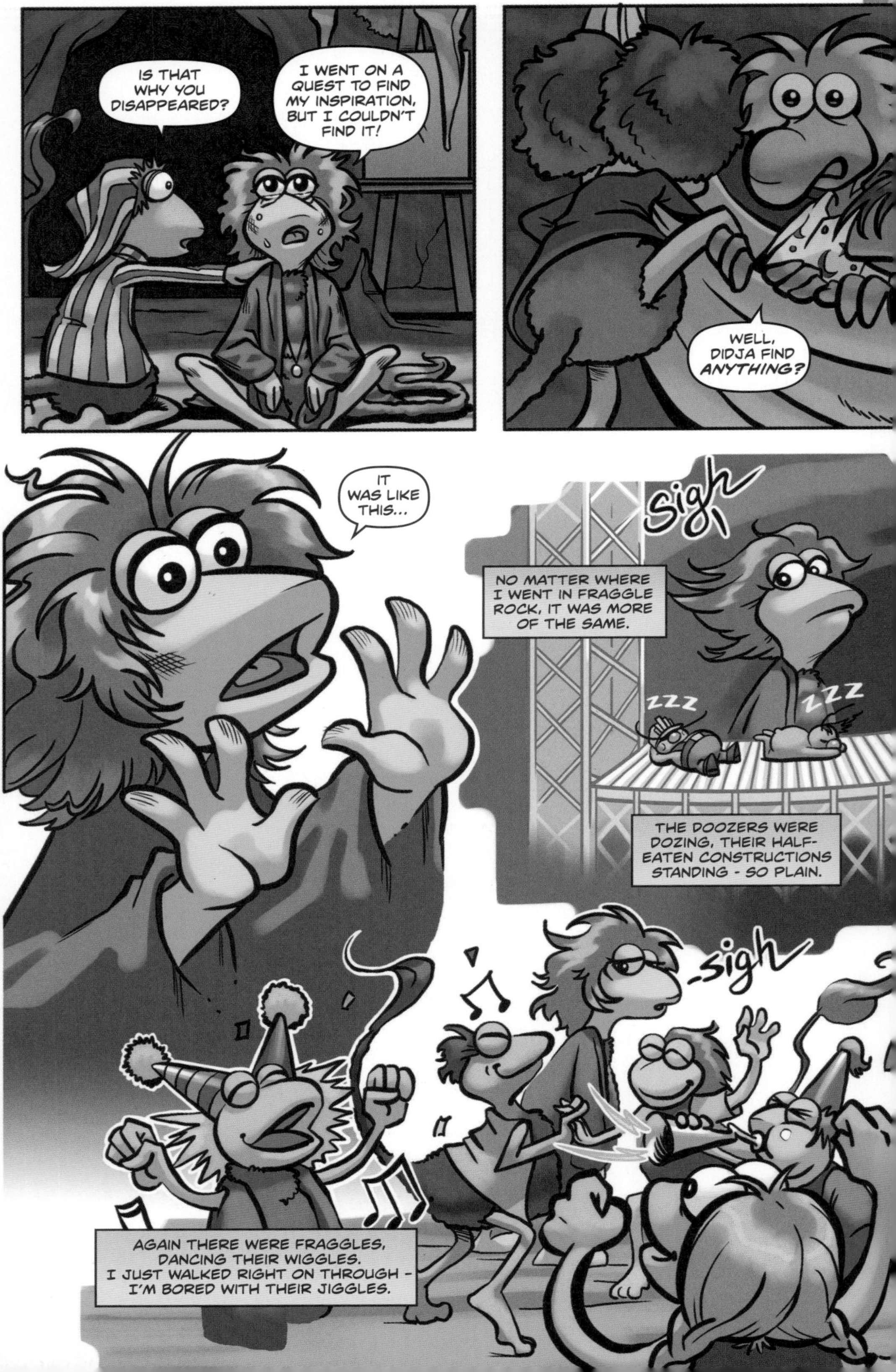
IS THAT WHY YOU DISAPPEARED?
I WENT ON A QUEST TO FIND MY INSPIRATION, BUT I COULDN'T FIND IT!
WELL, DIDJA FIND ANYTHING?
IT WAS LIKE THIS...
sigh
NO MATTER WHERE I WENT IN FRAGGLE ROCK, IT WAS MORE OF THE SAME.
ZZZ
ZZZ
THE DOOZERS WERE DOZING, THEIR HALF-EATEN CONSTRUCTIONS STANDING - SO PLAIN.
sigh
AGAIN THERE WERE FRAGGLES, DANCING THEIR WIGGLES. I JUST WALKED RIGHT ON THROUGH - I'M BORED WITH THEIR JIGGLES.

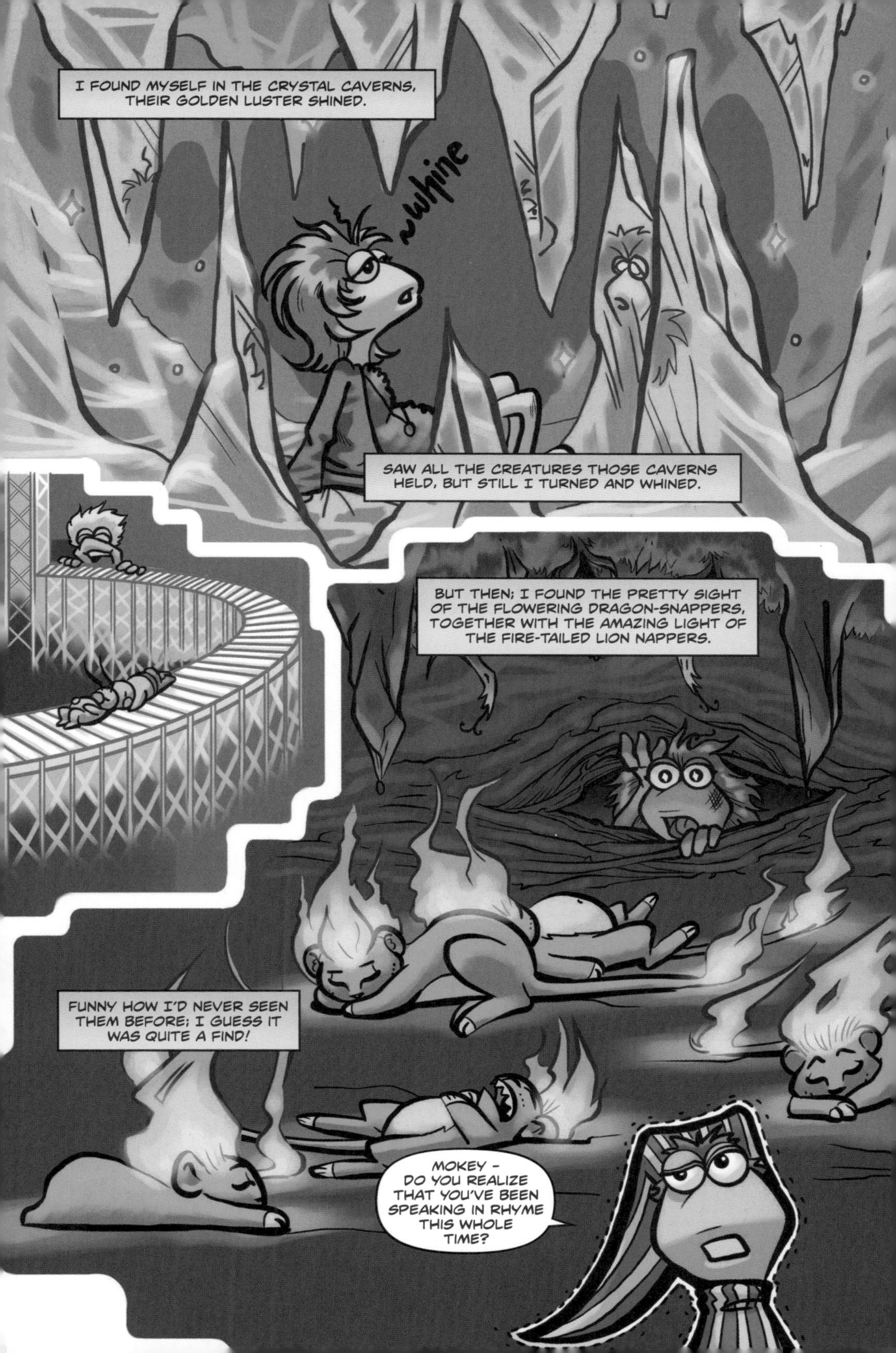
I FOUND MYSELF IN THE CRYSTAL CAVERNS, THEIR GOLDEN LUSTER SHINED.
~whine
SAW ALL THE CREATURES THOSE CAVERNS HELD, BUT STILL I TURNED AND WHINED.
BUT THEN; I FOUND THE PRETTY SIGHT OF THE FLOWERING DRAGON-SNAPPERS, TOGETHER WITH THE AMAZING LIGHT OF THE FIRE-TAILED LION NAPPERS.
FUNNY HOW I'D NEVER SEEN THEM BEFORE; I GUESS IT WAS QUITE A FIND!
MOKEY - DO YOU REALIZE THAT YOU'VE BEEN SPEAKING IN RHYME THIS WHOLE TIME?

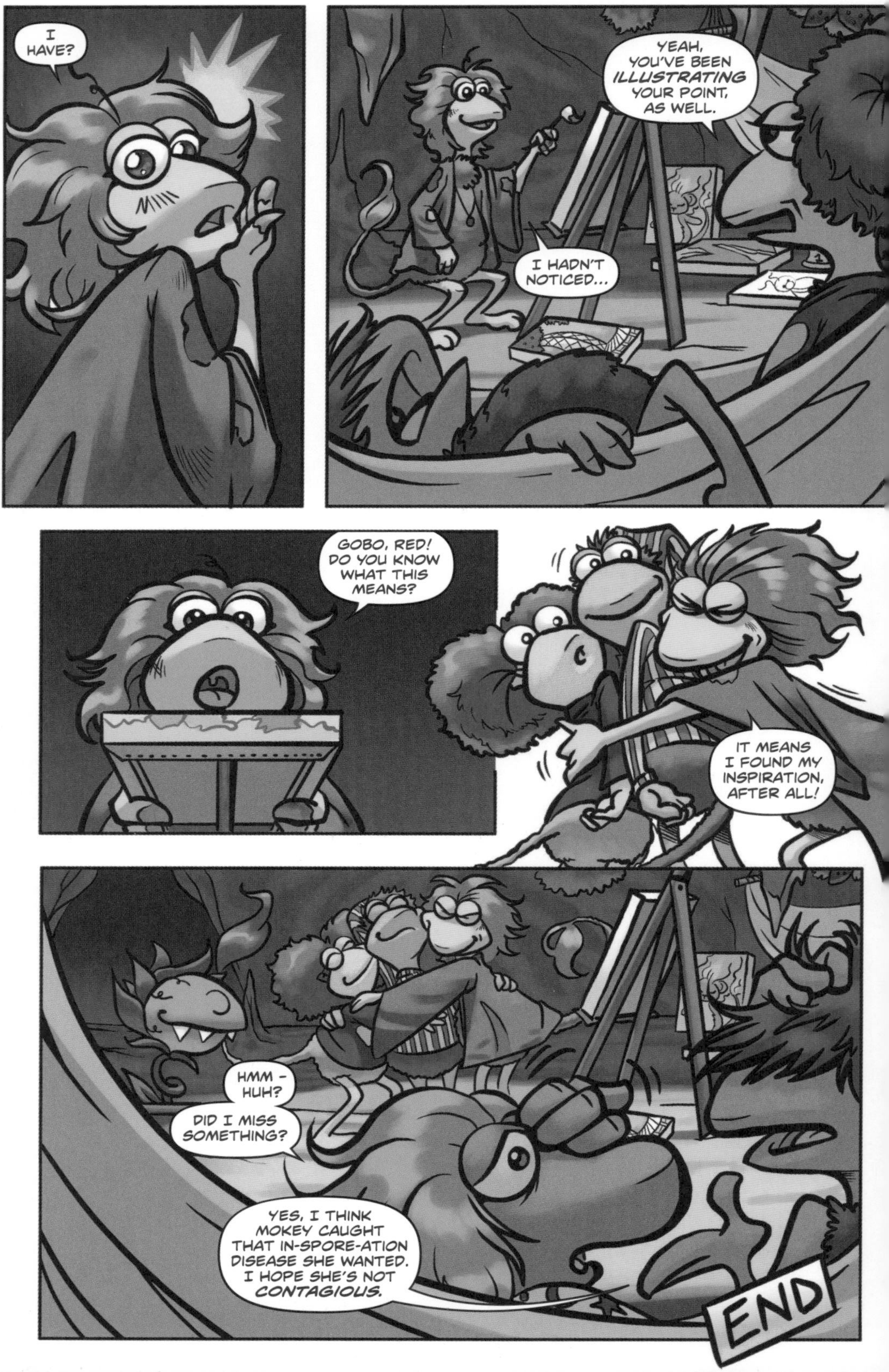
I HAVE?
YEAH, YOU'VE BEEN *ILLUSTRATING* YOUR POINT, AS WELL.
I HADN'T NOTICED...
GOBO, RED! DO YOU KNOW WHAT THIS MEANS?
IT MEANS I FOUND MY INSPIRATION, AFTER ALL!
HMM - HUH?
DID I MISS SOMETHING?
YES, I THINK MOKEY CAUGHT THAT IN-SPORE-ATION DISEASE SHE WANTED. I HOPE SHE'S NOT *CONTAGIOUS*.
END

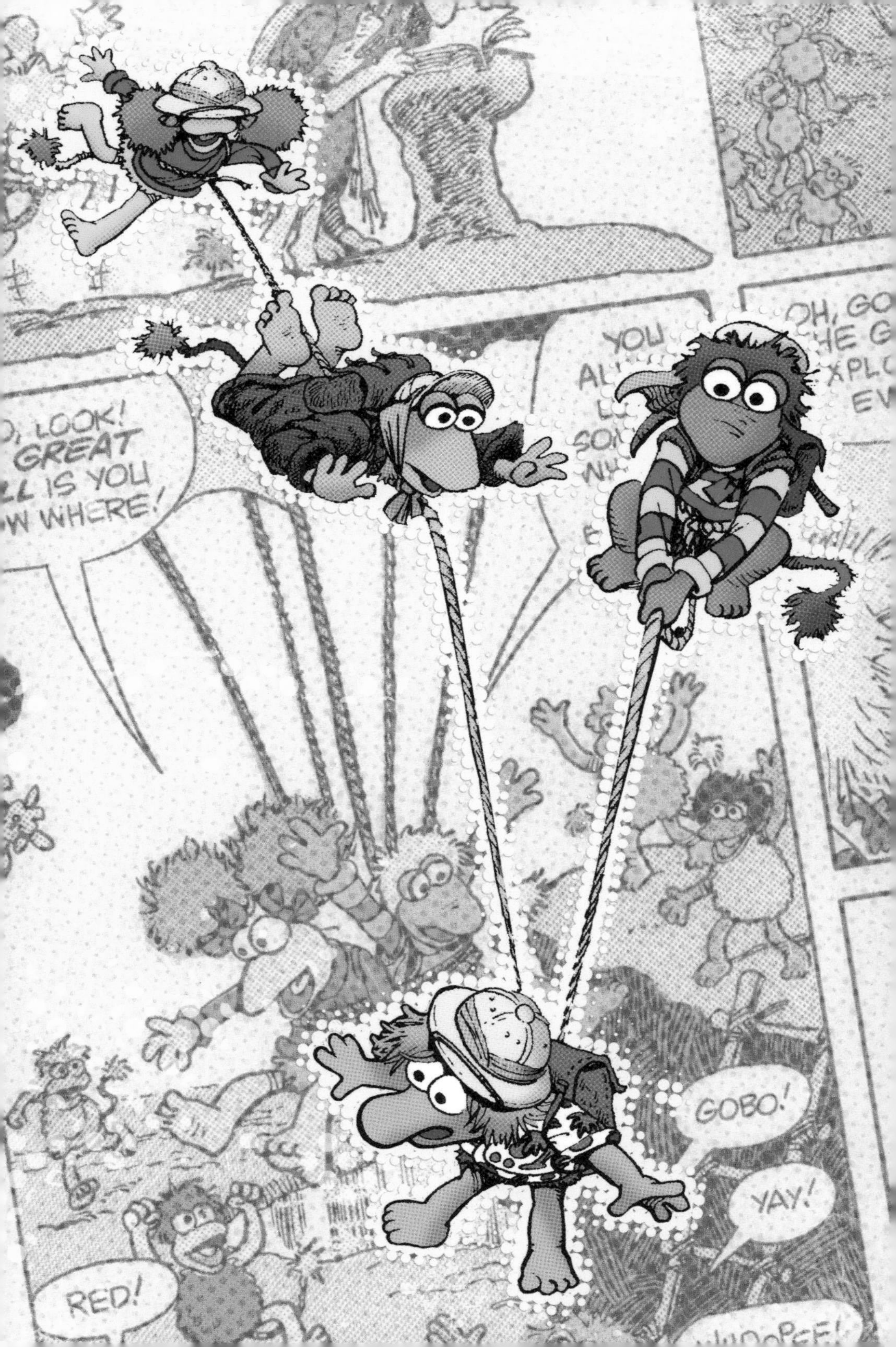
LOOK!
GREAT
GOBO!
YAY!
RED!

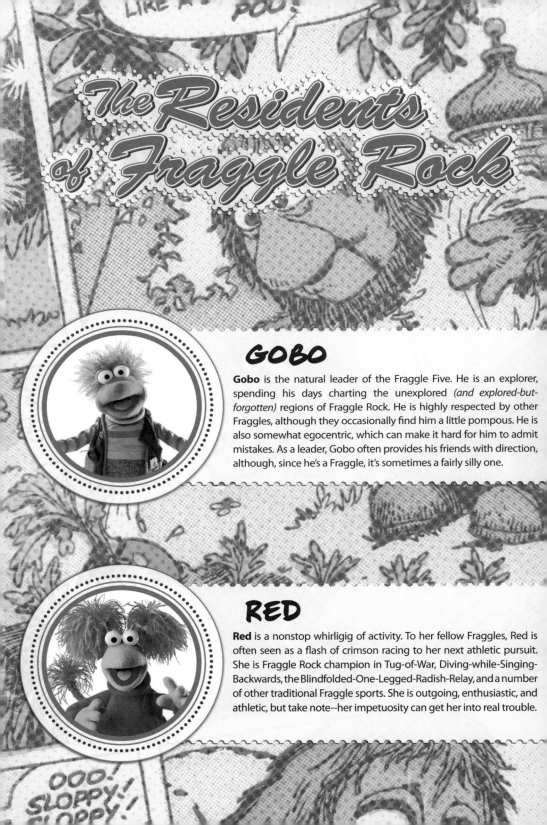

The Residents of Fraggle Rock

GOBO

Gobo is the natural leader of the Fraggle Five. He is an explorer, spending his days charting the unexplored *(and explored-but-forgotten)* regions of Fraggle Rock. He is highly respected by other Fraggles, although they occasionally find him a little pompous. He is also somewhat egocentric, which can make it hard for him to admit mistakes. As a leader, Gobo often provides his friends with direction, although, since he's a Fraggle, it's sometimes a fairly silly one.

RED

Red is a nonstop whirligig of activity. To her fellow Fraggles, Red is often seen as a flash of crimson racing to her next athletic pursuit. She is Fraggle Rock champion in Tug-of-War, Diving-while-Singing-Backwards, the Blindfolded-One-Legged-Radish-Relay, and a number of other traditional Fraggle sports. She is outgoing, enthusiastic, and athletic, but take note--her impetuosity can get her into real trouble.

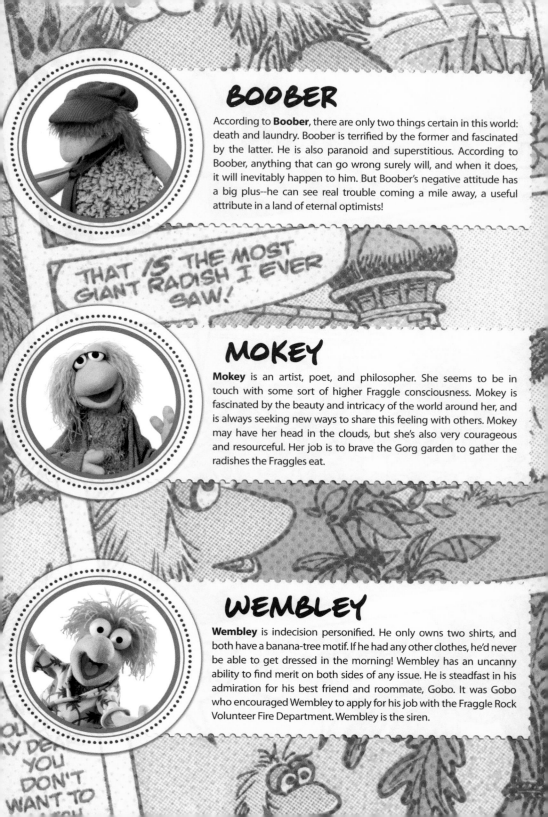

BOOBER

According to **Boober**, there are only two things certain in this world: death and laundry. Boober is terrified by the former and fascinated by the latter. He is also paranoid and superstitious. According to Boober, anything that can go wrong surely will, and when it does, it will inevitably happen to him. But Boober's negative attitude has a big plus--he can see real trouble coming a mile away, a useful attribute in a land of eternal optimists!

THAT *IS* THE MOST GIANT RADISH I EVER SAW!

MOKEY

Mokey is an artist, poet, and philosopher. She seems to be in touch with some sort of higher Fraggle consciousness. Mokey is fascinated by the beauty and intricacy of the world around her, and is always seeking new ways to share this feeling with others. Mokey may have her head in the clouds, but she's also very courageous and resourceful. Her job is to brave the Gorg garden to gather the radishes the Fraggles eat.

WEMBLEY

Wembley is indecision personified. He only owns two shirts, and both have a banana-tree motif. If he had any other clothes, he'd never be able to get dressed in the morning! Wembley has an uncanny ability to find merit on both sides of any issue. He is steadfast in his admiration for his best friend and roommate, Gobo. It was Gobo who encouraged Wembley to apply for his job with the Fraggle Rock Volunteer Fire Department. Wembley is the siren.

Complete your Jim Henson's™ FRAGGLE ROCK™ Library

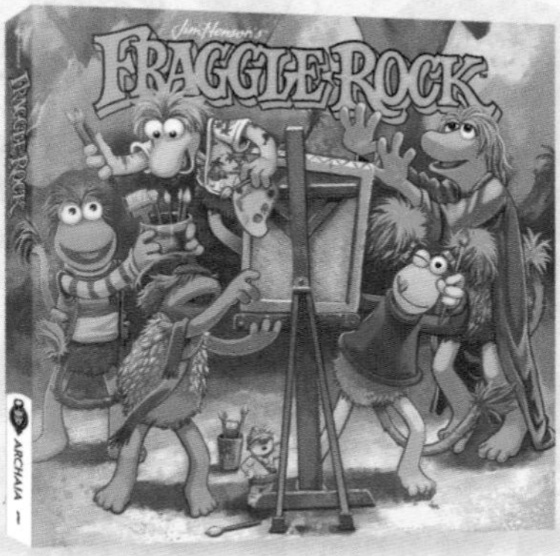
Jim Henson's
FRAGGLE ROCK
ARCHAIA 1

FRAGGLE ROCK VOLUME ONE

$19.95 • ISBN 13: 978-1-932386-42-4

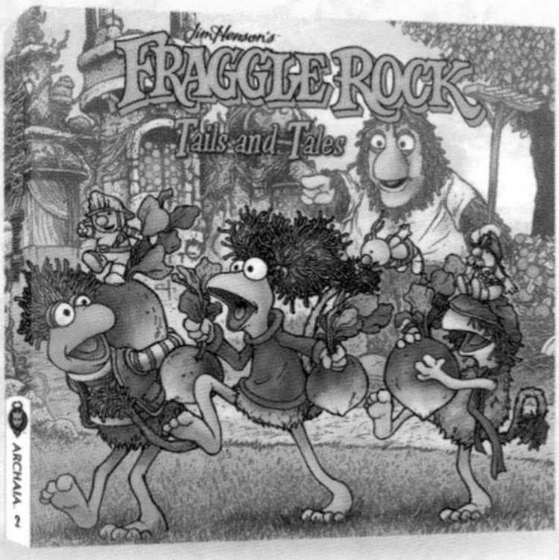
Jim Henson's
FRAGGLE ROCK
Tails and Tales
ARCHAIA 2

FRAGGLE ROCK VOLUME TWO: TAILS AND TALES

$19.95 • ISBN 13: 978-1-936393-13-8

ARCHAIA AND **THE JIM HENSON COMPANY'S** HARVEY AWARD-NOMINATED SERIES OF ***FRAGGLE ROCK*** GRAPHIC NOVEL ANTHOLOGIES, FEATURING ALL NEW STORIES FOR FRAGGLE FANS OF ALL AGES AND BROUGHT TO YOU BY A COLLECTION OF SOME OF THE MOST TALENTED WRITERS AND ILLUSTRATORS WORKING IN THE INDUSTRY TODAY.

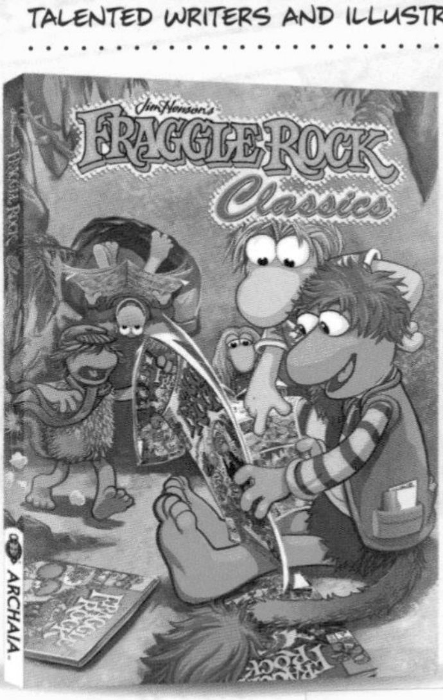
Jim Henson's
FRAGGLE ROCK
Classics
ARCHAIA

Available Now

FRAGGLE ROCK CLASSICS VOLUME ONE

DANCE YOUR CARES AWAY WITH THE FIRST VOLUME OF DIGITALLY REMASTERED 1980S ***FRAGGLE ROCK*** COMICS, INCLUDING STORIES SUCH AS, "THE MAGIC TIME MACHINE," "THE TROUBLE WITH BEING #1," "THE MONSTER THAT COULD BE ANYTHING," AND "THE DOOZER WHO WANTED TO BE A FRAGGLE."

$9.95 • ISBN 13: 978-1-936393-22-0